Motoo Eetee

Historical Fiction Published by McBooks Press

BY ALEXANDER KENT
Midshipman Bolitho
Stand into Danger
In Gallant Company
Sloop of War
To Glory We Steer
Command a King's Ship
Passage to Mutiny
With All Despatch
Form Line of Battle!
Enemy in Sight!
The Flag Captain
Signal–Close Action!
The Inshore Squadron
A Tradition of Victory
Success to the Brave
Colours Aloft!
Honour this Day
The Only Victor
Beyond the Reef
The Darkening Sea
For My Country's Freedom
Cross of St George
Sword of Honour
Second to None
Relentless Pursuit

BY DUDLEY POPE
Ramage
Ramage & The Drumbeat
Ramage & The Freebooters
Governor Ramage R.N.
Ramage's Prize
Ramage & The Guillotine
Ramage's Diamond
Ramage's Mutiny
Ramage & The Rebels
The Ramage Touch
Ramage's Signal
Ramage & The Renegades
Ramage's Devil
Ramage's Trial
Ramage's Challenge

BY DAVID DONACHIE
The Devil's Own Luck
The Dying Trade
A Hanging Matter
An Element of Chance

BY DEWEY LAMBDIN
The French Admiral

BY CAPTAIN FREDERICK MARRYAT
Frank Mildmay OR
The Naval Officer
The King's Own
Mr Midshipman Easy
Newton Forster OR
The Merchant Service
Snarleyyow OR
The Dog Fiend
The Privateersman
The Phantom Ship

BY JAN NEEDLE
A Fine Boy for Killing
The Wicked Trade

BY IRV C. ROGERS
Motoo Eetee

BY NICHOLAS NICASTRO
The Eighteenth Captain

BY C. NORTHCOTE PARKINSON
The Guernseyman
Devil to Pay
The Fireship

BY W. CLARK RUSSELL
Wreck of the Grosvenor
Yarn of Old Harbour Town

BY RAFAEL SABATINI
Captain Blood

BY MICHAEL SCOTT
Tom Cringle's Log

BY A.D. HOWDEN SMITH
Porto Bello Gold

BY DOUGLAS REEMAN
Badge of Glory
First to Land

BY R.F. DELDERFIELD
Too Few for Drums
Seven Men of Gascony

BY V.A. STUART
Victors and Lords
The Sepoy Mutiny
Massacre at Cawnpore

Motoo Eetee

Shipwrecked at the Edge of the World

Irv C. Rogers

McBooks Press
Ithaca, New York

Published by McBooks Press 2002

Library of Congress Cataloging-in-Publication Data

Rogers, Irv C.
Motoo eetee: shipwrecked at the edge of the world. / by Irv C. Rogers.
p. cm.
ISBN 1-59013-018-9 (alk. paper)
1. Survival after airplane accidents, shipwrecks, etc.—Fiction 2. Sealing ships—Fiction. 3. Ship captains—Fiction. 4. Pacific Islands—Fiction. 5. Shipwrecks—Fiction. 6. Sailors—Fiction. 7. Islands—Fiction. I. Title
PS3618.O46 M68 2002
823'.6—dc21 2002000234

Distributed to the book trade by
LPC Group, 22 Broad St., Suite 34, Milford, CT 06460
800-729-6078.

Additional copies of this book may be ordered from any bookstore or directly from McBooks Press, 120 West State Street, Ithaca, NY 14850. Please include $3.50 postage and handling with mail orders. New York State residents must add sales tax. All McBooks Press publications can also be ordered by calling toll-free
1-888-BOOKS11 (1-888-266-5711).
Please call to request a free catalog.

Visit the McBooks Press website at www.mcbooks.com.

Printed in the United States of America

9 8 7 6 5 4 3 2 1

FIRST EDITION

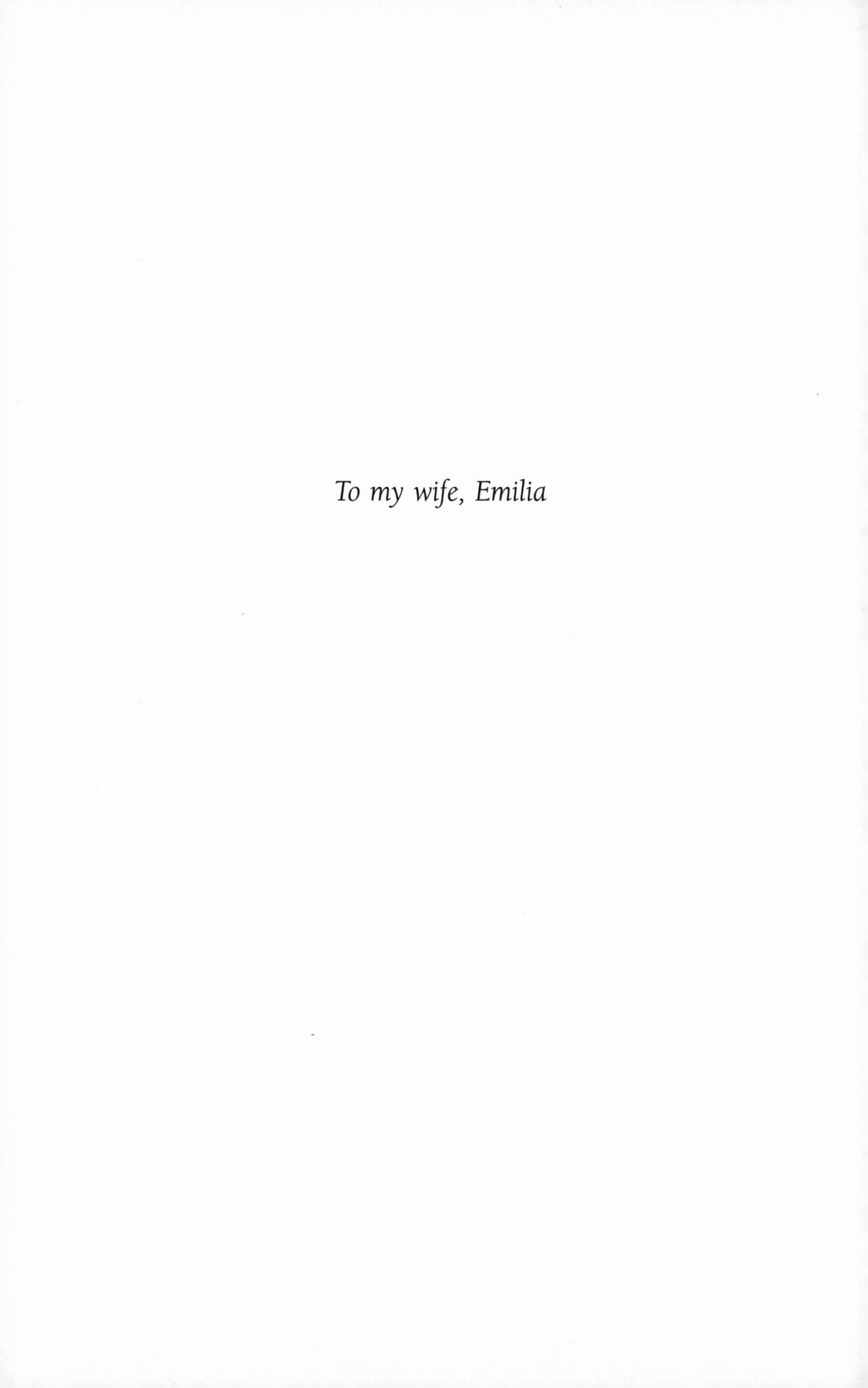

To my wife, Emilia

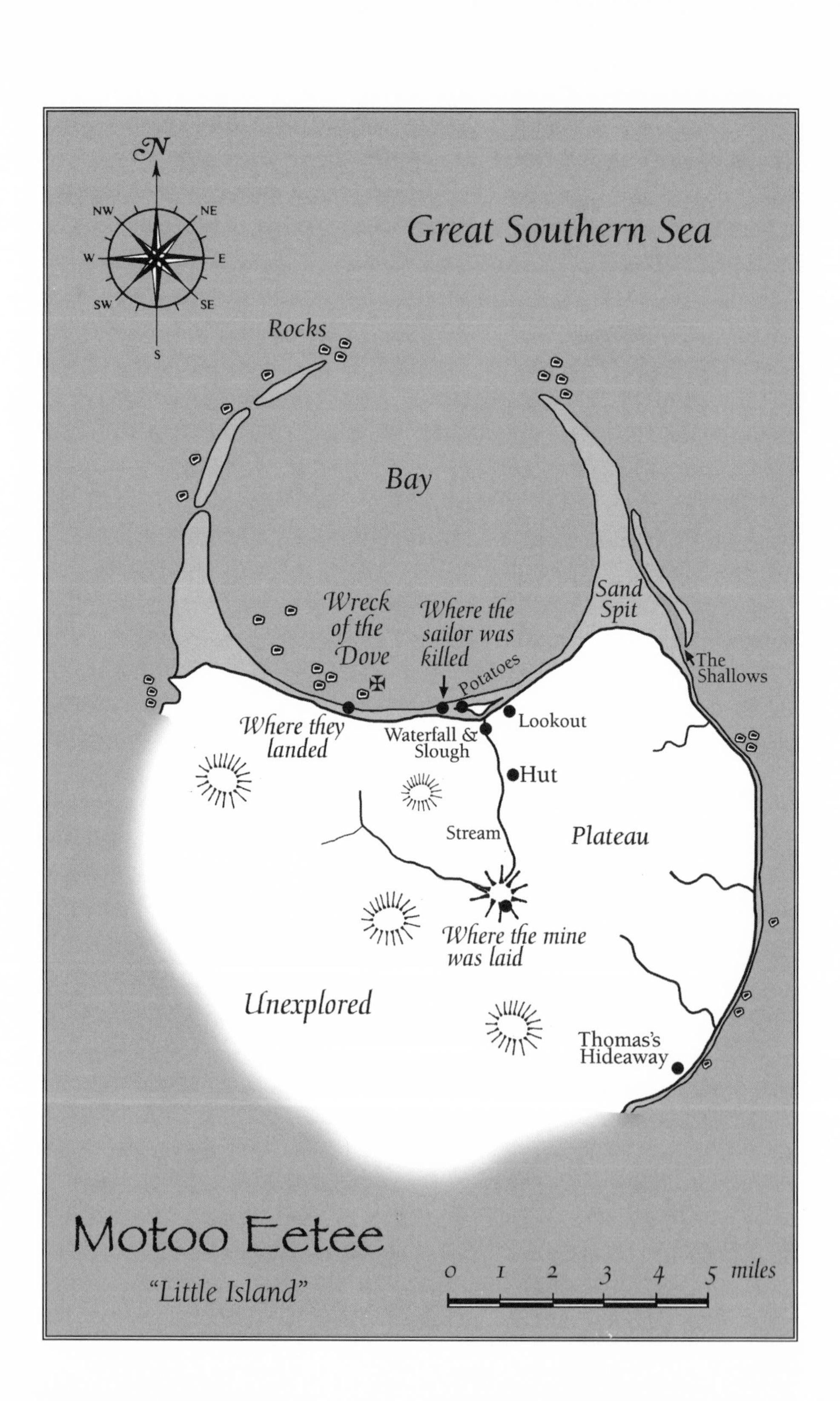
N
NW
NE
W
E
SW
SE
S
Great Southern Sea
Rocks
Bay
Sand Spit
Wreck of the Dove
Where the sailor was killed
Potatoes
The Shallows
Where they landed
Waterfall & Slough
Lookout
Hut
Stream
Plateau
Where the mine was laid
Unexplored
Thomas's Hideaway
Motoo Eetee
"Little Island"
0 1 2 3 4 5 miles

PREFACE

IN THE FIRST two decades of the 19th century, sealing vessels from America and the New South Wales Colony landed gangs on the lower coasts of New Zealand and on the remote islands far to the south of that country. They were a wide spectrum of men—New England farm lads, a few aborigines and kanakas (Polynesians), lascars, paroled and escaped convicts. In the earlier years, fur seals were plentiful and brought good prices, and even the green hands with log clubs and well-honed knives might earn far more than the ten or twelve dollars a month that was the seaman's wage. Yet it was a perilous life coasting in a whaleboat and making landings through the surf. Men were injured, killed by natives, and drowned in oversets. Little note was taken of the harshness of their lives or, beyond their immediate families, of their deaths and disappearances.

They lived for months in hovels and skinned the fur seals of their valuable hides while the vessel that had stationed them there went off to other islands. The location of a new rookery was never purposely revealed. Secrecy was necessary to keep competitors from moving in on the rich pickings, yet if the ship was lost, no one would be aware of the sealers left behind in the rookeries. Some men were rescued by other ships happening upon their isle. But others were marooned, some for as long as seven years, while surviving on seal meat, shellfish, and seabirds' eggs. Their individual histories were rarely recorded and, of those that were known, almost none was ever related in any detail. They have been lost to history, yet each one might have been as fascinating as that of Alexander Selkirk, the real castaway fictionalized by Defoe as Robinson Crusoe.

It was a short-lived "fishery" carried on at the edge of the known world. In little more than twenty years, the seals were reduced to near-extinction. When their ship had been loaded with skins and, in the later years, with the addition of oil rendered from sea elephants, the men faced a long cruise halfway around the earth to return home. The world was much larger then, when it was measured in voyages that lasted many months. In that larger world, secrets were more numerous.

IRV C. ROGERS
FALL 2001

ACKNOWLEDGMENTS

THE MANY PEOPLE who helped this book reach print are scattered from New England to California, and across the Pacific to Guam, New Zealand, and Tasmania.

Foremost among them are Barbara Manning, John Wylie, and the late George Seng, who supplied an unfailing optimism and proffered valuable suggestions for years. Andrea Sim of Auckland located and provided the key history of sealing that shaped the adventure. Frank Conley, a friend of long standing, gave expert advice on the weapons of the period. Descriptive material regarding the appearance of Stonington in the early 19th century was kindly sent to me by Mary Thacher of the Stonington Historical Society. Pam Eastlick of the University of Guam ferreted out obscure information about constellations that I was unable to locate in hours of searching. Judie Swartz, my daughter, printed out reams of copy and explained the quirks of computers to me. Others of my family gave encouragement and tolerated the books, papers, maps, and equipment that took over space in the house.

—I.C.R.

SALINAS, CALIFORNIA

DECEMBER 2001

CHAPTER 1

EVEN BEFORE rounding Five Fingers Point, the barque rose and dipped on the reaching, unhindered waves of the Great Southern Sea. With the swells came a fresh wind blowing through her rigging, never varying in its strength and direction. The stays, shrouds, and the lines of the running gear, each boused to a different tensity, produced a keening in the ears of those on deck every hour of the days and nights as their northerly course angled away from the abrupt coast of the Middle Island.

Old Will craned his neck and stared high overhead. Without shifting his eyes from the stunsail, he reached over and laid his hand on the boom brace belayed at the rail. His callused fingers curled around the line and held it in a firm grip.

"Here, Thomas," he muttered, "put your hand o' that." The old sailor lisped through a gap left by some missing teeth. He always swore he had not lost them to age but as a youth, when he was struck square in the mouth by a block that had parted its strap.

The young sailor grabbed the line above Will's grasp.

"There, d'ye feel the strain in the fiber?" Will asked.

Thomas clenched the brace tighter and felt its vibrations. The stunsail was bellied out drum-tight by the wind, and its leeches shivered and passed the tremors down the straining line to his hand. He nodded, agreeing with his watch-mate.

"She wasn't meant for a wind like this," Will grumbled and gave his head a shake. "No, we've too much on as 'tis, but ol' Tobit'll not be satisfied till he's got every mile. Damn! Never seen him t' carry on like this afore."

Will's bearded and wrinkled face remained turned up to the rigging. Thomas watched the old sailor's eyes narrowed against the cold wind. His attention shifted to Will's worn monkey jacket. Its collar was frayed to threads and both elbows were patched with scraps of sailcloth sewn on with neat overcast stitching. The jacket was buttoned to the top, and he had also wrapped a wool scarf around his neck to bar the cold and dampness. Its short ends fluttered erratically in the wind.

Thomas's clothing was in a like poor condition. Skinning the beasts and the boat work around the islands had been hard on his clothes, more so than the duties aboard the barque. He had patched his duck trousers over each knee and now even the patches were wearing through. Spots and streaks of tar were pressed into the once-white fabric from leaning against the standing rigging and from working tarred hemp in his lap. When he took them off and held them up, the creases and strained weave held the very shape of his body. He knew he must sew at least one new pair for the voyage home or look beggarly when he arrived in Boston or New York. He certainly couldn't return to the Longpoint in rags after such a success on the grounds.

Thomas leaned his head back to look at the sail Will was watching. "I hope it holds," he wished aloud. "I don't fancy reeving new lines before our watch is out."

"Ho, lad! We'll be up there 'less the wind eases," Will replied, then faced Thomas and complained, "Ah, don't grumble so. For sure I'm one that's too old to be 'loft. I'm not light and springy like you no more. No, not a wicker like you. My bones are brittle now and all damned sore 'tween 'em."

Thomas regarded the part of Will's face visible between his graying beard and the brim of his battered hat. Years of exposure to the sun and raw wind had ruddied his cheeks. Little red veins, fine as lint, formed a network beneath the skin, and from the outer end of each eyelid a pinch of small wrinkles fanned back across the temple. With his tarpaulin pushed back, the fore part of his bald head was always visible, and when he took the hat off in the fo'c's'le, his hairless pate had the shine of a glazed bowl in the lamplight. A beneficent smile was always there to soften Will's weathered face. Thomas recalled it from the first days of the voyage when the old tar's hands had guided his in bending a sail or reeving a luff tackle.

Most of the crew allowed he was the best man in the *Dove,* though pointing out that Gabe, Harrison, and Jack were good in their own ways. Will had been out many times for pelts and oil and, like Mr. Morgen and Harrison, had been in privateers during the war. Yet it was his gritty acceptance of his lot as a foremast hand that impressed Thomas. He had no other trade and would continue as a topman until he could no longer climb up the futtock shrouds or sidle out on the footrope. Perhaps he would then earn enough as a ship-keeper in New York or Boston to feed and clothe himself and buy his week's portion of tobacco.

"How many voyages have you made in the fisheries?" the lad asked.

Thomas knew, the entire crew, except the lascars, knew how many times he had been out. The old sailor had recited all his adventures in the night watches and in the fo'c's'le. He was almost the equal of Gabe, the master of the yarn in the starboard watch.

Gabe claimed to have seen monstrous creatures swimming in the sea and crawling around the rocks of uninhabited coasts. He told one story about a small island he had visited off the coast of Chile where the savages were so rude and unlearned they did not have fire and were terrified when they first saw it, thinking it was lightning springing from the earth. Once on a calm night far out at sea he had heard voices, women's voices. He swore to it, holding an open hand up to impress his listeners with the truth of it. "Sigh-reens" he called them, women close by but unseen who had breathed to him sweet and firm promises of their oyster baskets.

Will's tales were more believable. Thomas's question to him was simply to tease out another story. Will could guess that, but he never let on that he did, for he savored retelling and reliving all the times of excitement and awe in his life as much as his listeners. They all knew the destination of each voyage, the number of skins taken, and the amount of sperm and black oil rendered. Even a recital of those well-known tales made the watches seem shorter.

The old sailor kept his hand on the brace and lowered his gaze to the horizon. His head tilted a little to his left as he made the effort to recall his trips at sea. "Let me see. . . . First, three times after the whale. That was Greenland and the Brazils. Then it was to Masy Foora for skins and on to Canton for a China cargo." He let go of the line and counted on his fingers as he enumerated his voyages. "Then a year in privateers and coasters during the war. To the South Georgias twice for seal. Now, this time again for fur and oil. That will be seven times after the seal and whale, 'bout fifteen . . . sixteen year when we make Stonington again. Afore that it was the sugar trade."

"That was to Jamaica," Thomas prompted.

"Aye, Jamaica and Matanzas," Will answered. "Molasses, sugar, rum, and the fever."

"And pirates," the lad put in.

"Pirates, oh yes, pirates. Off Santiagy where you'd expect 'em for sure. I told you that tale."

"Yes, how they came up on you in the night."

"Aye, we suspicioned when we saw them with no light. We loaded our guns with bar and chain shot and carried away her rigging. Left the Spaniard in a trice. Hee, hee, hee. That was something we learned well from them." Will's laugh died away as he looked aloft again. He eyed the studding sail and tugged at the brace and warned, "Mark me, lad, something will part soon."

The wind driving the barque on her northerly course came from the west-southwest and struck the barque on her larboard quarter.

Thomas began coiling and stowing the extra line of the running gear. He looked over the rail as he worked and watched the white-capped swells rolling toward the ship from the same direction as the wind. On the leeward side of the vessel, their receding backs at any given instant appeared to be surfaces of chipped, smoke-hued glass.

When the subdued colors of dawn had spread over the sea that morning, scattered clouds had become visible drifting northeast and had grown in bulk and height from midday on, boiling up higher and higher.

The barque heaved forward into the troughs until the horizon could not be seen from the deck. She bore up sluggishly as each crest came under her keel, but the heavy press of canvas kept her heeled over.

Across the sternboard of the vessel were the words: "*Dove,* Stonington" carved out in raised letters and painted white. Below these was the figure of a bird also carved in relief. Its wings were spread as if in flight, and its head was turned to its right, showing a single eye. The eye was just a cavity in the wood that, at one time, might have been set with a bit of glass. Now, the bird stared blankly astern. The paint on it and on the names was weathered and peeling, especially on the harder grain. The sternboard was split in its entire length, and the wing tips of the bird had fallen off or had been knocked loose, making it appear dumpy and incapable of a soaring flight.

Thomas watched the stunsail again for any weakness, then his gaze moved up to the topgallant yard. He remembered he was up there standing on the horse the day they left Stonington Port. A chill wind was blowing out of the northeast when the newly painted *Dove* was cast loose and warped out. It had made his eyes water, and, in its crisp, icy feel on the skin of his face and hands, he felt the cold and severity of another coming winter or perhaps another strange year like 1816. In his ignorance he thought he was evading the harsh season, but many months later he had been plunged into worse weather far below the equinoctial line. From the height of that yard he had been able to see from a different perspective the town he had known since he was four years old. He had picked out the ropewalks, the shops, the churches, the kiln dock and the marshland beyond it. The trees in and to the northeast of Stonington were fast losing their leaves then. The blustering wind had stripped them from the branches and swirled them around the weathered houses and over rickety fences. In short lulls they had settled to the ground, only to be scooped again from the derelict garden plots, pig pens, and rutted roads, and carried toward the harbor. When they reached the dock, the leaves had sailed around and over the score of people gathered there to watch the *Dove* depart for the southern fishery. Then they had lost their momentum over the inlet and fluttered down onto the water. Between the wharf and the moving stern of the barque, hundreds of scarlet leaves patterned the dark surface of the harbor. More and more had fallen each minute in zigzagging descents to the water. The *Dove,* responding to the warp and nudged by the same wind that scattered the leaves, moved away from the land. In the eddies of her wake, the reddened bits of flotsam gyred into the murk.

Thomas had known nearly all the people who stood on the wharf that day, yet only his father and Isabel drew his eyes and held them. Father was taller than most of the others there and, unlike any of them, he had not waved to the departing crew. Thomas was puzzled, even piqued by that omission then, having thought they had come to an agreement. Or had Father changed his mind? Had the old melancholy taken him again? The men of both watches except those turning the windlass and tending the running gear had spread out on the yards to loose the sails and wave a hearty farewell to their shore-bound kin. They shouted hurrahs, fired with their prospects yet laden with goodbyes, over and over. Thomas didn't feel like such a display, but when he saw Isabel's face framed in the circle of her bonnet and saw her shake a handkerchief, he joined in. His right hand gripped his tarpaulin hat, and he waved it port to starboard in a wide arc over his head.

Ned, the smaller boy aboard, had overheard Mr. Morgen say it would be a two-year voyage. Jack guessed two and a half or three years, saying it would take that long to fill the hold. Seals had been scarce of late. No one knew for sure, not even the older hands who had been out for seal and train oil before. It would all depend on their fortune in the rookeries. Thomas remembered thinking he would not see Stonington again until late 1820 or even 1821. He had reasoned with Father that it was not too long a time to be away. He was almost sure to make more than wages in that time and might gain a small fortune. Many other lads had left for the grounds and had done far better than if they had stayed home. In addition to the cod men, the sealers were the ones who brought money to the port. In the fall of 1816, men from the *Meteor* and *Adventure* were paid off in Boston and got nearly five hundred dollars for their shares of two-year voyages. That was a hundred and fifty dollars more than what he earned making shoes in the same number of months. When *The American Victor* returned in 1817, the fifty-fifth lay was said to be six hundred dollars. Some of the Stonington men had carried silk, carvings, and such from Whampoa on their own account and what they sold them for they added to their share. Even before his sixteenth year, he'd seen that sealing, whaling, and the China trade were the enterprises to be in. Someone had told him once that no great wealth came from small shops, and he had repeated that to Father many times. But he had only nodded and continued cutting leather without looking up.

While most of those on the pier fluttered their handkerchiefs, waved or cried, Father had stood motionless and watched the barque fill away for the Brazils. Thomas, still waving his hat, had turned about and watched the line of well-wishers diminishing astern, losing the details of their clothes and features. Though he had waited with the others for more than an hour, his father seemed alone, not part of the little crowd. He had hoped that when his departure was made a fact by the loosing of the sails, Father would accept it completely. If he had waved, it would have meant he had seen the need of his leaving and made it a happier parting. Father never waved that day, but had turned and walked slowly to the shop.

"What are you thinking of, lad?" Will asked. "You're staring at the sky so."

The words pulled Thomas back to the present and he replied, "I was thinking of the day we left Stonington."

"Left!" Will sputtered. "Why, you oughtn't to be thinking o' that, but the day we return. We have our pelts. We have our oil. We need only to trade them for our China cargo, and we're homeward bound!" The old sailor's eyes sparkled with the memories of his past returns, and a smile, half-hidden by his gray whiskers, widened as he spoke.

The smile grew into a grin at the prospect, making the wrinkles on his temples deepen. "Think o' the day we drop our bower in Boston or New York," he snickered. "Hee, hee, hee. Oh, they'll be out to greet us. Ho! Lasses on each arm and the runners shoutin' to take our traps. Just think o' that."

Thomas tried to imagine what his return would be like. Who would want to hear how he had lived and worked in the rookeries of the high latitudes and called at cannibal coasts to wood and water? The stories of storms at sea and the strangeness of heathen China had been told over and over again. There would be no singular thing in his return. Father would listen politely, reassured by his recited adventures and dangers that it would have been better if he had stayed at home. He would then point out that he might as easily have perished as returned. No images formed in Thomas's mind of striding back to the shop with his sea chest and bag carried along after him on a cart. He had seen that all of his life, men who had gone to sea and returned in that fashion, but he could not see himself doing it. He could not picture himself with a gaggle of little boys following him up the road to the shoe shop. He didn't care to think of it. What threads ran back to the long, low Connecticut shore to draw him home again? Isabel's father would like him no better. All the money he could bring home would not alter that cool look of mislike he always gave him. In the smoke-blackened hovels on the sealing grounds, Stonington had become a half-remembered dream, a little port busied with its fishing and boat-building, but one that could not compare with the great doings and wealth of Boston and New York. It wasn't the place it had once been to him. He had sailed past the great stone peak in Rio de Janeiro and seen the blacks carrying their masters in palanquins. He had seen Table Mountain and the dark slopes of Van Diemen's Land.

"Oh, she's foul!" Will suddenly said. "Look at that weed, it hangs like ribbons."

Thomas leaned over the weather rail and watched the water draw away and reveal the streaming, green growth. Then he turned and looked aft. "We must keep a watch for Mr. Morgen. He's apt to come up soon," he warned.

"The ol' man wants a quick passage now," Will snapped, ignoring the lad's caution, "but he'd not spend a day scrapin' her. Can you see the shrewdness in that?" The old sailor slapped his hand on the rail and growled, "Ha! Perhaps he'll drop to his knees and pray awhile, and our foul bottom will be struck clean. I would like to see his fine religion do that, eh?"

The lad did not answer but returned to work and stole glances at the rising masses of clouds abeam of the vessel and far to the east.

"No, the good Lord won't make it clean for him. Now he'll have to carry on to make up for the loss. Hee, hee, hee," the old tar chuckled. "Then she'll part a truss or backstay. Oh, it's a shame to use a ship so." He shook his head at the prospect and turned away from the gunnel.

Thomas finished coiling and hanging the last of the running gear and went back to replacing the slings on an old buoy. Now and again he glanced up at the brace and clew. He could see the stunsail was catching the brunt of the wind. "When do you think we'll make the China coast?" he asked.

Will scratched his beard with the fingers of his right hand. "Oh, that's hard to say," he answered. "Now that we have this great load of skins and oil, we'll not call anywheres again 'cept to wood and water. By my reckoning, if we are not much becalmed and don't shorten sail at night, we could be there in two months. Aye, that would be rightly it, two months, perhaps three."

"You don't think it could be any sooner?"

"Oh, no, no. It will take that long to reach Canton. We can go nowheres else. We will do well to make five or six knots in this condition."

Thomas looked again to the east at the gathering clouds, then resumed working on the buoy as he spoke to Will. "We could have touched at the Derwent and laid her ashore there, or perhaps Port Jackson."

Will eased slowly down to kneel next to Thomas. "Oh, she should have been scraped long ago," he muttered, "but now she be loaded too much. She'd not take the ground easy." The corners of his eyes crinkled again, and a smirk grew wider and wider beneath his beard. Then he tittered, "Hee, hee, hee, now you don't think Cap'n Tobit would trust this crew that close to them rum shops in Port Jackson? No-o-o, we're the temperance ship. No-o-o. He wouldn't have that. Hee, hee, hee. He'd have no crew a'tall next mornin'. Maybe never see some of 'em again."

"But the men would lose their shares," Thomas pointed out.

"Lad," Will explained, "when your head is full of rum, there's no room for proper thinkin' and common sense. I've seen many throw away a year's wages and more for less spirits than would fill his hat."

The old sailor fell silent for a while. All traces of the smile left his face. Then he nodded and spoke wistfully, "Aye, lad, aye. I've done that myself. I've done it myself. It's just as well we didn't call at Van Diemen's again, m'boy. Those are evil places over there. Oh, evil places. Too many convicts and ticket o' leave men about. And they're the worst o' the lot. They might a' come aboard in the middle o' the night, cut our throats, and sailed the *Dove* to China themselves. They might 'a done it had we gone there and they suspicioned how much she was worth. Oh, no, lad. It was best we never called there with this great load o' skins and oil. Well, the worst is over for now. No more pullin' ashore on those chilly islands. No more huntin' bird's eggs out in the mizzlin' rain. You'll be glad o' that. You don't take too well to the skinnin' business, eh?"

"No, not too well," Thomas replied, turning to look again to the east. "This wasn't what I expected at all. That was surely the end of the Earth down there. We must have gone to every miserable rock and shore in that ocean."

"Aye. Just about," Will agreed, "but that's where the seals be. 'Tis the nature o' the business. But you'll not need to fret about it no more, lad. On to China, eh? We'll have a fine load for Boston: tea, silk, nankeen, fancy plates. Oh, they'll make a dollar on this trip. The blasted owners will be rich in a few months' time. A thousandfold on their money for profit. But no more clubbin' the creatures and smellin' the stink o' the rotten meat. No more boilin' sea elephants. The killin' part and the livin' ashore is over, and we won't land on another island 'cept to wood and water. Lad, are you sorry you left your cobbler's bench for this?"

Thomas did not answer at once. The question stirred his memories, and the image of the oil lamp hanging in the shop formed in his mind. Its amber glow spread over the scraps of leather, knives, awls, hammer, and marking wheel resting on his bench. The lamp illuminated the racks of lasts on the wall. He recalled the smells of cured hides and tobacco smoke that filled the shop.

"Sometimes," Thomas finally replied, "but Stonington is a dull place in some ways."

Will shook his head and said, "You young 'uns are all for adventure. You let your fancies carry you away. See, you have left a good shop back there, and you have left your father all alone while you sail on this stinkin' barque."

"But we made a good voyage, and I intend to go back and see how he is and give him half my share."

"Surely, lad, you will go back. But you will see it all differently then. I'll warrant you not leave again. You're not for this sealing business. It's not your callin'. No, it's for us what cannot read nor cipher and haven't the wits for a better trade. I've watched you, Thomas. You belong ashore, with a wife and little 'uns in a proper house. Aye, you belong there. You can make your fortune, become a gentleman, wear long togs, and have respect. Stay in the fo'c's'le, and you will be nothing ever. Once you get back, stay ashore."

"Ashore," the lad repeated, "perhaps, but not sitting cramped at a bench making shoes. I would go mad if I had to smile at another old lady or sew another stitch. No, I'll not be a cat whipper again. I might go up along the Mohawk or down the Ohio, but I'll not keep a shop."

"Was your father loath to have you leave?"

Thomas brushed a stray hair from his face and felt for the ribbon that held most of it at the nape of his neck. "I don't know truly how much," he said slowly. "We talked some about it. He always advised against it, but when I left he gave me that fine pair of boots I have."

"Ah, made them himself, did he?"

"Yes. He spoke very little after the colic carried my mother off. He was taken with melancholy the whole of that year. When I told him of my aim, he said it would be best I didn't go. He was satisfied with what the shop made in a year, but I meant to sail for the fishery and earn more than a narrow living. And I have done it."

Thomas kept a steady watch to the leeward for nearly a minute. Massive clouds were billowing up over the darkening sea to the east. In all directions, rain was falling in patches about the ship, but the heaviest rain was far off to the starboard.

Will peered at the horizon trying to discover what had drawn the lad's attention. "D'ye see the New Zealand coast over there?" he asked. "If you do, you have a fine pair of eyes. The steward heard Mr. Morgen say it was upwards of two hundred fifty mile away."

"No, not the coast, but I think something is over there. You see how dark it is directly abeam."

The two crewmen watched the gray curtain of rain that seemingly hung motionless between the base of the clouds and the sea. Thomas pointed to the horizon and asked, "There, you see that darkest place under the clouds?"

Will leaned his head back and squinted at the rain falling miles away.

"Back to work!" the lad whispered. "The mate's coming up."

Both men dropped to their knees and busied themselves with the slings on the buoy. They watched the mate with stealthy glances as he passed the helmsman and took up a station at the weather rail.

Will whispered to Thomas, "What you see over there is just the shadow o' the clouds. With all the rain it makes it dark so."

A strong gust of wind struck the *Dove* at that moment, heeling her farther over. The barque groaned in response to the added strain and recovered. The crewmen looked up at the spread of canvas being pressed by more and more rushes of the air. The stunsail boom strained at the brace and eased back again with each gust. The cleat where the brace was belayed was working badly and looked as if it would carry away at any moment. Thomas and Will both turned and looked aft at the mate.

"Damn!" Will sputtered. "Why doesn't he have us take it in?"

Mr. Morgen watched the sail but showed no concern and gave no order to have it struck. He lowered his gaze to the deck and spotted the two sailors looking at him. "About your work, you two!" he shouted. "You're not paid to take the air!"

The chastened crewmen instantly turned to the buoy again.

"A great bloody fool . . . a great bloody fool," the old sailor muttered in his beard. "We slave to get it up there, and in a few minutes we'll have to cut a mess down. Carry on! Carry on! That's all they know. When it goes, he'll make out it wasn't rigged proper. 'Aye, sloppy work. You're a mob of sojers,' he'll say. Right, lad?"

They finished, and each man reached behind his back and sheathed his knife. Thomas pinched up the bits of rope and seizings, got up, and walked down the slanting deck to the leeward rail where he tossed them to the wind. Will picked up the finished buoy and went off to stow it away.

Large raindrops began falling, slanting over the rail with an increasing wind, and in a few minutes the bare deck was shining with a bluish light reflected from the sky and the rising clouds. The ship plunged ahead and heeled over until the sea boiled up through the lee scuppers. The hissing of the water alongside could be heard over the drone of the wind in the rigging and the slap-slap of the halyards against the masts.

Suddenly, a loud *BANG!* sounded overhead and then the crack of loose canvas snapping in the wind. Everyone on deck looked up to the main yard. Lines were blowing free between the main- and the foremast, and the topmast stunsail was slatting and twisting from its stub yard. The lower brace had ripped the cleat off and the boom had carried away. A splintered end projected from the iron ring. In a second the mate was yelling orders forward to the men on deck. Thomas swung himself out onto the weather shrouds and started aloft, quick, monkey-like. Will followed but was slower, just reaching the main yard as the younger sailor crabbed his way out to the broken boom.

"Ho, mate!" Will called out as he came up to Thomas on the yard. "Here's a good lesson for Mr. Morgen. Let's hope he learns it well afore he makes firewood out o' all our spars!"

The lad nodded as he pulled at the heel lashing. The two of them worked the broken stub out of the iron. By gripping the jackstay with one hand, then sliding it along and carrying the boom in the other, they sidled toward the slings of the yard. Their jackets and trousers fluttered in the wind and were hit with scattering drops of rain.

"Now what are they about?" Will cried out. He was leaning over and nodding toward their mates below. The stunsail had been lowered to the deck, and a man was unbending the blocks from the other half of the boom. Another man was carrying a new boom along the deck.

"Why, they mean to send that stick up and set the stunsail again," Thomas replied.

"Damnation!" Will swore. "It'll only give way again, if we ever git it up a'tall."

"You, there!" the mate yelled up to Will. "Send that down by the girt line!"

"Aye, sir! Down by the girt line," the old sailor called back with a quick nod of his head. He overhauled enough of the line to hitch it to the broken boom. He then sent it down to the deck, grumbling as it went. "What clowns! They're in a lather to make another mile now. Old Tobit and the mate didn't make such a do when we was on Macquarie and Brister's, half-frozen and eatin' seal paws. They could damn well take their time then."

All around Thomas was the spider's web of rigging he had sorted out during the first few weeks of the voyage. He had learned that it was all in a state of tension and equilibrium. The shrouds were set up taut, the starboard ones countering the pull of the port ones. The backstays held against the forestays and the press of the wind on the sails. In all of the standing lines, not one could be hauled upon without easing off another that pulled against it, nor could one be loosened lest it caused its opposite to go slack. Each force was pitted against a counter force. The tautened fiber and the force of the wind thus bound the masts, spars, and hull into one rigid being. The construction of wood, iron, and rope vibrated as the wind swept through it. The long lines clapped endlessly along the height of the masts. The shadows of the mast, shrouds, footropes, and clewlines played with a slow rhythm, rising and falling on the bellying topsail, marking the limits of the barque's pitching. The cloths of the sail were yellowed by the late afternoon light and took on the shades and patterns of old, water-stained paper. Above him, the topsail yard hanging by its tye block was split for half its length and weathered by the two years at sea. Where the iron fittings were mounted on the spar, red-brown stains had leached onto the wood and mixed with the streaks of guano.

Beneath the bowsprit, the bluff hull rolled a whitened wave aside. The barque rode down the backs of the swells, carrying its little community of men northward. To the east the clouds had continued to swell into masses, the nearer ones covering the sky halfway to the zenith. Scattered curtains of rain from them obscured parts of the horizon. In his imaginative eye, the clouds became enormous peaks lighted by the lowering sun in places and shadowed in others by those west of the *Dove*. The deep clefts remained in cold grays, becoming misty gorges with the implied depth and traces of hidden views as in an oriental painting. What Thomas saw beneath the high constructs of vapor and light could have been an illusion or simply the downpour. He thought it must be one or the other. As the sun edged down, a straw-hued light streamed through the aisles between the clouds in the west to tint the whitecaps leeward of the barque. The darkened area beneath the largest squall became denser, solidly fixed within the veil of mist. It then assumed a defined shape, forming an outline that sloped up from the surface of the sea on each side and disappeared into the black cloud above. He did not sing out at once but waited several minutes while the rain there slackened. The low-angled sunlight penetrated farther and farther beneath the cloud. A thin, white line widened, narrowed, and widened again where the dark mass met the sea. Thomas touched Will's shoulder and nodded his head to the east.

Will turned and looked in that direction. "Oh, lad, you was right!" he exclaimed. "'Tis land for sure, high land!"

"What do you make it to be?" Thomas asked.

"I couldn't guess. We're not to make landfall so soon."

Thomas leaned out and shouted aft, "Land 'o! East by north."

The mate and the helmsman looked up at him and then to the horizon where he was pointing. All the men working on deck turned and searched the sea to the east. Even the little lascar cook ducked his head out of the caboose to see what the fuss was all about. The crew looked alternately over the waves and then up to Thomas as if they could see nothing beneath the massive cloud. Word got down to the fo'c's'le, and the watch below came up to see an unexpected landfall. They clambered onto the knight-heads and the windlass to get a better look. Every face that was turned to leeward was full-bearded except for those of the boys.

Mr. Morgen had his glass up to his right eye, but it was difficult to keep it steadied while the vessel plunged forward. He slipped his left arm around a line for support and managed to keep the glass trained on the horizon.

Thomas looked back to the east again. The white line was still there, swelling, then thinning down to a taut thread, marking an undeniable boundary between the sea and a shadowed land. The clouds, great puffs of vapor, were changing their shapes and hues. Peaked masses spread and took on the colors of firelight. In places the cloud-mountains gradually parted and opened new chasms and hanging valleys. The dusky shape beneath them now had that massy, unmistakable quality of land. It was no longer a black form within an obscuring fall of rain, but something that had solidity. Every few minutes lightning flickered at the base of the clouds or glowed within them. A narrow shaft of sunlight penetrated the decreasing rain and illuminated a speck of green above the line of surf.

There was a stir on deck. The mate had taken the glass from his eye and called to little Ned. The boy ran aft, listened to the officer's order and hopped off to the companionway. In a minute he returned leading Captain Tobit who came across the pitching deck in his old waddle. He seemed annoyed with the interruption as he came to the weather rail.

"Well, what is it?" the captain asked the mate.

Mr. Morgen pointed to the east and said, "It's land, sir. Young Thomas saw it from the maintop."

"You call me up on a fool's errand, Mr. Morgen! You know there's no land on this course till we come up to the Three Kings."

"I've seen it myself, sir. Here, take the glass."

"He's just seeing rain and clouds for land," Captain Tobit growled back impatiently. His thinning white hair was revealed when he pushed his hat up to make room for the instrument. "I see nothing," he announced.

"One point farther north," Mr. Morgen suggested, "there, where it rains the most and is the darkest."

The captain moved the glass slightly.

"Do you see it, sir?"

Little by little the end of the spyglass moved along until the captain had surveyed the entire eastern horizon. Then he returned it to the place the mate had pointed out. "Humph, land for sure," he murmured, taking the glass from his eye.

"Could it be the coast?" the mate asked.

"No! No! You know we could not have made that much leeway. There are islands in the Strait, but we are not up to it nor are we anywhere near the coast. There is no denying but it is an island."

"Perhaps we have met with a current setting that way, and there is a headland over there?" the mate ventured. "Cape Foulwind?"

"Certainly not! Take another look, Mr. Morgen," the captain snapped and handed the glass back.

The mate picked the land out again with the spyglass. He studied it for a few seconds and admitted, "Yes, I can see it now. It is an island. I'll make a note of it in the log."

"No!" the captain barked. "You'll not make a note of it in the log!"

"Why should I not record it?"

"I will give you reasons enough later. At present I wish to look it over. Now bring her about and make for it."

"But we have no need to. It's merely another island."

"To you it is only another island. Ha! I can believe that well enough."

"Can we afford the time now that we are . . . ?"

"Damnation, man! Order the helm about . . . there, three points. I'll not trade another word with you. We *will* have the time. *I will* make time as *I* please. Do you understand me?"

"Aye, sir," the mate answered weakly and crossed to the helmsman. He gave the order, and the vessel veered to a more easterly course. The crew braced the yards to be carried more squarely.

All the men off watch crowded by the cathead as their mates brought the *Dove* around to the new course. They studied the island that was now about a half point to the starboard of the jib-boom. One of the men looked aft along the deck at the captain who was staring at the bit of land veiled in the rain.

"Now what's he up to?" the crewman asked. "We have wood and water enough. We have our full load of skins and oil. Now he's going to poke his big beak over there. For what, I ask you, for what?"

"Well, Gabe," said the man beside him, "perhaps he don't trust his cypherin'. That could be the coast over there and he don't know why."

"Well he'd best find out afore we strike on some rocks," Gabe warned. "We need plenty of water under our bottom now. Damn! Twenty thousand skins and over two thousand barrel of oil and we're homeward bound. This voyage's o'ertopped all I ever made, and I don't want to be wanderin' about here. Let's be goin' our way."

"Maybe the chronom-eater has gone off," suggested another man at the gunnel.

Gabe turned and snapped, "Jack, he found Brister's an' Macquarie an' Dusky with the chronom-eater well enough. I say he's playin' the devil. Mark me, he's up to no good."

"He could be curious of the land. Just curious," Jack offered for another explanation.

"Ha, has he been curious about anything afore? No, not 'less there was money to be made by it. For two Spanish dollars he'd sail this barque up the Sticks."

"Sticks? Where's that?" another sailor asked with his head atilt and one eye winked shut.

"Why that's a river down there," Gabe replied, pointing over the rail. "There, Nat."

Nat took a step closer, leaned over the side, and turned back smiling. "Nothing there 'cept seawater, Gabe. Can't be no river there."

"Well, no, not right there. Way down below in hell. Below the sea."

Nat suppressed his smile, removed his hat and held it to his chest as if addressing a lady. He leaned farther over the side than before. He straightened up, and stroking his beard said, "No, can't see how that could be. A river there'd get all mixed up in the salt water, then there'd be no river anymore."

"No, you don't understand. Even under the bottom of the sea. A fella once told me there was a river down there in hell, and there was a man that got a boat and carried people from one side to the other."

Nat thought for a while, then asked, "Why would they want to get across, seeing as they was dead anyhow and couldn't go nowhere?"

"I don't know, but he told me that's how it was down there. It's not like in heaven where you can wander all around between the clouds and look down on all the live people. Down there you can't do nothing but cross this river, and they call it the Sticks."

Every man standing at the gunnel was smirking except for Gabe who shook his head, piqued at their failure to understand his words.

"The Sticks," Jack murmured, "that sounds like a brake where you'd cut wattles or there is willows or pollard trees. Don't sound like no river name. You sure you got it right? Are you sure it wasn't the

Mys-sticks River? Now that would put hell between Stonington Port and New London, and that would give those Baptist preachers the fits for sure. Hee, hee, hee."

Nat forced his smile into a sober look and asked, "If ol' Tobit chooses to touch over there, will you make your complaint to him?"

The rest of the watch kept smiling, and some broke into half-suppressed giggles. Gabe looked glumly at them and said no more.

"Now, I say we have Thomas set down your dissatisfaction on paper," Jack proposed, "then you can carry it aft and give it to ol' Capt'n Toby like a memorial."

The crewmen around Gabe broke out in howls of laughter.

"Aye!" Nat cried out. "He'll have you triced up to the shrouds and pull down your trousers. Then we'll wager what he'll do with the paper! Hoo, hoo, hoo!"

"Or maybe he'll make you eat it," another sailor cackled, "every last scrap with a half pound of salt to make sure it's well seasoned."

"Laugh now, you fools," Gabe mumbled. "There will be grief enough for us all later."

"Oh," Jack said, tossing another barb at Gabe, "perhaps he'll be kindly, forgive you being so plaguey forward and leave you there ashore with a tierce of flour and your club. 'Sleep under your boat and skin seals for a while,' he'll tell you, 'and we'll relieve you in a year or so.'"

One by one the grins and laughter ended, and the men turned to watch the dusky shape of the island rise and widen. The last pink tinge faded from all but the tops of the clouds. Below, they had only shades of gray, from the lightest to the darkest. The veiling rain was still falling over the island, and, in the failing light, the flashes of lightning grew brighter and broader within the clouds and rain. A few bolts struck below the obscuring mists, and their flashes revealed portions of wooded slopes. Several seconds later, muffled, fragmented thunderclaps reached them.

Captain Tobit scanned the island with his glass. Several times he lowered the instrument, grunted, and peered at the horizon with unaided eyes. "Mr. Morgen!" he called. When the mate approached, he asked, "Do you see that surf running north of the island about some straggling rocks?"

"Yes, sir. Something of a reef or shoal water there."

"Round the end of it, and we will lie in the lee of it for the night. Take in the stunsails, Mr. Morgen, and see to it there is a sharp look-out on the foremast."

"Aye, sir, a sharp lookout on the foremast," the mate replied. Then he muttered to himself, barely moving his lips, "I damn well don't need to be told that."

An hour later the barque was within two miles of the surf, and by the persistent twilight, the crew saw the sea pounding on a long spit that curved west from the island then turned north and finally north-east. It was composed of jagged, dark rocks with low sections of beach between them. The man on the foremast called down to tell the mate that there was another spit farther east, a mirror image of the first. Its tip was only three or four miles from the first, and thus they formed the heads to a large circular bay.

The *Dove* went east a half-mile beyond the tip of the western spit, then turned toward the entrance. Captain Tobit ordered her held full and by until she was brought to the center of the bay. Two boards were then made to bring the vessel nearer to the windward shore. The other watch was set to readying the buoy, getting up a range of cable and bending it to the chain.

Mr. Morgen then ordered the deep-sea lead brought up, and all got ready to make soundings.

CHAPTER 2

"READY FORWARD?" the mate called to the men on the bow.

"Aye, sir, ready forward," came their instant responses.

"Ready aft?" he asked, facing the starboard quarter.

The crewman standing in the mizzen chains shouted his answer.

"Then heave away!" Mr. Morgen ordered.

The lascar clinging to the end of the spritsail yard shoved the plummet forward. It swung out ahead of the *Dove*. When the weight reached the farthest point of its arc, the man on the jib-boom, holding the bight of the line, let it go. "Watch ho, watch," he called out.

The lead splashed into the waves beyond the tip of the boom, then plunged downward, pulling the line at a speed that made it hiss.

No bottom was reached, and the line was reeled aboard and the lead hove again and again as the vessel plowed toward the island.

"Got ground! Seventy-five fathom!" the man in the mizzen chains called out when the *Dove* was three-quarters of a mile from the shore.

Captain Tobit grunted and paced about, waiting for the lead to be hauled in. The crewman passed it to the mate and he in turn raised its lower end up and showed it to the captain. Very dark gray grains like coarse sand or cinders were pressed into the tallow arming. Tobit picked some of the granules from the tallow and rolled them between his thumb and forefinger. Then he opened his hand and looked at the grains for a few seconds. "Take her within four cable lengths and let go the bower," he said absently.

With his mouth half-open Mr. Morgen stared at the captain, unable to respond to what he had just been ordered. Tobit looked up and glared at the mate when he did not answer. "Well, why are you all struck aback?" he demanded.

After a pause the stunned mate asked, "Four cable lengths . . . four? But should it not be. . . ."

"Do you need an ear trumpet now?"

"But if the wind comes around to the north'ard, they'll not be room to veer away cable. . . ."

Tobit's face reddened, and he shouted, "Damnation, man! It isn't going to change. I said four, Mr. Morgen, and I mean four lengths. No more, no less. You understand? Now see to it!"

The mate ordered all but the fore-staysail, topsails, and mizzen taken in. The *Dove* slowed as sheets were started and each sail was clewed up and furled. Gabe and Jack bent over a heavy hawser, working quickly to bend it to the chain cable.

"He's mad," Gabe muttered. "He's altogether mad. The man belongs in Bedlam."

"Ah, we all can see that well enough," Jack agreed. "It will be a piece of work to beat out of this place in a north wind. No, we're in too far as it is. What do you think is ailin' him?"

"I don't know. It's a puzzle for sure."

"Maybe he's gettin' too old for this business. He should be home hoeing a garden and tendin' his chickens."

Gabe nodded and said, "He's been right strange since we got this great load of skins and oil. Maybe his share bein' a whole fifth works on his mind. That and how much increase over that he'll have on the China cargo. We have only our sixtieth lay to think about. Better he think about how we're to get home than how he be spendin' his money."

"Ho, mate that's a surety. He won't enjoy his fortune if he don't get it to Boston or New York. He'd better see this load to Whampoa before he dreams about what he's going to buy next."

Gabe stole a glance aft and whispered, "Watch him parade up and down. He looks like a great stupid bird waddlin' about with his hooked nose and big belly."

Each sounding with the deep-sea lead indicated a steeply rising bottom. When it was shallow enough, the heavy lead was taken in and the smaller plummet given to a man in the fore channel. He let out several feet of line, whirled the weight in large circles at his right side and, on the upward swing, let it fly forward. The lead arched up and ahead of the bow. It finished its curving flight and plunged into the water. His first call was for sixteen fathoms. At the required distance from the shore, the last call from the leadsman was a quarter less eight.

The *Dove* turned into the wind and slowed quickly. Within a few seconds, she got sternway, and the mate gave the order to let go the anchor. Then he shouted to the topmen, "Take three reefs in the topsails!"

By the last hint of twilight admitted between the clouds, the crew spread out on the yards, set the reefs, and furled the slapping canvas. From that height they looked toward the island, but they could make out nothing of the black shape above the swelling and shrinking of the white surf. They could only sense a brooding mass that threw back the hollow rumble of breaking waves. High overhead sudden glows rose in the clouds and a few moments later came a cracking, descending thunder.

Thomas swung down from the shrouds, and the moment his feet touched the deck, by long habit, he looked upward. Patches of stars showed, evidence that the sky was not entirely occluded. New stars appeared in portions of the sky while elsewhere they were blotted out. From overhead came the constant thrumming of the wind in the shrouds and stays and the noise of halyards and sheets whipping against the masts. Men on the deck had coiled the lines of the running gear and stowed them neatly away.

Mr. Morgen gave Thomas and Will the anchor watch, and the remainder of the crew made for their bunks. As Thomas passed alongside the caboose, someone placed a hand on his shoulder. "Aye, mate?" he asked, looking to see who it was.

"Still a chill in the wind," a soft voice said.

In the darkness Thomas recognized it as Harrison's. "There is that coolness, Chips," he replied. "I can feel it well enough in my bones."

"We're not out of the reach of those islands yet," Harrison noted.

"I won't believe we're on our way to China till we're up to the line."

Harrison said nothing for a moment but lingered as if he wished to say more. His face was not more than an arm's length away, but in the starlight his eyes were hidden in dark hollows and his beard was only an indistinct black smudge.

"Chips?" Thomas asked. "Is there something else?"

Harrison shifted in his stance, looked upward, and replied, "Perhaps. Sleep lightly when you turn in tonight. Sleep lightly, lad."

"Surely, I promise, but why, mate?"

"The wind most likely will change," Harrison added.

"How do you know it will?"

"It would be strange if it did not blow from another direction now that we are nearer the Strait. It's a contrary sea 'twixt here and New Holland. I served with a man who was out here years ago in the *Favorite*. He told me there was little accounting for the whim of the weather here."

"But if the wind comes round to the north, might it not start lightly and we would be able to beat out of this bay?"

"Perhaps, but it will be a risk in any case. We'd best be ready."

"What if we let go another bower?"

"Do you know what came up on the lead? Something light like cinders. Do you think even two bowers and the sheet anchor ahead would hold in ground loose as that?"

"I guess not," Thomas answered. He certainly would not dispute Harrison's opinion, for the man knew as much of the sailing of a ship as the chief mate, perhaps more; yet he was before the mast as the carpenter.

"Remember, sleep lightly, lad," Harrison warned once again and slipped away in the darkness.

"Goodnight, Christopher," Thomas called after him.

For Thomas there was almost an hour of the anchor watch yet to stand. He walked forward to the windlass and stood there for several minutes listening to the breaking surf and each crack and boom of thunder as it rolled down from the heights of the island. The constant notes of the hempen lines in the wind droned over those mixed rumbles. Then he stepped to the cathead and looked to the west. Weak star-shine reflected from the breakers rising and falling against the distant western spur. To the south there was nothing visible but the immense blackness above the white pulse of the surf. Someone touched his elbow, and he turned to see his watch-mate holding something out to him.

"A musket?" he asked, barely recognizing the object in the gloom.

"Aye, and all loaded and primed," Will said. "Mr. Morgen orders we are not to walk the same side and talk our watch out."

"He expects boarders?" Thomas asked.

"I'll lay old Tobit does. He told the mate there might be savages ashore there and to keep our watch as we did at Cape South and Dusky."

"Ha, are we to put up nettings too?"

"At least not that, lad, but we are to look under the counter and channels at every turn. You take the larboard for now."

Thomas took his weapon and rested it on his shoulder. For the remainder of their watch, the two men paced the length of the vessel, met at the bow and stern, and reversed directions. On the larboard side Thomas peered often at the island; but no light, no flicker of fire, no lantern showed. It remained hidden in its veil of blackness, throwing back the sound of the crashing waves and their rolling echoes. He wondered if the discharge of his musket would come back as one or many reports. What confusion there would be if, for the nonce, he did pull the trigger! A smile formed on his face, and he laughed inwardly as he thought of all the crew and officers dashing about looking for savages and shouting for lights. It would almost be worth it to see old Tobit, in fine fettle, giving orders like Bonaparte and then being piqued when no savages appeared. But he daren't do that. Tobit would work him up for the rest of the voyage. He would pay dearly for a little bit of humor to break up his watch.

What would they see of the island in the morning? A good guess was that it would be well wooded, much like the land about Dusky. They were not yet so far from there. He had seen that bit of green by the last light of the sun, and the lightning had revealed portions of mountainsides clothed in a dense forest. The idea that there might be savages ashore came to him repeatedly, and each time he stepped up on the spars stored on deck and leaned over the rail, he expected he might see men swimming below the channels. The first light would show the houses they dwelt in. At that time they might paddle out in dozens of canoes, wanting to trade crawfish and potatoes for arms and iron. Tobit would surely send them away. He had little to trade and swore he would not traffic with savages and allow them things that might permit them any increase in might.

Will rang eight bells and went below to rouse two men of the starboard watch. Thomas handed a musket to each when he came to the top of the steps. For a few minutes he took a last look around, listening for any alteration in the wind or in the sound of the waves breaking on the shore. If anything had changed, he imagined the wind had increased a little. He turned away and started down to his bunk, closing the scuttle behind him.

The fo'c's'le was lighted by the single lamp turned low, but in contrast to the spar deck above it, seemed well illuminated. Shadows created by the one source of light moved up and down on the white interior of the hull. Though it was in the quieter water of the bay, the barque rolled markedly. Little Ned was in his bunk just to the right of the steps. He had not pulled his curtain, and Thomas could see him lying at full length with his hands flat on his chest and his head bedded in its dark curls. The persistent smile, one that always seemed incapable of any deception, was gone from Ned's smooth face. He slept silently with his eyelashes forming thin crescents. Thomas stood on the bottom step and looked about the cramped quarters. Each man was in his box-like bed. All were asleep. Even Will who had come down only two or three minutes before was immobile behind his short drape and probably had already dozed off. There was no snoring or even a sound of breathing, though he was only a few feet from any of them. He pulled off his hat, boots, jacket, and scarf and crawled into his bunk. Then he took one last look around before he drew the cloth along the cord. In the months he had spent aboard the barque both in heavy seas and in calm, Thomas had rarely awakened during his watch below. When he rolled into his bunk, he was always tired and his sound sleep had yielded only to the ringing of eight bells and the call from the scuttle. This night, however, he did not drop off in the first few minutes after he put his head on his folded jacket. The slap of the water against the bows just a foot or two away was now disturbing, when before it had always lulled him to sleep.

Before eight bells sounded, the captain had opened his charts across his bunk and across the cabin table. He turned from the one on the bunk and looked again at the chart on the table, smoothing it out with his hands. It was weighted at the edges with a brass inkstand and his hat to hold against the insistent curl of the paper. The mate stood behind the captain, yet being taller still had a full view of the chart.

"Well, I can't see one thing that could be this landfall," Mr. Morgen said, shaking his head.

"No, you don't, simply because there is not a rock or an island that could possibly be it. We have made 134 miles from noon yesterday till noon today. Add to that about 60 miles since then. That makes 194 miles. That puts us here," Captain Tobit tapped the chart with a curved forefinger. "Even with leeway we could be no closer than 170 miles to the coast, but we are more likely the 185 miles away I show here." He picked up the dividers and measured the distance traveled for the second time and then marked it off from the previous day's position. "There, 167 degrees, 24 minutes east and 42 degrees, 12 minutes south. No doubt but it is a new island. It is not laid down here or on the Italian map, and there is nought of it in the *Oriental Navigator*, but that is old. It would surely be known had a ship of the John Company raised it." He stepped around to look at the chart on the bunk again. "No," he assured the mate, "it is not here, and I heard no report of any new discoveries while we were in Van Diemen's Land.

That is not to say another sealer from there or Port Jackson has not touched here."

The mate leaned forward for a closer look at the chart and asked, "So if it is a new island, what are we to do here?"

The captain's head suddenly jerked up, and he leaned back into the rigid stance he assumed when he was displeased or offended. "Damnation!" he sputtered in disbelief. "What have we been doing for these months? Skinning, Mr. Morgen! Skinning and boiling sea elephants!"

"You mean we are here to take more seals?"

"Aye, to skin. That is our business in the event you haven't noticed." The captain tinged the last words with sarcasm, then placed his right forefinger on the chart. "We are here. The island is here, but not laid down. There is a fair chance no one has touched before us. That would mean a great plenty of seals, and we will have first choice among the herds. Now, what do you make of that?"

"But there are no fur seals so far north on this coast," the mate protested.

"Do you know that to be a fact, Mr. Morgen?"

"No one has reported them much above Doubtful Sound."

"If you had found them this far up, would you be so much of a fool as to tell all? Would any sealer? Look, you will notice here that we are near to the same line as Bass Strait. How many fortunes were taken from there a few years ago? Well, we are going to look. We are surely going to look and take them if there be any!" Captain Tobit slammed his open hand down on the chart to show his determination.

"But where are we to put them? The hold is steeved full, and the steerage nearly so. The men are crowded there."

"I have my designs. Make the boats ready to be hoisted out. I want the men on the water before daybreak, all with their clubs. Be sure to send some arms with them. It is close enough for those heathens to reach here. The men are not to laze about. They are to search for the seals about every rock, to the west across that bar, and if we find none there, we will round the island. See to it, Mr. Morgen!"

"Yes, sir," the mate answered, "but could we not dispose of the load we now have and return for a proper kill? Then we might take as many as to fill the ship again."

"We shall take all we can if there are few. If there is a great plenty, we will land a shore gang and return after we have disposed of this load in Canton. Some ships have failed last season and I expect this season too, thus we will see much advance in prices."

"But that would be hard usage for those put ashore. Some of those who were on Macquarie, Cape South, and Brister's would have to spend another season ashore."

"They signed for a sealing voyage, did they not?"

"Yes, but some have spent a year skinning ashore. It would mean six months or more in this wilderness for them. Perhaps another year."

"What of it? They will be paid their lay."

"Why, sir, we have no stores to spare them. You mean to put them on this shore with nothing? They will have no relief for months. No crew has been served so by design."

"It is their calling, and every good Christian must work his best at his calling, however lowly. It is so ordered. They will do well enough with the good Lord looking after them. Do not concern yourself, Mr. Morgen, *I* will decide what is to be done when *I* find what our situation is here. And *I* will decide what is hard usage. Mind you that, Mr. Morgen, *I* will decide! We raised this land, and we will take from it what we wish. If we do not grasp this opportunity and a ship from Port Jackson finds it, do you think that there will be a pup or an old wig left for us? No! There is a great fortune to be had here. I believe we are the first to lay eyes on it, therefore any wealth is ours by right, and I mean to have it! You see to it the boats are on the water before daylight."

"And what of another bower ahead? It would be best to have it out now, at least with its cable bent to it and ready to let go. The wind might shift and blow fresh from the north'ard."

"Damnation, but you persist! The wind is not going to shift and make against us. It has been blowing these many days. I'll not risk a fouled hawse to humor you. If there are seals on this island, I mean to have their skins. We are here because I want the men to kill seals and not to pull a league to shore and off again or clear cables. Have Mr. Wilson rig the boats, Mr. Morgen, and I'll order out the other bower if it is needed."

"I'll see to the boats," the mate muttered and started out of the cabin. He paused at Mr. Wilson's cuddy and knocked. The second mate opened his door and looked out annoyed and sleepy. "Get dressed and come above," the first mate ordered and then climbed the steps to the deck. There he found one of the anchor watch and sent him forward to call up the rest of his mates.

Thomas felt as if he had been awake for an hour when he heard the scuttle open and someone creep down the steps. Thomas's hand nudged the edge of his curtain aside, and he witnessed a man call the starboard watch. He made an effort not to wake others and walked around and shook each one he wanted. That was rare consideration, Thomas thought; four hours of unbroken sleep was such a sweet thing on board. There was a stirring, muffled and deliberate, as the other watch dressed and filed up the steps to the deck. The scuttle was closed quietly by the last man.

A few minutes later, Mr. Wilson, now dressed, approached the first mate on the spar deck. "We must have the boats ready to hoist out by the first light," Mr. Morgen ordered as the other officer neared.

"Now what the devil are we to . . . ?" the second mate protested.

"Never mind why we are doing this. Just ungrip them and rig the lines. Break out the clubs and put them into the boats. And set one man to loading a half dozen muskets. They must go along in the morning with extra ball and powder."

"Are we to fight a war?"

"To your duty. I have enough to vex me," Mr. Morgen snapped and paced forward to the bows. Overhead, the masts and bare yards obscured and revealed the stars as they moved to and fro. The spit to the west was still a varying band of white that waxed and waned with each wave. Gaps in the band showed where unseen rocks stood. Beyond the larboard cathead was the high mass that blotted out half the stars in that portion of the sky. The surf at its base extended eastward and westward, fading into the darkness. He knew it ran unbroken around back to the north where they had entered, and that their vessel was lying within two hundred and eighty degrees of surf, rocks, and sand.

"We're embayed for sure," he whispered. Their only escape would be north if they could not hold ground where they were. Nothing was visible in that direction, and if the wind veered and blew fresh from there, they would have a task to claw off. Suddenly, he turned and marched quickly along the deck past the men rigging the boats. A dim light showed through the cabin skylight when he reached the aft of the barque. He went softly down the steps and faced the captain's door. Mr. Morgen's right hand reached for the latch and his left doubled up to rap on the wood. A sliver of light flickered between the edge of the door and its frame. The captain was moving inside and casting his shadow around the cabin. A deep muffled cough sounded from the interior, and the mate dropped his hands to his sides. He stood for a moment longer, watching the play of light and shadows at the edge of the door. Then he raised his left hand again as if to knock, holding it an inch from the oak panel.

Abruptly, the captain's voice came from inside. Mr. Morgen took a step back, wondering if the captain had suddenly acquired the gift of second sight. He might be aware he was standing there and yank the door open and accuse him of spying. The words he could hear were half-whispered and unintelligible. By turning his head and leaning forward, he could just make out what the captain was saying. The rhythm of the speech was slow, measured, unlike his quick barking of orders. The voice rose a little and he heard Tobit speak the words, ". . . and for all this, I thank Thee, oh Lord." The mate pressed his ear to the wood, and listened intently. ". . . such opportunities have been given me and in such measure," the captain continued, "that I cannot but believe that I have been chosen. I know that it is my duty as a true Christian to seize these prospects and turn them to Thy greater glory. I swear to make my good fortune to work for Thy holy design. As one raised up, I shall be diligent, humble and true." The mate backed away from the door and stood motionless for several seconds. Then, he turned suddenly and mounted the steps to the deck. At the hatch he found the second mate still readying the boats to be hoisted out.

He tapped him on the shoulder and ordered, "Let this be for a while and rig out the slip line. To it now. I want no delay!"

"Ah, so he's had a change of mind. I thought he'd come round to it," the second mate snickered. "We are to stand on and off all night!"

"No, we are not to slip our cable. Just rig the line, Mr. Wilson, and keep your notions to yourself."

"Aye, Mr. Morgen, aye," the second mate replied.

The men of the watch worked quickly and brought the line in through the hawsehole and then bent it to the cable. The remainder of the line was taken aft outboard of the chains and in through the stern port. Mr. Morgen inspected the work as it was finished, checking the buoy and running his hand over the line where it was bitted. When he straightened up, he found the second mate there beside him.

"A fit job?" Mr. Wilson asked.

"Yes, now you can return to your boats."

"If we are not to slip, what is it to be in the morning?"

Mr. Morgen remained silent for a moment, then started his answer slowly, "A long pull for the men. He has it in his head that this island is covered with seals. If we find none here, we are to round this rock and search about the south shore."

"Do you expect to find any?"

"None at all this far up the coast. Perhaps the odd one has strayed here from the south'ard isles and sounds. Our gangs were probably the last to get a good cargo. There have been too many ships and nearly every pup and clapmatch has been taken. There are too few to continue the breed, and I fear the fishery has been near destroyed."

"Aye, we may have caused their finish, but had we never landed, the other gangs would have done the work and the money would be in their purses. Well, if the wind shifts, we won't be bothered to look for the animals in the morning."

"I don't care for either choice," the first mate grumbled, "but if we must claw off a lee shore, we are ready. Now finish with your boats."

"That I will," Mr. Wilson replied.

"Be sure to call me if there is the least change in the wind before my watch."

"Aye, first thing, Mr. Morgen."

CHAPTER 3

NOT ONCE did Thomas feel the expected, welcomed drowsiness advancing over him. After the other watch had been called, he remained alert and could only lie there and think of how the voyage had progressed. It had seemed interminable, as if they would never reach the rookeries, and then when landed on those hazardous shores that they could never skin and boil enough animals to fill the hold of the barque. The constant wetting in the surf, pulling the boat in and out even when it was snowing had left him chilled and stiff. Thomas knew his share should be a fine sum, but it had been a struggle each day to find the seals and get to them. Something always conspired to delay their return journey. He had thought they were homeward bound when they loaded the last of the skins and oil at Brister's. His clothes were greasy and filthy with soot when he rowed away from that accursed little beach for the last time. Then Tobit had decided to look in again at Dusky, determined to get every skin possible.

After half an hour, he peeked out once more even though he knew that no one else in the fo'c's'le stirred. The rest of the crew, mostly hidden behind their curtains, slept without the least murmur or movement. He lay in his bunk and watched the clothes swinging on their hooks and the pattern of light and shadow moving up and down over the hull, the chests, and across the planks of the deck above. By its sounds, it seemed the wind had not slackened in the least. The creaking of the spars and rigging of the vessel and the wash of the waves against the hull were, if anything, louder. Just overhead, the cable groaned as it strained against the roller and then eased. His entire body, lying full length in the bunk, sensed a change in the way the barque dipped forward and rose again.

Doesn't anyone else feel she's riding hard? he asked himself. What was it exactly? Perhaps he was merely imagining a change where there was none, finding something odd to fill up the minutes when he couldn't sleep. He tried to think of something else that would put his mind at ease. China, he thought, yes that would do it. They had yet to call at the factories at Whampoa. What would that be like? Would the stories he had heard told in the Port and Mystic be true or had they been exaggerated to impress or hoax boys? Were certain people there always carried about on the backs of others when they went out, and did all the men have hair that reached to their ankles? He would see it all for himself in time. Perhaps he might have the luck to buy some pretty shells, ivory, or some jade pieces there that he could sell in Boston. If he could make such an adventure as that, it might return a tidy bit to add to his lay.

Suddenly Will whispered from the bunk above, "You awake, lad?"

He was surprised at the voice but glad someone else was up. "Yes," he replied and then asked, "did you hear the other watch called?"

"Aye."

"What have they been sent for?"

"The other bower and range of cable, I expect. We'll hear when it's done and know for sure."

"I'd rather it be to turn the windlass. I want to be on the way home, but this delay is all my fault. If I hadn't sung out when I saw the island, we'd still be making fair for China."

"Oh, no, no, lad. You did right there. We might have been far out o' our course. They would have to know what land 'twas to set us aright. No, you did well to sing out."

"But look where it's put us. We don't know how long we'll be here."

"Likely it won't be more than a watch or two. Are you that keen to see Yankee Land again?"

"Aye, as much as you are. I want to be on my way after all these months killing and skinning and shivering the whole while."

Will jollied him, "Ah, is it only that, or is there a beamy lass there in Longpoint waiting for you?"

"No, mate."

"Oh, now I've heard you mention a name. What was it? My memory has gone poor of late. Now, what was that name?"

"Isabel, you mean? She simply lived at the other end of the road, and I have known her for some years. Her father has much property in New London, and he let me know in his way that she was not in my walk. I could never have asked her to be my intended."

"Why not? You had the shop."

"Father and I scarce made a living out of it. It was one penny at a time. I would rather risk all on some enterprise than plod away at that bench in Stonington. No, I would not drudge away her life as well as mine."

"So, now you drudge away your life here on this barque. A fine advance you have made."

"I intend to try my fortune in other places."

"You gave up one good trade to start a poor one," Will reproved him, shaking his head. "You make a good marlinspike sailor, but your condition is no better. Thomas, you have fine wits, and you can read and cipher well. You shouldn't lay that aside. Mind me lad, don't sail on ships 'less you intend to be master. Ask yourself what your share will be when we get home. Then ask what the captain's share will be, then add to that what he may get from what he carries on his own account. It will be a hundredfold difference and more."

Will stopped speaking. He looked up, listening to the thump of the feet moving along the deck above. "Most midships. No cable coming up. What are they about now?" he whispered. The old sailor leaned farther over the side of his bunk and asked, "Do you feel there's a longer sea running and how she's slow risin'?"

Thomas pushed his curtain all the way back and answered, "Yes, what's wrong with her?"

"It's the great weight in the hold and the cable holdin' her. Those make her act so. But there's somethin' else that's strange, and I can't make out what 'tis."

"Harrison said the wind might change. He was almost sure of it."

"Then it most likely has," Will said, looking down at Thomas. "He knows as well as those aft, better maybe. Damn! I didn't think ol' Tobit would touch here. I would have laid a few dollars out that he wouldn't, but he's been strange of late."

The *Dove* was heaved up by a swell, and the hull popped and creaked more than usual.

Will looked at Thomas and asked, "Do you feel that?"

"Aye, she's laboring."

"I mean, did you feel her come up easier?"

"Yes, a little," Thomas admitted. "Was it the bower?"

"Surely! Oh, I don't like it. I don't like it, lad. I'm goin' above and see what's afoot. There's something strange here." Will eased down from his bunk, guiding his bare feet to step on his sea chest and then to the deck. He climbed the steps to the scuttle and opened it slowly. The full sound of the wind came through the opening as he left and quieted when he pulled the scuttle closed. The noise did not rouse any of the men, and they remained solidly fixed and silent in their bunks.

A swell came under the bow and the barque responded, rising with less hesitation than usual. Thomas felt a vibration in the wood of the vessel. It came through the beams and planks and added to the creaks caused by the straining cable. It lasted only a second and ceased when the hull dipped into the next trough. He rose up on his elbow and remained motionless and tense in that position, waiting for the call for all hands. In all their months at sea he had not seen Will uneasy about the *Dove*. The older hands had had little anxiety even when the barque was plunging into a head sea off the Cape or being buffeted by the howling gales of the high latitudes. Now, next to an unknown speck of land they feared a shift of the wind. Certainly, he knew they were in more danger there by the land than out in the empty ocean. After several minutes, no call came, and the rigid pose he held made his muscles ache. He rolled back onto the straw and stared at the bottom of the bunk above him.

His thoughts drifted out of the fo'c's'le, and he saw himself at his bench in the shoe shop close by the window, just as he had been two days before he boarded the barque. It had been late afternoon with an overcast sky that required the lamp to be lit to see the work. He was cutting a tap from a large hide and gripped the knife tightly as he forced it through the stout leather. Then he became aware that someone was watching nearby, and, looking up, saw his father standing just outside the door and barely within the glow of the lamp. He did not move or offer to speak as he watched. He had stared back, unable to think of something to say. When he finally returned to his work, he saw that the knife had slipped, and the sole was ruined.

A gust of cold air struck his face and aroused him from his strange dream. Will had just closed the scuttle and descended the steps. He walked in short quick steps, hunched over like one stealing about in an attic.

"Thomas," he whispered, "the wind has rounded to the north as Chips feared, and it's blowing fresh. Did you feel the bower give some a few minutes ago?"

"Yes, are they going to let another go?"

"No! They've ungriped the boats and broke out our clubs! When they're done, the anchor watch is to walk fore and aft again like we was behind Fisher's Island. Then we're to go for seals at daylight. We have the veriest lunatic aft!"

"What's Mr. Wilson doing, sleeping?"

"No, he is awake, but he has orders not to touch a line or cable. Mr. Morgen is up too and talking to him. They are both for slipping and clawing off now, but I heard them say Tobit will not have it. I fear he's wholly mad. There is something dreadful wrong here, lad. If nothing is done soon, we'll be driven ashore!"

The shadow played across Will's wrinkled brow in time with the rolling of the hull. The old tar's grave face and his wide-eyed stare at the deck above unnerved Thomas.

"Damn! And we can do nothing!" Thomas hissed out.

Ned groaned and sat up in his bed. He looked sleepily about and saw Will crouched by Thomas's bunk. "What? Who's that?" he asked and then closed his eyes and sank back.

The men in the other bunks, disturbed by the voice, stirred and muttered. Will and Thomas spoke not a word while they waited for them to settle back into their full sleep. They both listened to the sounds of the vessel and now and then looked at each other.

The *Dove* snugged into the next wave, and when the bulk of the swell came under her keel, she rose easier than before. The vibration came through the wood again. Will grabbed the edge of Thomas's bunk with both hands. They felt the barque slip back, hold for a second and slip a second time.

"Oh, Lord!" Will exclaimed in hoarse words. He leaped to his feet and dashed for the scuttle, shouting, "She's draggin'! She's draggin'!"

The curtains were thrust aside one after the other, and white legs and brown appeared over the edges of the bunks. Thomas rolled out and followed Will up the steps to the scuttle. Behind him he could hear bare feet slapping onto the wood of the deck. He burst out into the night and into a swirl of wind and noises. A man from the other watch came running forward, bumped into Will, recovered, and shouted into the fo'c's'le, "Ahoy! Ahoy all hands! Up and make sail!"

Captain Tobit bellowed from the waist, "Lay aloft, you topmen! Fore-staysail, topsails and mizzen, Mr. Morgen! Mr. Morgen!

"Aye, sir!" the mate answered from somewhere aft.

"Mr. Morgen, bend the slip rope!"

"The slip rope. Done, sir, done!" came his immediate answer.

The captain was now near the bow and among the crew rushing along the deck. "Are you all deaf or asleep? Move!" he yelled, "Move!"

The topmen swung out onto the shrouds and others went to pull the sheets and braces. Men going aloft were on each other's heels. Below the fore and main tops they bunched up as those in the lead were slowed at the futtock shrouds. Thomas was the first out on his yard and pulled at the wet, swollen ropes while the cold wind buffeted his body and whipped the fabric of his shirt and trousers.

More men reached the yard and spread out to help loose the sail and overhaul the clew- and buntlines, but the sail didn't drop far and slatted aback against the topmast. The crew on deck then sheeted it home and hoisted the yard. At almost the same time the fore-topsail was loosed, and its yard swung back by the starboard brace. At the bows, the cable whipped out through the hawsehole and splashed into the sea. The vessel, gaining sternway, cast onto the starboard tack. With the yards braced and the bowlines hauled, she began to ease forward, plunging whale-like into the troughs and rising dully on the swells. Thomas knew the slip line aft would be unbitted next and would run out the stern port. They would leave only the two buoys bobbing about in their wake. The men slipped along the yard to return to the deck. Thomas moved after them, checking the points as he went. Will waited for him and shouted something, but the sense of the words was lost in the noise of the wind.

Will called again as he got nearer, "She'll not do it close-hauled! She's never any good on a tight bowline!"

Thomas nodded.

"Tobit knows that!" Will shouted. "We all know it!"

Along the horizon to the far west, the surf was noticeably higher. A broader band of white swelled on the spit between the black sea and the stars above.

The *Dove* labored through the waves, west by northwest, bowlines taut, and gaining a little to the windward. Swells passed under the hull and went on, leaving the vessel heeled over. The masts pitched in arcs fore and aft. Thomas took a look at the sea from astern around to the west and to the north and saw nothing but black water and a few whitecaps around the barque. The wind pulled his hair from the ribbon holding it and swirled it about his head and across his face. He was chilled and started to go to the deck when he spotted a hazy patch on the sea ahead of the *Dove*. It was larger than any whitecap and moved like a mat on the water. He thrust his hand toward the white blur and shouted, "Look, there! Forward!"

Will peered ahead and discovered the blossom of foam. He turned and screamed toward the helm, "Ahoy, there! Rocks ahead!" The noise of the wind overpowered his voice and there was no response. Together, the two shouted, "Rocks ahead!"

Will reached out and grabbed a backstay. "Stay here and keep a good watch," he called out. Then he wrapped his legs around the line and slid down out of sight.

Within seconds the headsails were let go. Then the fore-topsail went ashiver. The barque veered slowly to windward, and he gripped the jackstay as if he could force the bow about with his hands and will. He felt that it was minutes before his yard was braced about and the slapping sail filled. Slowly his grip eased when he saw she had made her stays and was on the larboard tack. Thomas sidled out to the starboard earing again and held onto the stunsail boom. They would be making some leeway, and he reckoned it would be better to watch from that side. With the *Dove* heeled in that direction, he was over the sea and watched the whitecaps pass below as the vessel eased ahead. The jib-boom rose and dipped, probing the darkness, and Thomas, looking forward past it, searched for any sign of rocks or shoal water. He hoped he would not see that broad blossom of white again. The thought of the forefoot striking on the rocks made him shudder. Would they get her off if that happened? If she could not be freed or if she was stove, could they launch the boats in the swells without damage?

And if they managed to land on the island, what would they meet with there? A way to escape might be found, would have to be found if there was little to eat and no shelter. There could be little thought of rescue from an unknown island. If the boats could be got ashore, some men would have to sail one somewhere for help. Frightful stories of wrecks on cannibal islands had been told and re-told in the fo'c's'le and in the huts of the rookeries. Yet there had been an arch look on the face of the man telling the tale and also on those of some listeners, clues that the details were exaggerated to impress the boys and green hands.

He had to believe there was some bit of reality, some true event that gave the stories durable lives. He had seen the tattooed faces of the natives and the short clubs they carried. Once, off the coast of Tovy Poenamoo, a canoe passed the barque in which there were a dozen of the savages shouting, waving their paddles, and twisting their faces into rude and fierce looks.

Jack had related how he met a survivor of the brig *Betsey* who told of landing on the shore of a rookery with five mates and being attacked by an entire tribe. The man managed to hide in a cave concealed by a thick growth and survived for four months by eating fern root, birds' eggs, and a few raw shellfish. During that time all his mates had been captured and eaten.

Gabe had his favorite yarn about three men taken in Bligh's Islands and kept crouching in small cages for so long their clothes rotted from their bodies. They were well fed, even forced to eat all they were given. They could guess their fate and would have suffered it had not the captain of another ship learned they were there and exchanged many trade goods for them. Once freed, the prisoners could no longer walk and spent the rest of their lives as dirty beggars crawling the streets of London.

Why was he thinking of such horrid tales? The vessel was there, sound beneath him and going full and by. He put them from his mind. Each dip and rise of the bow was carrying them a little farther from the shore. Ten or fifteen more minutes and they should be out of the worst peril. Getting past the heads would mean much tacking, but once out they could lie to all night. Then perhaps Tobit might forget about the island and they could make for China.

In any case it was going to be a miserable night unless the wind let up. He was shivering, had been shivering since he had loosed the sail and now wished he had paused long enough to put on his jacket and his boots. If it was going to be all hands for the night, he would have no chance to slip below and get them. He tried tensing his muscles and swaying from side to side to make some warmth in his body, but it did little good.

Suddenly, his grip tightened, and he thrust his head forward to peer into the darkness. He thought he saw another white shape rising and falling on the sea, or was it merely a larger whitecap? He squeezed his eyes closed for a half-second and opened them. A wide patch of foam appeared among the smaller bits of white riding the surface of the sea. Thomas twisted back and shouted to the deck below, "Ho, rocks ahead! Rocks ahead!"

The danger must have been spotted from the bows for there was a flurry of shouted orders, but they were not intelligible over the howl of the wind. The barque was answering the helm, and he could see they were veering to the leeward of the rock or reef hidden under that whitened sea. It looked as if she would make it. Yes, he thought, they would ease past!

The hull rose on the next swell. As she dropped forward into the trough, the yard jerked up and back, and he doubled forward over it. Instantly, he rebounded. The boom was ripped from his grasp, and he was flipped from the footrope, tumbling aft from the yard.

"Oh, let there be water below!" he begged as he plunged. The air rushed past his ears as he continued to turn head over foot. There was no up or down, and he could see nothing. It occurred to him that he might have already struck on the deck or the rail. Was that instant passed? Was this death: blackness, limbo, no heaven, no hell?

A stinging shock hit his body. He had slammed into the water. A sensation of heat covered his entire back from the impact, and cold sea swirled around his face. He felt the water going up his nose and heard the gurgling of it in his ears. Without thinking, he began to swim, but something was around his wrists like string or rope that fouled his efforts to swim. Thomas found that his worn and patched shirt had split up the back and washed around, entangling his arms. Fiercely, he ripped it off his wrists. Freed of the rags, he tried to pull his way to the surface. Then it flashed in his mind that he might be beneath the hull or that some current was holding him down.

He reached out, feeling for the side of the *Dove.* Nothing, in any direction. Though he swept his arms through the water, he found not a rope or a plank. Without some clue, he did not know if he was facing the surface or the bottom of the sea. He was suspended in blackness, and pawing his way through the water was tiring him quickly. Then he tried lying still, hoping that he would rise to the surface, though his lungs burned and he ached to take a breath.

Suddenly, he could hear the wind again. His head was above water. Air spewed from his mouth, and he gasped for his next breath. He whipped his head from side to side to clear the hair and water from his eyes. He saw only waves until he turned about, and there was the *Dove,* forty feet away, down by the stern and wallowing in the swells. Waves struck her far side and rolled across her deck and cascaded over the starboard rail. Amidships, the boats, freed from their gripes, had been swept against the mainmast shrouds and the rail, and remained there capsized. Above the hull, the maintopmast had fallen in a tangle of rigging against the fore-topmast, and the angle between the foremast and the jib-boom appeared too narrow. Even if the *Dove* were got off the rock and did not sink, she would be a hulk that could only drift with the wind to the shore of the island. Too much of her rigging had parted and was hopelessly fouled.

Thomas worked his trousers off and started swimming toward the bow where some of the crew were gathering. Two men had gone aft to free the trapped boats and were struggling to right one when a wave spilled over the far side and pinned them against the rail. It drained away, and they turned to the boats again but were there only a few seconds when an even larger rush of water came at them. One man was carried off the barque, but the other managed to stay aboard by clinging to a shroud. Thomas watched the man in the water. His dark head showed sharply against the foaming sea as he moved closer.

"She's split!" the man shouted. It was Harrison struggling toward him.

"The boats?" Thomas called back.

"Stove . . . all!" the carpenter cried out.

A large swell lifted the barque a little and forced the stern to the south. There was a grinding sound that was felt as much as heard. The whole vessel had a loose movement fore and aft.

"She's broken! Swim for shore!" Harrison yelled and started for the island.

Thomas watched the carpenter swim to the south, then turned back to the barque. Each wave rolled farther forward covering more and more of the deck. The sea now completely concealed the helm and the waves were washing as high as the deadeyes of the main shrouds. Some of the crew had gone out on the bowsprit to escape the water at least for a few minutes. He wondered if the *Dove* would continue to sink or if the hull would settle onto the rock or reef it had struck. Even if it did not sink, it would be battered to pieces if the swells from the north did not soon abate. She kept settling as he watched and in less than a minute the entire deck was covered. Two men had climbed from the bowsprit up the forestay and appeared as two black lumps on the line. A powerful wave slammed against the far side of the bow, and the two were shaken from their holds and dropped into the water. The masts heeled over a little farther with each swell.

Thomas began swimming away from the wreck. It was difficult in the heaving water. He was dropped into the troughs, where he could see nothing, and then carried up on the crests and buffeted by the spoondrift. He had not gone far when he felt he must look at the barque once more and stopped swimming when he rose on a wave.

Overhead, the broken rigging, a snarl of ropes and spars, was easing lower like the jaw of a ponderous trap. He saw the danger he was in and started for the land again. That top-hamper with its web of lines and spars could snare him and carry him to the bottom. Thomas pushed on as fast as he was able. Harrison was out of sight. Nowhere was he able to spot a dark head moving in a patch of white. He saw nothing except the swells as he paddled ahead. All he could do in the darkness was follow the wind. If it had not changed direction, it would be going toward the closest land. He swam with the wind at his back, away from what he reckoned was its source. It was difficult to tell unless he paused for a moment. He gasped for breath and felt it was safe to take a rest and look back.

The *Dove* had rolled onto her beam-ends. All aft of her main chains was under water, and the larboard bow and bowsprit were washed over by the largest swells. Her masts were lying in the water with their yards protruding from the surface at all angles and moving in response to the currents below. Waves surged around the wreck, swirling into thick, white foam. He could not see a single man clinging to the remainder of the barque or struggling in the sea. He was totally alone. A sudden twinge, a hollowness struck in his chest, and his pulse drummed in his ears. It was both fear and fatigue. If he saw another man, even if he was yards away, just discernible in the gloom, he would rejoice. The waves lifted and dropped him as he searched about. Should the *Dove* continue to slip lower, then the only things visible would be a few stars and the patches of foam on the heaving sea. There was nothing to do but resume swimming, though at a slower pace to spare his strength and keep a watch ahead. Perhaps he might catch sight of the carpenter or another crewman. That would reassure him and put more spirit in his struggle toward the shore.

He knew that after the *Dove* had struck, everything had happened quickly. In a minute or two she had rolled over and settled in the water, yet it seemed to have taken much longer, that he had been in the sea for an hour. To him, the whole disaster had been a succession of drawn-out incidents. He continued at his steady pace and changed direction when he suspected there were rocks ahead. The wreck was no longer visible. With the wind as his sole guide, he tried to keep before it. If it had not veered around to another point, he must reach the shore soon. If he was heading in some other direction, the cold water and fatigue could be his end. He could last just so long. He might die a few yards from the shore.

His worries faded in a moment when he stopped for a rest. Far ahead there was the muffled sound of the surf. Its rumble permeated the blackness. Thomas was elated. It assured him he was swimming toward the nearest shore and was no longer lost in a tossing world of wind and water. Solid ground, perhaps rock, was halting the ponderous roll of the swells ahead of him. He might—no, he would walk on the earth again. He might find his mates there, waiting for him, to grasp his hands and help him out of the waves. The rumble of the breaking waves was there before him and he worked toward it alternately swimming and resting. As the surf increased to a booming, new energy flowed into Thomas's arms and legs. There was nothing more he wanted than to feel the hard, unyielding beach under his feet. It might rage and blow all night, all week, if only he and his mates were on that shore. Slowly, a band of white became visible each time he rose on a swell. It extended into the gloom in either direction.

"Huzzah!" he managed to croak. The goal was in sight, and his limbs now moved automatically, seemingly without his will. Ahead, the swells peaked as they rolled on, tipped forward, and crashed into a chaos of foam and spray. Certain larger waves slammed down with a thunderclap and sent white fountains shooting skyward. He stopped and watched the confused water race toward the shore. No breaks appeared in the row upon row of waves where he might slip through to the shore without being injured. They looked too violent. They could dash a man against the bottom or tumble him over and over until he drowned. Back to the north was nothing except more waves coming. No crewman's head bobbed in the swells.

He was alone in a nearly lightless world, and he might become the sole man to reach the shore. If he became the lone castaway on the island, only the miscalculation or curiosity of some captain might bring a ship close enough to see his signal of distress. That might be only after a stay of years on that speck of land. But first, he must pass through that booming water that barred him before he could become a survivor on that shore. He had to enter the breakers soon, for the longer he delayed, the more chilled and fatigued he became. One by one the swells rolled on and broke over the backs of those gone before them. Thomas paddled to keep his head as high as he was able and watched for any coming swell that was lower than the rest. He hoped Harrison had already made it through and was somewhere on the shore and perhaps watching for other survivors. But he could as well be in that churning water being rolled back and forth. A smaller swell was approaching.

He struck out swimming at his fastest pace, but he had waited too long. It passed under him and he sank into the next hollow. A second wave did the same, broke beyond him, and spread up the slope of the beach. A third one rose to a peak sooner than the others, and he was suddenly swimming down its forward slope. It steepened until he was being hurled forward in the nearly vertical face of the water. Twisting about, he tried getting into the body of the swell. The wave slammed onto the boiling back of the one ahead. He was tumbled toward the island, then halted, and dragged as swiftly seaward. Rocks raked his back as he was carried away. Slowly, he floated up and broke the surface. The seething back of the wave was stretching up the slope. In the other direction, the next swell was rushing at him. It curled over and smothered his head in froth.

The cycle was repeated again and again. Each time, he was carried along the bottom and came to the top, only to be covered by another wave. Beneath the sea, he could only hear the gurgling mixture of air and water. Above it, the breaking surf roared and the wind howled. Thomas was covered and carried down once more. As he was rolled and drawn along, striking against the rough bed of the sea, he wondered if he would ever get a whole breath of air. Make an end of it, he thought, or let me reach the shore. I ask nothing else. His body could as well be fixed and the sea and the island whirling about him. There was no firm, unyielding point to be reached and grasped. He was being ground to meal as if he were between two millstones. If he didn't escape soon, would he be more than a battered carcass? In an hour, there would be nothing left of him, just his bones on the bottom of the sea being drifted to and fro with the surge of the water. The thunder of the surf struck his ears. He was again at the surface and gulped a deep lungful of air. He panted while his head was above water. The sea pulled him from the beach, then pushed him toward it. His feet touched the bottom, lost it, and touched once more. He kept his footing for half the time. By struggling against the haul back of the waves, he kept some of the headway they gave him on their landward rush. He managed to work his way in until he could dig his toes into the beach and hold his place as the water raced back. With each wave he gained a yard or two. He was staggering forward in thigh-deep water when he was knocked to his hands and knees by larger waves dashing up the slope. As they drained away, the foam and water boiled against his body and flowed around it. He thrust his fingers deep to grip the shore. Exhausted by his efforts, he remained on all fours, fighting upward and coughing out seawater. He felt as if he was a beast striving to get out of the sea, a reptile clawing its way landward. He wondered if there was anyone watching while he crawled slowly up the beach to where the lips of the waves barely reached. The shore appeared black in contrast to the white froth. Fits of coughing shook him, and he remained there with his arms holding his body off the beach. He spat out grit. The sand of the shore, or whatever it was, felt coarse and loose in his grasp. It was a delight, an assurance that he was safe for the moment. It had been a terrible trial. How many others would make it to the island? Those who could not swim would certainly drown. Even if they clung to some bit of wreckage, an oar or a broken plank, their chances of getting through the surf were slim

"I have done it," Thomas whispered between flurries of coughing and spitting. "I hope the others reach this shore too," he said a little louder and crept a few more feet upwards. He felt his fatigue fully and moved each hand and foot one at a time. After a few seconds, he collapsed and rested his head on the beach. His whole store of strength was gone, and he could do no more than lie there and listen to the boom of each breaker as it crashed. Some were as violent as cannon shots, and their startling reports rolled far down the shore and back again, returning as if they were echoing through an enormous cavern.

CHAPTER 4

THE WAVES battered the land. With each one that slammed down, the beach vibrated, and Thomas felt it along his entire body as he rested there. Given enough time, he thought, such a pounding would carry away the whole island. How did he ever pass through that violence? What quirk of fate saved him, got him through all the terror? Was he truly alive and on the edge of this dark, shapeless land? He could as well be in the ocean dreaming the visions of drowning men, but he felt the shore beneath him shuddering with the assault of the sea. Was that part of the dreams too, an artful charity of nature to make his death more bearable? For all he had seen of it, the very island might be an illusion. Then again, if he were truly on a beach, what of the others? What was the fate of Christopher, Will, Gabe, Nat, Jack, the lascars, and the boys? Could they have reached the island or were they still out there clinging to some wreckage and hoping the wind would carry them to the shore.

Suddenly, he realized that the tumbling waves had stripped all his clothes from him. His naked body pressed against the wet beach. The cold wind was sweeping over him from his feet to his head and dashing raindrops against his skin. He rolled onto his right side and peered into the darkness. That is east, he thought. There the white, pulsing band of surf faded away into the distance. He could see nothing else. In the other direction, the view was the same, just the blurred image of foaming waves dimming to nothing in the blackness of the night. So there he lay cast on his beam-ends.

Exile would be hard indeed, if no other crewman survived. It would not be like the sealing grounds. There would be no one to gam with, or to help with the building of a shelter and the gathering of food.

The days would pass ever so slowly. How would he live on the island alone: eat, sleep, and piss in the bushes day after day? He would exist in the sunlight and the long nights like some unthinking animal. There would be no holidays to celebrate. Days and weeks would have no meaning for him. Nothing could have meaning then. He could never be part of that flow from father to child to grandchild, going from the past on into a time he could not imagine. He would huddle next to a fire when it was cold. One morning he would not wake, and all would be as if he had never been born. Or he might fall from some precipice and his bones would be covered by layers of rotting leaves and sink from sight, perhaps never to be found and puzzled over. No one to note my passing, no one to tell Father.

Then again, there might be savages on the island. Would they welcome him or knock him on the head and put him in their cooking hole? In the darkness no light had been seen, yet that was no proof they were not there. They might be shrewd ones, remaining in the underwood until sailors felt themselves safe and came ashore. They might befriend him at first, then slay him. He had heard stories of such villainy.

Along the beach to the west he could see something small and dark floating in the foam and water. Was that wreckage or was it one of the crew? Though he was still panting for air, Thomas pushed himself up onto his haunches to get a better view. The thing separated into two halves that drew farther apart as he watched. The hope that the objects could be his mates roused him, and he struggled to his feet. The two spots vanished and reappeared as the breakers rolled in and receded. He walked to the west and suspected he might have seen an arm rise and fall as he neared the closer one. He strode faster and angled from the beach into the fanning border of the wave. The shapes, barely showing in the water for a few seconds at a time, were not wreckage but the heads of men. He saw that both were pulling toward the shore, though yards apart and each fighting alone. The nearer man was having the worst time of it. A wave struck his back, and he hardly recovered before the next was upon him. Thomas waded deeper and pushed against the incoming water. A hand stretched out for him. The draining water pulled the man out of reach. The next breaker brought him back, and Thomas managed to grasp the hand.

"Been hurt!" the man cried out.

Thomas recognized it as Gabe's voice, but it was weak and strained.

"Where?" he asked.

"Legs!" the sailor cried.

Every receding wave pulled at Thomas and Gabe, holding them back until the water paused and turned. Then they made a few feet in with the aid of the next rush of the sea. Thomas looked back at Gabe. He felt the pull of the man's entire body. He sensed Gabe was in a bad way. He's not helping enough, he thought. The sea swept around the two, and they were forced to retreat a few yards. Another breaker curled and rushed forward on the back of the previous one. It caught them and carried them toward the land. But when it made its retreat, Thomas felt Gabe's fingers weakening. The clasp of their hands broke, and Gabe slipped from his feet. He was carried away, then covered by the next flood of foam rolling in.

"Gabe! Gabe!" Thomas screamed. The sea swept in and out once more but his shipmate's head never broke the surface again. "Gabe!" he repeated, but he knew it was useless. He had felt Gabe weakening through his failing grip. That hard, calloused hand would never have let go from mere fatigue. He must have been badly hurt, or he would have clapped on for a week. Gabe had gone as if he had been pulled under. He could not even guess where he might be in that rolling froth.

Forty feet away the other survivor was just holding his own. Thomas waded toward him but looked back, hoping to see Gabe bob up once more. He and the other survivor held out an arm to each other. They neared and locked hands. There was white hair on the man's head. He had hold of the captain. The two men staggered, trying to keep their footing as the broken waves rushed back against them. The sweep of the water inshore and out was making Thomas giddy and unsure of his balance. Often, they lost in two seconds what they had gained in fifteen. Suddenly the captain slipped and dropped beneath the foam. Thomas kept his grip, tugged him to his feet again, and they slowly made their way up to the shallower water.

When Thomas scanned the surf once more, there was still no sign of Gabe, no hand, no head, or bit of clothing. There was only the tumble and boil of white foam. Down the beach even farther west, he saw two more men fighting their way ashore. He shook the captain and pointed to them. Tobit nodded once, indicating he had seen them. Thomas pulled the captain just above the place where the waves stalled and drained back to the bay. The two men halted there. The lad's legs began shaking. He tried to stop them, but they went on, defying his will. Then the rest of his body started to shiver, starting with his shoulders and extending down to his arms and hands. That shiver passed through his grip to the captain. Even by clinging to each other, they could no longer stand on their quivering legs, and both dropped to their hands and knees.

Thomas waited for the spasms to stop that he might crawl farther up the beach. They came in surges, growing intense, then weaker. Between the worst of them, he moved one arm and leg forward at a time, then paused a moment before he moved again. The captain was following behind him. The pair inched their way up to the higher part of the beach and collapsed. Thomas lay with the left side of his head resting on the shore. It was a strange perspective with the surface of the land now vertical in his view.

To the west, the other survivors were holding on to each other and formed a small lump in the surf. They moved slowly, and when they gained the upper reach of the waves, they dropped and remained motionless. If he had not seen them come out of the sea and stagger up the beach, he would have taken their shapeless outline for a drifted mass of rockweed.

He raised his head and looked back into the eye of the wind. There was nothing of the barque to be seen. No wreckage was yet being blown ashore or any other crewmen swimming through the surf. Close beside him, he could hear the captain's deep wheezing over the boom of the breakers and the rush of the wind. A wave flowed up around their feet, but neither Thomas nor the captain moved when the water touched them. Thomas imagined for a second that the sea was rising to recapture them, but he remembered the wind had been blowing onshore for hours. The surf might get higher, and also, the tide was perhaps on the flood. The reports of the collapsing waves traveled along the beach, degraded in the distance and returned in hollow, desolate echoes. Only high ground or a cliff could throw back the cracks and booms like that, Thomas thought. Beyond him, to the landward, was a great dark mass, indicated more by the reflection of those sounds than by what he could see.

He pushed himself up to sit on his heels, then looked at Captain Tobit. The pale body and white hair of the officer contrasted with a beach that was totally black in the weak starlight. A trickle of blood came from the captain's scalp and was washed across his temple by the rain and into his right eye. His clothes had been taken off or stripped from him so that he too was wholly naked.

"Captain!" Thomas called over the noise of the surf. The captain moved his head a little, indicated he had heard. "Captain!" he repeated, "two men ashore there . . . g-going to see how they are!"

Tobit continued his labored breathing and did not respond. Thomas touched Tobit's shoulder, and the officer then managed a small nod. The lad stood up in the chill wind that whipped around his body. It was no longer a steady gale from the north. It had shifted a little to the northwest with some recurring gusts from the west. He started toward the other survivors lying on the shore. As he walked, he caught the scents of damp earth and wet, green plants. They came and went as flaws of the wind struck him. Somewhere to his left, on that hulking mass, he heard the unmistakable sound of the wind soughing in trees, not a few trees but a large coppice or an entire forest. At least they had not been cast upon a barren island, he thought. It would be hard fortune indeed to lose their mates and vessel and then have to forage on a barren shore. The shivering of his body lessened. He warmed with the effort of walking and that gave him new strength.

He found it easier to walk in the lips of the waves where the foam halted and sank away rapidly into the loose material of the beach.

Thomas watched the two figures lying nearly together on the beach. They remained motionless, resting on the black shore in the close and lax manner of dead men. Breakers tumbled and fanned up the slope far enough to flow around the bodies before sliding back. At a distance of ten yards he saw that the men were lying on their sides. He ran up to them, dropped to his knees, and laid a hand on each body. Thomas was relieved. Their chests rose and fell in deep, rhythmic breathing. From a distance, their stillness had made him fear they were dead or dying. He rolled each man enough to reveal his face. One was Mr. Morgen and the other was Christopher. Their bodies, like his and the captain's, were stripped of all clothing. He shook them, but their only responses were groans and deep respiration.

Thomas remained kneeling beside them, and while there, rested and looked out over the bay. He was hoping to see some fragment of the *Dove* floating shoreward with some of his mates clinging to it, but nearby he could only see the bare backs of breakers rolling in. To the east and west the vague white line of surf was visible until it faded into the gloom half a cable's length away. Beyond that there was nothing. Overhead the clouds blacked out more than half the stars.

What a damned fool! What a simpleton! Thomas growled to himself. How could this happen? How could a ship's crew, all sane and able men, let that muddling oaf bring them to this calamity? An hour ago they were safe aboard the barque, and now it was shattered and sunk. Here were four men exhausted and stripped naked on the shore of an unknown island. How many of their company were drowned and drifting back and forth with the waves? And the worst might be yet to come for them. Savages might be awaiting somewhere in the darkness, ready to rush out and smash skulls with their clubs. Death would be a tragic end for the voyage, but to be beheaded and eaten! Thomas hated even to think of it. He turned and stared into the blackness to the south, just to make sure savages had not already appeared. There was nothing there. But he worried that they might be hiding, peering out, savoring their intended meal, and plotting how to divide his flesh amongst them.

He looked down at the two men. “Are you hurt?” he asked. A groan was all the answer he was given. “Are you hurt?” he questioned each as he shook him.

After a short pause, Harrison gasped, “Thomas, lad?”

“Yes, Chris,” Thomas replied. “Are you all right?”

“I believe so.”

“How is the mate? Is he injured?”

“Think not,” Harrison said. He rolled up into a crouch and added, “He's been knocked about like me, but no worse. He was strong in the water, but when we got near shore, he was spent. Never seen a man so winded.”

“I pulled old Tobit in. He's about the same,” Thomas said. “I had Gabe, but he was hurt badly. He slipped from me. He's gone.”

Harrison gripped the lad's arm to give urgency to his words and shouted over the thunder of a breaking wave, “You must find someplace in the lee. We cannot be long in the wind all wet and naked as we are!”

Mr. Morgen stirred and murmured.

“He's coming around,” Thomas said.

“I'll see to him. You go fetch the captain here. Then you must find shelter, back there amongst the rocks, trees, or whatever you may find.”

“But shouldn't we look for our mates first?”

“I can feel you shaking,” the carpenter explained. “None of us will last in this wind. We will be of no use to our mates after much longer out here. They are no worse off than we are. They must look to themselves for help.”

“Let me go down the beach. Just a-ways to see if anyone else got ashore.”

“No, you will be chilled through. Cold breaks the reason. Soon you will not know which way you are going. Do what I tell you. We can wait no longer.”

Thomas thought for a moment. He knew Christopher was right. He had been shivering for most of the time he had been on the beach. He rose to his feet and started back to the captain. He walked fast, hoping the effort would warm him. Being partly rested and with the wind now partially at his back, he covered the distance in half the time. The indistinct form of the captain, showing a dull white in the starlight, appeared ahead on the shore. Tobit hadn't moved. He was still on his left side with half his face in the grit.

Thomas knelt beside him and spoke close to the captain's ear, "We must go now." Tobit remained still. Surely, Thomas thought, he must have recovered by this time, but the captain was the oldest—by far—and the least fit of all on the barque. He might have died of an apoplectic fit while Thomas was away talking with the carpenter. He turned his head and listened. The rasp of shallow breathing was audible. He grabbed the officer's shoulder and called, "Captain, can you hear me?"

A long, low groan was the only answer.

Thomas shook the captain and said, "I'll help you to the others. Then we must find a place out of the wind."

"No, no, leave me be. Want to rest."

"Those yonder are M-Mr. Morgen and Harrison. I h-had Gabe for a minute, but lost him. He went under . . . never came up again. Get on your feet. We must f-find a place to shelter."

"Done in, lad . . . can't move." The officer's words came out faint and wavering, nearly in a whisper. He never opened his eyes while he answered.

"I will search for a place in the lee and come b-back for you. Then you must be ready to move."

"Good lad. Let me rest for a w-while longer."

Thomas listened to the boom of the surf and the hiss of the waves as they neared and hauled back. It didn't appear that the captain could rise and walk. He got to his feet and started up the beach toward the dark mountain or cliff that blotted out all that part of the sky. Away from the foam of the waves and its reflected starlight, he could see nothing. He slid each foot ahead to avoid tripping or stepping on any sharp thing. Some deadly serpent or animal could be on the shore, and he would have no warning if either attacked. As he edged forward, he held his hands palms out before him. Step by step, he advanced. There were pieces of what must have been driftwood that he pushed aside or felt with his foot and stepped over. His left hand touched the leaves and branches of a tree or bush. In an attempt to pass around it, he discovered more to the right and left. The growth presented a continuous, stiff, and intertwined barrier at the back of the beach as he edged along. When he tried to force a way in, twigs poked his face and body. He feared he might have an eye pierced. Then he eased to his hands and knees and attempted to crawl in under the bushes. The lower limbs were as numerous and tangled. He could smell wet leaves close by. It was damp under the bushes, and drops of water fell from the leaves and limbs when he pushed on them, but he could find no entry. The bushes seemed to have grown in crevices between the rocks, but below them was sand or soil that could be hollowed into a rude shelter. Even if he found or dug a space large enough for the four of them, he thought, they would not be wholly sheltered from the wind and would have to lie or squat on wet earth. Thomas moved to his right and, instead of twigs and leaves, he felt the cold surface of a rock. It was rough and pitted and higher than he could reach. Farther on there was more of the dense growth and yet another great boulder. Now that he had traveled a bit in the dark he could sense, like a blind man, that a great rock fall lay along the back of the beach and all the narrow openings in it were filled with tough, springy bushes. He could only keep moving and hope to discover a hollow at the base of one of the rocks or some place they could build up a wall of stones and driftwood.

While he felt his way along, with his feet meeting and sliding over broken branches and stones, images of the *Dove* flashed into his mind. Her weedy but sound hull had carried them through all manner of storms in the tropics and the high latitudes of the grounds. Most of the time, they had been dry in the fo'c's'le, if not comfortable. He would give anything to be back in his bunk with a blanket spread over him. But in less than an hour Tobit had caused the barque to strike.

"Damn him!" Thomas cursed. "Damn that infernal fool! Why did I ever pull him from the surf?"

Now, if he ever got off the island, he would have to sign for another voyage skinning and boiling blubber or return to Stonington Port penniless. At best, it would be a year or two more before he reached home, and he would be worse off than if he had stayed in the shop and made shoes all that time.

Before thinking of any return, though, they must be rescued or find a way off the island. A steady wind now came from the west and he shuffled along in that direction, touching the boulders and feeling in the bushes for some cavity that would serve. His shivering increased again. Rubbing his arms and body helped a little, though his jaw muscles rattled his teeth, and nothing he tried would stop them. He crouched at the base of one of the rocks and scooped a little depression in the cinders. Huddled there, he felt less of the wind. The rain had waned to a mere drizzle. Harrison was depending on him to find shelter for all, and he knew he must get up soon and go on. In a few minutes, the shivering fit suddenly lessened. That encouraged him to rise from the hole and continue his search. He could wedge himself into a few places between the boulders and the bushes, but they were neither large enough for all nor much out of the wind.

He came to two high rocks separated by a gap about two feet wide. One rock rested closer to the bay, making the opening between them almost parallel to the beach. Thomas stepped into the gap and was halted by a tree trunk. The tree had grown against the landward rock, but the space between its trunk and the other rock just admitted his body. Slowly, he squeezed between that rough wall and the tree, sliding his right foot before him to feel for what was ahead. Anything might be in that crevice, he realized—some fierce cannibal, an animal with great fangs, poisonous spiders. It was totally black and where he looked made no difference, except directly overhead where a few dim stars flickered through leaves whipped to and fro by the wind.

For a few seconds, he remained motionless. Hardly a wisp of air stirred, and by that he guessed the other end of the cavity must be closed or blocked off with thick bushes. A sudden feeling of warmth spread over his body as he stood in the calmer air. If there was room enough for all, even if they had to stand, it would be better than anything he had found so far. With his back to the one boulder, he inched farther in. One sidestep, then another.

Suddenly he froze, hardly daring to breathe except in shallow, silent respirations. Something feathery was touching his arm! Was it the hair of a beast? . . . The plumed headdress of a heathen? Even through his open mouth, the sound of his breathing seemed loud. His blood thumped in his ears. What was he to do? Wait . . . till when? . . . Dawn? Until there was enough light to see what it was? Should he back away and leave? No! No! He had to find shelter now. Harrison was right. They might not last the night out in the open. Continually chilled, the captain would surely expire soon.

A little puff of air came in through the narrow opening and moved the soft thing that was touching his arm. He whipped his hand to the side and grabbed at it. His fingers clenched what felt like a long feather. It did not come free when he pulled. Gripping it tighter, he broke the center rib or quill in his hand. A stout tug and he knew it was rooted in the ground. Fern! Yes, yes, ferns! There would be many here, just as there were at Port William and Dusky. He felt others when he swept his hands around.

Thomas took the measure of the space he was in. It was eight paces long and at the far end another wall blocked any exit. From just within the tree at the entrance, the walls diverged until they were two and a half paces apart. He could feel by the matching lumps and hollows that they once had formed a single boulder. He guessed the rock to the landward side was the greater of the two, and the other was a portion that must have broken away. A split had opened and created the two walls. Another fracture had come from the outside and met the first at the far end in a right angle. Thus, the far end was blocked by a portion of the landward boulder. A section, almost flat on one side and one end, had been forced away and created the slim wedge-shaped void in which he was standing. The walls had to be taunt for the wind had almost no effect in that little space. He sank to his knees and felt about with his hands. Except for the clumps of ferns the floor of the space was coarse grit or cinders. Good, he said to himself. It was better to sit on that than on a mat of wet, rotting leaves. If they huddled together, they might even manage some sleep before dawn. The wind was excluded. The rain would not be. It would fall upon them like the light of the stars. The thought came to him that if no better shelter was found, a roof constructed above could make the place into a serviceable, though cramped, den.

Thomas got to his feet and slipped out past the bole of the tree. Instantly, he felt the renewed chill of the wind around his bare body. He moved directly for the bay, shuffling his feet across the surface of the beach. On the way, he picked up a long piece of driftwood he bumped with his foot. Just above the reach of the waves, he pawed a hole and set the wood upright in it. He packed it in tightly and thought, it will be my marker, it will lead me to the crevice.

While seeking shelter at the top of the beach, he estimated he had gotten west of the mate and Harrison. Thus he should meet them before he reached old Tobit. Thomas scanned the surf and beach westward as far as he could see by the starlight. There was nothing there, nothing that looked like a man. A march a few yards farther in that direction might yield more of the crew, but then it might not. As Christopher had said, this night each must look to his own security. It was not the time to search. The four of them were cold and exhausted, and their first need was to get out of the wind. He turned and headed for the mate and Harrison somewhere out in the blackness before him. The wind had become westerly, and the rain driven by it was now only intermittent dashes against his head and back. Foaming waves spread up to his pacing feet in slow, rhythmic succession. He peered right and left, looking for any human form or wreckage from the barque. Several times he detoured when he thought he saw a body lying in the sweeping foam or up on the beach, but the shadowy forms always proved to be a clump of rockweed or the drifted branch of a tree. He reckoned more of the crew had got ashore, though they may have landed farther west or east. Thomas felt he had traveled far enough on the shore to meet the others. Had they moved higher up the beach or gone looking for shelter themselves? If they had, he would have to search for them and delay all. But Harrison would not do that. He would stay where he could be found, close to where he had waded out of the waves.

The land smell of vegetation and wet earth was now constant, carried by the wind veering and crossing over more of the island. A few more minutes walking and he detected a whitish lump on the black surface of the beach. Thomas took longer strides, wishing the object to be the mate and Harrison and not a drift log or pile of weed. The lump appeared to move as he neared it, and he ran forward to find it was indeed Mr. Morgen and the carpenter crouched there.

"Christopher," Thomas asked, "have you seen any of the others?"

"No, n-none at all. You?"

"Not a one."

"M-may find one or two in the m-morning," Harrison said. "Don't think we can h-hope for more."

"Where's the captain?" the mate demanded. "Did you b-bring him?"

"He was too tired . . . wouldn't move," Thomas explained. "Left him. Went for shelter."

"Did you f-find any?" the carpenter asked as he rose to his feet.

"One that will serve. It's m-murky back there away from the surf, but I f-found a close place between some rocks we may squeeze into."

"We . . . we'd best hurry," Harrison warned. "Anything that is in the lee w-will do."

Mr. Morgen struggled to his feet. "Thomas," he ordered, "run b-back and f-fetch the captain."

The lad did not answer, and even in the dim starlight where faces were mere smudges in the gloom, Thomas's reluctance could be sensed.

"You hear me?" the mate demanded.

"I hear," Thomas replied, "but he has put us here, and the old buzzard should. . . ."

"Thomas!" the mate barked.

Harrison stepped between Mr. Morgen and Thomas and spoke quietly into the lad's ear, "We w-will settle this later. Say nothing for now. B-bring the captain here."

Thomas backed away slowly into the darkness and returned a few minutes later leading Captain Tobit, who was dragging himself along.

"Let me rest for a-a-a-w-while," the captain stuttered and dropped to his knees beside the mate.

"Only for a m-minute," Harrison warned. "We cannot stay out here m-much longer."

"Feel the wind now?" Mr. Morgen asked. "How it b-blows about in flaws?"

The carpenter turned and faced the gusts for a few seconds. "Coming from abaft the land," he explained. "That's w-what is breaking it up . . . now have a wind from the south'ard."

"That will not help our mates get ashore. How will they know which way to swim?" Thomas asked.

"'Less it gets lighter, they will not," the mate added. "I could see nothing. Just went to leeward all the w-way. They do the same now, they w-will be going the wrong direction."

"I hope they find something to hold to and can last till morning," Thomas said.

"We can do nothing before the light comes." the carpenter pointed out. "Must get to our shelter. Captain, w-we are chilled through . . . cannot stay here longer. Must go!"

"Ju-ju-just a m-mite longer," the captain protested.

"No! Up with you!" Harrison commanded.

Mr. Morgen reached down and slipped one hand under the captain's arm. "Here, help him up. His legs are weak. Thomas, lead us to this place you have f-found."

The mate and carpenter pulled Tobit to his feet and started off after the lad. All four men walked along just above the highest reach of the spent waves.

"I must s-stop. . . . Re-re-rest," the captain begged after only a few minutes marching.

"Not now!" Harrison snapped. "If you cannot walk, we will carry you. If we cannot do that, we will drag you!"

"B-but must rest. I-I-I am tw-twice your age."

"You must keep on," the carpenter growled. "We are all shivering. Soon none of us will be able to m-move. Only hope is to keep going. The effort will warm us. Walk! Walk! Walk!"

The captain dropped to his knees. "Legs are lead," he whined. "C-c-cannot move."

Harrison and the mate grabbed the captain's arms and buoyed him up again. In that fashion, walking three abreast, they moved on once more. It was awkward and limited them to short steps. Thomas marched ahead, but he had to stop repeatedly and wait until the others caught up with him. The men kept the captain moving for ten minutes though he complained constantly that he could go no farther. At times they bore his entire weight or dragged him along like a petulant child. When it was a few yards away, Thomas spotted the stick he had planted in the beach. It showed black against the white of the surf farther down the shore.

"We turn in here," he announced, when the captain was brought up to him.

"How do you know?" the mate asked. "Looks the s-same to me, like the inside of a b-barrel."

"Here," Thomas said, and put his hand on the upright piece of wood, "here is my mark."

"Where are we?" the captain asked. "Wh-where is this place?"

"Just up there, between some rocks," the lad answered and started up the pitch of the beach. He did not find it when he reached the bushes on his first try. In the short walk up from the marker, he knew he must have drifted a little to one side or the other. He searched to the west, turned back east, and finally came upon the rock. Then he felt along around its corner and located the cleft. "In here," he called back. "There is a tree nearly blocking the way. We'll have to push the captain through."

Thomas worked his way in and tugged on the captain's right arm.

"Ahh! Ahh! Stop!" Tobit cried. "Rock is cutting my back."

"Turn about and put your damned b-belly there," the mate growled.

The captain backed out, turned, and wedged his left side into the opening. With the lad pulling from within and the mate and the carpenter pushing from without, they managed to get the captain past the tree but not without Tobit crying out at each shove. Harrison and Mr. Morgen squirmed through after him.

"No w-wind in here," the mate noted. "Ahh, I feel none at all. Good thing. W-warm compared to out there. Yet we are going to have a d-devil of a time. I'll lay we will be shaking all night."

Harrison felt his way around the others and went to the far end, touching the walls as he went. "Nigh a cave. You've done well, lad. This will serve for tonight and perhaps longer," he said.

"If we only had f-flint an' s-steel an' tinder," Tobit chattered through his teeth.

"All is wet," the carpenter pointed out. "No fire tonight. Tomorrow, perhaps. Now let us dig a bit and see if it is drier down a-ways." He knelt and pawed out a hole at the base of the rock on the bay side of the crevice and announced, "Aye, better. Feels better. Let's dig a place for us all."

Thomas, the mate, and Harrison crouched side by side and scooped out a depression large enough for everyone.

"Put the captain in first," Mr. Morgen ordered. "Harrison, you sit on one side and I'll sit on the other. He needs the warmth. He's in a bad state."

They pressed close to each other and drew their knees up to their chins to hoard the heat of their bodies. After they made the first adjustments to their gritty seats and to each other, they were quiet for several minutes. Thomas was the first to speak.

"Listen to that sea," he murmured. "Sounds like thunder. It's doom for someone."

"Don't say that," the carpenter objected. "We've had enough ill luck for this night."

"Aye, boys," the mate broke in, "b-best we not talk. Should rest as w-well as we can. Daylight comes, we must search for the rest of the crew and salvage what we can of the *Dove*. And watch for savages all the while. Let's sleep for now."

The little group fell silent again. Throughout the night, the booming of the surf lessened a little each hour. A few raindrops fell on their heads and shoulders sporadically. Instead of the constant wind, separate gusts tore through the tops of the trees above them. They ceased at intervals, then resumed later with less ferocity. The periods of near calm became longer. Often they felt a few leaves land on them that had been torn from the treetops. Now and then the men shifted their arms and legs to ease their cramped muscles. Each one slept for a few minutes or half an hour at a time, then awoke to shiver or groan. Captain Tobit had fitful dreams. He mumbled snatches of scripture and then coughed and grunted an "Amen."

After several minutes of a good nap, Thomas suddenly jerked his head up. There was a reverberation, a quivering in the air that lasted for a second or two. He was unsure if he felt it or had truly heard it. Was it real or was it the last scrap of a dream? If it had been a dream, he couldn't recall anything about it. He couldn't place that noise or sensation. It had not sounded like anything he had ever known before. He meant to concentrate on it should it be repeated. He listened, focused on the sounds about him, but soon he was drifting toward sleep. A half-minute later, he yielded and dozed off.

CHAPTER 5

THOMAS had no idea how long he'd slept when he awakened again. It felt as if it had been an hour, but probably had been much less. There was no way to mark the time. He raised his head from his arms, crossed on his knees, and stared directly overhead where there was something other than the few dim stars to be seen. In the narrow slot between the stone walls, the sky had lightened slightly. He inferred black clumps of ill-defined leaves when they moved and obscured the dimming stars. He put his head down again wishing to sleep a little more.

It was hopeless. His back pained him from the bruising in the surf and his muscles ached from being in one position without shifting. All night the others had jostled him awake after what felt like only a few minutes drowsing. The sound of the waves had grown quieter and now, without the thunder-like reports of huge breakers, was only a steady rumble. The wind had abated too, but still tossed the trees overhead. After what he thought was a half an hour, he looked up again. The sky was perceptibly graying, yet all that was visible was that irregular strip above. The leaves moving back and forth had become defined into silhouettes, yet the vaguest shape could not be detected in the blackness between the walls. He thought he might discover how the island appeared by the pre-dawn light and rolled from his sitting position to his knees. He put a hand on the rock to aid his rise to his feet. Only the dim light above gave any reference for a sense of balance. It was a trial walking on legs that been pulled up against his body all night. They were stiff and would not bend properly at the knees. Step by step, he forced them to move in a tottering walk toward the entrance. He slid his left hand along the wall, and with his right he felt for the tree that partially blocked the entrance.

Something was amiss! He felt it the instant he put his hand on the trunk. There was no longer enough space to allow him to pass. The tree was now in the middle of the opening. It was about a foot in diameter, far too ponderous to be forced aside. The wind veering in the night and working against the upper limbs must have shifted the trunk leaving openings on each side of the tree that were impossible to pass through. The four were trapped in their refuge. They must seek another way out when there was more light. Perhaps they might climb to the top of the walls and drop to the beach. He pressed his head to one space between the rock and the bole of the tree and saw the white edge of the surf. The beach was invisible in the darkness and each whitened wave appeared to flow unsupported into black space.

A deep note suddenly throbbed in the air all around him. Perhaps it was the noise that had awakened him an hour or so before, a sound plucked on a length of twine just taut enough to vibrate. Nowhere could he see a likely source. Then another one was repeated three or four seconds later, with the same pitch and for the same duration. Now he was sure it was what had broken through his sleep, and he must have heard the last bit of it before he was fully awake. His heart beat rapidly and his pulse thumped in his ears. Ah! A long bow he now suspected, one not tightly strung and plucked softly. The single notes came evenly spaced at the same intervals. There was no change in pitch so it was not meant as music. He imagined a savage somewhere in the darkness signaling to his fellows. Facing different directions, Thomas turned his head and listened, but could not determine where it came from. Each note was struck some distance away and pervaded the air around him. He felt his way back to the others and shook each of them.

"Keep still," he whispered.

"Uh . . . What is it?" the mate murmured.

"Listen closely."

All the men remained motionless. The seconds passed while they waited in a long silence. Thomas then wondered if he had not imagined the sounds. Perhaps a dream had spilled into his half-wakened mind. Perhaps the one making the notes had stopped.

"I hear nothing," Mr. Morgen said softly.

"Shhhh," Harrison cautioned and touched the mate's shoulder.

A moment later the deep note came wavering in the air.

The mate questioned Thomas, "What do you think it is?"

"I don't know. I've never heard a thing like it."

The captain hissed, "Cannibals! They have discovered us."

The mate then asked Harrison, "What do you make it to be?"

The carpenter did not answer at once, but waited motionless in the gloom, listening to each note as it came at its expected interval. Then at last he said, "I believe it is a bird."

"No, no," the mate objected, "it is like a large viol! The lowest string played. Birds chirp and sing their songs."

"But the crow, the gull, and the goose? How sweetly do they sing?" Harrison asked.

"Aye, they make their coarse cries," the mate agreed, "but this is no bird or fowl. It is a man sound."

Suddenly another identical but more distant note broke the measured interval between the first notes. They listened. The two sounds alternated, one seeming to answer the other without change in pitch or volume.

"Ah! Ah! Savages! Cannibals!" the captain croaked. "They are all about us!"

"If that is so, we'd best leave somehow. This is a trap we are in. We cannot get out the way we came," Thomas explained. "The wind has shifted the tree. We must climb out."

"Are you sure? Let me see," Mr. Morgen demanded and rose to his feet. He felt his way past the others and to the entrance. After reaching around the tree he whispered, "Aye, lad, it has. We can only get out above. Feel for a way up."

After a few seconds searching, Harrison reported, "There are no limbs I can reach on the tree. The rock is pitted, but there is nothing either large or deep enough to grasp. Perhaps we could stand on each other's shoulders. Or we might be able put our backs to one wall and our feet to the other and force our way to the top."

"Ach! My back is far too sore to do that," the mate complained. "Even if we three could do it, the captain could not be got out."

"A vine. We get out and lower a vine for the captain, and hoist him in a bowline," the carpenter proposed.

"Are we sure we may find a vine? There might not be a one on the whole island," Mr. Morgen pointed out.

While the others were crowded near the tree, Thomas went to the far end and ran his hands over the cross wall that blocked that end of the shelter. He discovered the surface was as the carpenter had described it at the other end, pitted but not so deeply as to give a handhold. At the base of the wall he found there was a cavity in the material of the beach. He pressed his head into it and felt a slight breath of air against his face. Thomas backed onto his haunches and announced, "I think I have a way out. Help me dig." He pawed at each side to enlarge the hole, drawing out handfuls of material and passing it back to Harrison, who in turn pushed it on to the mate. After each scoop was removed, a little more light came through from the beach outside.

The wedge of sky visible above the walls was graying, and the waving branches and leaves were growing more distinct. In the small space the fern fronds formed out of the darkness. They could see from what they were digging out, that the shore on which they had landed must consist of coarse, dark cinders. For nearly a quarter of an hour, the three men worked on the hole. Thomas surveyed it and pulled out one last scoop. Suddenly he dived in and wiggled forward until he was partially outside in a shallow depression. He raised his head cautiously to the level of the beach. With a quick look to the left and right, he saw nothing on the shore except a few hanks of rockweed and branches of driftwood. There were no beached canoes, no tattooed savages carrying spears and clubs. As far as he was able to see in the morning mist, the shore in each direction and the bay was tranquil and empty of any man. The cinders of the beach were slate gray on the dry part and nearer to black where wetted by the waves.

A few white birds stood immobile along the shore just above the reach of the waves and watched them wash in and recede. Someone called to him from inside, but his body still blocked most of the hole and the words were muffled and meaningless. Thomas thrust himself ahead and up in an effort to rise out of the cinders.

"Ah! Ah!" He cried out in pain and winced as the rough stone above scraped his back.

"What's amiss?" Mr. Morgen called from inside.

Thomas could hear the captain saying something about cannibals.

"There is nothing on the beach," he called back to the mate. "I chafed my back against the rock. Take care as you come out." He crawled the rest of the way out and stood up to get a better view of the shore. It was a little clearer to the west, and he saw the turn of the beach where it swept to the north forming the base of the spit. The high, hulking shape of the island was partially visible in the gray light. At the foot of a dark bluff were the scattered boulders embedded in the dense bushes that he had explored in the blackness of the night. Eastward, the shore and the remainder of the island faded away into the surf haze. No huts there. No savages yet.

Good he thought, and others of the crew might be somewhere along that coast. A grunt drew his attention back to the hole. Harrison was just squirming out, and he was surprised by the carpenter's appearance. His hair and beard were still damp and ropy with seawater, and there were crusts of dried blood and cinders sticking to his knees and shoulders. When Harrison turned about to help the mate out, Thomas saw scrapes on his back that had dried some in the night and had been set to bleeding again by his struggle out. He inspected his own body and saw the same abrasions and oozing cuts on his arms and legs. Through the night, he had felt some pain and the sting of salt in wounds, but he had not suspected the surf had given him such a tumbling.

Harrison and the mate each had a grip on one of the captain's arms and were pulling him up. Dark patches of cinders clinging to his naked body made the skin appear as white as bread dough. The sagging flesh contrasted with the lean, hard bodies of the other men and seemed alien amid the surroundings of tangled scrub and coarse stone. He was drawn up by the mate and Harrison and left standing on his feet.

Mr. Morgen stepped around and viewed the captain's body that bore its share of bleeding cuts. "We've taken quite a raking," he said after inspecting himself and the crewmen. He backed away from the boulder in order to get a view of the bluff above it. The rest did the same and then searched the trees to each side and far as they could see down the shore.

"You saw no one when you first looked out?" the carpenter asked Thomas.

"See for yourself. Same as now. Nothing has changed," he replied.

"And what of the savages?" Tobit asked. "You saw nought moving?"

Thomas shook his head. "There were only those bits of rockweed here and the birds as far as I could see. Who knows but they are in the trees and making those noises."

"We must be doubly careful," the mate cautioned. "They are all cannibals on these coasts, all, and I don't fancy being eaten."

While Harrison looked along the shore to the west and the east, he announced with measured words, "I doubt there are savages on this island. I am almost convinced there are not."

Mr. Morgen turned to the carpenter, his mouth half open as if he couldn't get his words out. A second later he asked, "What makes you say that? Have you been here before?"

"No," Harrison replied, "I have not been here before. But I expect the west coast beyond that spit and the south side of the island are ironbound. Even if they are not, the swells from those quarters must raise a heavy surf there. This bay then is the natural, the sensible place for the savages to beach their proas or canoes."

The captain pointed a finger at the carpenter and said, "Just so, but we may still meet them. There is much yet to explore. If there are no savages here, then what is making those noises?"

Mr. Morgen was peering into the bushes on each side of the boulder and then higher up into the trees on the bluff. "Yes, they are plucking a length of twine or gut," he insisted.

The men listened for each succeeding note, anticipating them as they sounded after the interval of silence. Even outside the narrow crevice they could not fix the source of either one. They seemed to come from everywhere back of the beach.

"It's most like a drum with the head a little slack. That could possibly be how they are being made," the captain suggested.

"I believe I have heard them before," Harrison said.

"Where?" Tobit demanded. "Where have you heard them?"

The carpenter eyed the trees on the steep slope above the boulder and listened intently. The others watched his expression, waiting for his answer. Finally, he nodded his head once and declared, "Yes, it is a bird. It's a certainty."

"It can't be," the mate objected. "The sound has too low a pitch. How could a bird make such a call?"

"I don't know," Harrison continued, "but it is a large, green parrot, the size of a goose. It does not fly, but can only walk about and climb a little. In Port William I heard one much farther away, and one was pointed out to me there."

"I never heard of such a parrot," the mate snapped.

"It's not a common thing," Harrison explained. "It stays far out in the woods and is very shy."

The mate nodded and said, "Well, bird or savage we shall soon know for sure. When it is lighter we must search for the others that may have got ashore, but we need something for arms. We cannot go about empty-handed, and we must keep a sharp watch all 'round. Harrison and Thomas, find what you can that will serve for weapons. Show little of yourself as possible."

"Aye, sir," the carpenter replied. He turned to Thomas and motioned for him to follow. They headed west, keeping close to the rocks and bushes at the upper border of the beach. Both scanned the shore as they went, looking for some fragment of their vessel. "Not a stitch," Harrison observed. "It has all been carried north, perhaps even out of this bay. I cannot even see our buoys. But we must find something. We cannot live here with naught."

A hundred yards away from the officers, the lad patted his stomach with both hands and sauntered along aping Tobit's rolling walk aboard the barque. He tilted his head back and asked pompously, "Well, what will serve best, Mr. Morgen, muskets or hangers? Remember, whichever you choose, I want them well-polished. Perhaps you could muster some swivel guns and cartridges and shot. That would put us in a good posture, wouldn't you say?"

"I expect so," the carpenter chuckled at the lad's aping of the captain. "But for now it can only be clubs or spears. Look for what has washed up and what we can break out of the bushes."

The two walked slowly, pausing to scan the shore and peer into the thick growth at the foot of the bluff. From the driftwood they selected the straightest pieces. Less often, they discovered a dead limb they were able to break out of bushes between the boulders. Several hundred yards from where the officers were crouched, they stopped after having gathered seven sticks that were a fathom long, as thick as an anchor cable at their larger end and tapering to an inch at the opposite end. They dropped them from their shoulders onto the beach. Harrison sorted them out and chose the four straightest ones.

Thomas was looking farther west along the shore. "No one out there," he said, "and not one footprint or sign that anyone has passed here. Not even a scrap of the *Dove*."

"They could not have got so far west," the carpenter said. "We shall not find them out there. If they were not drowned, they would have gained the shore close to where we did. Come, lad, we must sharpen these sticks so we can thrust and parry with them."

Thomas picked one up, hefted it in his hands, and nodded his approval. "The butt end is heavy enough to fetch someone a hard knock on the head," he said.

Harrison leaned over and selected one for himself, then picked at its surface. "Perhaps manuka," he declared. "Aye, good stout wood."

Carrying his stick to a large rock, Thomas rubbed its small end back and forth to form a sharp point. He turned it a bit at a time as he forced the wood across the rough surface. When it looked properly finished, he gripped it with both hands and lunged at an imaginary opponent. He whipped about as if there was another man behind him, jabbed in that direction, and then shifted his hold. His imagined attack went on, and he made wild swings using the stick as a club.

A wide grin formed under the carpenter's beard as he watched the lad's trials with the weapon.

Thomas heard Harrison chuckling and quit his fighting stance. He spun about and asked, "Is it so comical?"

"Aye! Hee, hee, hee! Aye, surely comical. How do they say, risible? I watched you and had a thought: if we should meet with natives on this island, we would appear the more like savages. Why, look at us, all naked and smeared with blood and you prancing about with a club! If we danced about a fire, we would be the very picture of heathens. We might frighten a company of dragoons or Turks with our beards and wild hair."

Thomas stared at the carpenter's bare and bloodied body and at the long stick he was holding. It is ridiculous, he said to himself and then snickered aloud, "Yes, you are right. Without a stitch of clothes and your roger swinging in the breeze, you are a cruel sight. We look more dreadful than the fiercest of them, but it can't be helped for now. We were in luck to reach the shore in any condition."

"I agree with you there," Harrison said, "but I doubt these weapons are needed. They will only serve to reassure the captain and mate."

"We can't suppose there are no cannibals here simply because we see no canoes on the beach. There is much more of the bay to see. What of the other parts of the island? They may be up there hiding in the trees above us."

"Why should they hide? They could not have missed seeing the *Dove* entering the bay and would have watched for us to land. This morning there was no boat ashore and no vessel. So what would the savages think?"

"That we had left in the night."

"Thus, no need for them to keep to the bushes. Doesn't that follow?"

The younger sailor nodded. He could find no fault with the carpenter's reasoning. He took another stick and began shaping it; when it was sharp enough to suit him, he touched the point with a forefinger. "Hardening them in a fire may help," he suggested. "Later, we might fix a point of iron on them from the *Dove*."

Harrison looked up from his work and asked, "For what purpose? To spear fish?"

The carpenter finished working on his stick and stood viewing the shore to the west where it to curved out to become the spit. A wind-smoothed field of dark dunes filled that junction behind the near-perfect arc of the beach. It extended as far as could be seen, possibly to the west coast. Along the spit there were angular spires of dark rock. Closer to the island they were forty or fifty feet in height, but farther out they grew shorter until, at the end, they were barely visible above the white froth of the breaking waves.

"There," Harrison said, "the coast is beyond those dunes, and I'll lay there's a high surf there always." He faced about and pointed to the beach to the east and added, "If any of our mates got ashore, it would be there. None could have got out this far."

To the south, on the bluff, the tops of trees showed through a moving mist, and the island, they saw, was like the slopes around Dusky, wooded with densely leaved trees. Except for the subdued green of the trees and bushes nearby, the scene was a monochrome shading from the white surf to the expanse of gray sea to black rocks. There was a much higher part of the island, the dark form that they had seen from the deck of the barque, but they were too close under the foot of the bluff to be able to see any of it.

Harrison touched the lad's shoulder and pointed down the beach. Mr. Morgen was hurrying toward them in a low crouch.

The crewmen gathered up their sharpened sticks and started back toward the mate. Mr. Morgen waved a hand landward, indicating he wanted them to stay close to the boulders and bushes.

"Could they have seen any of our mates?" Thomas asked as they trotted along the beach.

"Aye," Harrison responded, "a man or two. I don't think we can hope for more. It was a long swim from the *Dove*."

The mate stopped and waited for the crewmen to approach.

"What have you found? Some of the others?" the carpenter asked when he came close to the officer.

Mr. Morgen shook his head and answered, "None as yet. Hurry along, the captain wants to start looking for them. Give me two of those. The captain wishes to see if they will serve." The mate took the two sticks Harrison was carrying and started back.

"Ha, he will see if they will serve!" Thomas mocked the mate. "He had no idea of what he wanted. Now he will say they are not useable."

"Oh, let him act his part. It will do no harm," the carpenter said with a wave of his arm. "We can suffer him to play the officer. What can it matter to us?"

"He looked quite the captain when he marched about the deck. Now, without his clothes, we can see what a clown he is and, worse yet, what he is not. Those bandy legs look as if they will give way any minute."

Harrison smiled, then sobered his look and added, "Yes, his underpinning does look weak."

"Why, they look like sticks propped under a sack of flour," the lad snickered, "and if the Boston girls saw his little worm, they'd giggle for a week."

The gray sky was taking on a bluish shade, and the sun hinted where it would rise over a part of the island still mist-covered. Individual trees on the top of the bluff revealed their details. Some were so tall their trunks stood out against shadows and the dark foliage of the lesser ones. It was obvious that, ages ago, the great boulders had tumbled from higher up and had landed on the beach. Since that time dense bushes had grown up between them forming the nearly impenetrable wall he had faced in the night. Farther along that shore, Thomas suspected there might be a dozen secret places perfect for an ambush. A few savages with a will could overpower them in a trice. Despite Harrison's reckoning, he was still wary. Even if there wasn't an entire tribe, it was possible a few cannibals were lurking about.

Captain Tobit was holding one of the sticks upright at his right side and waiting for the crewmen to approach. "You have found nothing?" he asked, apparently not expecting any surprising reply.

"No man and no one thing of our barque," the carpenter answered.

"Well, we will search to the east. We will stay close under this bluff. We must not show ourselves out on the beach. Keep a sharp eye and hold your weapons at the ready."

"Aye, sir. We are set to go if you are now fit?" the mate asked.

"I am well fit!" the captain snapped back. His thick jaw was set firmly as he looked the other men over. "Now, let us show some life," he ordered. "Follow me and look all about. Listen for those sounds . . . if they follow us or cease." He spun about and started off.

The others fell in line. The mate followed Captain Tobit. Thomas was next, but held back some extra paces that he might talk to Harrison who came last. Their pace was slow at first. The officers warily sidled forward close to the boulders and greenery. During their search for the weapons, Harrison and Thomas had worked the stiffness from their muscles, but the mate and captain still walked with unwilling strides that showed the effect of their struggle through the surf and the hours sitting up in the damp sea air. Captain Tobit carried his stick at the ready, prepared to lunge at any beast or man that might confront him. The mate followed two paces behind and aped his stance. Anyone watching the men's attempts to hide would have judged them absurd. Their pale bodies showed white as paper against the slate gray rocks and the green bushes. Thomas crept along half-erect five or six yards back. He kept his weapon pointed at the bushes until he looked back and saw the carpenter sauntering behind him with his stick across his shoulders and his hands hanging over each end of it. Then Thomas stood straight and put his stick on his shoulders too.

Mr. Morgen stopped, turned half around, and said, "Look sharp, lads, for any sign of our people on the beach or in the trees. They would have got between the rocks and bushes last night as we did."

"Must he treat us like children?" Thomas whispered to Harrison. "We are doing that just now. We can think well enough for ourselves."

"Oh, he must say something to remind us that he is the officer," Harrison replied.

"Yes," Thomas agreed, "and pretend he knows better than we."

The castaways weaved their way around the blocks of stone, some no larger than a keg and some that could conceal a coach and team. The captain stopped and crouched behind each boulder, peeked out, then slipped crab-wise to the next bush or rock that would provide cover for half his body.

Captain Tobit suddenly turned back to the others and jabbed his finger several times toward the surf. There, just ahead in the firm cinders of the lower beach was a line of footprints leading up and inshore. The men crowded behind a rock with the captain and stared at them. In the dry portion of the beach, they were mere pockmarks, but in the damp cinders just above the wash of the sea, they still had the outline of bare human feet.

Thomas smiled and tapped his chest with the tips of the fingers of his right hand. "Those are my footprints," he explained. "This is where I came up to look for shelter last night."

"Oh, yes, yes," the captain whispered, as if he had known what they were and was simply pointing them out to the others.

"The sounds have stopped," the carpenter said. "I swear they are parrots that make those calls, and we will not hear them again today. I believe they only sing at night."

"There is no proof it is a bird," the mate objected. "Even if it be a bird, there still may be cannibals. You two keep a good watch behind and make sure we are not followed."

The captain peered ahead and started off again. At each rock and thicket they paused and looked the shore over for any footprints or the least fragment of their ship.

To their right the high bluff grew less steep as they traveled eastward. Now, no longer diverted by such a high mass, more wind swept from the south over the island and poured onto the shore, fluttering the leaves of the trees and larger bushes and revealing their lighter-colored backs. An infrequent gust, bending limbs, brought with it sounds of stirrings in the forest above the bluff and a mix of smells: wet earth, lush greenery, and rotting leaves. Directly ahead, at the horizon, a yellow glow appeared. It diffused in the mist and droplets cast up from the breaking waves, and grew into an intense nimbus as the moments passed. The men narrowed their eyes against the radiance that burst upon them. For several minutes what they could see of the shore and the bluff in that direction was tinted with a gold light. The halo shrank as the sun rose higher. Mists evaporated in the warming sunlight and details of the shore appeared. Waves rolled in one after the other, rising and thinning to a translucent green, a veil of spray blowing back from their curling tops as they rushed shoreward.

For an hour and a half, the castaways kept at their creeping progress along the shore and close to the bluff. At one of their many halts, while the officers studied the way ahead, Thomas took his stick from his shoulders and turned back to see how much distance they had covered. The haze was almost gone, and every tree, boulder, and breaking wave was now sharp-edged in the clean morning air. He extended his arms to each side in an encompassing gesture and exclaimed, "Did you ever see such a green and wonderful place!"

Harrison swept his gaze from the beach behind them, over the wooded slope, and to the shore yet to be explored ahead. He nodded a few times and replied, "None, lad. For sure we are cast away on a rich and bosky land. Our little island. How would that Otaheetee man at Port William name it? Motoo Eetee? We will want for nothing here. There are surely fish in the bay and birds and animals in the woods. We are not in such bad straits on this island."

"Do you think many of our mates reached shore?"

"I can't say, but I fear most are lost. So many did not know how to swim, and if they seized an oar or cask, why, the wind carried them north when it shifted. Nothing that floated free has yet come ashore. There was nothing we could do and nothing we can blame ourselves for, lad. Do you fret about our future here?"

"If there are no savages to deal with, no. I would rather be here for now than on some rocky shore stretching hides and smelling the awful stink. How does it suit you?"

The carpenter scratched his beard and answered, "Much the same. We have all we may need, and we are in no danger but what we make for ourselves."

"What do you mean by that?"

"I say we are alone here. There is no danger lest it be our doing. You are as secure here as if you were sitting on Grant's Hill."

"So you still believe there can be no cannibals here?"

"Aye, more than ever. Have you seen any sign thus far?"

"No, but we have a long way to go. There is the whole of the island to be explored still."

"Just so, lad, just so! Yet if savages reached here, they would have explored and been to all parts of this land and left their marks. We have not seen one broken twig, not one footprint other than our own, or one thing made by man, heathen or Christian. We see all this just as it was left after the Deluge. We are the first to behold this island. Think of that. It is like a gift to us, the greatest gift we could hope for. We may live here like fighting cocks."

"But it is not home!" Thomas objected.

"True, it is not home. But you will see home again. A ship will call here, a whaler, another sealer, or a colonial from Port Jackson. They are about these islands."

"How soon might that be? A year? Or five years? We could be graybeards or dead by the time someone stumbles upon us."

"Then we shall build a boat, a little sloop, a pinnace. We are fit and there are trees of all kinds."

"But we have no saw," Thomas protested. "How can we pit logs and cut planks? There is no ax or adze. No wedges or froe to rive with."

"Then we dive to the *Dove* to get them, and blocks, line, and what iron we may need. If we cannot do that, we will hollow a log for a hull. We can make lines from the bark of saplings to rig it with boomkins and a spar as a proa. Once it is done, there will be naught to do but run before the wind for a few days, and then we must fall in with the Middle Island for certain. From there we will make for the Bay of Islands, or we might meet with a whaler before then. I heard they take whales about Cook Strait. Ah, you shall walk the roads of Stonington again. No need to be a Jeremiah, mate."

Thomas listened to Harrison as he listed their choices with cheerfulness and made out the building of a vessel to be a simple and speedy thing. Considering that they had been cast ashore naked and bruised with not even a sheath knife, his words and voice seemed far too hopeful. And perhaps they were so simply to hearten him. He suspected that was the carpenter's intent, but he was not that much of a marine and knew full well what their plight was.

With the sun now higher, a few gulls soared over the surf. At the top of each sweep, they twitched their tails and teetered on the wind.

Thomas rubbed his chest and murmured, "Ah, that sun is good on the skin. I seem to have come alive again."

"Everything looks better now that it shines full on us," Harrison added. "You'll feel better by the hour."

"Do you smell what's on the wind? The trees and the earth. Ah, that's the good land smell."

"Think how fortunate we are, lad. We might have fetched up on some dismal rock with nothing from which to make shelter or togs. We would have died of the cold in a few days time."

"If only our mates were ashore, I wouldn't fret so much about the wreck."

"We passed the rock we split upon long ago," the carpenter muttered as he looked out over the bay. "The farther we go, the less chance there is of finding any of our crew."

"Then you have given all the others over for lost?" the lad asked.

Harrison shook his head slowly and then pointed behind them. "You see the distance we have gone?" he asked. "We went from the ship straight for the shore; but to reach this place, a man would have to swim three times as far. If any went this way to find a refuge in the lee, where are their tracks? They would have crossed where we have since walked to find shelter. Oh, it is possible one or two are yet to be found. It is a slim hope though."

Thomas glanced over the bay from the west to the east and saw nothing on its surface except the flecks of whitecaps. The arriving swells peaked, collapsed, and ran tier upon tier toward the beach, each renewing the lace work of bubbles on the blue-green water.

"Do you see something out there?" the carpenter asked.

"No, nothing," the lad replied, "I was just watching the waves. I hoped there would be some bit of the *Dove* floating about, but I suppose we are too far from it now. Odd that there is nothing. Surely gear washed free, but we've not seen a scrap."

"It was the wind that shifted after we got ashore. We will see nothing of it 'less it blows fresh again from the north'ard."

The two officers had drawn ahead and were now hunkered behind a low bush. The captain and mate peeked from their hiding place to the beach ahead of them.

"They have found something!" Harrison blurted out and trotted forward.

At that moment, Mr. Morgen turned about and motioned to the crewmen to keep close to the rocks and stay low. Both men bent low and rushed ahead. At the bush they dropped to their knees.

"What is it?" Thomas whispered.

The mate beckoned for him to come up and see for himself. Thomas crawled forward and peeked through the leaves. To their right the angle of the bluff became less steep and farther ahead it curved away to the south. On the flat ground between the beach and the receding slope was a stand of flax plants. They were taller than any he had seen in Dusky. Some smaller, scattered plants grew nearer the shore, but behind them the vertical, sword-like leaves formed a wall eight to ten feet in height. They were so thick it would be slow labor to force a way through, and at every step they might risk ambush in the dense growth. Thomas's eye followed the beach line. It kept its curve around the bay, but beyond the field of flax a quarter mile on, he saw the edge of a lagoon or slough. The beach at that point became a barren bar that separated the bay water from the slough. It was bare for its entire length until it rejoined the high ground a mile and a half away.

The carpenter moved up beside Thomas and pointed to the gray-green flax and said, "Ah, lad, there is our rope and marline. Good as Russian hemp. With work and patience we may have all we want."

Thomas sat back on his haunches. He looked at the captain and Mr. Morgen, then asked, "What are we waiting for? There are no savages?"

"No, no signs as yet," the mate explained, "but you see we cannot go farther unless we show ourselves out there. There is no way to get through those plants on the land side. They are thick and there could be much danger in them."

The captain agreed with a nod and declared, "We'll not go out there. We could be seen from half the island."

"Then what are we to do now?" Thomas demanded.

For several seconds, Captain Tobit gave him a scornful look and spoke his answer with slow words like the beat of a drum. "Do not forget who I am. We must wait here until dark. We have no other choice."

"And leave our mates out there?" Thomas cried. "No, I'll not do that! We've seen no cannibals . . . not the least sign of them!" He leaped to his feet.

The mate grabbed at his arm to pull him down to the cover of the bush, but Thomas wrenched free and dashed out into the open.

"Damn you!" the captain shouted. "Where are you going?"

"To find my mates!" Thomas yelled, turning half around as he marched off. "I'll not cower here whilst our men and boys are lost!"

"Damn and blast you! You betray us bolting out there!" the captain screamed and rose to his feet.

The lad halted and looked defiantly back at the two officers standing behind the bush.

"You have made our deaths near certain!" the mate cried. "These savages feast on strangers!"

With a contemptuous swipe of his arm, Thomas shouted back at them, "Go hide in the trees. I will search for our crew alone."

Captain Tobit stepped from behind the bush and walked up to the young sailor. He stared into his eyes. "I will settle with you," he hissed in a low voice and brought his stick up and gripped it with both hands before him like a quarterstaff.

Thomas gazed back unblinking. His mouth had a slight upturn, as if he welcomed any move of the captain to strike him.

"Not now, but later," Tobit promised. "Don't think I shall forget how you defy me. I'll not rest till I have you spread-eagled. You are still under my command. You have no discharge from me. I will teach you who is officer and who is man. I will cut that out on your back!"

Thomas looked down on the captain's face, blotchy and red with rage. His hair was a welter of white tufts peppered with black grit. He was about to answer when the officer pushed past him and headed for the bar. Immediately, the mate hurried out to join the captain.

Once more the four men moved along the beach with the officers leading and the crewmen following. The pace was faster now that they were visible from a greater part of the island and not delayed by their efforts to hide. Harrison and Thomas slowed until they were out of earshot of the mate and captain.

"He has no ship," Thomas growled, "therefore he is captain of nothing. He can no longer order what I do."

The carpenter remained silent as he strode along and searched the shore ahead and the island to the right.

Thomas waited a half-minute for a response and then argued, "We signed for a voyage aboard the *Dove*. Now it lies at the bottom of this bay. How do we continue the voyage? How do we take seals and boil sea elephants?"

Harrison answered deliberately, "As you say, our ship is gone and now he commands nothing. But we are not in Boston or Stonington or even near our continent. I am not sure, but as he says, he has not given us a discharge."

"If the law were such, he could keep us at his will for the rest of our lives. No, I say the voyage is over. He has no command of us."

"Lad, you must consider this: if we work together, we will make our time here easier. Someone must command and direct our work."

"But why that beef-witted old fool, the very one who brought us to calamity? We did well enough on Macquarie by ourselves."

"Because he is our captain," Harrison replied, "and he and Mr. Morgen will be set against our fending for ourselves."

"He can do nothing. There will be only the two of them against the two of us and any others who have survived."

The carpenter shook his head slowly and warned, "If a vessel calls here, we may be clapt in irons, carried home, and tried for mutiny. It will happen if he wishes it."

"It cannot be mutiny. There can be no mutiny if we are not on a ship."

"Ah, my boy, you must understand it is mutiny if they choose to call it such. Tobit will swear you refused your orders and plotted against him before the wreck and thus it will be mutiny, ship or no ship. They know how to bend all to their favor." Harrison paused in his stride to pick up an empty shell. He hefted it in his hand and then examined each side. "It is like a cockle," he mused. "Perhaps they will make our supper. We will not go hungry on this lovely isle."

"A master cannot keep an apprentice beyond his time," the lad noted.

"No, he cannot, but at sea, law is different. All those in the fo'c's'le are considered to be rascals, and laws are drawn up with that in mind. You will find no justice there. You will see less grief if you keep quiet."

"Damn!" Thomas spat out.

The carpenter tossed the shell aside and said, "I think he has no authority, but they must put us in the wrong by some means. Let's not chafe the officers. It will better if we obey. All will go easier and we might reach home sooner."

The two of them then marched along in silence. The curving expanse of the slough between the bar and the bluff could be seen entirely. It was a long body of water filling the space behind the bar. At its western end and along the southwest side the shores were covered with the dense flax growing at the foot of the high bluff. In comparison to the heaving water of the bay, its surface was ruffled only by wind coming down the slope.

Thomas turned about again and walked backwards, peering at their starting point. He hoped to see some of the crew running along the beach toward him, but had to admit now that there was little chance any of them were alive. Harrison had pointed out that they could not have crossed the shore without leaving some mark, so he faced forward again.

The higher portion of the land hidden above the bluff became visible as they went farther out in the open. Rays of the rising sun slanting across the slope accentuated the forms and details of the land. A thickly forested slope extended upward, perhaps forming a high peak or many peaks in the interior of the island. They would have to travel farther to the east to gain a view of what they had only seen in black outline the evening before. The eastern foot of the slope rested on what appeared to be a level ridge that extended from the back of the slough for miles toward the eastern spur.

Harrison turned aside to a pile of wet rockweed in the wash of the waves. He poked his stick into it to scatter it over the beach. Thomas followed him to help search for any small bits of their vessel but found only a few roots and small pieces of driftwood. They abandoned the effort and hurried ahead to close the gap between themselves and the officers.

On the bar where the four men now marched there wasn't a bush, tuft of grass, or a single low, hardy plant clinging to life in the sterile cinders that would divert the eye of anyone watching. From the higher parts of the land they would be dots moving along the dark, narrow strip between the surf of the bay and the slough, and if there were savages ahead at the rejoining of the bar to the shore, they would witness the approach of four wild men. At first their nakedness and crude weapons would be recognized. As they neared, the added details of their tangled hair blowing about their heads and the untrimmed beards would define them as brutes who only had the shape of men.

Thomas nodded his head toward the flat ridge running toward the eastern spit and inquired, "What do you think is up there?"

"Ummm. . . ." the carpenter hummed a little note while he pondered the question. "There could be anything; a valley, a lake, or perhaps it is quite narrow and the shore is close on the other side. Most likely it is all level, a plateau. You see there along its edge, between the trees, it has a layered appearance." He suddenly halted, raised his arm, and extended a finger to point south across the slough. "Look there!" he cried out.

Harrison's words stopped the mate and the captain, and they turned and looked where he indicated.

Just above the far shore of the slough there was a deep cleft in the face of the ridge. Within that cleft was something white, moving like a long strip of cloth in a whisper of wind. Then they realized what they were looking at and picked out all its details.

CHAPTER 6

"A WATERFALL!" Mr. Morgen called out to the others.

The four castaways stared at a stream that was pouring from the top of the level part of the island where it joined the mountainside. It spilled over a series of step-like rocks in flat sheets, from one level to the next. Tree ferns on their thin trunks arched over the water where it spread out on the tiers. Mats of bright green, perhaps small ferns and mosses rooted in crevices and watered by a wind-blown spray, covered the rocks on each side of the fall. From the last step, the stream made a long plunge to the slough below. The mixture of air and water struck the surface of the slough and dashed a thick mist out in all directions. They had seen the like at Dusky Sound. Behind the lower two-thirds of the fall was a cavity, and the shadow in it made the falling, white plume stand out sharply. They all stared at the lake, the cascade, and the washed greenery. A few fluffy clouds peeked up from the far side of the island, but the remainder of the sky was unblemished blue. "It's set so far in," the mate pointed out, "you can't see it until you are near this place. Most of the water from the island must drain this way and into this lake."

The carpenter walked to the shore of the slough, pitched his stick aside, and dropped to his knees. With his hands, he scooped up a little water and tasted it.

"Is it salt?" the mate asked.

"Sweet," Harrison declared. "Sweet as you will, every drink."

"I would have sworn it would be salt being so close to the surf. Some waves must break over the bar," Mr. Morgen suggested.

"Yes," Harrison said, "but for most of the time, the water from the fall carries it away, so it is sweet."

The three others kneeled beside the carpenter and drank. When they had finished, the castaways rested on the cinders and scanned the eastern shore of the bay they had yet to explore.

"We must be the only ones to reach the shore," the mate said.

"Aye," Harrison agreed and shook his head. "None could have got this far by swimming. If they laid hold of some gear, they would have been carried north as the wind shifted."

The mate looked eastward along the beach between the bay and the bluff and muttered, "It would be a wonder if anyone got ashore beyond here. There is scant hope we will find a one from here to the end of the island, but we must look."

They were all comfortable resting on the bar and warmed by the sun, but after only a few minutes' rest, Thomas rose to his feet and picked up his stick. Seeing the lad get up, Tobit put the point of his weapon into the beach and used it to pole himself to his feet. "Look lively," he grunted. "We may discover some of them yet." He began walking stiffly toward the eastern spit.

They had traveled for no more than five or six minutes, when Thomas stopped and raised his left hand head-high with the palm open. He stared straight ahead.

"What is it? What do you see?" the carpenter asked.

Thomas put his finger to his lips for silence, and the others stopped and listened. They scanned the far end of the slough and looked back at Thomas expecting him to explain his caution. A faint sibilance in the air seemed to surround them. The four men searched all about, over the bay, back along the bar, across the lake, overhead. The sound had no source and gradually increased in volume until it resembled the wind rustling leaves.

Harrison nodded toward the east end of the slough and whispered, "It's from over there."

At once they stepped back from the water's edge. Something odd was happening to it at the far end. A long, low wave was rising up and moving rapidly toward them. They backed still farther from the shore and stared awe-struck as the wave defied gravity and separated from the surface of the water. Its dark edge continued to lift higher and slowly separated into a multitude of dots.

"Ha!" Harrison shouted, "I have never seen so many at one time!"

"What is it?" the captain demanded. "What is it you see?"

"Fowl," he answered. "Aye, fowl. I can see them, a great cloud of them."

The wave continued to rise into the sky and spread toward the men. The beating of thousands of wings created a drumming in the air. It was mixed with the honking and quacking calls. Then, at some undetectable signal, the birds all started turning in a wide circle just as they passed overhead.

"Ducks and geese!" the mate called out.

"All sorts," the carpenter added. "They will make a good number of meals for us."

"If you catch them. You will have to catch them first," warned the mate.

"Oh, we will take them, never fear," Harrison assured him. "We will seize them while they sleep or snare them or shoot them with arrows if we must. Nothing eats so sweet as these ducks. See there, some are the same as we got in Dusky. But we must hurry and take them before they leave here."

The four men all stared overhead at the great bounty, dizzied by the birds wheeling around and around. Thomas leaped up and swung his stick as high as he could reach in an attempt to strike a bird down. The ducks easily evaded his weapon, for it was too heavy and unwieldy for the purpose. The lad tried repeatedly. He spotted a duck flying toward him and slashed at it, but it veered at the last second. They were all now rising out of reach, so he gave up the effort and watched the potential feast, flapping and squawking, lift higher into the sky. Then he turned and started walking toward the east end of the lake.

Captain Tobit saw him and called out to the mate and Harrison, "This is not a Sunday stroll. Step lively."

He hurried past Thomas and again led the group along the bar. The thousands of birds, much higher now, beat their wings and swept around in a wide gyre. Slowly, they settled back to the surface of the lake and landed with flusters of beating wings.

The beach beneath the men's feet became firmer as they advanced along the shore. The dark gray of the cinders became mixed with a white, fine-grained sand, and the castaways found it noticeably easier to walk, even on the drier parts.

To the right side of the waterfall the slope rose steeply and joined the high central portion of the island. From the fall on to the east was the level portion of the island. Its face formed a rampart around the back of the eastern part of the slough and was covered for the greater part with smaller trees and bushes. There were some larger trees where its base met the beach. Thomas again wondered what was up there and beyond. As Harrison guessed, there might be anything just over that level edge, possibly the far shore close on the other side. What was remarkable was that it hardly varied a yard or two in height from the fall at its west end until it tended away out of sight far to the east.

As the four men approached the end of the slough they saw it narrowed until, at the rejoining of the bar and the shore, it turned and fed into a stream spilling across the beach. It was the exit for the water entering the lake from the fall. They approached the bank and watched the water ripple in a shifting path through the sand and cinders and disappear into the waves. Thomas was the first to step into it, meaning to wade to the other side, but he could not ignore the pleasant feel of the knee-deep outflow on his skin. He stopped and jabbed his stick into the streambed. Then he sat in the water and scooped up handfuls to splash on his shoulders, thoroughly pleased as the stinging salt was carried from his wounds. The other three men, seeing his example, stepped in and did the same, washing the encrusted blood and cinders from their bodies. They all dipped their heads into the stream to clean the grit from their hair. For a quarter of an hour they sat and let the fluid swirl against their skins. The condition of their sore and bruised bodies became more evident in the soothing bath.

It puzzled Thomas that they had not thought of bathing when they first discovered the lake was not salt or brackish. They had been so intent on finding their mates, he thought, and seeing what the island was revealing to them that none had considered anything else. Captain Tobit was the first to rise out of the stream. He picked up his stick from the bank and waded to the far side to wait for the others. There, his pale, flabby flesh stood out against the rich green boskage on the slope. Mr. Morgen got to his feet and went to join him. The carpenter and Thomas lingered in the stream when they saw the officers begin to talk. Harrison swept his hands back and forth in the water. He peered in it and then over the surface of the lake.

"What do you see?" Thomas asked. "Fish?"

He seemed not to hear the question and continued to feel the water about him. "It's warmed," he remarked, "not greatly so, but it has more heat than I would expect the sun to give to it."

Thomas replied, "Aye, it's warm and will always be a ready bath for us."

Harrison shook his head, mystified. Then he grabbed his stick and waded out toward the officers. Thomas, stroking the beads of water from his skin with one hand, followed directly.

"We will go as far as those rocks," the captain announced. "From there we might see something of the eastern shore." He pointed to the nearest of the dark monoliths that nearly formed a spine to the east cape. The line of them appeared to be the scattered remnants of some great ridge that once stood there. Thomas turned and looked in the other direction, back along the expanse of shore they had just explored. It curved away miles to the west, fading in the distant haze and becoming liquid in the heat of the sun. What composed the center of the western portion of the island was now visible to them. There were high peaks there. They had been hidden from the castaways at the start of their search by the nearness of the bluff. Now, from the end of the slough they had a good view of the whole central mass of the island.

"See how they are shaped and lofty," the mate noted, "like the Mount of Pelee."

Dense stands of trees and bushes grew on the sides of the peaks three-quarters of the way to their summits then merged into a band of low shrubs. These in turn thinned and stopped abruptly, and above a certain height there was nothing to hide the bare rocks. The verdant covering resembled a thick quilt draped over their slopes. Though the heavy greenery softened the lower parts of the peaks, they did not conceal the erosion that had worn deep gullies into their sides.

"That's very odd. Nothing grows at the summits," Harrison noted. "What leaves the tops naked while the sides bear such a forest?"

"The soil must be very rich on the lower parts about this island," Mr. Morgen suggested. "But if there is naught but stone up there and snow collected for most of the winter, it would not admit trees to grow."

The carpenter nodded and agreed, "Most likely, but what else is strange is that while that part is made of mountains as it is about Dusky and Chalky Bay, the other is so flat, like nothing we have met with in these seas."

The castaways stared at the panorama of the island, which was discernible in every detail. The peaks and the hills with their covering of thick verdure were outlined by the smooth blue of the late morning sky. Patches of different greens and textures on the slopes proved there was a variety of trees and shrubs. Most were a deep green, some were lighter, paling even to near yellow, and a few others silver- and gray-green.

In the clumps of flax, growing a few feet back from the slough's edge, dark blossom stalks grew out of their centers a foot or two higher than the tips of the leaves. Each stalk held two dozen or more red flowers an inch and a half in length. Harrison walked to one and pulled it down to him. He pinched off one of the red flowers, peeled back its long petals, and sucked up the sweet fluid. The others saw what he was doing and soon all were at it to get the sip of nectar from each blossom. It was sweet and appetizing, but far from enough to sate the hunger of the men. They soon tired of the tedious effort required for what little they gained, though some flowers yielded almost a half-teaspoon of nectar. Captain Tobit gave it up first and called for the men to follow. The others tossed the last blossoms to the ground. Their fingers and moustaches were smudged with yellow pollen.

They felt much better after their invigorating bath and the mite of nourishment and tramped along the beach faster. Trees high on the face of the bluff appeared lower and more tangled as the castaways progressed eastward. Sections of the layered rock became visible at the rim of the bluff between the tops of the highest trees.

Thomas pointed up at it and again asked, "Why should that be so unlike the other parts of this island?"

The sun had risen higher, and in the distance, the beach rippled where its heated surface began the sweep away from the island to form the eastern spit. Blue-green swells in the bay rolled toward them, rose, and tipped forward. Glints of sunlight flashed from their curling backs. Thomas narrowed his eyes to bar the glare from the white foam. Again he looked back to see how much of the bay's shore they had traversed. The western cape two miles on the other side of their starting point was now six or seven miles distant. He tried to imagine any of the crew still clinging to wreckage out in the bay. He could see nothing. A man's head, an oar, or even a grating would be lost amid the specks of foam rising and falling across the miles of dark sea. If they saw a man, they would be helpless to aid him. How long could anyone last out there? It was a desperate hope. They had found neither footprints nor scrap of their vessel. He had to admit it: the four of them were the only ones to reach the shore. They must find their food and clothing on the isle and live with small hope that they would escape or be rescued soon.

Captain Tobit kept going even after they reached the first of the rocks and led them on to where the bluff tended away eastward. From there they could see across a broad field of gray dunes to the open sea on the far side of the island. The coast there appeared to be a low one, perhaps made of shallows and sandbars where little or no surf broke. The peaks of the island sheltered that side from the swells and a portion of the wind.

For a minute the captain studied the view, then grunted and went on to a taller rock. Thomas guessed the portion of it above the beach to be thirty to forty feet in height, and from its shape it appeared an equal part or more of it was buried. The castaways paced around it, inspecting its deeply pitted surface. Its colors varied from a charcoal to a brick red and those in turn were flecked over with green mosses and gray and crimson lichens. From any distance it looked merely a dark, dirty brown or black as the light struck it from different sides. All of the monoliths scattered from there northward had the same color and primal shapes.

The captain took a position standing with his back to the huge rock and faced to the west where they had started that morning. "All gather before me!" he suddenly commanded in a near shout.

The others were startled by his loud command and looked at each other with questioning glances. They had no idea what to expect, and without thinking, obeyed and stood before him.

"We have found nought of the others," Captain Tobit announced after a short pause. Then he asked, "Are we all agreed that we have made a proper search for them?"

No one responded. They bowed their heads and stared at the sand at their feet.

Thomas felt that to answer yes would be to abandon their mates and any hope for them. To think that was one thing, but to speak it openly had the power to negate any unforeseen and miraculous rescue. Yet he had seen how the drier surface of the beach was lightly crusted and how the weight of a foot broke it apart. Wind and rain could not have erased every footprint in the few hours since the wreck, and any castaway would have crossed into the trees to get out of the cold and left his certain mark.

Then the captain asked, "Thomas, is it your wish we should search further?"

The young sailor looked up at the captain. A question to be answered with an opinion and not an explanation was a surprise to him. He was sure whatever he replied to the officer would make no difference. It was a clever move by Tobit, he figured, to involve him in the obvious decision to end the search. In the future he could never complain about it.

The captain's jaw was clenched and his eyes were fixed on Thomas, waiting for a reply. "Well, answer me, do we search beyond here?"

Thomas knew that any more time spent looking was futile, and with the others watching him he could only shake his head slowly.

"Harrison," the captain continued, "have we hope of finding more of the crew?"

The carpenter looked up and answered quietly, "No sir, no hope."

"We are all agreed," the mate volunteered, "that since we have not found the least sign of the crew, further search is useless."

"Then we can do nought more," the captain declared. "We can only despair of finding any alive about this island. They have apparently departed this life for a better one in this year of our Lord 1820. Now we must pray for their souls that the deserving among them shall find their rest and repose."

He grunted as he began to kneel and used his stick to help lower his scraped knees to the beach. The others followed his example and knelt. After a couple of coughs and a long clearing of his throat, Tobit began his prayer.

"Though the bodies of these men are lost beneath the sea and lost to our sight, at the last Day of Judgment those of the true believers will be quickened again and raised unto glorious life with the Lord in Heaven. Thus is the reward of those who are obedient to God's will, but take heed those who stray for they will soon lament their sins of pride and arrogance. Punishment awaits those who do not admit the righteousness of our true faith and the true God. Amen."

The others repeated "Amen" weakly and rose stiffly to their feet when the captain finished his prayer. They brushed the grit from their legs and stood about in perplexed silence for several minutes. The loss was now a stated fact. Hopes, however earnest or fanciful, could not be spoken with any sincerity. They could no longer expect to see the faces of those with whom they had shared a long and dangerous voyage. They were the only castaways, the four survivors, the ones who must live for some unknown span of time on the island, and perhaps return to tell their dismal story.

Thomas wandered away from the rock and went out to where the edges of the waves reached up the slope, paused for a second, and drained back under the next one spreading toward him. He recalled the moment the night before when Gabe's grip on his hand had weakened and given away. The image of Gabe's head sinking into the boiling foam flashed in his mind. Each event that had occurred in the dim starlight came back to him in disjointed scenes. Twenty-one men and two boys, he repeated to himself, twenty-one men and two boys. The Lascars, Will, Jack, old windy Gabe, and lively little Ned. They had all spent two years on ice-cold seas and rocky shores. Some of them had lived a year in the blackened hovels of laid-up rocks and sod, surrounded by the putrid carcasses of the seals. And what would be the whole of their wages? Their poor widows and mothers would be reduced to charity. He remembered the dark figures being shaken from the forestay, men wrestling with the smashed boats, and the upper works of the barque heeling inexorably down to the water.

The waves flowed up to his feet, ran over them, and swept back to the bay as he paced to the north. It was an injustice, he said to himself, that his mates, having shared such a hard life, should perish so. It was even worse to know that they had died because of Tobit's stupid and lubberly handling of the *Dove.* He suddenly stopped.

On the sand before him was a tangle of rockweed with something white caught in it. He stooped and pulled at the wet mess, hoping it might be some part of the *Dove.* He worked the white thing free and discovered that it was a piece of a large jawbone set with several rows of teeth. He had seen one like it before but one that was unbroken.

"Thomas!" the mate shouted.

When he looked up he saw the others were coming toward him and looking curiously at the object in his hand.

"What have you there?" Mr. Morgen asked. "Something from the barque?"

"No, it's part of a great fish. The jaw."

"Ha! What do you want with that stinking bone?" asked the mate.

"Why it is the very thing!" Harrison burst out. "Aye, the very thing! We must have blades to cut with. These will be our sheath knives." He stepped closer to Thomas, reached for the jaw, and turned it over and over in his hands.

The mate and captain crowded around the carpenter and touched the teeth, testing them for sharpness. The rows of thin, triangular teeth were well anchored in the bone at their bases, and two sloping edges were surprisingly sharp. It was apparent that if they wrenched them out they would have two dozen or more good cutting tools.

"I have heard that the savages in some islands fix these teeth in staves and use them for swords," Harrison remarked as he handed the jawbone back to Thomas. "This is a great find for us. We should look for more."

Captain Tobit gave a shake of his head and declared, "First, there is the matter of the cannibals to be settled. We will now search the most likely places. Then, if we find none, we will concern ourselves with food and such."

"But we have seen no marks of natives here," the carpenter objected. "Look where the sun is. With that much daylight left to us, we might build a little hut. There is flax by the lake. We could at least have a roof thatched by nightfall and not fear rain."

"Perhaps there are no savages here, but we are not going to risk not looking. We will search above that bluff here and near the fall," the captain replied and beckoned for the others to follow.

Walking side by side, he and Morgen started to return to the west.

Thomas and Harrison gave each other a knowing look and paused before they followed them. The carpenter held his hands out to each side palms up and then let them fall. An exasperated breath gushed from his mouth.

The sun had now moved past the zenith and a strong light beat down from it. Ahead, the heat created a mercurial layer above the sand and cinders. The younger sailor watched the captain enter the mirage where his thin legs softened and shifted from side to side, yet continued to support his sagging buttocks. The officer's shoulders were pink and the color was spreading down his back. The skin of their all bodies was becoming sunburned except on their hands and faces. Those had long since turned to the russet color which months in hazy sunlight and cold wind produced. A few more hours in the open and there would be more pain added to their scraped backs and legs.

Captain Tobit and the mate searched the face of the bluff looking for a way up through the tangle of bushes and vines. A few places looked promising, but the growth at the foot of the bluff was so dense they couldn't reach the slope. Mr. Morgen probed his way into the small trees and scrub each time he suspected there might be an opening but was stopped by a tangle of vines and long, snaky limbs that ended in clusters of spiky leaves. The plants had threaded their way through the bushes and around the tree trunks. Halfway back to the slough, the mate found a gap by which he could advance through to the foot of the bluff, and then called for Thomas to take the lead and break a way to the top. The lad handed the jawbone to the carpenter and started to work his way up. It was slow going. He had to force the limbs aside or, if they were small, smash them down with his stick and trample them under foot. If they were too stout, Thomas crawled under them on hands and knees or climbed over. He advanced, pushing the greenery back and beating it aside. The captain, who managed to keep ahead of the others on the shore, was a liability picking his way up through the heavy growth. He was continually gasping for air and had to be helped over limbs and up the sides of rocks. They stopped repeatedly and sat and listened to the warbling of the birds while they waited for him to catch up.

"Why not rest awhile here?" Mr. Morgen suggested. "When we find the way up, we will return for you."

"No! No!" the captain snapped. "We will all travel together. I want no stragglers, nor will I have that young one getting too far ahead. If we are scattered about, savages may take us easier. We will all rest and all go together."

The mate and the crewmen could only wait for the captain to

recover and then proceed when he said he was ready. They estimated the elevation of the bluff to be about three hundred to four hundred feet, yet it took the four of them an hour and a half to fight their way near the top edge. When he broke out of the trees, Thomas was dismayed. He was facing a sheer wall of stone. It was higher than it had appeared from below, nearly twice the height of a man and weathered smooth. There were chinks where its layers met, but none would admit more than a finger. Without any holes or projections that would serve as handholds, it blocked them like a bulwark.

The carpenter peered at it closely. He hammered the heel of his fist against it twice and said, "Limestone. I would say limestone, wouldn't you?"

Thomas nodded and uttered an agreeing, "Ummph."

It extended to the right and left so far the two crewmen saw it would be useless to attempt to edge along its base. The growth there was tough and springy. With a saber or a hanger, they might have cut a way through slowly, but they had none. Beating with their sticks had little effect, and they had no choice but to return to the foot of the bluff and try somewhere else. All their efforts had been for nothing.

Once they reached the shore the captain and the mate waded out knee-deep into the waves and scanned the rim of the bluff for a lower portion of the wall that had blocked them. Trees hid some of that obstruction, possibly where there was a break in it. They started west again and could only make guesses that they had gone far enough to try once more. Each man pushed into any promising gap in the trees and underwood, hoping to find some possible way up. They were vexed time after time. Under the trees at the back of the beach, they met with sections of a low cliff and between those, huge stones tumbled one onto another, overgrown with bushes and tough vines in a tangle. That blocked passage to the men who could only attempt to batter a way up.

The carpenter took more time with his searches and lagged behind.

Mr. Morgen stepped out from his last try. He looked up the beach and back and asked, "Where is Harrison?"

Thomas turned and looked about too, then said, "He was just back there a-ways. I saw him a minute ago."

"Find him now!" the captain demanded. "I said I wanted no stragglers."

All three men instantly started back, searching the bushes at each place footprints showed someone had entered before.

"Blast him!" the mate swore. "Where has he got to?"

Thomas led the officers in the hunt, running ahead from place to place, poking into the scrub and trees. Then it occurred to him that cannibals might have hidden in the trees, seized Harrison, carried him away to some camp. Then he felt foolish to have considered it possible. Savages would have covered the island with their footprints. Their canoes would have been drawn up on the beach and they certainly would not have made their camp in such a thicket when they could take their choice of any part of the island. He found the next set of prints and followed them between two trees. A limb had been forced aside and partially splintered. He pressed on for another fifteen yards and suddenly entered a clearing beneath a rock overhang. The space was three fathoms deep and six or seven long. Harrison was at one end scratching in the earth with his stick. Following Thomas, the officers pushed their way in.

Harrison looked up and smiled. "Our home," he announced, waving his free hand around to present his discovery to them.

"Aye, if this is all the island offers, then it must serve," the captain replied.

Harrison tilted his head and looked at Thomas with one raised eyebrow. The lad knew what he was thinking: that the rock overhang was far better than the huts of stacked stones roofed with old rotted sails where some of the crew had lived for a year. The place was a wonderful find, yet old Tobit must make a belittling remark about it.

The castaways walked all about the shelter. The thick greenery between it and the beach blocked the wind and the air was nearly still. A few stones of two and three hundredweight had to be moved out, but once that had been done, they would have a level, sandy floor. Lank and pale plants were growing under the overhang, reaching up and out for light. These they quickly uprooted and cast out. There were no droppings or a spoor about, no traces to suggest that some animal used it for a den or casual shelter.

The carpenter explained, "If there have been Indians on this island at any time, they would have put this place to some use and left marks of their stay." Then he pointed to the lines he had drawn in the sand. "We can wedge limbs or saplings between here and the rock above and tie sticks athwart them. With flax leaves we can thatch the whole and that will make a snug place of it. We would then only need a fire."

"If we only had a flint and steel or a burning glass," Thomas wished aloud.

"We may find flint here, but if we cannot reach the *Dove,* there will be no steel," the mate pointed out.

"Then we use the bow and drill," Harrison suggested. "We can make the cord from the flax to turn the drill. Then we will roast ducks from the lake and fish from the bay. We can dig a cooking hole like those we had at Port William."

Thomas remembered how, on that shore, they had dug out the bundles from their cooking holes and inhaled the steamy aroma when the charred leaves were unwrapped. With no kettle or tools except rocks and sticks, that would be their sole way to cook foods like clams and crawfish. He was jarred from his thoughts of eating by the captain.

"First, we must finish our search," he ordered. "Only after we do that can we return here and think of our comforts." The captain grunted and threaded his way out through the trees and bushes. Mr. Morgen stepped across and followed him out to the beach.

"The demented fool!" Thomas growled through his clenched teeth. "We shall have another cold night. There won't be enough time to make fire or gather something for our beds."

"Tush, lad. It won't take that long. Come, let's find the savages for our captain," Christopher said.

They assembled on the beach and started their search again. Captain Tobit took his place and led them toward the slough. For half an hour the men followed, stopped, pushed into the scrub, and when they found no entry, went on.

The carpenter came out from one of his searches and called to the captain, "Here, I think I have found the way."

He led them through the bushes he had broken and wrenched aside. After they climbed up on boulders and pressed through a thick tangle of bushes and vines, they reached some taller trees. The dense canopy of the leaves overhead had shaded out much of the underwood and made it an easier climb. Except in a few places where slim, vagrant rays of the sun filtered through and played across rocks and moss-covered logs, the slope was all in shadow. Ferns of all sizes and shapes grew in the diffuse light. Some were only knee-high and others were ten- and twelve-foot tree ferns with trunks concealed by skirts of dead fronds still clinging by the stems. Small green birds twittered and flew just above the men's heads. To each side and up the slope was an unbroken chorus of them. The murmur of the surf from below mixed with the songs of the birds.

The mate picked his way around the stones that had fallen from above and had come to rest on the slope and said, "This looks the best yet."

They grasped the supplejack vines from the trees when they happened to be hanging in the right places and pulled themselves through the ferns and up the steep incline. Near the top of the bluff, the trees thinned out and the men were again in the sunlight, but they were also facing the stone wall that had been the obstacle before.

"Damn!" the mate swore. "There must be a way to the top!"

"I believe we need only go a short way further," Harrison suggested. "There looks to be a crevice, a gap. Yes, two. I see two." He pointed along to his right.

The mate sat on a low limb and rested with Captain Tobit.

Thomas and the carpenter began breaking a route through the bushes at the base of the barrier. The growth was as tough as before, but this time the crewmen believed they were close to an opening and the labor was worth the try. Harrison was forcing his way between the face of the rock and the bushes. The method was working. What branches he failed to push back or break, he battered down with his stick. It left enough of a passage for the others if they shuffled crab-like past the splintered ends. The carpenter reached the opening, but standing directly before it he saw only a niche that didn't penetrate the natural bulwark. The wall at its back was little lower than the face on the front. The second opening farther on was more promising. It was filled with bushes, but it led upward as a winding corridor. Its walls also lacked any cracks or holds large enough to aid a climber. Thomas and Harrison were pushing at the thick scrub at its opening when the mate came puffing along with the captain.

"Is it passable?" the mate asked.

"Perhaps. We cannot see the end," the carpenter explained, "but I think this is it." He climbed in and used his new method, slipping his back against the stone and pushing the brush away with his feet. Thomas followed and widened the passage a bit more. The crevice was about sixty feet long and the earth in it rose as they progressed. It ended against an eight-foot wall.

"Well, now what are we to do?" Mr. Morgen asked.

"Give me your sticks," Thomas said. He gathered all four and forced his way to the end. He pushed the sharpened ends of the sticks into the earth about four to five feet from the wall. Then he leaned the upper ends to touch the rock. "Here Chris, stand on the side and give a hand."

Gripping the carpenter's hand for balance, the lad walked up the sticks with short steps. When he reached the tops of the sticks, he thrust himself forward onto the rounded edge of the limestone. Then he wiggled forward until the others could see only his feet. Slowly he rose to his knees. Finally he stood up and looked quickly to his right and left.

"What do you see?" the captain asked.

Thomas ignored the question as if he had not heard it. The wind was blowing his long hair about his head while he remained there unmoving and looked south.

"What are you staring at? Is there any danger?" the mate demanded.

He turned at last and smiled at the men down in the crevice. Then he kneeled and reached a hand toward them. With Thomas pulling up and the mate and carpenter pushing from below, they managed to boost the captain to the top. When the other three got on the ledge, they could see what had amused the lad.

CHAPTER 7

THE FOUR NAKED, bruised castaways stood in a line on the bare stone ledge and surveyed the entire eastern half of the island, detailed in brilliant sunlight. Land covered with tall grass extended for miles to the south and east without the slightest rise or dip. The ocean was visible beyond, but the expected line of white surf was out of sight below the far rim of the plateau. Two great peaks rested on the western border with a truncated one nudged in at their foot. They appeared to have spilled onto the plateau in some past age. A thick forest that grew on their slopes did not extend out into the grass, making the border between the mountain and flatland even sharper. Another higher mountain rose behind the first peaks, veiled with a blue haze that was evidence it was much farther away. There were no huts, no cultivated fields, no orchards or any mark of man on the expanse of grass dipping and rising in the sea wind. A few dark brown birds flittered upward, then swooped low to catch invisible insects. It was all as devoid of human sign as the shore.

"Ah, it has a pleasing look," the mate sighed, "like the fields and pastures of Christian lands."

"Perhaps a prophecy," Captain Tobit said. "Look sharp, lads, for any marks of the savage."

Mr. Morgen answered, "I can see nothing, not one thing you could say was made by a man."

"Look south, there, toward the far verge," the captain asked and pointed in that direction. "Is that a line of trees or might it be huts?"

Mr. Morgen squinted for a moment, and replied, "I would say they are bushes. Perhaps they grow along a branch that carries water to the coast."

The captain grunted, accepting the answer only conditionally, and shifted his attention to the dark edge of the trees at the foot of the peaks. He pointed to them and said, "Those trees there must conceal a brook that feeds the fall and the lake, and they may also conceal some number of Indians there."

Thomas gave them a glance, turned and looked at the bay. In the western spit there was one, perhaps two places where the waves might wash over the bar. Except for the entrance at the north side, he could see no other large break in the capes of sand and rocks that held the quieter water within their curving arms. Harrison and the mate scanned the peaks and the plateau, taking note of all they were now able to see. Mr. Morgen ended his search facing the bay with Thomas and remarked, "It is curious . . . a circle nearly without defect, as if it were drawn with a trammel. What do you make of that?"

Thomas did not reply, but Harrison faced around and said, "I believe it was once a volcano of tremendous size."

The mate frowned, thought a moment, and asked, "But it is merely sand and rock all about a great hollow. What has become of the mountain?"

"It must have cast everything far out into the ocean or it may have fallen in on itself. See how the rocks around the edge were once part of a large peak. They are sloped on the outside but steep toward the bay. That must be how it came to be as it is. The light is perfect now. You can see the depth of the water and how the bottom drops away."

Mr. Morgen was unconvinced and objected, "How could an entire mountain disappear in that fashion? It would be nothing short of magical."

"They say some of Vesuvius was once carried aloft and scattered about Naples. In this part of the world where nature is the more odd and violent, it could happen that a whole mountain could be blasted away and never found."

"Well, if it was ever a volcano," the mate declared to Harrison, "its fires are certainly quenched by the sea forever."

The carpenter pointed along the shore to the west and added, "If we climb up on the mountain just there, above where we struck, we should be able to look down and see the *Dove*. Then we can dive to her. We must have all we can get out: lines, clothes, most of all iron."

Each man turned back to the vista of the plateau. Patches of grass bowed and rose again in response to the wind, and each presaged gust rolled toward the castaways and struck them, cooling their faces and naked bodies. They breathed in air carrying the scents of the grass and the sun-warmed earth.

Suddenly, Thomas leaped forward and sprinted into the grass, weaving to the right and left out on to the flatland. Harrison bolted after him, and the two men raced, sweeping their hands through the leaves and stems as they went. Only the upper halves of their bodies were visible above the tops of the grasses.

The mate and captain watched the crewmen run. Captain Tobit rubbed his right hand over his face, the only adult face that had always been clean-shaven aboard the barque. Now there was white stubble there. His eyes narrowed. "They frolic and run about like children," he said.

"Aye, like children," the mate repeated.

"Whatever our situation, we must not lose control of them. It is not a good thing for the men to have idle time. That makes for mischief as surely as heat breeds flies. They will have no watch to stand here, therefore we must see they are always kept at some work, that they heed God's wishes, and keep the Sabbath. That is the first thing they will neglect . . . the worship of the Lord."

The mate agreed with several nods.

"That lad is surely going to be trouble if he insists on being impudent. The young are more open to the devil's lures, Mr. Morgen, and are wont to become slothful. I must punish him for the insolence he showed at the lake. If he is not reminded of his place, we will see more of it. Let him defy me again and I will break him like a horse! See how they run about with nothing but animal spirit, with no thought of their duty to God. It is a misuse of their lives on Earth."

The captain stiffened his posture and announced, "Though the *Dove* is gone, I am still in command and I am responsible for all."

The mate kept his eyes on the crewmen running across the plateau and muttered, "Perhaps you should have borne more of that responsibility last night."

The captain faced the mate and snapped, "And what do you mean by that?"

"I mean you should not have embayed the ship. We should have stood on and off throughout the night."

"Tush! We were in a good situation."

"But we struck upon the rocks, didn't we?" Mr. Morgen asked, turning around, holding up a finger in accusation. "The wind was not going to change. You were so sure of that. Now you will have to answer for the loss when we return. I will see to it."

"Ha! You have such a small intelligence. Ha! Answer for it. Our lives are meant for more than mere trade. There is something greater afoot here. Do you see nothing in these events? You see no design when we came upon this island no one else has seen? We struck upon a rock we could have passed with ease. All these happenings were meant to be, caused by the power of the Lord. It could not have been otherwise."

The mate turned his head slightly and gave a sidling look as he listened to the captain. He then burst out, "Been otherwise! We would be on our way to China if you hadn't chose to call here. The ship would still be afloat if you hadn't insisted we anchor so close."

"Another island, another place," the captain added in a low, measured voice. "What does it matter? We have been drawn here to do a great duty. I can feel a new strength in my body, in my arms. You will know it too. There will be other signs for us to acknowledge, signs you will not be able to deny. Think on it, Mr. Morgen. Think on how all has come to pass as if by some wondrous design." Then he turned to watch the men out in the grass. Both had stopped and were leaning over, searching the ground for something. They dropped from sight into the grass. Then they rose up, and each went wandering around in a different direction, still looking down at the earth.

The carpenter stopped and held his hand up high to show an object in it to the officers.

The captain said, "They have found something. Let's hope it's not some sign of the cannibals."

The crewmen started back toward them, walking slowly and searching as they went. Harrison held out his hand to exhibit his find as he approached.

"What have you there?" the mate inquired.

The carpenter displayed a dark lump between his thumb and forefinger and answered, "Droppings."

"Droppings, yes, I can see that. What sort of droppings?" the captain asked.

"I don't know. Something has been eating the grass out there," Harrison explained. "It is not large, perhaps the size of a goat."

Tobit took the dropping from the carpenter and rolled it over and over between his fingers. "You saw nothing else?" he asked without looking up.

"Just the place where the animal has rested and nibbled the grass," Harrison replied.

"Were there hoof prints on the ground or burrows in it?" Mr. Morgen inquired, looking at Thomas.

The lad shook his head once and looked back at the wide expanse of waving grass.

"So, we have a mystery here, lads," the captain said and handed the dropping back to the carpenter.

Harrison looked it over again and broke it apart with his fingers. "It feeds on the grass," he noted. "It may possibly be good to eat."

"We will have to catch it and kill it before we taste it," the mate grumbled.

"It could be many things. It is much larger than a hare," Harrison suggested. "We can see that by the size of its turds. There are no hoof marks so it's not a sheep, goat, or deer, or a swine. I would say it may be like those animals that live in New Holland and Van Diemen's Land."

"Let's hope you are right about that," the captain warned. "Until we know for sure, keep your sticks ready by your sides. It may eat more than grass."

Mr. Morgen looked at the sun that was now midway between the zenith and the horizon. "Captain, we had best start making our beds for the night," he suggested. "It will take some time to clear the rocks out and gather something to lie upon."

The captain squinted at the sun, then looked to the southwest and to the juncture of the flatland and the base of the peaks. "Humph," he snorted as he considered the hours of daylight left and the dark forest on the mountainside just a mile or two away. "Aye," he conceded, "we will do that for now, but we must keep a good watch all night." He pointed to the foot of the peaks and added, "Any number of savages might be hiding there. We will look in the morning. Yes, first thing. If we find none there, we may suppose we have the island to ourselves. Now, we will return to the shore."

The men climbed down over the rock edge, then picked their way to the shore, following the broken branches and trampled ferns. They exited where they had entered the trees and returned along the beach to the overhanging rock.

Mr. Morgen set the crewmen to work levering out the stones embedded in the sand and cinders. The cavities they left were filled in and leveled by raking their sticks across the surface. He directed how each rock was to be moved and where it was to be placed. The men rolled the largest ones out beyond the overhang, but had to bring some back when the captain decided they might serve as seats and tables. The carpenter and Thomas then dug trenches near the back wall to use as bed sites. They would, Harrison said, be warm when filled with grass and leaves, warmer than lying on flat ground.

Captain Tobit paced around the cleared and leveled ground

and grunted his approval. "Enough, yes, that's well," he said to the carpenter. "Now, see what can be got for bedding, but don't stray too far from here. Keep a cautious eye on all."

Harrison picked up the fragment of the shark's jaw and placed it on one of the large stones. With the point of a stick he broke two of the largest teeth out of it. He kept one and handed the other to Thomas. The two men set off immediately on their errand.

After about an hour and a half, they returned carrying crude baskets stuffed with dried leaves and fern fronds.

The mate met them as they came in and felt the side of one of Harrison's baskets. "Ah, woven of the flax," he noted.

"Aye, from those growing at this end of the lake," the carpenter explained.

"The fish teeth cut them easily?" the mate asked.

"Oh, fair. It takes a bit of sawing and the fingers tire," Harrison explained. "We split the leaves and wove them so. They are poorly made, but will serve. These leaves have good hemp in them and we may make our yarns and ropes of it."

"And perhaps thatch too," Mr. Morgen pointed out. "With it, we can make a fit place to sleep here."

"But we still lack fire," Thomas objected. "We must have fire to dress our meat and fish once we find them. I have seen no flint, nothing here that would strike a spark."

Harrison nodded and promised confidently, "We will make fire in some fashion. If we find no flint, we will make it with a drill."

The crewmen emptied the baskets into the depressions and went out to gather more loads. They found the best place to gather the material was under the small trees along the back of the beach. The wind had driven leaves in between them, and in certain places, against rocks and logs, drifts of them were a few inches thick. It took a half dozen baskets to make a pile in each hollow before the captain deemed it enough.

"That will do for tonight," he said as the last load was dumped. "Now what offers for vittles? Ducks?"

"I would be happy with a piece of old salt horse and a biscuit," the mate grumbled, "but the fowl. . . . I see no way to take them unless we come upon them asleep. Then one quack and they'd all be off. There isn't a nut, fruit, or berry to be seen. So far we have had nothing but sips of nectar. Now, roots. . . . Thomas, Harrison, do you know of any here that can be eaten?"

The carpenter thought a moment, then suggested, "Fern, some of their roots can be eaten, but they need to be parched on coals. I would say try for clams. There is not more than an hour or two of good light left. They will be the quickest to find if any food is to be got in that time. Fern roots, they are found under trees mostly and must be dug out with sticks and fingers. It would be black in the woods before we got a meal, and the roots would do us no good, as we have no fire to roast them.

The captain pushed out his lower lip as he mulled his choices.

"We will try for the clams," he announced and picked up his stick.

The crewmen gathered their weapons and a basket and followed the officers out to the beach. At the edge of the waves, the captain pointed to Thomas and Harrison and said, "You two will gather the clams and cast them ashore. And you, Mr. Morgen, will pick them up."

Harrison and Thomas dropped their sticks and waded into the waves until they were waist-deep. They moved parallel to the shore going west. The two felt for the clams by sweeping their feet across the bottom, watching every few seconds for breaking waves. For the first quarter of an hour, neither man found a live clam. The first objects Thomas came up with were empty shells and a few rocks, which he disgustedly threw farther out into the bay. The sun had set and they were under a twilight sky that was reflected as scribbling patterns on the water. Thomas thought they had traveled far enough to find dozens, and he called to Harrison, "Perhaps they are no longer here."

"Why should they not be? Their shells are here and on the beach. We have just begun."

"Might they be farther out?"

"That is possible, but we can't manage in water that deep. The tide must ebb more before we can try there."

The bottom became firmer beneath their feet. Thomas imagined they were approaching a part that was mixed with more sand and less cinders. He was tiring from wading and forcing his body through the water. He was getting colder too. If they didn't find something soon, he must get out and warm himself.

"Ha!" The single word came from the carpenter.

Thomas looked up and saw him holding a small clam in his fingers. He waggled it at the lad.

"Quite a feast," he called to him with a little sarcasm.

"Patience, there will be more to find," he advised and tossed the clam to the waiting mate.

A few minutes later Harrison found another. Immediately after that, Thomas felt a clam with his toes and ducked under to dig it out. He knew by the heft it was a live one, and he displayed it to Harrison. Then he pitched it ashore and resumed his hunt. Feeling the lips protruding slightly above the sand was difficult as they swept their feet along and at the same time watched for waves that might knock them off their feet. But every few minutes either the carpenter or Thomas found a clam.

North, beyond them, the surface of the bay was a deepening blue, and to the south and west the land had darkened against the twilight in the sky. Thomas's foot touched the lip of another clam, a large one. He scooped it out of the sand and held it up. It was about three inches across, and the two halves were firmly clamped together. Its weight was assurance of good flesh inside. As he threw it to the mate the captain waved for them to come out of the water.

"Ho!" Thomas called, "C-Christopher, time to go."

"About time. How many did you g-get."

"Sixteen. Seven large ones and n-nine about so," Thomas replied, holding his thumb and finger making half a circle.

"I got twenty-one. That's thirty-seven. Not a feast b-but we will do better tomorrow."

Once out of the surf, the carpenter and Thomas swept the water from their faces and bodies with their hands. Both stomped their feet to shake more of the drops off and warm themselves with the effort.

"Come, let's be on our way," Mr. Morgen ordered.

"One minute," Harrison said and ran to the trees at the top of the beach. He searched about for something. Soon he returned with a short stick, pushed it into the cinders, and left it standing there. "Just so. That's where we may start again and not go over what we have already searched."

Captain Tobit looked at the stick for a moment. "That will be a certain sign to the savages we are nearby," he growled, seized the stick, and pitched it back into the trees.

"But our footprints are everywhere now and we. . . ." Harrison objected.

The captain ignored him and started back toward the shelter. The crewmen trailed behind the officers and looked at each other, smirking and shaking their heads at the preposterous logic of the captain.

After a few minutes marching, Thomas asked, "Chistopher, d-do you think we can dive to the barque?"

"Oh, surely. She struck upon a rock and may not be too deep. We will make a raft of logs and dive from it to the wreck. There is our canvas, iron, and rigging. We will sail from this island in a few weeks and in less than half a year we will be home. I have known men who have done it. Aye, and their situation was worse than ours." He slapped the lad's shoulder and added, "Don't despair, lad."

"If we can't reach the *Dove,* how can we build a canoe with only a f-few fish teeth to cut with?"

"Why, as I have said, we will do just as the savages do in these islands, hollow out logs with fire and make a proa, perhaps even a catamaran."

"And the sails? How do we make the sails?"

"Ah, those too. Just as they make them, by weaving the leaves of trees or the flax, see, as we have made that basket you carry."

Thomas wondered what bothered him so about Christopher's

cheerfulness. He was right about the island, but anyone could see that. It would yield for all their wants. Indeed, in a few hours they had found a place that would keep them dry and from the wind. They had found a little for supper and they could look forward to taking the fowl and netting fish. There might be seals from which they could make clothes. But why was he so sure they could reach the barque? They saw from the plateau that the bay was deep. If the *Dove* slipped from the rock, it would sink far beyond their reach. With no rigging to be got from there, making lines from flax would be tedious and consume hours of their time. Christopher was too confident and too certain all would go well. Yet he had made many voyages and had great experience. So he said. Perhaps it was to give him assurance. Thomas considered the length of the sloop or canoe that would carry the four of them from the island and sail for a week or more. It would be about that many days before they fell in with Tovy Poenamoo. He guessed a canoe should be at least twenty-five feet long and allow a beam of, at the least, two feet. Was there a tree of that size on the island? Even to fall it and get it to the shore would tax all their strength and wit. There would be much to make: oars, water butts, lines, seizings, the sails, a mast, and boom. The problems multiplied as he tallied all they must create if they could not reach the wreck. They had nothing but their hands and, lacking iron, nothing to cut with save a few fish teeth. We are naked and empty-handed, he was thinking, when the carpenter grabbed his arm.

"We are here," Harrison said. "You are lost in your thoughts." He led Thomas between the trees to the entrance of the shelter. There, in the deepening dusk, they watched the officers divide the clams into four piles on the largest rock they had rolled out from under the overhang.

"Here, we are ready to eat," the mate said, pointing to the clams.

"Stand before me, and I will say grace," the captain announced. "Mr. Morgen, step over here to my right."

The men gathered around as they were ordered. Captain Tobit bowed his head and held out his hands, palms up before him. He began his prayer, "Oh, almighty Lord, we give thanks to Thee for sparing our lives and casting us upon this most fertile land. We see Thy design in this and will work to Thy purpose. That Thou hath spared us is a sign that we are destined to do Thy work and preserve the natural and intended order of this world. Our duty lies before us, and we stand prepared to fulfill it. Each of us in his particular capacity pledges to do Thy will, to stand firm in his appointed place, however humble, and against all the enticements of the devil. We shall form a rampart from which no man will absent himself. Oh Lord, we partake of this food Thou hast provided us that we may gain the strength to work to Thy greater glory. Amen."

"Amen," the others mumbled in response.

There were nine clams in each pile except for the captain's share, which had the extra clam. They were, considering the varying sizes, fairly divided, but looked a pitiable meal for hale men.

The captain reached down for a stone and cracked open the first clam. He scraped the broken shell against his lower teeth to scoop out the animal. The others used the same method, breaking open one clam after another and raking the flesh into their mouths. Juice ran into their beards, through their fingers, and down their arms to drip from their elbows, but they ignored it and ate until every shell had been emptied.

"Ahhh," the mate sighed, "hardly a nibble, but we shall have many more to eat tomorrow."

The pile of shattered shells was left on the rock, draining the last of their juices. They were barely visible now that the faintest bit of twilight was nearly gone and the brighter stars were claiming the deepening blue. The four men sat silently in the gathering gloom.

Harrison reached down and worked a length of flax leaf from one of the baskets. He smoothed it to its full length on a flat part of the rock, and, with a broken clamshell, he scraped the green plant flesh from each side of the leaf. What he had left in his left hand were long white fibers with bits of the green still clinging to them. By laying the fibers across his thigh and rolling them together under his right palm, he created a string a foot and a half long. "There," he declared with satisfaction, "with this and a few sticks of wood, we will have a fire tomorrow and cook our food and sleep by a warm hearth."

Mr. Morgen took the string from the carpenter, and with an end of it wrapped around each hand, he snapped it taut. "Umph, good," he muttered, and handed it back.

After a few minutes, the captain stirred from his seat on one of the stones. He started for the beach and motioned for all to follow him. At the edge of the trees, he announced, "We are in a precarious way here. A watch is to be kept just as on the *Dove*. Thomas is to take the first four hours. Being it is clear, you may guess the time by the stars. Harrison will take the next four. Mr. Morgen, you will finish until it is light. You will keep your watch here from within the trees, just so you can see up and down the beach. Do not walk about, and be sure to call me if you sense any danger."

Thomas watched the officers return to the shelter and then growled to Christopher, "What a fool waste of time this will be."

"Perhaps not," Harrison suggested. "If a ship should come into the bay. . . . Not a likely happening, but still, if it did, one of us would be here to see it."

"They could not be so daft as to come into the bay at night. If they came to wood and water, they would certainly stand off and on until they could see properly."

"Yes, Thomas, I know, but let us do our duty. Keep old Tobit's spleen from us."

Harrison lingered on the beach, and he and Thomas witnessed the stars increase a thousandfold across the entire sky. They walked out near the small waves that stretched up the beach and feathered out before they reached their feet.

"Why so gloomy, lad?" the carpenter asked after a few minutes when he saw Thomas staring northwest.

"I keep seeing the two men drop from the forestay. I can't forget our mates and the boys. They needn't have died so."

"Aye, I shan't deny that."

"If we had foundered or had been run down in a fog, I wouldn't feel so angry, but it is so maddening to have lost them because of a fool. What a confounded ass he is!"

"I believe as you do, Thomas, yet what can our anger do for those who are lost? We can best spend our time finding food and seeing to our comforts. Don't dwell on it all, lad. Time spent in anger is wasted time, and there is too little for any man. If we are to get home again, we must think how it is to be done and all work together."

"We will do better without old Tobit. We are cast ashore and our mates are drowned because of his pigheadedness. I swear I will move against him in the courts when we get home. I swear it!"

Harrison shook his head slowly and said, "Thomas, you know no one before the mast can do that. We are in their power. They always have the weather gage in the law."

"I don't see why that should be so. Why must he have the advantage of us? It's an outrage."

"I agree, lad, that it is unfair, but everything will be arranged against you in the courts. They will see to that. You have no one in a high position to speak for you. They will ask why they should believe you, a green hand and a shoemaker, instead of an experienced officer. It is dangerous for them to have their authority even questioned. The judge may feel his position is in some way being tested too and thus favor the officers. They will not have their power put in jeopardy for any reason, so those from the main deck must always be wrong. You are young and you are angry now. I would not tell you that you have no reason to be bitter, just that you will get no satisfaction in the courts. When we signed the ship's articles, we put ourselves in that position."

"But we are no longer aboard the barque. Where are the articles? He has no command over us now."

"Perhaps, I am not sure, but he may have. Our voyage is not over, therefore lawyers might claim he does. If we do not obey him in all ways, he may say it is mutiny. Remember the words of the agreement: that during the whole of the voyage we must go to any island and up any river and remain there to work as the officers command. It said nothing of shipwreck."

"We have no ship and no boat. We cannot take seals and beam and dry their hides or salt them."

"Ahh, but it does not say we must only do the skinning business. We have done what the officers appointed over us ordered us to do. We mended and tarred the rigging, worked the ground tackle, heaved the lead, and made spun yarn. Whatever is needed we must do, and they now require what will keep us until we are rescued."

"If we are rescued, what will be our wages, our lay for such service to that witless ape?"

"Nothing, lad. It is the risk all must take. If we'd reached Canton and then brought the China cargo home, we would have had gold enough for any common man. Such are the odds for the men and the officers alike in this business."

"But the owners don't risk their lives, just their dollars."

The chill of the damp night air made them both shiver, and they walked back and forth on the beach to warm themselves.

"But you see how he sets our tasks," Thomas noted, "yet he doesn't turn a hand to help. We don't need that pair. You and I can shift for ourselves, aye, as those of us on Macquarie, Cape South, and Brister's did. Let them find out what it is to fend for themselves. The mate will do all right, but that booby will starve if left alone. He will spend his days praying for food and expect it to appear before him."

"Ah, no, Thomas. It is better we do our duty. This is your first voyage. You must learn you cannot oppose the captain and not pay for it. I have seen men who did, and they suffered terribly. Besides, it is best we stay together. We will see how it all goes in the days ahead. Lad, we must not forget rescue. If any ship raises this island, they will most likely call here, for it is not on any chart. Then we will be standing for home."

"I am sure things will go no better," said Thomas. "He thinks he is still parading around the aft of the *Dove,* but he will learn that fish and fowl will not leap into his hands at his order. He expects savages behind every rock and tree. Why does he dwell on them when he can see just as well as we that there are none?"

The carpenter stopped walking and thought for several seconds and then explained, "If he talks continually of cannibals, he obliges us to think of them and of little else. He draws our eyes about as a conjurer does with one hand whilst the other does something we never see. It's quite useful for such men to have an enemy, whether it be a witch, a devil, or a savage. If he claims to be for all that is good, then he may call all who oppose in him in any way evil. The more devilish he paints his enemy, the more righteous he may appear to be. Soon he can cast suspicion on anyone he chooses."

They strolled along the shore for another half-hour in silence. Then Harrison halted, leaned his head back, and looked around the glistering dome of the sky. "Good night, Thomas," he said. "Wake me when the sail of the Argo is about there. That will be the start of my watch." He pointed to the position a little past the zenith with his outstretched arm.

Thomas spied the familiar constellation and murmured, "Yes. The Argo."

"Aye, and there the Hunter, and the Dog and Hare," Harrison added.

"Good night, Chips," Thomas said.

"Good night, lad," the carpenter called back as he started for the shelter.

Thomas kept walking, sometimes even trotted along the shore, and then having warmed himself, sat in the bushes until he felt the cold again. He repeated the process until the Cross rose above the bluff and the appointed ship Argo began its decline. He thought of it sailing endlessly and hopelessly around the southern sky seeking fortune. Not once did he believe that there was another human on the island, and, though he expected none, he looked up and down the shore and out over the bay till the end of his watch.

Under the rock overhang, he shuffled in the blackness to the right and along the back wall until he found the pile of leaves that was

Harrison's bed. A touch and the carpenter was awake and sighing.

"How did you sleep?" he whispered.

"Terrible."

"What's the fault?"

"You'll find out soon enough," Harrison replied and went out to stand his watch.

Thomas did find out as soon as he buried himself in his pile and lay his back against the leaves. Immediately, the stems poked at the wounds and his sunburned and tender skin. He stirred about and managed to find and remove those that pained him the most. Sleep was composed of only short naps when his fatigue overcame his constant discomfort. He realized he had slept longer the night before. They had been exhausted then and had huddled together for warmth in the narrow crevice.

It took him several seconds to realize where he was when he opened his eyes in the morning and a few more to determine he was facing north. The first light of the day was an irregular strip of gray between the rock above and the tops of the sheltering trees. He had awakened from a dream. In it he had been back in the Port, walking carefree on Pendleton Dock.

Harrison and the captain were buried in their covering of leaves and were vague shapes in the gloom. They had turned often, rustling in their nests in the early hours of the morning, but they were quiet now and he thought they must be asleep. They must find better bedding, he thought. No matter how he had shifted and turned during the night, there were always a few stems poking his sensitive skin. Dried fern fronds might be best if stripped from their stalks. They seemed warmer and scratched the body less.

What, he imagined, was on the island that would serve for clothing? They must deal with their nakedness soon. When winter came, there would be a great need for some sort of covering for their bodies. In the colder months, they could not shelter under the rock all the time. They must search for food and work in the chill wind. Even if so much as a staysail washed ashore, it would provide enough fabric to clothe them all. Then they would require a needle. That could be made from a bird bone, and thread could be unraveled from the sail. Even a simple cloak of canvas would be some protection from the sun and wind. In the next few days some parts of the ship might float free and be washed ashore. They must keep a watch on the beach opposite the rocks where the *Dove* struck.

Sealskins might do very well for clothes once they were worked up. Certainly, fur seals and even hair seal skins would keep their bodies warm. There must be at least a few of them about the island. The animal that ate the grass on the flatland might serve, but they would have to find it and see what sort of pelt it had. If it was the size of a goat, it would require perhaps five or six skins to fit one man with a suit.

More light was entering and he looked about the shelter again. There was much to do to make it habitable. An invisible breath from the sea drifted through the trees and underwood, and its dampness made the cold more annoying while they slept. Harrison's proposed wall of thatch would stop that, and with a small fire inside they would be cozier than they had been in their hut of stones on the sealing grounds. At least they would not be blackened head to foot as with the smoky blubber fires they had made there. They must be warm so they might sleep well and rest for the next day's labor. The better they worked the sooner they would sail from the island. Certainly they were in a desperate way, not having sheath knife or a scrap of clothing. The savages on the islands wherever they had called were in a better situation. At least they had clothes and tools to make whatever they wished. Naked and empty-handed, he and the others were now less than the meanest of Indians.

More details became evident in the increasing light. The captain and the carpenter were lying quietly under their mounds of leaves and ferns. Overhead, the rock ledge was showing more of its stained surface. Towards the bay the light brightened and the twigs and leaves of the trees became sharper in their outlines. The mate, he imagined, was out there just beyond the last small trees walking back and forth in a cold, senseless vigil as he too had done.

The surf had diminished in the night for it was only a whisper.

Harrison was surely right about the savages. Were there any on the island, they would have seen some of their houses, tilled fields, or even the images of their fiendish gods. But they had not discovered the smallest mark of them. The island was theirs alone, fresh and unblemished as if it had risen from the depths of the sea. They could work unhindered and without fear of attack. Once they had explored along the foot of the peaks and the rivulet that fed the falls and found the animal up there to be no danger, why keep a guard all night? It would suffice to watch the bay for any vessel, and that would only require a glance two or three times a day. Dotty old man, Thomas said to himself, he imagines danger from cannibals where there are none, yet had ignored the obvious danger of a lee shore.

Suddenly, there was a rustling of leaves. He raised his head and saw the captain stirring in his makeshift bed. Tobit sat up. In the morning light he looked many years older. Bits of the leaves were caught in his mussed hair. He stretched his arms above his head and yawned. His flesh, all patchy pink and white, sagged on his bones. Only his paunch showed any fullness beneath the skin. The pouches that sagged below each eye were now puffed with fluid.

The captain caught him staring. "Fetch Mr. Morgen here!" he snapped.

Thomas rose out of his covering of leaves and started for the beach.

"Are you forgetting? I just gave you an order!" the captain growled.

He looked back at the officer's scowling face. Suddenly, he understood the meaning of the remark and answered dully, "Aye, sir. Oh, yes, aye, sir. Fetch Mr. Morgen." He turned and left without another glance at the captain. Thomas returned in less than a minute, following the mate who was rubbing his hands over his body and stomping his feet.

"Ach! We must have a f-fire," he said, chattering slightly, "I cannot suffer another night of this."

"We shall have fire in good time," the captain replied, "when we are assured that there are no savages up there on the flatland. We will have no meal this morning but go directly to it. I want to search those trees and find the source of the branch. When we have done that, we shall have our fire."

Harrison had gotten up and was out under the edge of the rock, eyeing the distance between the overhang and the ground. "Uprights two paces asunder and crosspieces a yard above each other to the top," he muttered. Then he looked back at the others and added, "If only we had an adze or an axe, we might have the thatch up in a day. But we shall have it, though it takes a bit longer. Lad, fetch me the fish's jaw."

Thomas went to the back wall, picked up the jaw and brought it to the rock that served as their table. He and the carpenter huddled over it, working out more of the teeth.

Captain Tobit beckoned furtively to the mate, and the two officers walked out onto the beach where their conferring voices could be heard through the trees but their words were only muffled syllables.

"We will have no meal . . . we will have no meal this morning," Thomas aped the captain's words and pompous stance. "Is he going to approve every breath we take?"

"Pay no heed to that," the carpenter answered. "When he finds there are no savages here, he will change."

"He will not change!" Thomas objected. "He will be no different. He can't put aside the idea of his great importance. He will give us trouble until we reach Stonington again. Or perhaps because of him, we will never see home."

"Or he may have an apoplectic fit," Harrison countered. "He is old and may not fare as well as we. But for now, let us obey him and say nothing."

Suddenly, the mate appeared and ordered, "Take up your sticks and lay out on the beach."

Thomas spun about to face Mr. Morgen. He wondered how much of his conversation with Harrison had been overheard.

"The sun is about to rise over the island and he is loath to wait. Come along smartly," the mate ordered and turned for the beach.

The crewmen picked up their sticks and followed the mate. As soon as the four men were gathered together, the captain started off leading them west along the shore at a brisk pace. The exercise warmed Thomas's body in the cool, misty air. Even the usually dry portion of the upper beach was dampened with a little dew, and the leaves of the trees dripped when shaken. They arrived at the stream that emptied the lake, and there the captain turned in and followed its bank.

Northward, out on the bay, the waves were catching the first yellow beams of the sun while the whole of the lake and its shore the men walked on were still in shadow.

They passed the scattered clumps of flax from which Thomas and the carpenter had cut leaves to make their baskets the day before. The land on which the flax thrived was not sand and cinders but a damp mixture of fine soil and ashy material that yielded perfect imprints of their feet, even to the wrinkles in the soles. Harrison paused and clawed up a handful of it. He squeezed it in his hand and then, curious of its qualities, broke the wad apart with his fingers. It was the first soil of its kind they had seen. On the plateau, the grass grew from much coarser material, and the trees and ferns of the bluff were rooted in a mixture of rocky earth and rotted leaves. While the carpenter and Thomas had paused, the officers had gotten ahead.

"Look at the mist!" Mr. Morgen exclaimed from the other side of a line of plants.

The crewmen rushed ahead through the flax and saw what had surprised the mate. He stood in a gap between the plants where he had a clear view of the entire lake. In the recess where the fall plunged to its surface, there was a layer of fog. It spread out for a distance, thinned, and then evaporated or was dissipated in the light breeze.

"Ah, the chill of the night air on the slough," Harrison said. "It must be warmer there than where it runs to the bay."

Mr. Morgen waded into the water and swished a foot around. "That it is," he said, confirming the carpenter's words. "There must be a hot spring under this lake, something to heat it."

"No, no, it is above the fall. See how the water falling steams," Harrison pointed out.

"You're right. I can see it," the mate said. "We might have a spa up there. I would like that."

The bluff on their side of the fall was a series of ledges the height of a man. Farther on, near the cascade, the ledge tops narrowed and the vertical surfaces came together to form a sheer precipice. In the hollow behind the fall was a dark pool that appeared to be very deep. They could not proceed much farther. The shore waned in that direction until there was nothing left upon which to walk.

The captain stopped and searched for the easiest way up. A tangle of ferns, vines, and plants grew on the tread of each giant step. Where water seeped over in places, the stone faces were covered with worts and bright green mosses.

"Here," he said abruptly, "we will scale the rock here and when on top, follow the branch to its source." He then pushed his way through the flax and ferns to the face of the first ledge. With the mate's help, footholds in the rock, and a provident vine growing within reach, he climbed onto the top of the huge step. He panted after each effort and had to rest for several minutes, but he would not permit any of the others to pass him and lead the way. Those below had to look up at his sagging buttocks as he struggled over each edge. The tops of some of the ledges were covered with patches of muck and rotting leaves. Their feet sank into and sucked out of the stinking, black mire. In addition, the men had to pick their way over fallen fern trunks and tangles of fronds and the long, snaky trunks they had met with the day before. At the last ledge to be climbed, the captain stood perspiring and gasping for air.

"Lads . . . we are . . . near the top . . . keep silent and watch me," he hissed. He rested a few more minutes and started up over the edge. With the mate pushing from below, he pulled himself up by a frond and managed to squirm over the lip. Slowly, he got to his knees and then to his feet.

Thomas nudged the carpenter's arm and whispered, "Now he knows there are no savages and plays the great leader. He will only annoy the birds."

Captain Tobit turned and beckoned to those below. They pitched their sticks up and helped each other to the level of the plateau. There they faced a thick boskage. There was no path, no natural opening where they might stroll through.

The sun had risen higher and its light now fell on the bar and part of the slough. With that increase in light, the morning on the island was in its full measure. The light rustle of a breeze in the leaves about them mixed with the splash and rumble of the fall striking the surface of the water below. A few white gulls soared over the shore. As the men rested, they became aware of sweet twitterings in the bushes. Some small birds fluttered close about their heads, eyeing the men with curiosity. Thomas watched the little things flapping and hovering. They had done that at Port William and Dusky Sound, yet these birds seemed even more intrigued, as if they had never seen men before.

The captain pushed his way into the thicket, working his way west to intercept the stream above the fall. Even before they expected it, they broke through to its bank. The growth along it was knee-high ferns and small bushes. It offered an easier way and the captain followed the bank upstream for a hundred yards. There, the bushes became thick again and forced them out to wade in the water. It was little more than knee-deep and flowed over a gravel bed. Each red and black pebble and rock showed clearly in the warm and transparent fluid. They formed a pretty pavement underfoot, but they were also angular and hurt the men's bare feet. Each step had to be cautiously tried before they moved ahead. They reached some larger trees growing on each bank, and in places, their limbs met overhead, creating a tunnel-like space above the stream. Where their roots grew out and were bathed in the water, they held streamers of a fine green growth waving in the current.

Harrison looked at the limbs and leaves overhead and guessed, "Beech, I believe."

By grabbing the ends of limbs with one hand and using his stick in the other hand to aid his balance, each man could force his way against the current.

The mate turned back and asked Harrison, "Do you feel the water is altogether warmer here?"

The captain stopped and held his hand up, warning them to be quiet. He slowly turned his head, attempting to locate some faint sound. A distant roar or rumbling became detectable to their straining ears.

"The fall," the mate suggested.

"It's from the south. From the other way," Harrison whispered.

"An echo coming round about?" Thomas asked.

Harrison shook his head. "Too even," he pointed out. "It doesn't wander or waver as it should in these mountains."

"Ah, I have it, steam coming from the ground?" Mr. Morgen speculated. "I have seen it do so in Naples."

"Perhaps," whispered the captain. "We must approach with caution and with our sticks at the ready."

The four started wading again in single file with the captain timidly leading them around each new bend. The carpenter and Thomas peered into the thicket on each bank without the least apprehension. After a half-mile of travel up the stream, the foliage thinned. They passed openings in the trees and, through them, part of the slopes of the peaks on the right side were visible. On the left, they saw nothing until they came to a large gap in the bushes and trees. Through it, they had a good view of the grass-covered flatland they had discovered the day before. The rumbling in the air had become louder as they had worked their way up the stream. Captain Tobit led the men out of the water through a patch of waist-high ferns on the bank. He went out as far as the edge of the grass and looked all about. With his left hand, he motioned the others to gather closer.

"Harrison, you come with me," he commanded. "We'll continue in the stream. Mr. Morgen, you'll take Thomas and follow our direction, but in the bushes near the grass. Stay hidden as best you can and watch for any danger from that side." The captain faced about and led the carpenter back to the branch.

Thomas put his stick on his right shoulder and started picking his way through the brush and ferns.

"Thomas! You come back here instantly!" the mate barked.

CHAPTER 8

THE LAD spun around and saw that the mate's face had the testy look he always gave those that he considered the shirkers of the crew. The frown on his forehead drew his dark eyebrows together, making a deep furrow between them.

"I'll not waste words with you!" he spat out. "Since we have landed on this island, you have become insolent. Captain Tobit and I have talked about you. This is your first voyage, therefore I am giving you a caution. From this moment on, you will answer the captain and me respectfully, and you will mind our orders strictly."

Thomas stared at Mr. Morgen with his mouth half agape.

"You will make no more outbursts as you did the other day," he warned, pointing his finger at Thomas. "You signed the *Dove*'s articles of agreement. You are still a member of her crew and must remain under our command unless you have our leave!"

Thomas took the stick from his shoulder, stepped toward the mate and asked, "Where is the *Dove* and her articles? They are down there in the bottom of the sea!"

"Remember, when you signed them, you did it in the presence of the owners and people of position. Take care what enemies you make. Yes, and you gladly took your advance."

"Ha, we all worked off that dead horse nearly two years ago. I owe you nothing! You have no ship. Your command is gone. . . . Poof!"

"Nothing has changed. You are still under our authority and will be until we see Boston or Stonington again."

"Look at me and look at yourself. We are shipwrecked, cast ashore on an island no one knows of, wandering about naked as the savages, and you prattle about command." Thomas turned and started through the ferns and bushes.

"You are in sore need of a thrashing!" the mate shouted. "That will give you respect for your betters."

The lad halted. He turned back and faced the mate. In a slow move, he lifted his stick and held it with both hands diagonally before him at the ready.

Mr. Morgen took a slight step back. Thomas had come aboard the barque as a thin youth. Morgen recognized now how the work had caused him to fill out in the two years since. The lad was now well put up with a deeper chest and thick, muscled arms and his hands had a firm grip on his stick.

Thomas stood motionless with his feet planted apart. His jaw was clenched, and his unblinking eyes bored at the mate. The two men remained facing each other.

At length Thomas said slowly, "I will do what is needed to survive and get us from this island, but no more." He kept his eyes on the officer as he turned to resume his walk.

The mate saw the corner of Thomas's mouth turn up slightly as he faced away. He watched him wading forward, thrusting the greenery aside. Suddenly, he bolted after him and stretched out his paces to catch up. They had not gone forty yards when Thomas made an abrupt turn and headed toward the east. As the two marched farther from the stream, the bushes became lower and sparser and gave way to the pure stand of grass. To the south, the slope of the smaller mount was visible. The trees on it were larger and more thickly leafed than those growing on the taller peaks. Those two other mountains appeared to have risen in a later time and encroached on its western side. For half an hour they walked through the grass.

Thomas halted and pointed a finger at the level top of the lower peak. A diagonal line of white patches just below its summit bobbed up and down from behind the greenery and limbs. There seemed to be limits to their motions.

The mate stared at it and asked, "What could it be?"

"Water," Thomas declared. "A cascade of water."

"A branch up there? How could it be so high."

"I don't know, but that sound is coming from there. Hear it?"

Thomas took a long look at the plateau from one side to the other. "We must tell the others," he said and started for the stream. He pushed his way into the bushes and ferns toward the bank. When they broke through and stood at the edge of the water, the captain and Harrison were not in sight.

"We have traveled faster than they did," the mate explained.

Thomas stepped into the water and waded with the current.

Mr. Morgen followed and called softly, "Captain Tobit," as they rounded each bend.

After traveling the winding course for several hundred yards, they saw the captain when he appeared from behind a bush that overhung the creek. He was poling himself ahead with his stick. Harrison waded a few paces behind him. The officer was surprised, even piqued, that the mate and Thomas had gotten ahead of him.

"We have found the source of the noise," the mate called out as they approached.

Captain Tobit instantly put up a hand and motioned for him to be quiet.

"We have found no savages," the mate assured him. "There is not the least sign. We may talk as we wish."

"Well, what have you discovered of that rumbling? What makes it?" the captain demanded.

"It is this very branch. It falls from near the top of the mount ahead of us. We can see it from out on the flat," Mr. Morgen said and led them out through the trees and into the grass. There, he pointed to the cascading water visible through gaps in the forest covering and proposed, "It must arise in the higher peaks. There can be no other source for so much water."

The carpenter, with a puzzled look asked, "Aye, the fall of rain must be greater up there, and there may be snow in the winter. Yet how can it show there at the very crest?"

"We will follow it up that far," the captain said, and re-entered the bushes and headed toward the stream. They found where the cascade from the hillside was rushing onto the flat. At that point, the water, racing down during heavy rains, had thrown aside the stones, and even some large boulders, and scoured out a pond sixty or seventy feet in length and twenty in width. As the stream flowed in, an equivalent amount drained out at the other end as the source of the branch. Its water was dark under the shadows of the leaves overhead. A few vagrant rays of sunlight moved back and forth on its rippling surface.

From the pool, the castaways climbed up the steep slope, always keeping close to or at least within sight of the frothing water. In places, the liquid boiled from beneath boulders and swirled around others. Where there was no other path, it dashed over the stones, limbs, and any logs that had fallen in its course.

The trees and ferns, large and small, were rooted between the jumbled stones that formed the slope. The men had to find their way around boulders and up through a tangle of vines and fronds. They seized any limb or rock to keep their balance and as grips by which to pull themselves up. Thomas left the trail-blazing to Harrison and the mate and stood below them, holding their sticks while they found footholds on the mossy rocks and wrenched limbs aside. It was an unvarying clamber upward. The pursy captain called for those in the lead to halt when he could no longer keep up. The others waited in the shadows and diffuse light, watching the frothing water in its downward rush to the flatland. All about them was the roar of the cascade and the chirruping of the birds.

"What a damned sulphurous smell," the mate swore.

Harrison nodded and added, "Aye, I caught a whiff of it a while ago."

A foul odor came to them more often as they worked their way nearer the top. The mate cursed the stench each time the breeze carried it to his nose.

It was past the middle of the morning when they approached the top. They had seen hints that they were nearing it. The trees had become smaller, and there were fewer of them. Soon they broke out into the open where bushes and ferns were only a knee-high covering over the rock and cinder slope. The mystery of the cascade was solved. The low peak was indeed a volcano, and its crater was filled with a lake.

The men stood on the rim panting for breath and watching vagrant wisps of steam drift across the water. The smell of rotten eggs was inescapable. A notch had been formed or washed in the north wall of the crater not twenty yards from where they stood, and there the water poured out between thick ferns growing on each bank, and on down to feed the cascade. Thus, they saw that the lake was the origin of the fall and the slough below. Except at the west and southwest sides, the crater was nearly circular. It would have had that shape if the two high peaks had not joined and encroached on that quarter of it.

Thomas pointed to the steep wooded valley between them and said, "There, that must be the source that fills this crater. Any rain falling back up in the highlands can only come this way."

"Yes, it enters on that side beneath those trees and spills out here," Harrison said. "It is like a great cup pouring its contents out but never empty."

The entire plateau was spread out below and extended unbroken, except for a few trees marking the route of rivulets, to the eastern shore of the island. Gusts of wind gliding across the flat were made visible as the grasses bowed and rose again in moving patches. Each man scanned the whole of the flatland out to the sea and around to where it met the slope of the high peak to the south.

"Even from this height, we cannot see the surf beyond to the east and south," Mr. Morgen pointed out. "The shore must be close in under the bluff."

"Aye, so there will be little or no beach there. That settles the question of savages," the carpenter reasoned. "They would not choose to have their village on the windward side where canoes could not be got off or landed without danger or where the sea broke onto rocks."

"Ahh, we may sleep easy tonight. No cold watches on the beach," the mate added with an obvious sigh of relief.

"The only secret left now is the animal out there. What is it and what may it yield for us?" Harrison asked.

"Well, I have no worries about it," the mate replied. "It is not large and if it prefers grass to eat we are safe enough."

All around the lake the lip of the crater was uneven in height, and in places its top narrowed to a mere fathom, hardly space for a path.

Harrison pointed to a small hole on the inside of the crater rim from which a little mist emitted. It was two feet above the water's edge. Rocks around the opening were yellowed as if painted with the most brilliant pigment. He carefully selected his grips and footholds on the crumbling rocks as he climbed down toward it. The stink intensified. From a few feet away, the carpenter saw that a delicate, fuzzy structure of fine crystals had formed from the hot breath blowing out. They were easily broken when he touched them. A few yards farther away he discovered another cavity like the first with its yellow halo and escaping steam.

"Brimstone!" he called up to the others that had remained above. Mr. Morgen nodded he understood and waved for him to return. "I think it's all about the crater," he said while he crept up to the edge again.

Once Harrison joined them again, the captain picked his way carefully over the jagged rocks. Their bare feet could be easily cut by some of their sharp edges. He tested each step, placing his weight slowly forward. Sometimes he backed away and tried another spot before going ahead. He led the others around toward the side of the nearer peak that had impinged on the crater. The rest of them followed, limping over the clinkered edge. Captain Tobit doggedly kept ahead of them and traveled halfway around the lake, pausing now and then as if he were searching for something. Finally, he stopped and peered into the trees on the outer slope.

"Is he still looking for his cannibals?" Thomas snickered. "I think he will be quite put out if he finds none."

They were surprised to see the captain drop his stick and deliberately step over the steep side and disappear.

Mr. Morgen started off again, hopping gingerly ahead to the place where the captain had gone over. Thomas and Harrison trailed after him, glancing down the slope to discover what had attracted the officer.

"Captain! Captain!" the mate yelled as he leaned out and scanned through the trees.

They could hear the captain below breaking through the underwood and kicking rocks loose that clattered into the trees far below.

"What have you found?" the mate called out. The captain did not answer and continued thrashing through the greenery. "What the devil is he up to?" Mr. Morgen growled through his clenched teeth.

"It's very steep here," the carpenter suggested. "Perhaps he has injured himself?"

"What have you found?" the mate repeated and waited for an answer.

After a pause, the reply came as a faint word from the forest below, "Nothing."

The men on the rim listened intently. In a few minutes there was a stirring in the bushes, as if the captain was scrambling back up. The noise stopped and resumed again many times. They waited nearly ten minutes before he came into view, grasping at limbs and fronds to aid his climb and hold his balance. Mr. Morgen eased his way down to aid him, but the material of the volcano was loose and kept rolling from under his feet. Only the well-rooted plants gave the two men enough purchase to pull themselves to the top.

The captain's face was a deep red when he stepped onto the rim. He labored to get enough air into his lungs. Perspiration dripped from his jowly chin and the tip of his nose. Small leaves and bits of stems adhered to the wet skin of his arms, shoulders, and back.

"What did you expect to find there?" the mate asked.

The captain waited until his breathing slowed, then pointed to where he had been below. "Side is . . . very thin there. Water seeps out . . . makes a runnel."

Harrison and Thomas looked at each other and then at the captain with baffled expressions.

Mr. Morgen leaned over the side and, with a frown on his face, inquired, "What has that to do with us? What advantage might it give?"

Captain Tobit turned away and murmured, "Later, later." He then cautiously picked his way down the inner side of the crater to the edge of the lake and waded in. Slowly he dipped up handfuls of water to wash himself. The others pitched their sticks aside, descended after him, and found places where they could sit in the lake waist-deep. Harrison swirled his hands about and smiled, saying, "Our very own spa. A hot bath whenever we wish it."

The mate agreed with him, adding, "Yes, and if it weren't for that damnable stink, it would be ideal."

Thomas ducked his head beneath the surface and rose up again. With both hands, he wiped the water from his face and hair and then looked across to the far shore. The wind was coming from around the mountains in broken airs. Their effect was to drive the wisps of steam on the water first one way and then another. Every few minutes a cluster of small bubbles rose to the surface and burst, increasing the smell.

The return to the shelter took hardly more than two hours, for the descent from the volcano was far easier than the climb. In addition, their crossing of the grassland was a brisk walk for the captain no longer had any reason to sneak through the bushes and peer around rocks as he had done walking the stream. Their only halt on the way was at the edge of the plateau where the castaways searched the entire bay. There was no ship on it nor any minute indication of a sail out on the hard, blue line separating the sky and sea.

Just after the middle of the day, Thomas knelt on the sandy floor of the shelter and frowned at the bow in his hand. Its string had just snapped. He tossed it aside. His first try at making a fire had failed.

Harrison handed him another one of the three bows he had prepared. Thomas twisted the string of the new bow around the foot-long drill stick and again poked the tip of it into the notch cut into a short piece of a splintered limb. In his left hand he held a small clamshell, which he cupped over the top of the drill. His right hand pushed and pulled the new bow back and forth. The string spun the stick rapidly, reversing its direction with each stroke. Harrison, also on his knees, gripped the limb with both hands to keep it steady.

Mr. Morgen and the captain stood over the crewmen and watched intently as the drill whirled. The smell of charred wood rising in the air was evidence Thomas's effort was taking effect. On the sand beside the carpenter were a handful of dried fern fronds and piles of twigs, sorted by size from the thinnest to ones thick as a finger. Lying next to them was a coil of cord he had made an hour before and the last bow, ready for use. Thomas sawed away with long, steady strokes. A dark brown wood powder was forced out of the notch, and a wisp of smoke curled from it. The young sailor increased his speed, whipping the bow back and forth at a furious pace. Dense smoke boiled from the tip of the drill. More charred fuzz tumbled out of the notch onto the smoking pile. Thomas tossed the drill and bow aside and crouched on his left elbow. He cupped his right hand around the smoldering powder and puffed lightly on it. A red spark in it swelled with each breath, then gradually shrank and winked out. Thomas mumbled a curse and picked up the bow again. Twice more, he had the glow started before it increased enough to add some crumpled bits of fronds. The new fuel began to blacken and curl. Little sparks popped up and a tongue of flame suddenly wavered over the glowing leaves.

"Huzzah, lad!" Harrison cried out. "You've done it."

Smoke wreathed around Thomas's head. He abruptly pushed himself back onto his haunches and gasped for clean air. Tears filled his eyes and ran down into his beard. Thomas selected the smallest twigs and placed them gently onto the flame. When those were well ablaze, he added the next larger ones. In a few minutes the fire was a foot high, and the mate and Christopher were feeding even larger sticks to it. The castaways stared at the orange flames. Tobit leaned over and added his token bit to the fire. The crackling and popping and the sight of the smoke rising to the rock overhead gave Thomas a feeling of achievement. Whenever their little oil lamp went out in the seal islands, he had used a flint and tinder or even a mite of gunpowder to restart fires. Now that the flames were secure, he and Christopher rose to their feet. All four stood around and felt the radiating warmth on their naked bodies. It was a delight and a security. Their great need had been filled. Now with fire they felt in complete possession of the space beneath the rock.

Mr. Morgen angled his open hands over the blaze as if to direct its heat toward his body. He boasted, "We shall sleep snug enough from now on. We only lack clothes and we shall manage those soon enough."

Thomas recalled how he had shivered the night before, even under his covering of leaves. Now he could rise whenever he became chilled and warm himself. With the igniting of the fire, there was a change in his spirit and expectations. Fire was a comfort and a most useful tool. He felt more in control, more assured of escaping from the island. They might float out to the wreck and dive to it, now that there was a means to cut logs for a raft. Burning them was as good as severing them with a saw or an axe. Clothes, iron, a boat, all were possible now that the *Dove* was within reach. They were now much more than helpless, suffering castaways on a bit of land no one might discover for years.

Smoke from the blaze rolled up and spread out against the overhanging stone. Then it flowed to the outer edge and upward toward the sky. Harrison watched it merge with the afternoon air. "We must leave an opening for that when we thatch up the wall," he muttered.

Thomas selected a stick from the fire and blew off the little flame that was clinging to its tip. At a smooth portion of the back wall, he made two marks with the smoking end. "Two days," he said. "How many more before we leave here?"

"I will tend the fire," the captain declared. "Mr. Morgen, gather all that is needed for the wall."

The mate instantly set the men to work. They discovered the required straight saplings were widely scattered, and they had to search for them in the trees at the foot of the bluff. To cut them was the most tiring and difficult task. They forced more of the teeth out of the shark's jaw, and the ones left made a crude saw. With it, they scored all around the saplings, then wrenched them back and forth until they snapped off. They used the same method to trim away any branches. Many times they wished for one small hatchet that would have cut the sticks with no more than one or two blows. That simple tool would have shortened their labor to a few hours. It took the carpenter and Thomas the rest of the day and the first hour of twilight to cut enough parts for the uprights and crosspieces.

The next day, the enclosure took shape rapidly, and by evening, all the framework was lashed firmly in place with narrow strips of twisted flax leaves and the first rows of thatch bound to the cross members.

Clams were the only food that they could gather without net, snare, or arrows, and the captain sent the mate off to find them at low tide. He gathered enough for each man to have a dozen or a few more. Though at first they had eaten the clams raw, once the fire was made Mr. Morgen intended to cook them. While the crewmen worked on the wall, the mate dug a hole several yards away, lined it with stones, and built a large fire in it to heat them. When there was nothing left but ashes and red coals, the officer placed his clams, wrapped in fern leaves, in the pit and covered them with sand. That evening, he scooped the sand aside and pulled out the charred bundle. Harrison placed it on the largest rock and plucked it open. Inside were the partly opened clams, exhaling a delicious aroma.

"Ah, nothing could be better," Mr. Morgen said, reaching for one of the largest shells. "They taste so sweet."

The captain stepped forward and placed his hand on the mate's arm, and in a low, hoarse voice said, "Do not let your appetite cause you to forget your obligation." He repeated his usual words of grace, but at the end added, "We know this food is not simply for us to relish. All our vittles, meager or ample, are given us that they may sustain us, that we may worship Thee and serve Thee alone. Amen."

After he had eaten, Harrison entered the half-finished shelter and built up the fire inside. The others came in and paced around, admiring the construction.

"To have the fire and the wall," the mate purred, "to have the fire, food, and the cave. What fortune! It could have gone badly for us."

"Better than our wretched hole on Macquarie," Thomas muttered.

Harrison gave a short nod. He had spent a few nights in that hovel of stacked rocks roofed with a broken spar, several boards, and a half-rotted sail. "Aye, 'tis better," he agreed, "and we'll not have to blacken it with blubber fires. We will live like decent men in this place. Our wants will be met in time."

"And all by God's great design," the captain suddenly injected while he sat on his rock and stared into the fire with absent eyes. They were surprised when he spoke. He seldom addressed them now except to give an order or ask a question. Then, with his eyes still intent on the flames, he added, "He has denied this island to the heathen. He intends this to be a Christian land and for those who continue in it, to save all worthy souls."

Their crude ladder, constructed of two poles and a few sticks, was taken down at mid-afternoon the next day. The wall of fresh, gray-green thatch was completed up to the shelving rock.

Harrison tugged at the long bunches of leaves and the ties that held them in place. "We must hitch them on again after they dry and shrink. They will not cover half as well then. Many bundles, oh, it will take many bundles before it is a finished home," he explained.

To celebrate the completion, they quit early, opened the cooking hole, and feasted on an extra helping of clams.

"Now we must think of clothing ourselves," the mate said after he had had his fill. He picked up one of the bows lying at the back of the shelter and plucked its string. "We would have to dress a quantity of this and build a loom to make the meanest of cloth."

"Indeed," Harrison replied, "it would be weeks before we had anything to cover our backs, and it would make an indifferent coat at best. The answer can only be skins. I would say find the animal that is on the plateau."

Mr. Morgen objected, "We do not know what sort of beast it is, or if it has a pelt at all."

"Then it must be seals," the carpenter suggested. "We might search around the rocks on the coast to discover their rookeries."

"We know how to kill and flay seals well enough," the mate boasted. "We will make a sortie along the east coast tomorrow. That will be the nearest place we might find them, and if we follow the shore around, we will not miss any of their haunts."

A FEW NARROW openings, small defects in the wall of thatch, were revealed as light pierced the dark interior of the shelter the next morning. Thomas felt he had rested comfortably, and each time he had dropped off the episode of sleep seemed longer. During the night he and Harrison had risen and spent a few minutes reviving the fire. It may have been the thought of the wall blocking the damp sea air, or the pop and crackle of the burning wood that made him feel he had gotten a better night's rest. The pain of the sunburn had diminished, or he thought it had, while he slept. At any rate he felt hale and ready for the day's search as he lay in his bed.

Mr. Morgen stirred from his leaves and went to move the thatched frame aside that served as the door. Light poured in. Captain Tobit rolled in his bed and began a short fit of coughing.

Harrison and Thomas arose without a word and prepared to find seals. They gathered up the sticks needed to kill the animals and a few of the shark's teeth to skin them. Thomas glanced at the baskets for a few seconds, and then grabbed both. The carpenter saw them in the lad's hand and said, "Good, a good idea. We may take many hides or find better bedding."

The captain knelt by the ring of stones and nudged the smoking ends of the driftwood closer together. "I shall remain here and tend the fire," he announced as if he was taking on a great responsibility.

The two crewmen followed the mate as he ducked out of the opening. On the beach, Thomas leaned toward Harrison and mimicked the captain's voice and words. "'I shall remain here and tend the fire.' Now he is sure there are no savages here, I'll lay he will spend most of his days in the shelter," Thomas said. "He will become a piece of old smoked meat."

Harrison was scanning the horizon from west to east. He held a finger to his lips and nodded toward the mate marching a dozen paces in front of them. They strode on the curving shore and searched the waves and beach for any bit of the barque that might have floated free in the last few days. Thomas peered into the trees at the foot of the bluff and inspected the beach near them, but there weren't any newly bent or broken limbs where someone had forced their way in. There were no strange footprints pressed into the damp cinders and sand. None of the crew had got ashore days after the wreck by some miracle. A shipmate would not exit from the greenery, fit and smiling, to surprise them. For nearly an hour, Mr. Morgen led the men toward the eastern extremity of the island. Ahead of them was the dark rock where, the day after the wreck, the captain had prayed for the souls of the lost men. In the barren landscape of the sea and the dunes, the tall, rough stone stood as a cenotaph.

From that time, when the deaths of the rest of the crew were undeniable, dreams had come to Thomas in his sleep. In them he had seen bodies entangled in cordage and torn sailcloth and swept to and fro in a black sea. There was also the image of Will's wrinkled and grinning face and the images of the boys working the spun yarn winch. They all flowed, mixed, separated, and mixed again until he awoke waving his arms in an effort to swim. He came back from his dream memories just in time to follow the mate as he turned to the right.

The broad field of dunes was before them and extended to their left as they traveled toward the eastern shore. Mr. Morgen skirted the wooded face of bluff, fifty yards away on the right. The far side of the island, at least a portion of it, was proving to be what they expected as they labored through the sand and cinder mixture of the low dunes.

It was a low-lying coast of shallow water and tidal flats. Sandbars and inlets were aligned along the coast by the current coming around the island and sweeping north. Driftwood and clumps of rockweed had been carried to the calmer water in the lee of the island. There, it had all fetched up in rotting piles with clouds of insects buzzing over them. The men wandered out onto the soft beach and picked through the smelly heaps.

"Nothing save what grows about the island," Harrison announced as he finished pulling apart a heap of rockweed.

"Damn! Not a fid, toggle or stave from a cask. Naught from windward," the mate complained. "It's as if we were not in the same sea as the other islands. I would expect something from Van Diemen's or from the ships that pass 'twixt there and Port Jackson."

The flats extended for miles north along the spit. Nearby, they were whiskered with sea grass in places. At flood tide they would be covered, or perhaps only the tips of the grass would show between the small waves. Wading birds wandered to one side and the other probing their bills into the fine sand and muck. Overhead, squawking gulls wavered, dipped, and rose in response to changes in the wind.

The carpenter was walking beside one of the inlets and eyeing the water in it. He turned and beckoned to the mate. "Fish!" he called out.

Thomas and the mate rushed to his side. Harrison proudly pointed to three dark-backed fish little more than a foot in length moving their fins and tails slightly to hold their place in the water.

"There must be more we cannot see," Harrison said. "A snare would work here, wouldn't you say?"

The mate estimated the width of the inlet and gave his head a slow, indecisive shake.

The carpenter gestured with his hands as he described his idea. "There," he said briskly, "from there where it is about knee-deep, we build a fence of wattles from each bank and angle them until they nearly meet in the center up there. Then we wade in and drive them into one of our baskets held at the opening."

Mr. Morgen gave an understanding nod and said, "They should

provide a meal or two, but we do not have the time." He turned around and peered south where the tumbled rocks of the bluff met the shore. "Captain Tobit expects us to discover seals if there are any. We must explore as much as we are able today. Tomorrow will do for the fish."

"The fish are here now," Thomas objected. "Tomorrow they may be gone and there will be no meal or two."

"Quite true, lad," Harrison agreed.

The mate looked at the inlet and then south to the rocky coast. In that direction the sandy shore on which they stood narrowed to nothing, and the ocean washed over a shore of stones and boulders.

"Aye, the fish may leave today," Harrison warned, "but the seals, if they are up, will not for they will be pupping."

For a moment, the mate appeared undecided. He checked the position of the sun and said, "We have most of the day yet. No, we will go on and return here if there are no seals and then build a trap." He looked once more at the rocky shore. "It will be foolish to travel on that jumble. We must climb to the plateau," he said, and started off.

The crewmen faced each other and then extended a hand out in an extravagant invitation to invite the other to proceed ahead. Thomas took the initiative and went first, shaking his head as he marched after the mate. They picked their way up through the trees. It was a good choice. Travel on the plateau's level surface was ideal. They were able to see long stretches of the coast as they walked along the rim. The entire eastern shore was composed of tumbled rocks with slim patches of sand where there was a little protected water. The steep incline from the brink of the flatland down to the shore was covered with trees, and it appeared no different than that on the other side on the bay. It was not quite noon when they reached the peak that blocked their way. The southern edge of it and of the mountain beyond had fallen into the sea, and the fractured coast tending away to the west showed as sheer faces of stone. Frothing surf broke between boulders that had fallen from above. They saw that, at low water, they might crawl antlike over those rocks but would be trapped if they did not return before it was on the flood. Any further exploration was barred at that point. There were no rookeries within their sight and no space not washed at high tide on which fat-bodied seals might haul out. If a seal was discovered, there was no way to reach it. Even with a boat it would be a precarious task.

"We are baffled here," Mr. Morgen lamented, and gave a beckon to them to follow him back the way they came. They had marched about six or seven miles from the shallows almost without a pause. On the trip back the mate kept an easier pace, and they stopped at one of the two streams they had crossed on the way to drink and rest.

Before they started off again, Thomas swept his gaze around the horizon. There was a clear view of it, except for that portion hidden by the highlands to the west and northwest. He tried to resolve bits of clouds into the sails of a ship, but they always remained clouds or evaporated. He saw that the others were doing the same, peering into the distance beyond the island.

To keep a beacon fire going constantly, at least one that might be seen any distance, he knew was nearly impossible. During fair days, the peaks themselves were far easier to detect with a glass. It might work on rainless nights if they could gather enough dry wood and drag it to some high point. Even then, the peaks would hide their fire from six points of the horizon. He and Harrison would spend entire evenings tending the fire. Only rain would give them any respite. They might spend months or even years at it and never be any nearer relief. Best to forget any vagrant ship happening upon the island. A boat of some sort was the only sure way home. Better to make shift and try their skill, than to wait for some vessel that might never arrive.

The sun was still high when the men descended from the bluff to the shallows. There was time to set up Harrison's fish trap, and they spent the greater part of the afternoon gathering enough sticks to build the fences. Each man ranged along the shore, picking up branches and pulling wood from the drifted weed. These were pushed into the soft bottom of the inlet to create the walls of the trap.

In three tries, beating the water up the inlet to the apex of the fences, they snared eleven fish. They resembled a herring and were all more than a foot in length. The trap was a great success despite the escape of several fish.

"Ha! With a little work, it will be even better," Harrison said with some pride in his voice. "We can make other traps farther along. We will have nets at the ends, and the fish will snare themselves while we are away. We will need only come to gather them each day or so."

The mate looked at the length of the shore and muttered, "It is so odd that we have found nothing, absolutely nothing. I have been to many shores, as far the South Sandwiches and even there, some bit of wood, bottle, or rag has fetched up." He shook his head and said, "Well, lads, time to go."

They gathered up their long sticks, shark's teeth, and baskets.

After taking his first steps, Mr. Morgen halted, turned, and stared east over the ocean. Thomas and Harrison also stopped and scanned the horizon, but saw nothing from the shore to the sea's junction with the sky.

"What is it?" the carpenter asked. "A ship?"

The mate shook his head and, still intent on the horizon, muttered, "Tovy Poenamoo."

"In the right season, and with a stout boat we will reach it," Harrison predicted. "We are fortunate it is all to the leeward once we set off. No beating to windward, and we can't miss such a long coast."

The mate stood more erect and leaned his head back as if that would allow him to see that far shore. "That part is a wild coast, I hear," he said. "What welcome can we expect from the savages there? Perhaps it would be much wiser to wait for relief." He turned and set off for the shelter.

•

THE FOUR MEN crouched around the cooking fire outside the new thatch wall and waited for their meal. Each one had a fish impaled on a forked stick, which he turned slowly above the bed of glowing coals. The aroma of the cooking flesh drifted around them, increasing their hunger. They had hiked many miles, nearly a quarter of the way around the island by their estimate, and were tired and eager to taste their catch. Every fish taken from the heat of the coals had its fins burned crisp and was nearly black. Each of the castaways laid his meal on a frond and picked it open. He lifted out the backbone and pinched up the steaming flesh with his fingers.

"Mmm, far better than sea bird eggs and seal paws, eh, Thomas?" Harrison asked.

Thomas nodded and replied, "Aye, we ate enough of them."

"There is better food on this isle to eat," the carpenter said. "Perhaps we will find some new thing, some dainty at the other end."

Mr. Morgen broke in, "But tomorrow it's seals we're after. We need clothes to put on our backs and soon. It's vexing that on the whole of that shore we found nothing."

Thomas wiped his fingers with some leaves and remarked, "Even when we find skins, it will take some time to dress them."

"You can do that?" Tobit asked. "I mean, make soft leather, soft enough that we can wear it in comfort?"

Thomas sucked his teeth and nodded once. A looked of studied indifference crossed his face and he answered, "Oh yes, I have seen it done often enough."

"And what will you need?" the mate asked.

"Oh, tubs, the right bark or leaves, some things to scrape with. . . . Clamshells will do. Ashes, things of that sort. Nothing we cannot get."

"And how long will it be before we might tailor our clothes?"

"Oh, days or weeks, depending how it be done. There is much work to it."

During the cooking and the meal, the wind began to work through the trees and stir the branches. Thomas and the carpenter turned to look north when they felt the air stirring around their bodies.

Mr. Morgen sat thinking for a while. He glanced at the lad several times when the youth's attention was drawn away. The officer eyed him, perhaps admitting to himself that he had received the worst of the exchange up on the plateau. The boy was stout and growing willful, and in time would become unruly. There was no crew any longer to back him and keep order. He knew he and the captain must devise some restraint on that one.

Harrison rose to his feet and walked through the trees to the beach. Thomas got up a half-minute later and followed. Out in the open, the two men watched pink and blue-gray clouds driving across the sky. The wind was kicking up a poppling sea across the entire bay. Along the bluff, the flaws rolled into the trees, swished through their leaves, and bent limbs back and forth.

"Well, no ship standing in and it's to be a wet night out," the carpenter noted. "How miserable it would be for us if we didn't have that snug nest back there. Sleep well tonight. That was a long trip today, and we have another tomorrow if it clears."

The two crewmen returned and built up the smaller fire inside the shelter. All the castaways sat on rocks around it and spoke very little. When the flames shortened and were about to die, one man or another would nudge a burning stick farther in or add more wood. For minutes at a time, they were motionless, yet patterns of the firelight and the outsized shadows of their bodies pulsed and wavered on the rock on one side and the dull green of the thatch opposite. Later, after they snuggled into their beds, they heard the rain pelting the trees just outside and thunder mumbling in the highlands.

In the first light, Thomas was up and walking out through the dripping bushes and trees between the shelter and the beach. By habit, he first scanned the horizon back and forth. Then he leaned his head back and watched the last scattered clouds being blown eastward. Mr. Morgen and the carpenter came out to join him, and, armed with their sticks and carrying baskets, they started for the western end of the island. Sunrise at the men's backs threw long shadows of their figures ahead on the beach, and as each foot lifted and fell its attendant shade pumped up and down.

The meal of fish the night before and a good rest had given them vitality and they were their old selves again. Their injuries, now well scabbed over, were healing rapidly.

The mate set a fast pace. It was six or seven miles to the rocks of the west coast where they hoped to find seals. At the lake, they waded the stream rippling from the lake to the bay and then they hurried along the bar. Opposite the fall, they marched along and watched its plunge, but there was no slowing in their strides. The castaways made only two short stops on their way.

The first was opposite a boil of foam out in the bay that had to be the effect of a submerged rock. There was no indication of the wreck there, no dark shape beneath the waves and not the least fragment of rope or man-shaped wood floating or on the beach. They could not be sure it was the place the *Dove* had foundered.

The next halt was at the split boulder, their shelter the night of the disaster. All three of them peeked in past the tree that blocked the entrance. No paw prints were on the cinders or in the pit they had huddled in that night. It was all unchanged, just as they had left it six days before, except for a scattering of spent leaves.

A rumbling became audible a good mile away, even before they entered the dune field at the base of the western spit. It was a clue that high surf was breaking on the west coast. Halfway there, the ocean became visible through the heat ripple on the sand. It showed between the hummocks: deep blue, heaving and falling and thickening into a line of white as waves broke. The three naked and bearded men arrived at a beach between the bluff on their left and the first great rock of the cape on the right. They stood holding their baskets and sticks and mutely facing into the wind. Each wave rose, rolled toward them, and then broke on the back of the previous one. Three or four in their final rush appeared as layer upon layer of boiling foam. After surging up the shelf of cinders, part of each wave soaked in and the remainder drained away.

There were no seals there. It was strange. The beach, its location, and the pounding waves made it a place the seals would chose to come onto the land, but Thomas's young, sharp eyes saw no dark, tumid bodies sunning on the spit near or far.

After a quick look about, the mate announced, "Damn! Some ship has discovered them and killed them all."

"No bones," the carpenter reasoned as he pointed up and down the shore. "Had there been seals at any time there would be the bones of those few that always die on the shore, and if any sealers had reached this beach it would be covered with those remains."

The bluff extended beyond the beach and farther into the sea and blocked their entire view to the south. Mr. Morgen scanned its top edge.

"Well, lads, onto the cliff. We must climb over it if we are to find covering for our backs," the mate said and turned toward the bluff. The three dropped their loads of sticks, baskets, and shark's teeth when they reached its base.

Harrison glanced around and overhead. "All the birds!" he exclaimed. "Eggs, we may have eggs for our supper."

"We have to discard those now in the nests and wait for fresh ones to be laid," Thomas said. "It will be some days till we enjoy them."

Many more sea birds were flying overhead there than on any part of the island they had yet seen. Nellies, gulls, and some smaller birds sailed over the ocean and along and over the bluff extending into the sea. Their numbers and behavior were in contrast to the sparse and slow waders on the opposite coast.

Thomas started up first, digging footholds and grabbing ferns and roots to pull himself to the top. Harrison and the mate followed. The climbing dislodged stones that bounced down the side to the beach below. One dropped past the mate's head.

"Damn!" the mate shouted. "Are you trying to kill me?"

Harrison and Thomas looked down to the officer's scowling face.

"Don't blame Thomas," the carpenter said. "That one slipped from my hand. I must apologize for that."

The mate's dark look eased at the carpenter's explanation.

Harrison turned his head up and motioned Thomas to the right. "Go to that side," he suggested. "Veer off there, and the dirt and rocks won't drop on us below."

It was a prudent change, for the protruding stones and caked cinders broke away in their hands half the time they grasped them. They struggled up to the edge and finally stepped onto the original slope of the peak. Its precipitous angle lessened as it spread out toward the coast. The entire west side of the mountain was covered with a low, thick scrub sheared by a constant wind to a uniform thickness. The limbs and twigs of the growth were tough and wiry and scratched the legs and thighs of the men as they pushed into it. A few small trees that had managed to grow higher than the bushes leaned with the gusts and bore leaves only on their leeward sides. Their lopsided greenery was pruned smooth as if by a gardener.

Down the slope to the west, they saw that the side of the peak did not continue as far out as expected but ended at a break beyond which no surf could be seen. That meant another, steeper slope was there. They rested for a few minutes and then angled across to find what sort of coast formed the unseen western margin. They hoped to discover rookeries below on that hidden portion and, if they existed, find some route to approach them. Even before they reached the edge, they heard a continuous roar of surf from below. Overhead, white sea birds sailed on the wind gusting upward. They wheeled and plunged, disappearing below the rim, then were carried up again and again. That was a clue to the shape of the coast. Thomas forged ahead, thrusting his legs through the dense bushes. He was the first to reach the edge and was struck by a sudden blast of air against his face and naked body. Despite his expectation, Thomas was not prepared for the panorama of the western shore.

He stood at the top of a curving cliff of black and reddish stone. It ringed the sides of a cove a quarter of a mile wide. There was no beach, and the sea surged in a white band a hundred yards wide at its foot. He estimated the slope of the peak on which he stood had once extended nearly a mile farther out, but the long, hollow swells had pounded against it without pause until there was only that remaining vertical drop to the sea. Mr. Morgen and the carpenter reached the rim beside the young sailor and stared at the buttress of the island being battered by the waves. Huge boulders of all shapes were scattered out from the foot of the enormous wall, and the breakers surged around and over them in a sucking mass of foam. Each wave smashed against the face of the precipice, surged upward, and on its return poured between the black rocks like milk over a great toothed jaw. Far to the south, more coves scalloped out of the mountains tended around to the east and out of sight. Between each headland were long hollows, filled with the haze of the surf.

At the base of the cliff there were no seals, not one old, ailing wig nor an abandoned pup to be seen, and no place for a rookery. Not one rock or shelf below had space for more than one or two seals. Even were they there, the men had no means to reach them. A boat would be swamped or stove there in less than a minute.

"Defeated again! Damn!" the mate swore.

"I would guess it to be near thirty fathom down to the water," the carpenter said.

"Aye, at least that," the mate agreed.

Scores of sea birds swept back and forth before the wall of black- and brick-colored stone. They soared and dived, and the enormous void constantly echoed with their piercing cries and the crack and rumble of the waves. The steep face, still in the cool shadow of the morning sun, was speckled with white birds nesting in cavities and on stone shelves. From each nesting site, streaks of guano had dribbled down and dried on the dark rock. By the length of white droppings and their thickness, it was apparent the birds had occupied the nests for decades, perhaps centuries.

Harrison pointed to where the cliffs faded away to the south and east. "It must be the same all round and join to what we saw yesterday," he suggested. "We have seen all the useful parts of this isle, save the highlands. I doubt we will find much of use to us up there."

Thomas's shoulders shuddered from the chill of the wind and the giddiness of being on the verge of the empty space. The vision sprang into his head of a ship striking on that shore. Had they wrecked upon that coast there would have been no survivors, only battered bodies washing to and fro. Nothing could live in that huge, natural trap, a certain destroyer of vessels and men. Perhaps some ship had come upon it many years before in darkness or thick weather. Beneath that tumbling foam there might be the rusting ironwork of a ship and the bones of sailors hidden amid rockweed. He put the dread thought from his mind.

He would think of what they might use for clothing now that they had failed to find a single seal. Fur or hide to wrap around their bodies was essential. None of them could guess how cold it might become on the island. They would have to be out nearly every day to gather food of some kind. Winter storms, if they were like those on the sealing grounds, could bring sleet and snow. They would suffer much when outside the shelter and far from the fire.

Thomas had been relieved when the captain declined joining their searches. It was always annoying to wait for him and help him over rocks and fallen trees. His presence alone made Thomas uneasy. Many times he had looked up and found old Tobit was watching him. He didn't like his stare and that wait-till-it's-my-turn look. Was he devising some cruel punishment? he asked himself.

The captain had shown himself to be inept or wholly careless by the loss of the barque. He had shown himself to be a coward on the beach when he feared to walk in the open to find the crew. Mr. Morgen had seen it all, but chose to ignore it and remain silent. Officers will always close ranks to protect each other. He had sent Tobit into such a rage that day when he shamed him. He might forgive a weakness or sloth in a crewman, but he would never forgive any challenge to his authority. Thomas was sure the captain was in a slow ferment and biding his time. Well, let him, he thought. Once he attempts to punish me or order me to some pointless labor, I will simply leave and set up for myself far away. He can do nothing then.

The castaways worked their way back down to the beach and picked up their baskets and sticks. It was still only about midday. By the time they got back to the shelter, there would still be time enough to gather clams. Thomas felt an increasing hunger after the long march and the climb up and down the bluff. He wanted a big meal. He was sure they all did.

CHAPTER 9

"NOTHING occurs in this life but the Lord knows of it and wills it not to be otherwise. Is that not so, Mr. Morgen?" Captain Tobit inquired in his Sabbath voice and rhetoric.

The mate, sitting on his rock by the fire, raised his head as if to answer but remained silent. He returned his gaze to the short, evanescent flames flickering over the glowing coals.

The captain asked once more in his measured words, "Well, would you not say that it is true?"

Mr. Morgen looked at the captain obliquely, and, though he nodded his head, it was an indifferent response.

The captain strode slowly around the inside of the shelter and resumed speaking, "We made much leeway. Aye, we should not have been this far east, but we made leeway and that put this island in our path. Do you not find that most strange? Why has it not been found before? Have we discovered a stitch from our vessel or any other?"

"No, and I have searched the beach at every turn. You are right there. No single thing," said Morgen.

"Thence, we are here by His will. Would you grant that is so?"

The mate turned his head and kept his eyes trained on the other officer. He was again tardy with his response, and at length, following the captain's logic, he mumbled, "Possible, in the way of punishment perhaps."

"This life we are now in accounts for little. It is only a brief moment, a mere preface to our glorious existence in heaven, but it is when we are to have our faith put to the test. Your religious education has been deficient." When he reached the end of the shelter, he turned and clasped his hands behind his back. "You have not thought enough about your salvation. You do not realize it, but your soul is in danger, oh, much danger. Yes, yes, yes. And so are many other souls in this world," he said as he advanced toward the mate.

"Thomas and Harrison, you mean?"

"No, they are the common sort, lesser men apt to fall prey to falsity or the devil in some guise. They were never destined for the after life with the Lord, but only are meant to serve in their calling. Their place is appointed and they like others are poor, for only then are they the more obedient to God. The devil works ceaselessly to lure the good and the holy from the walk of righteousness." He passed the fire and paced on as he warmed to his purpose. "It is a constant trial. It is a never-ending labor to save the deserving souls and defeat the Lord of Darkness." He faced about and stood considering the mate through the thin column of smoke curling up from the smoldering branches.

Mr. Morgen rose to his feet and asked, "What has all this to do with us here? We must now build our boat and escape this island."

"Escape, Mr. Morgen! Escape to where . . . to Tovy Poenamoo? Escape to a land where the uncouth savages will not hear the word? It is their habitude to dance and sing and forever indulge in carnal frolicking. Aye, they kill, they devour the very messengers of the Lord! We are in the darkest, most forsaken part of the globe. By the richness of His grace, you and I are raised up from the rest of mankind that are yet in ignorance and sin. The Light of His Word must be carried here."

"What do you intend? Aren't we to build a boat or some sort of piragua?"

"In time, in time, but there are other matters we must attend to first. They will be revealed to us presently. All that has been visited upon us is a revelation. You might have drowned with the others, and if you had, would you have been ready? But you were spared, Mr. Morgen. Did you ask yourself why? You were spared that you might be of particular service to the Lord and by that service, prepare yourself, indeed render yourself fit for heaven." The captain stepped around the fire and leaned close to the mate. "Be aware, Mr. Morgen," he breathed sotto voce, "be aware that you and I are different from others, much different. You and I are clear of sight and have wit and wisdom and cannot be deceived by false religions. Is that not so? We have been given our mission. Our continuance on this island must be used to the advantage of the Lord. I sent the crewmen away that I might speak of this to you."

The mate thought for a moment. "So I was spared," he mumbled. "Thomas and Harrison were too. Are they to serve in this mission also?"

"Everyone has his place. For some, it is a humble calling, but humble or not, each must hold fast in his singular service, each must stand at his appointed post faithfully to hold the devil at bay. But here in this place, here amongst the very heathen, we will do more than that. We will thrust him back! Such is the charge given us in this special time and place."

Mr. Morgen listened to the captain and nodded his head. Then he asked, "Will we build a boat or some canoe in the next months?"

"Be aware!" Tobit bawled out. "Our good fortune in the fishery where many others have failed of late is a sign. It cannot be otherwise! That we are natural leaders is an indication that we are to be God's instruments. Do you not see the Lord has cast us on this shore to do His work? If we fail him, we will be found wanting and not deserve the glory of Heaven! We will raise here a fortress of righteousness. From it, the Word will be spread into these heathen islands. The savages will topple their false idols, those beastly signs of the devil, and the true church will rise in their stead. Think of it! Think of the triumph of the Lord here amongst cannibals! You will then be assured of your place in Heaven. You may take your choice, Mr. Morgen, eternal life if you succeed in what the Lord has chosen you to do, or eternal damnation if you fail Him! Watch for the sign. It will be revealed to you soon!"

THOMAS and Harrison were at a loss to know where to go next. They stood scanning the flatland. By Tobit's order, they had climbed the giant steps of limestone near the falls and weaved a way through the underwood to the grass. For an hour they had marched south, alternately searching the earth at their feet and the grass waving in the middle distance.

"No droppings. Not a sign of them," the lad complained. "If we knew what sort of animal it is, we might guess its habits and know where to find it."

Harrison pointed to the coast and asked, "See where those brooks drain over the edge? When we looked for the seals, we passed the flax and bushes there, but we did not look upstream. They may be hiding somewhere along them."

"You try toward the coast," Thomas suggested. "I'll go along there under the mountain. They may live up in the trees and come down only at night. We have not been up here in the dark. Let's meet back at this spot no later than midday." Thomas turned toward the small volcano to continue the search there.

It must have the nature of a sheep or deer, he decided, but be smaller and lack the cloven hoof. It might browse the bushes on the slopes and descend at odd times to feed on the grass. He hoped it was not fierce or armed with claws, but he had his stick and, if he did not come upon the creature unawares, it could be clubbed like a seal. Harrison was already half-hidden in the waist-high grasses and heading toward the dark line of small trees and flax clumps. Thomas skirted the base of the small volcano, searching for any disturbed grasses out beyond the trees and bushes. He came to where the larger peak had spilled over the lesser one and the two sides formed a gully. During the rains, freshets had rushed down and washed the loose soil of the flatland away to reveal the underlying stone. A small trickle still ran through it. He stepped down into the void, across the water, and up through ferns on the opposite bank. After traveling a cable's length he discovered several stalks of grass in a line bent over in one direction. He stooped and studied them.

The wind could not have bent those few and none of the others. Birds could not have done it. Only an animal could. A hare might, a large hare leaping in that direction. The striding legs of a taller creature might snap the stems to that angle and just that height. It must be the trace he wished to find. Farther ahead he made out more of the stems lying over in the same direction. In damp soil, beneath them, he made out vague paw prints of a size and shape that could have been left by a hound. Now there was a trail to follow. Thomas walked faster, keeping his eyes searching ahead for the next kinked stems. Some appeared to his left, converging on the ones he was following. After traveling fifty yards more, he came upon a patch of grass nibbled to the ground, then more of the droppings and places where the animal had lain and matted the grass. Beyond it was a defined path of trampled and broken stems. He followed it as it tended south for a while and then made a turn toward the foot of the high peak. He was positive he was going in the right direction.

The trail was becoming more evident from the passage of many animals. A few fresh turds were scattered along the way. He believed he should fall upon the animals soon if they were not in the greenery high on the slope. Thomas took the stick from his shoulder and gripped it with both hands. The trail before him entered the bushes and smaller trees that concealed the foot of the slope. He shouldered his way through the growth and found himself in an open space of nibbled and trampled grasses that barely survived by spreading shorter shoots lying close to the earth.

The far side of the space was a line of gray-black rocks of all sizes. Atop the rocks were several strange animals sitting back on their haunches. Not one had turned to flee or showed the slightest fear when he entered through the bushes. Their thick bodies were covered with fur that had the color and texture of a hare's. They were all the size of a lamb but with larger heads and shorter legs. One facing to the side revealed it had only a stump of a tail. All sat in the same unconcerned pose, with their forepaws held out before them as if readied to catch any object tossed in their direction. Their eyes, small and black, looked at him without concern. One animal chewed slowly. One twitched its short ears and scratched its belly with a paw.

Thomas stared at the stolid animals. They reminded him of small bears, though with large heads shaped like a beaver's. Yet they were not, he suspected, relations of either. He had been to a menagerie in Boston and, of all the strange creatures there, he could not remember one that looked anything like those sitting on the stones before him. He gripped his stick by the smaller end, raised it shoulder high, and edged toward the nearest animal. The creature resumed munching something already in its mouth and watched without a blink as he neared. Thomas began each short step gradually, expecting the animal to leap aside and flee at any second. He came within striking distance, only two paces away. Still, the oily eyes stared at him. His fingers tightened around the stick, and he swung with all his strength.

Time seemed to run down. The large end of the weapon started around with an absurd slowness. He saw it moving past the bushes and rocks as it arced toward the large head. But the animal remained on it haunches and the club smashed against its skull with a satisfying thud. His quarry tumbled to the earth, one leg kicking spasmodically. Blood trickled from one nostril to form a puddle on the ground.

It surprised Thomas that none of the others fled but remained on their rumps and watched the twitching body. They shifted their gaze to the lad again when he took half-steps toward his next victim. He stared into its eyes while he lifted his cudgel again. He repeated his powerful swing and that creature was felled and lay thrashing on the ground. It tried to get up, but Thomas raised his weapon high and bashed it once more. The jerking of its body slowed and then ceased. The two remaining animals, sitting a few yards away, turned their heads a little and shifted their feet. He sidled toward the nearer one and clubbed it in the same fashion. At the lad's approach, the last animal hopped from its perch and wiggled into an opening between two large boulders.

Thomas saw that the piled rocks must have tumbled down the slope and came to rest on the flatland, thus providing the creatures with a ready-made warren. The packed earth and stunted grass in the clearing were evidences that they had lived there for many years. Even the edges and tops of the boulders were worn smooth by the constant passage of their footpads. He surmised that that would have taken a century. Close under the sides of the rocks where the creatures could not tread was a thick, cropped stubble. Their droppings and urine had made it a rich green. He walked about and peeked into the openings between the boulders. There were animals crouched, immobile in each of the cavities, their eyes reflecting the light that slipped past Thomas's body. Unless they came out into the clearing, he would have no way to take them. He returned to the last animal he had killed, knelt beside it and pinched up a fold of its skin. He rolled it between his thumb and fingers and felt the fur, fine and warm to the touch. Once they had many pelts dressed, they would all sleep rolled up in that fur. They would no longer suffer the scratching and poking of the twigs and leaf stems in their beds. The skins could be made into passable clothing, perhaps better than some made of seal. With the fur on, they might be too warm. Ashes, he thought. Yes, rolling them in ashes should make the hair slip, or if that did not work well, they could scrape it off. Thus they could have two suits of clothes, one with fur for the winter and one of plain hide for the warmer seasons.

He had heard from the whalers who had been to New Holland of the great leaping animals, the kangaroos, which lived there. He had even seen a drawing of one, but those that were lying on the earth before him were smaller and differed in many ways. Their heads were larger and they had no huge tails, indeed, almost no tails at all. He reasoned there might be many curious beasts in the unexplored lands in such a strange part of the world.

I must tell Christopher, he thought, and walked out through the bushes to signal him that he had found their quarry. In the distance he could see Harrison still walking toward the sketchy line of trees that marked the first little runnel. He shouted, "Hoy, Chris!" A couple of seconds later when the sound reached Harrison, he stopped and looked back. Thomas waved his stick, beckoning him to return. When he had reached within a pistol shot, Thomas called out, "Found their dens! Slain three as well!"

"What animal?" the carpenter asked in return.

Thomas leaned his stick against his chest and held his arms out wide with his hands open to show he had no idea what creature he had discovered.

The two men pushed through to the clearing and back to the three bodies.

"I've seen nothing so odd," the lad explained, "and what is so strange, they showed not the least fear of me. They made no bleat or call. They must be totally dumb or only make a mewing. Even after I killed one, the others sat there foolishly. I simply stepped to the next and fetched it a blow to the head too. I killed the third before the last went into its den. Have you seen any beast like it?"

"No, nothing. It's a strange creature for sure, but we might expect to see its like here. You say there was no fear in them. Then there is no other beast that eats them and causes them to be wary."

Harrison knelt and lifted the head of one of the animals. He turned it from side to side and saw that the dark eyes had gone dull with death. His hand slid to the neck, gripped the fur, and tested it as the lad had done. "It should tan well and be soft as that of a sheep or more so," he judged.

Thomas dropped to his knees beside him and felt the side and haunch of the body. "And the flesh," he asked, "would you say it will eat well?"

"Most likely. I would imagine it would be like goat. The young and the females will be the more tasty. Old males might not make such a good dish." Harrison rolled the animal on its back and ran his hand down its belly to find its gender. "Ha! Here!" he exclaimed. "Look here, it has a pouch!" His finger was inserted in the skin of the belly. He lifted it and leaned over to see what was inside. "Its kits are in there. Two of them," he explained, and leaned back to allow Thomas to see. "It has the nature of a great opossum or has a pocket like one," he added. "It's sure to be good to eat and we will soon be dressed in its skins."

The lad rose to his feet and declared, "Well, our needs are met! Let's pack them home."

Harrison got up slowly, still studying the bodies, and asked, "What shall we call them. They should have a name."

"Bears, I suppose. They look most like bears. I can think of nothing else."

"But they are not bears," Harrison objected.

"They are not like any other beast. It hasn't the look or size of an opossum or kangaroo. 'Bear' will do. You will know what I am speaking of, when I say 'bear.'"

Each shouldered his stick and one of the animals. With their free hands they carried the third animal between them, one holding a hind foot and one holding a forefoot. As they started to leave, a few of the beasts crawled from their holes and sat on their haunches and watched the men.

"Look at them," Thomas said with a toss of the head, "they don't fear us. They merely sit and watch like ninnies."

"Ha! We shall be back and cure them of watching," Harrison promised.

The men started awkwardly toward the fall with their loads.

At the shelter, the mate inspected the "bears" minutely, but the captain merely poked their bodies once and nodded and grunted a passing approval.

Thomas and Harrison then tied the carcasses to the limbs of trees with strips of flax leaves and skinned them. They sliced off strips of flesh and set aside the portion to be eaten that night. The excess they planned to preserve by smoking. Thomas flipped the hides onto a boulder and alternately inspected the fur and flesh sides of each one.

"Humph," the lad mumbled, "little fat, very little fat on them."

Mr. Morgen looked at him and asked, "What do you say? Will these skins tan well and serve to make our clothes?"

The crewman turned from the hides and, without the least deference in his expression, glanced at the officer. Aboard the barque, he had started as a green hand, instructed every minute by his watchmates as to which line to let go, which line to haul on, how to make seizings, and how to use the serving mallet. Now, he was at his old trade or nearly so. He had gone to the tanyard often and watched the process that would yield a decently cured skin. He reviewed the various stages in his mind. So much of the essential gear was wanting. They had explored the portions of the island that were most accessible and seen from a distance those which promised to have anything of use. They had no vats, no hogsheads, but a log might be hollowed. A tree trunk would serve for a beam and scrapers could be made from seashells. Bark and leaves from one of the trees might give a tea powerful enough to cure. They had seen black pools of water lying in low places between the stream and the foot of the mountain. He guessed they held some strong liquor leached from the forest litter. They might simply soak the hides in that natural decoction.

"Well," he answered the mate, "the skins are not thick. We must take care while beaming them. It looks as if they would taw well, but we have no alum. I would say to cure some quickly, slip the hair and brain-tan them. When they are dry we may smoke them for a few days. Then we may make our suits."

"And to make furs for our beds?" the mate asked. "Use a tanning bark?"

"Yes," he replied with the air of an expert and an arch look on his face. "They must be soaked in the water with a bark or leaves or anything that might prove better. In any case, it will take time, much time. First, we must find a log with a cavity or hollow one with fire."

THE WORK during the days and the long hours of twilight then settled into a routine. At the very first light Thomas or Harrison went to scan the bay and the horizon, and if no one had been on the plateau or working on the shore at the end of the day, the ritual was repeated at sunset. For the carpenter and Thomas, time was divided between dressing hides and gathering food. The skins were scraped and put to soak or stretched on frames. With that done, they were free to collect clams or fish.

The trap at the shallows was reset by the crewmen and one more built in another inlet. They were stronger and more effective, and so arranged that they required little work. Their narrowing walls led to a pocket. Thomas made a piece of netting from the twine of flax, laid it across the bottom, and tied it up to the fence of sticks that enclosed it. When the fish were driven in, they need only gather up the net and remove their prey.

On each return to the shelter from their tasks, the men carried back some firewood if they had an empty hand to hold it. They piled enough of the lighter and shorter limbs and driftwood inside the thatch wall to last for several rainy days. They were able to drag back larger pieces and the trunks of trees and left them outside to be used to heat the rocks in the cooking hole. The crewmen took the leftover ends and charcoal from those larger blazes to use inside the shelter.

Harrison fitted and tied some sticks together to form a crude, four-legged frame and then centered it over the stones of the hearth inside the shelter. Three feet above the flames it had a horizontal rack on which they placed the extra fish and strips of the "bears'" flesh. The food thus preserved was intended for the days of heavy rain when they could not go out or when their sources failed them. They preferred the smoked fish to the fresh, thinking it had better flavor and was more satisfying.

As Thomas had predicted, Tobit took charge of the fire and tended it most of the day. On some occasions, the mate joined him and they talked for hours while the crewmen worked the hides or gathered food. The captain managed to keep a few coals going until the evening meal, when he piled small wood on them and the hearth blazed up again. Thomas did not complain for it was a bother to make a new fire with the drill. In any case, someone had to sit by and place the raw food on the rack to be smoked. The chore defined the captain to the men as less than an able-bodied and effective officer. It suited the crewmen to have him there rather than outside, carping about how work was being carried on.

During the early evening, the four castaways sat on rock seats and faced the fire. Conversations began and trailed off. They all concerned the animals and fish, tanning the hides, the chances of rescue, and what might be happening back home. After each subject was taken up and left off, they were quiet for a while. They talked about what sort of jacket or coat was the best or the easiest to make. Harrison guessed it would require five or six hides to make a suit for each of them, depending on their finished sizes. One additional hide would be needed if they wished to make a hat or add a hood to their jackets when the weather grew colder.

While Harrison and the mate talked about the clothing and their other concerns, Thomas spoke hardly one word to their ten. For most of the night his terseness was pointed and almost sullen. From the day the wall was finished, it became a habit for each to sit on his chosen rock. Thomas had selected the one opposite the captain and moved it a little farther away from the fire than the others. He kept his hands busy, usually rolling flax fiber into twine or making the twine into cords. With his attention needed for his work, he could listen but it would be less noticeable that he spoke so little. When he rarely did glance between the legs of the rack and over the fire to the captain's side, the officer's face gave no hint as to what he was thinking. To Thomas, the captain's stolid expression was the facade of a man who believed he was infallible, and permitted no doubts from others in his mind. Tobit seemed to consider surliness and disaffection fit reactions to his position, always expected and even desired from his underlings. Such feelings arising in his men confirmed his authority and his proper use of it. Captain Tobit now treated Thomas as small beer. That pose made him proof against ill will. He could not be hurt by something he considered as a scant annoyance.

While there was still twilight, Thomas always went out and took a turn up and down the beach, sweeping his gaze north over the bay and what little he could see beyond each spit. Most of that view was to the leeward and any captain would near the island from the leeward or with the wind on the beam if he could, particularly at night. Fortunately most of the coast hidden from his view was on the windward side except for the shallows. Then he reasoned that any ship that approached meant to overhaul the island or to wood and water. The east coast and the shallows seen from offshore would look least fit for either purpose. Men on an approaching ship would see they must enter the bay to do those tasks well. He hoped that it would be so. On his return to the shelter, he saw that the little openings and slits in the drying thatch of the wall leaked points of orange light. At the top of the wall, the vent hole let out a band of illumination and a boil of heated air and thin smoke.

The men slept easier each night in the warmed shelter. If they found clumps of grass or dried moss in their travels they carried them back to make the beds softer. Harrison wove a mat to place over his nest of litter and found that it felt better against his naked skin. The next night they all had mats.

Mr. Morgen returned one afternoon with one of the "bears" and let it slip from his shoulder to the ground. He walked to the carpenter who was scraping a hide and held out his right hand to him. In his grip was an angular black rock the size of a fist. Harrison reached for it and examined it closely, rubbing its shiny facets with his finger.

He looked up to the mate and exclaimed, "It's glass! Aye, not clear but glass all the same."

"Volcano glass," the mate assured him. "I saw it lying in the stream when I went there to drink. We may discover more if we search the length of it."

Harrison turned to Thomas, handed the glass to him, and said, "We will make our tools from this if we can't reach the iron of the barque."

"I believe that is what we must do," the mate said. "I have climbed the bluff above where we struck and could see well into the water. There is no shape there that could be our barque, no buoy, not the least spar or plank. She must have fallen into a deeper part of the bay and carried all with her." He pointed to the dark lump and explained, "That will now be our knives and scrapers. We must make some axe or adze from it too. I will look for the ship again, though I have little hope it is where we may reach it."

Harrison turned the piece of glass over and over in his hand, trying different ways to grip it. He settled on one hold and looked about on the ground for something. Suddenly he reached into the bushes, picked up a small rock, and with it, he struck at the volcano glass twice. A chip flew off. He bent down to retrieve it and, rising up, tested its thin edge with a tapping finger. "Keen as any sheath knife I've seen," he observed and handed the chip to the young sailor.

Thomas held the sliver up to the sky. Along the thin edge it was transparent, but at its thicker part the light dimly passed through smoky gray bands. He also judged its sharpness by brushing his thumb across it and then by using it to cut a twig. The green wood was easily sliced in half.

"It's delicate and will break often, but we can make new ones, as many as we need," the carpenter declared. "If we can find large pieces, we can fit and bind them to hafts and they will be our axes."

The crewmen had been scraping skins for an hour the next morning when the officers exited from the shelter and watched them at their work. The captain inspected a nearly finished skin, turning it over and back again and feeling its softness. At length he muttered grudging approval as he left and walked out toward the beach.

Mr. Morgen waved his stick and announced, "I'm going to bring back another one of the bears. You look to the fire. You have enough to keep you busy until I return." He then marched out to join the captain.

"Oh, yes, we can't know what to do without him," Thomas sneered when the officer had left. "Ha! The work will go faster while he is away. We should be planning our escape and building our boat, but he and old Tobit can only wander about on the plateau whenever they fancy. What do you say, Chips?"

"Everything in good time, lad. You see how our situation here has changed in the days we have been here. We washed ashore naked and hurt. Now our wants have been met. Soon we shall fit ourselves with clothes and sleep under furs, then we will take up the task of building our boat."

"We should begin the boat now," the lad argued. "The sooner we start, the sooner we will be on our way home."

"Patience, patience. We have been here but a little while, and we have much to think of before we make a boat or a canoe. We will need rope and small stuff and something that will hold our water. If nothing else offers, then these skins must serve for sails. No, we must not be in haste, lad. We must consider all our needs closely. Each part of our boat must be made with care, for once we set off to the leeward, there will be no returning. We may be able to sail to the windward, but with no compass or naught else, how could we ever find this island again?"

"Tobit could do something other than wander about. What has he been doing up there these last days?"

Harrison shrugged his shoulders and replied, "I can't say. He doesn't confide in me."

"We'd best see what he's about," Thomas warned. "He should be doing something to help us from this island. Who knows what he may be thinking about."

Harrison stopped scraping the pelt lying on the log before him and arched his back to relieve his cramped muscles. "A little caution on our part may be in order," he said. "Our captain has changed some since we have landed here. Yes, a little caution to see if some disorder works on his mind."

A WEEK LATER, Thomas and the carpenter worked dressed hides over the end of a stump until they were dry. They placed them beneath a teepee of green boughs where they were smoked for a few days. Then, Harrison fitted the first of the cured hides around Thomas's waist and legs and marked out the shapes with the charred end of a stick. With a sliver of glass, he carefully cut along the black lines. The mate and Thomas took the cut sections of leather and sat in front of the shelter and each punched holes in their edges with the sharpened end of a bird bone.

"A tolerable fit," Thomas declared after he slipped on his new clothes. He tied the drawstring that served as belt and hunched and dropped his shoulders several times to accustom his back to the feel of the jacket.

Harrison had sewn the pieces together temporarily with flax thread and, his latest accomplishment, a carefully crafted bone needle. Thomas laced the jacket up with thongs while he walked about. The mate and carpenter halted the lad and picked and tugged at the seams, inspecting the fit. As Thomas was the largest of the castaways, Harrison planned to use his suit as a rough pattern and reduce it for the others.

"We can make buttons of wood or bone," a pleased Harrison explained, "and when it turns colder, we will attach the hood just here. That will make it snug for the chill weather. Let's take it off and I will lay out the next."

The mate watched Thomas slip off the garment and then tossed one of the baskets toward him. "There is no need for you to be idle. Go gather our supper," he ordered.

Thomas glanced at the basket and slowly bent over to pick it up. He turned and walked out to the beach. For a minute he halted to search the sea and the sky, then wandered westward to the clam bed. He never intended to wade into that cold water. There was plenty for their supper, and he and Christopher planned to go to the shallows for fish the next day. He knew the mate had given him the order simply to see him obey.

"Blast him!" he said aloud. The words had slipped out. He never meant to speak them and was surprised by their sounds. "Well, blast him!" he repeated, then added, "And damn old Tobit for good measure."

He approached the stick he had placed to mark the limit of the last harvest of clams. The tide was on the flood. It made little sense to try for the clams, he thought, and pitched the basket aside. Then he sat on the beach and watched each wave tumble up the slant of the shore, slow, and slide back under the next rush of water. He stretched out to lie there, and the dark, sun-warmed cinders yielded, conformed to his bare back. Everything around him was a contrast to the fog and the mist on the sealing grounds. Though naked, he was warm lying there. The sky was blue and not the continual gray of the islands to the south. There were no trees on Macquarie or even a bush, but here behind him on the bluff, a light wind chaffered through the forest. In the other direction were the cyclic, lulling hisses of the waves as they spent their last energy in spreading up the shore.

Indeed, their little company had landed on a fortunate island and could not have wished for a better refuge. It was favored with green mountains, the grassland, the shallows, and would provide all the food they would ever need. It was only marred by the presence of the mate and Tobit who fed on authority and had a deep desire to order others about. They conceived a world forever divided between the owners and officers and all those who had no fortune and would never, as they always predicted, gain any. From the first day of the voyage, he had witnessed how the captain and mate paced the deck, thrusting tight-jawed and humorless faces to the wind, and then posed at the weather rail in studied reserve, well aware that the crew watched them with glances that never quite centered on their persons. The officers labored at their footing with efforts that became obvious and even ludicrous when Jack aped them in the fo'c's'le. Jack had a knack of parading around with his chin up and clasping his hands behind his back that brought howls from the watch. The lascars, barred from comprehending many of the jokes by their scant English, had broad grins on their dark faces the minute Jack pulled his hat low on his forehead and practiced Tobit's waddle. Thomas even snickered aloud when he remembered the deft mimicry his shipmate made of Mr. Morgen trying to keep his cigar lit in a half-gale. They had all seen the mate make three trips to the galley to relight it. After the last lighting, he returned to his post at the weather rail with a hand cupped to protect the smoldering tip. Jack re-enacted all the mate's contortions in protecting the cigar. The officer had then unwittingly turned to the windward, and the cigar blossomed over his face. Every man on deck had turned his back and shaken with silent laughter as the leaves of tobacco flew over the far rail and disappeared downwind. The mate was perplexed for a moment then discovered a brace not set to his liking and sent men to round it in. Jack repeated the mate's look of damaged dignity dozen of times, yet it remained a favorite with the crew.

Perspiration beaded on Thomas's forehead and arms. He sat up. Down the beach, a clot of rockweed rolling in the edge of the surf, and he got to his feet to inspect it. It had a few sticks in it but nothing he had hoped to find. He paced farther west at the highest reach of the waves. One larger than usual flowed around his feet, and, feeling the cold water, he looked down as the foam drained away. In the loose cinders, he discovered the gibbous back of a drab shell. It was over five inches across, larger than any of the clams they had gathered. The color of the convex surface closely matched that of the beach, making it barely detectable. He stared at it for a moment. A shell of that size would make a useful container, a dish, or a tool they could use to dig or scrape. He leaned over and picked it out of the sand and cinders. A line of holes ran along one edge.

Ha! A sea ear, Thomas thought, just like those they had gathered at Dusky Sound. He turned the shell about to look into its hollow. Blue and blue-green reflections met his eyes. Opalescent, jewel-like patterns covered the interior. There was a depth to them, with one set before another, and the illusion of a space between each. He imagined he could see within the wall of the shell itself. One sample in his hand implied that more sea ears were clasped to the rocks at the far end of the bay. It was their habit to live and thrive under crashing waves and not in sheltered places. Current and waves had carried the shell some miles from where it had lived. On calmer days at ebb tides they might go to those rocks and, with a bone or stick, lever off a new food. The empty shells would become bowls to hold their meals, and with them, they could scrape out the charred wood from a log when the time came to make a canoe. A fortunate wave had washed that shell to his feet. It was a great find, and he dropped it into his basket.

Whitecaps were speckling the surface of the bay. He scanned it and the farthest edge of the sea. There was nothing there, no faint outline barely darker than the haze kicked up from the waves by the wind. The chance of meeting with an errant whaler or sealer was nearly beyond the limits of hope. They would have to make for the Middle Island and reach it on their own. Harrison's child-like belief that they might fetch Tovy Poenamoo in a few days, he suspected, was indulged in for his benefit, for anyone with the least mother wit would know better. If he were in Stonington he would sail a whaleboat to New York and back and think little of it. But even where they now were, far above the rookeries, the sea rarely had its smoother hours. To be out on its pitching swells for days and nights, bailing water from a small boat was an ominous prospect. The trip to the Middle Island loomed more perilous as he mulled it over and listed the things that might go awry. Their little vessel would be no more than a chip of wood, a mote lost amid the patches of foam scudding before the wind. They might be overset. They could be blown off course, or that wind might make against them until they died from thirst and their bodies lay lifeless in the bottom of their crude vessel. If they meant to leave the island, they had to risk death. To remain there was no better than banishment, albeit a secure one with all their wants, save consort with others, met with a little labor. The events of the world would pass, a new Bonaparte might arise, America might have another war with England or the Algerines. And all the while they would be living a dull existence on a speck of land far away from a course traveled by a ship of any fishery or the John Company. That was their choice: to sail off for the Middle Island in a rude craft or live most or all of their lives as unwilling hermits.

Thomas picked up the basket and started west, thinking it was better that he stayed out on the shore. Walking on the beach and searching the horizon appealed to him more than returning to the uneasy company of the officers. They would not abandon their vanity and be mates, even in the calamity of shipwreck, nor would he want them to do so. True mates were men who shared each other's fortunes and misfortunes for months and years. True mates were those who, once in the safety and snugness of taverns, relived all their shared labor and peril, raised their glasses to each other in rough, partially concealed regard, and entertained each other with lies no one was expected to believe. Those who lived in the cabin aft could not do that. They were too conscious of their self-made dignity, reveled in command, and could never comfortably divide their last biscuit with someone to whom they felt vastly superior. Where he and Christopher were mates, the officers could only be allies, joined by the need to present a seamless wall of command to the men forward.

Thought after thought poured through his mind as he walked into the wind. He considered their situation, the great boon the island was to them, supplying such a wealth of things, yet it was no less than their prison. Suddenly, he stopped when he realized he was out on the bar that confined the lake and had crossed its outlet to the bay without noticing. Hundreds of water birds were resting on its surface, and more were constantly turning in wide circles in the air, flaring their wings to land, or making flapping runs to get airborne.

Thomas watched them. Snares or arrows, he pondered. How could they best be taken? A squad of ducks waggled their tails and waddled along the inner shore of the bar. A net supported on poles above bait of some sort and dropped at the proper moment might trap a brace or two. If the birds learned to avoid the net where it was set up, it could be moved to a new place so they might have plenty of the fowl to eat until the day the birds took it into their heads to quit the island.

He paced again along the top of the bar. Birds standing in his path and those swimming near the shore moved cautiously away as he advanced westward. When he reached the wide field of flax at the end of the lake, he turned and walked between the edge of the water and the border of smaller plants. There were no trees, bushes, or other sorts of plants growing there, thus it was a pure stand of flax that extended around the inland shore almost to the fall. Between the plants and the edge of the water, the damp earth was all patterned with the webbed prints of the ducks and their droppings. Feathers and bits of down were trampled into the wetter portions and caught between the leaves of the flax.

Thomas continued on, watching for places where they might set up a weighted net and hide in the plants. From such places they might watch and release the cords when the ducks and geese were enticed under the net. Simple, he said to himself, a simple task anyone could manage, but one they must do soon for the fowl might not stay much longer. He wandered along that sloping strip of wet earth farther than he had intended. Flecks of bright green on the shore near the flax plants drew him farther ahead. They resolved themselves into heart-shaped leaves at a distance of twenty paces. He approached, leaned over to pick one and held it by its thin stem. For a moment he contemplated the familiar outline and color. Then he kneeled and dug his fingers into the soil. He scooped up wads of it and cast them aside as he searched for the tuber he suspected was the source of the leaves. His probing fingers found one swollen root the length of his hand and of a thickness not quite circled with thumb and forefinger. Thomas washed it in the water of the lake and held it in his dripping hand. His thumbnail scratched the thin skin and under his nose it had an earthy, pleasant smell that recalled markets crowded with baskets humped with turnips, potatoes, and beets just brought in from the farms. He broke it in half and nibbled its white flesh. A pleasant taste, he thought, just the thing for a garden sauce to relieve their steady diet of fish, clams, and roasted meat. There were many leaves scattered across the band of soil, and in all he dug up seven of the thick roots and dropped them into his basket. Having found something better than a few clams, he retraced his steps back to the bay. With the wind at his back, he returned along the beach to the shelter.

"No clams! You've brought no clams!" Mr. Morgen barked out when the empty shell and tubers rolled from the basket onto the ground.

The captain stepped forward, held up his open left hand to quiet the mate and extended his right to the young sailor. Thomas read his meaning, reached down, picked up the root he had bitten, and handed it to him. The officer turned the object over and over in his hands as he moved to the doorway to view it in better light. He gave a grunt of approval every few breaths, and an expression, grading into a smile, played across his face for a second or two. "Ah, I see you have tasted it?" he asked, pointing to the bitten end. "Do you think it is poison?"

"The taste is good and one I know," Thomas replied, "and I'm still alive, not even ill. It's sort of a sweet potato. The leaves are near the same."

"And where did you discover them?" the mate broke in.

"At the far end of the lake between the flax and the water," he answered, "and the earshell washed up on the beach just down a-ways."

Harrison was holding the shell and admiring the colors in its hollow. "A fortunate find for us. Something more to add to the larder," he said, glancing over at the potato. "The island yields all for our needs."

"Let's see if it yields a boat for our escape," Thomas muttered. He looked at Tobit and the mate, but they were inspecting the tubers and did not hear, or perhaps they had no wish to hear his remark.

"How many plants are there by the lake?" the carpenter inquired. "Enough to feed us all?"

Thomas answered thoughtfully, "It's hard to say. I can only see leaves and vines scattered about, but I would guess upwards of two score."

"We could plant them all about and have enough to eat every day and more," Harrison proposed. "If they thrive on that end of the lake, they should grow on its shore everywhere. The soil is rich and fine, and the water is warm. The plants must need warmth as they do in the West Indies."

"Aye, that makes good sense, else they would have covered the island had there been heat enough," Mr. Morgen added.

"There is no soil near the bottom of the falls," Harrison explained. "They cannot spread in that direction, and the waves casting far up on the bar make it too salt for anything to sprout there. Thus they are held to the far end of the lake."

"Yes, yes, yes!" the captain said in a voice far more buoyant than his usual grumble. He held the potato out before him and ordered,

"We must gather them up and spread them about, plant them immediately. It is a great addition to our chief dependence, the flesh of the 'bears' and fish. This is the sign, the key to it all!" With a few quick steps he was through the opening and on his way out to the beach.

The others were taken aback by Tobit's sudden burst of energy, and it was seconds before they moved to follow him.

"The baskets!" the mate snapped to Thomas and the carpenter, and then exited after the captain.

The crewmen picked up the containers and left the shelter.

Captain Tobit led the castaways along the bar, not in his old lobbering walk, but in a spirited stride that took him to the end of the lake before the others. He wheeled to the south past the bunches of flax bowing and fluttering in the sea breeze, and came to the leaves that had attracted Thomas and to the holes the lad had dug in the shore.

"We thank Thee, oh Lord. Yes, yes, we thank Thee," he mumbled as he paced around and inspected the vines on the earth. "Mr. Morgen!" the captain commanded when the mate arrived, "Have the men dig the potatoes with care. Have them break off the roots and plant them where there are now none. Then do the same with the vines." The captain fussed about the men as they worked, instructing them in an almost pleasant voice where to place each bit of root and how deep to set it. Once all the better parts of that shore were planted, he had the crewmen gather the remaining vines and follow him to the opposite end of the lake near its outlet. They set them out there in the same careful manner.

When the planting was finished and given the captain's approval, the men started for home, walking in the light of the sun that was halfway to the horizon.

Thomas kept his eyes on the officers walking ahead to be sure they were beyond the sound of his voice and asked the carpenter, "Isn't it peculiar, Christopher? Has old Tobit ever gone at anything like this, hip and thigh, lest it was something in which he saw a fair gain?"

"No, lad," Harrison answered, "but I think he sees the value of the potatoes. They are for all our good. They will add to our meals and they are said to cure the scurvy. We will have to carry some vittles like them when we leave the island."

"Is that what he's truly thinking of? I wonder. If half the plants we set out yield but two or three potatoes, we will have enough for the Boston market for a month. Once all our clothes are made, we can begin our boat, but I'll wager he will put it off with some excuse. He seems to be thinking of something other than our escape from here."

"Perhaps he believes his prayers will bring a ship to this island and we will be saved the labor of building a boat and the trouble of sailing it to Tovy Poenamoo."

"Aye, he overprizes his religion. Prayers will bring him nothing but sore knees. His Sunday rants aboard the barque didn't prevent us from striking on the rocks, and much good it did that poor crew of swearers."

"Ah, patience my boy. If we rush off in a weakly-built boat, we put ourselves in needless danger, and we may miss any ship that might call in the next month or two. We can wait that long and then, if none appear, why then we will have a well-found boat for our escape."

"Christopher, sometimes I think you have the mind of a child. Old Tobit brought us to this pass. What other disasters might he lead us into? What is he thinking of when he stares into the fire at night? There is something in that look he gives me that I don't like."

"Perhaps he dwells on how you defied him on that first day ashore. That's likely not happened to him before. He is vain and forgiveness will come slowly from such a man." Harrison put his hand on the lad's shoulder and said earnestly, "But it will come in time. Do your duty and obey him and Mr. Morgen in everything. He is a religious man and will see forgiveness is what he must allow you in the end."

Thomas looked aside to the carpenter and shook his head and replied, "You are a child. He's a man taken with his importance and mean with greed, and you don't want to see it."

CHAPTER 10

THE CAPTAIN'S trousers were the first to be completed and ready to wear, but there was something amiss the minute he slipped them on. Harrison had overestimated the material needed to cover his backside, and had cut the seat so full it hung in the rear like a pouch. Tobit was unaware of the poor fit, being wholly intent on tying the drawstring to prevent the trousers from falling. He tried pulling the waistband above his paunch, but there wasn't room enough in the crotch to allow that. Even with the drawstring taut and knotted, they slipped a little at each step, and the captain had to grasp them with both hands and wriggle them back up. For the rest of the day, he coped with the problem. Thomas and the carpenter looked away when they could not repress their smirks.

Thomas leaned toward Harrison and whispered, "It's high time for him to furl his mizzen topsail. The only wind that sail will catch is from his arse."

The carpenter doubled over and his back pulsed with suppressed laughter. He came back up hawking for air. "Thomas," he gasped, "you could ship for a clown. . . . Don't say more or I will choke."

The lad ignored Harrison's caution and frowning with a feigned concern added, "I see he's coming about on the larboard tack. Watch that. . . . Ach! He's missed his stays. See how that sail has gone ashiver . . . or is it just another one of his great farts? Ho, there, Mr. Wilson, send your topmen aloft to take it in!"

Harrison bolted for the beach, holding his hand to his face to hide his grin.

"What's the matter with him?" the mate asked as he watched the carpenter dive through the bushes and trees toward the beach.

Thomas turned to Mr. Morgen with an opened-eyed look of innocence. He circled his stomach with his right hand and muttered, "Ah, a little of the flux, I think."

The mate looked at the swaying bushes Harrison had just slipped past and shook his head, nonplussed.

The next day the captain ordered the carpenter to make a pair of galluses. This he did in less than an hour, cutting two straps, sewing them to the rear of Tobit's trousers, and then rigging them in front with small wooden toggles neat as a pair of topsail sheets.

For the next two weeks, it rained off and on, and the castaways' lives were ordered by the weather. Plans for the day's labor were made each morning after consulting the look of the sky. Low, dark clouds moving in swiftly meant they would have to keep close to the shelter. On fairer days, the officers climbed to the grassland in the morning and returned in the afternoon with another slain "bear." Thomas and Harrison were sent to work the traps, to clam, or to search for sea ears at the far end of the island. Rain, at least the heaviest downpours, kept them confined to the rock overhang, but there was enough to occupy them in the daylight hours. Hides had to be beamed and stretched. The thatch, drying to a fraction of its bulk, had to be retied with more added to make up for the shrinkage. Though they were constantly dressing hides or walking the length of the island to gather eggs or fish, it was becoming a more comfortable existence. Their suits of hide conformed by wear to a good fit and made the nights lying in their beds far more bearable. Harrison sorted through the scraps of hide one day and cut and sewed a pair of loose boots for each man to wear while sleeping. With the boots on their feet and their knees drawn up, they were warm enough to dream away the night almost without waking.

During the wetter days, they all sat under the overhang just outside the thatch wall, scraping a hide or making twine as they watched the rain pelt the earth and spill in streamlets from the edge of the limestone. It was cozy with the fire blazing up and warming them as they worked. Tobit sat on his rock, eyes closed and his fingers interlaced across the middle of his belly. The only excursions the crewmen made on those slaty, rainy days were to the shore of the bay to look for the sails of a ship. But they were only short dartings out past the trees where they usually saw the bay and all but the nearer part of the beach hidden in a steady rainfall. Their hide suits absorbed water readily, and it required nearly an hour standing and turning before the fire to dry them.

Thomas began weaving a net with which he planned to snare the fowl around the lake. Harrison scraped flax leaves and rolled the fiber into twine, then Thomas took it from him and wound it around a short stick. He started his mesh from a thin sapling stripped of branches and mounted across two uprights. The lad used the width of his hand as a gauge and worked his way back and forth along the stick, tying each loop of the cord with a sheet bend. He made enough in two hours to serve as a proper trap and then took the net from its supports and laid it on the ground.

"There, saplings all around, making a frame to keep it taut and give it weight. Two sticks will hold up one side and when we pull them out at the proper instant, we will have a fat duck or two to put into the cooking hole," Thomas said proudly.

"Ahh, a bird steamed to tenderness and full of juice," the mate muttered and slid his tongue along his upper lip. "These animals, these 'bears' are too lean for my taste. Give me a fat goose or duck and I'll strip its bones. Ha!"

The carpenter coiled his last length of twine, inspecting each fake as he gave it an adroit twist to make it hang neatly in his hand. The fire had dwindled, and the mate pushed the smoldering ends of the limbs onto the center of the radiant coals. He leaned back from the heat and smoke as he added more sticks into selected gaps. Short, wavering flames flashed over the new wood, consumed the rising smudge, and burst into a tall blaze. Brighter light suddenly reflected from their faces and the drying thatch.

Thomas kneeled and rolled the finished mesh around the sapling, then stowed it next to the wall. The next fair day would be soon enough to find and cut his other poles, he reasoned. Let it rest there until the sun shines.

The growing light of the next morning entered through the smoke hole and a few slits in the thatch, and its brightness and hue were hints to the castaways that the dark ceiling of clouds had broken. They filed out to the shore and saw that it was true. The rain had ceased in the night and the dawn presented a sky with only an afterguard of tattered clouds drifting northeast.

Mr. Morgen eyed the surface of the bay and the horizon, but as on all the mornings and evenings before, there was no ship within the spits and no sail beyond them. He turned to the crewmen. "See to the traps," he ordered. "This weather might have damaged them."

Thomas and Harrison gathered up their baskets and began their trip along the shore in an unhurried pace. A visit to the shallows was a respite from hours of bending over dressing hides or scraping flax, and they also looked forward to each foray to any place on the island. Lackluster days of rain had, without their perceiving it, dulled their thoughts and movements. Their spirits were soon lifted when the edge of the sun took its first bite above the horizon and a burst of clean light flooded across the bay. The last of the night's rain, beaded on leaves ahead of them, caught some morning rays and gave random glints as the men, with renewed energy, walked past. Behind them on the slopes of the peaks, low-angled beams of the sun lighted the wisps of vapor lingering just above the washed green.

At the shallows they found that the traps had suffered little damage from the wind which had accompanied the rain, and the only noticeable change on that side of the island was some knots of rockweed that had washed ashore. They pulled them apart and found a few sticks they could use to repair the traps, but nothing that had not grown on or about the island. Harrison and Thomas began their ritual by removing their trousers and wading in at the open end of one snare. They drove ahead slapping the surface of the water, kicking up clouds of fine sand with their feet along the bottom, and herding the fish through the slot where the fences met. Once the prey swam through that opening, they were in the small net, which the men raised and emptied into a basket. After their third sweep of the second trap, they looked into the mesh where they expected to see their catch, but the effort had yielded nothing.

"Well, that was a waterhaul," Thomas complained.

"We have over a score, laddie. We have all we shall get today. Another time. Another time."

Each man skimmed the water from his buttocks and legs and pulled his trousers on. With baskets in hand, they faced into the wind and trudged through the field of dunes to the bay. Their pace along its shore was leisurely. Neither could recall any chore that needed their prompt return. They often turned aside, poking into the bushes and trees at the foot of the bluff when something caught their eyes that might prove useful or edible. Both men halted, dropped their baskets of fish, then meandered out to where the waves thinned and sank away. Their feet pressed into the surface of the beach, came up specked with the dark cinders, and then were splashed clean by the lip of the next slowing wave. They roved in unhurried, whimsied steps, knowing that the labor needed for each day's living was lessening. A warm sun now shone on their backs, and the sea breeze tossed the hair of their heads about. Except for a dribbling of clouds at its joining with the northern horizon, the sky was a clean, limitless blue. Along the length of the beach, birds swooped and soared above the froth of the spreading waves.

To the two men, the aspect of their island had altered. It was no longer a small, fortunate refuge, but a portion of the globe that had not been peopled, an unclaimed piece of earth clothed in rich green. The shoreline sweeping into the distance, the leaves of the trees shivering in the sea wind, and the waves overriding waves onto the beach were evidences of how the whole of the planet had appeared when newly formed. To be the first men to behold it, to wander its unmarred, primal earth, and to rest at will under its arbors was to feel completeness, a longing gratified though not wholly grasped. They recognized this was the undeniable call of empty and unknown lands, one never to be framed in words and imparted to others. The castaways savored a fragile sweetness in each pace they made on the arcing shore, an amalgam of soft air, the scent of wet greenery, and the quality and angle of the light. It was a perfect moment of their existence they at once kenned and would never forget.

They became undiminished boys again and started weaving chases after each other with their bare feet splashing through the skims of the waves and each one shouting twits to the other. With both hands, one scooped up water again and again, flinging it at the one ahead. The other just as often turned and surprised his pursuer with the same dash. Suddenly, by unspoken agreement, Thomas and Harrison halted to recover from their running. They panted and viewed the island as the drops of seawater dribbled from their faces and beards. The distant peaks under their faint blue haze were limned against the sky. It was all fixed in their memories in its sunlit detail. What a favored place, Thomas thought, what a land of Cockaigne that could, from its peaks and shores, fill all the needs of a man.

The two retrieved their loads of fish and started off once more, wandering on until they were within a quarter of a mile of the shelter.

"Wood!" the carpenter declared suddenly and turned up the beach to the trees.

All the fuel lying on the beach near the rock overhang had been gathered for their fires, and it now had to be searched out farther away in places between rocks and under trees. The men left their baskets and pressed their way between the trees to break off dead limbs or find driftwood that been cast farther up. Each one picked an opening and snaked out the deadwood, dropped it, and returned for more. The larger pieces were prizes to be dragged home, for once ignited they smoldered all night and in the morning could be puffed into a blaze again with ease.

"Ahaaa!" Thomas shouted.

When no other word followed, Harrison asked, "What have you there?"

"Ha, come and see," Thomas called back.

The carpenter pushed his way into the trees again and found the lad freeing a log from the leaves and litter. It looked as if it had been thrown up against the rocks before the bushes and trees had grown to any size. "Oh, way too large, "Harrison said abruptly. "It's upwards of two foot through and far too heavy to move."

"Well, certainly to take for the fire. But I didn't mean that," he explained with a grin. "Look, it's four fathom long, straight, and not a limb anywhere."

"Ah, for a canoe you mean! Yes, it would serve if there is no rot or split on the underside."

They broke off branches that were in their way and leveled the sand and cinders on the bay side of the log. With limbs selected to use as levers and fulcrums, they rolled the bole over inch by inch. Harrison hammered the sides of the log with his makeshift lever and declared, "Sound wood all through, mate, and free of splits."

Thomas hopped onto the log and gestured with his hands while he spoke. "Burning out the center will reduce the weight by three quarters," he declared. "Then we can float it right before the shelter. We bind two boomkins athwart it here and fix a spar at their ends and she will carry a sail."

"Step the mast about here," Harrison broke in, pointing to a spot on the log, "and then we can move it fore and aft till she has the proper steerage."

Thomas turned to his mate, and, with a smile, asked, "What do you say, Chips? A month and she floats on the bay all rigged and ready to stand for the Middle Island?"

Harrison was near the center of the log, and he let his gaze range along its length several times, judging its potential, picturing in turn each step required to create the vessel they needed. Then he dropped to his knees and smoothed the wood with his hands, as a sculptor would feel his stone. Several minutes passed before he stood up and placed a foot on its side. Then, with one short nod, he murmured, "Perhaps, lad, with a sail made of flax leaves or skins, it might be ready then, but I doubt it. We must remember the fall season will be here soon, and we know what that means. Even in a proper, decked boat it would be a risk in that season if early storms came upon us. We should leave next month or must wait till November."

"But we will have spent the best part of a year on the isle by then," the lad objected. "Couldn't it be ready in one month, if we worked every hour of daylight and made our lines by the fire at night?"

The carpenter studied the log again, trying to envision the work required to transform it into a tractable craft. "Oh, Thomas, think of all there is to do. How are we to fasten the booms securely? And how will we fix a rudder to it?" he asked. "Those are things that will take much time. The sail, the thimbles, some sort of butts for our water will have to be devised. There is so much to make, and we have no tools save volcano glass and fire. It will be difficult to do in two months. But we could start a-building, and when the weather becomes better, we will have a fine canoe with everything properly made."

"Well, come then," the lad urged. "Let's show the mate and the old pelican this log. I doubt we will find better around the whole of the island."

THE CAPTAIN stood at one end of the log, dull-eyed and slowly pushing out his lower lip in doubt. The mate showed more interest, walking its full length and tapping it with a length of driftwood.

"Yes, sound enough," the mate declared, "though it could be larger."

"Aye, sir, but we have found none," Harrison replied.

Mr. Morgen then muttered, "Well, we will keep this one in mind and hope to discover one longer and with more girth."

"The two of us could just roll this one," Thomas complained. "If it were any larger, we might as well try to launch a first rate."

The mate extended his arms, each pointing to an end of the log and said, "There are four of us. See how cramped we will be."

"Then two hulls!" Thomas promptly suggested. "We hollow two

and lash them side by side four or five feet asunder. Then we shall have all the room needed."

"Let us begin to hollow this one," the carpenter proposed, "then if we discover better, then nothing will be lost but a little time spent burning it out."

Captain Tobit suddenly broke in, "Yes! That is quite the point. Time will be lost. Before we turn a hand to this, we must move ourselves and all to the plateau."

Thomas and Harrison turned and looked at each other. The young sailor's mouth hung half open as he stared at his mate.

"Move, sir? Build another home so far away?" Harrison asked. "But why?"

"We have found no danger from within the island. Well and good," the captain explained, "but now we must be wary of a danger from without."

"Danger!" Thomas blurted out. "What danger?"

"Yes," Tobit continued in what seemed a rehearsed speech. "Yes, at any time convicts may stretch over to this island from Botany Bay. They have done it . . . seized ships and even got to the Indies. They are men who have given themselves over to every wickedness and crime, thieves of every stripe, wastrels, murderers!"

Thomas recovered enough to protest. "Then we must leave as soon as possible," he reasoned. "We can be gone from here in a few weeks. Here is the means, here before us." He lifted his right foot and planted it on the log.

The captain was warming to his subject, and, not having finished his speech, ignored the young sailor. "Apostates," he continued. "Godless creatures, worse than the heathen who have never heard the word, for those fallen ones have received the Light yet abjure it. They are doubly damned. If they discover us, they will either slay us or force us to their evil habits. Aye, take us on board and raise the black flag! One morning we may wake to find they have landed in the night, and we must face these convicts, men armed with muskets and hangers. How will we defend ourselves then? Tell me?"

"There will be no need if we are gone from here," Thomas replied, stomping his foot on the log.

"We shall build a new shelter up there where it cannot be seen," Tobit announced. "It will be a safe haven the criminals will not suspect is there, if they see no mark of us on the shore. A watch set upon that height can spy a sail far sooner than one here. When we are safe at night and can have warning by day, then we will commence work on a vessel. You hear me!" The officer's usual pallor was blotched with red. He leaned toward the others and in a monishing whisper added, "Who knows what terrible evil may approach from the sea?" He drew a deep breath and straightened his body. Looking at the men through narrowed eyes, he warned, "They are scoundrels who have known every vice and crime. Ah! Some may have signed the devil's book and they are loose in these seas!" When he finished his last remark, his jaw set firmly as if he had recited an unassailable article of faith and would receive a chorus of amens. He wheeled about and picked his way through the trees to the beach.

Mr. Morgen looked at the crewmen, banged the log once again with his stick, and tossed it to the earth as his final comment. Then he followed the captain.

"Damn him!" Thomas snorted. "Damn him! Damn that fool. With a little mummery he intends to keep us on this island for months more. I do believe he takes delight in chafing us. Building a new home far up there will take the best part of three weeks. We must carry all the thatch and sticks up or find some other supply. Then by the time we finish our canoe, it will be too late to leave. The chancy weather will be upon us."

"But look, that will be no tragedy," the carpenter objected. "What are a few more months' delay if we arrive in Tovy Poenamoo safely? Perhaps his words are sound warning. Perhaps you and I are too trusting. We were given no leave to go ashore in Van Diemen's. We don't know how vile these men may be, and all the captain warns us of may be true. How could we face these convicts if they are armed? If they land and learn we were here, they might choose to stay and pursue us. Then we could only hide somewhere on the island and hope they grew tired and decided to leave."

"I might believe him," Thomas growled, "if he didn't speak it all in such a passion."

"It's his way of thinking. He has a suspicious nature and can see evil where we do not. His age makes him so and perhaps his long service as a parson. It might well be we have been fortunate that none of the convicts have arrived here thus far."

Thomas sat on the log and ran his hands over its surface at his right and left. It had been stripped of its bark by a long rolling in the sea and surf. "I can see it," he said, "all rigged with sail, water skins, oars, all that we need. Ha! I tell you, Chips, I am ready to set up for myself on this island and build my own canoe."

"That would be a challenge he could not resist, an opposition he must surely meet and overcome. No, no, the captain will have his way. He and the mate will break up what you make until he decides it is time. A boat will be built when he orders it to be done and not before."

"Then you and I must join together to fight them and escape from here. He may never wish to leave!"

Harrison sat beside Thomas. "Must we waste our time in battling them?" he pleaded. "One of us would have to be awake at night. We could not separate lest they attack our canoe. How could we hide our fires or go about to gather flax and wood to build with? How could we feed ourselves? No, we'd best make a canoe all together, even if it is a few months later. Then they could not accuse us of mutiny. Be patient until the new home is finished in a few weeks. There is small chance a ship calling here will be manned by Botany Bay convicts, and should they come to wood and water, they will not spend time searching about. They want nothing more than to speed away from New Holland, and we will be safe up there on the plateau. But if we are still here on this beach and they find signs of us, come upon us unawares, they will want our skill to sail and to set their course. If we refuse, they will kill us to make sure no one learns anything of their strength or that they called here. They may be evil, but they are clever, sly as any man or beast."

Thomas shook his head and growled, "Wasted time! It will all be wasted time!"

"Not at all. It may be that some whaler or sealer will call here while we are a-building our new home and the canoe. I would rather wait out the winter weather and hope for rescue than make a mad-brained dash too soon." Harrison clapped his hand on his mate's shoulder and asked, "There, am I right? Have I convinced you it is best we obey Tobit and join our efforts?"

Thomas remained quiet for a minute and then hammered his fist on the log. He rose to his feet and slowly nodded his head. With measured words he said, "Perhaps you are right for now, but we must begin the canoe as soon as the new shelter is built. I will not suffer another delay."

"Nor I. He cannot refuse after we are situated up there. If he does, then he is surely moonstruck. Come, we have our wood to fetch home."

MR. MORGEN and the captain climbed the limestone tiers the next day, intent on finding a hidden and suitable site for the new home. From the top of the fall, they set off to follow the course of the stream up to its source at the foot of the small volcano.

"I want the hut well hidden in the trees on one side or the other of this branch and near enough that we may bathe and go for water with ease," Tobit said.

The west bank of the stream was a slope of boulders that had tumbled down from the high peak edging the plateau there. Between the huge rocks were pools of dark, motionless water with surfaces patterned with fallen leaves. Higher up, the few other open spaces were aisles between the moss-covered trunks of the trees with an understory of tall ferns. Overhead, a dense canopy of leaves admitted a filtered, slightly green-hued light. A few narrow rays of the sun broke through the trees, and their entire paths from the source above were made visible by the misty content of the air. The openings in the leaves admitting them widened and narrowed by the breeze and the light played across the rocks and fronds. They could see there was no level site for a hut there and no warming sunlight for them in the morning. The officers waded out of the stream and onto the east bank, continuing their search along the edge of the open grassland where walking was easier and forays could be made in at places that appeared suitable. They moved south and, after many tries, entered the border of trees to find a promising spot for the new home. The mate stepped up onto a barrow a fathom higher than the plateau, twenty yards long and eight wide. It was a mile from the fall and well hidden in the trees. If, during heavy or prolonged rains, the spates of the branch spilled out onto the plateau, they would not flow into their hut.

"We have it!" the mate barked out and stomped his feet on the cinders to celebrate the find. "There are enough trees to hide us from any direction," he boasted. "We will be safe enough here."

The captain looked toward the grassland, raised himself on his toes as best he could, but failed to see over the trees and bushes. In that the mate was correct. If they did not build the new shelter too tall, it could not be discovered by anyone walking on the plateau. Tobit wandered about, poking through the shrubs that covered the mound to determine its useful extent. The mate's more deliberate pacing outlined the area that had to be cleared for the house and a work yard as large as they had on the shore. The barrow had space to spare on its top. By tugging at some of the smaller bushes, the mate found their roots were not well anchored in the cinders. Clearing would be easier than it appeared at first.

"Now we must have thatch. Is there some nearer than the lake?" the captain asked.

Mr. Morgen pointed to the east, though they could see nothing through the greenery in that direction. "There is some flax growing where the runnels drain off the plateau," he said, "but it is farther away. It would be better to gather it on the shore and lug it up here."

"That will leave stumps, marks. Someone might see where it has been cut."

"Ah, but I have thought of that. If we make a trail from the fall down along the slope to the west, we can reach within all those plants at the end of the lake and cut what we need. Anyone walking the beach cannot see it. That is, if they don't go far into the flax and they will have no reason to do so. Wood and water is what they will be looking for and naught else."

"Humph," the captain grunted an approval and added, "We must remove all the old shelter and conceal all signs we have made. There must be no trace for the convicts to find."

"The men are not keen to move up from the shore."

"They know no better. Had they heard the tales of murder told on the Derwent, they would not stay a minute longer down there. It is a cesspit in Van Diemen's and New Holland, filled with criminals spared from the gibbet and transported, the distilled evil of England seasoned by the lash. They are cunning and have taken ships from under the very noses of their guards."

"But if they call, it would only be for wood and water."

"Aye, there is nothing to keep them here: no rum, no jades, and no vice of any kind. They may have need to cut a spar or two, no more. Yet if we are found, it is a surety the convicts will make us their prisoners and force us to sail them to where they wish. Once there, we may be killed that we can tell no tale. They would even delight in our deaths, even make a sport of it! Come, we have found our place and it is well hidden. We must prepare for the move."

The next day Mr. Morgen led the carpenter and Thomas along the bar and into the great stand of flax to lay out a trail by which they would move all of the old shelter up to the plateau. He weaved a way through the smaller plants close behind the beach. Farther in, where the bunches of leaves were taller and grew closer together, the men hacked off bunches of leaves with hafted blades of volcano glass, then cast them aside to get through. The mate planned to carry them to the plateau later and use them as thatch. The remaining leaves formed gray-green walls eight to ten feet high on each side of the passage. From the foot of the slope, they cleared a long, diagonal path to the top on the west side of the fall. It crossed the stream, edged the grassland, and ended at the tumulus that was to be the location of their new shelter. It was a longer distance to travel, but it was far easier to carry loads on that route than to struggle up the face of the bluff or up the tiers of limestone. With the route finished, the men began dismantling the wall that had formed their snug retreat under the rock overhang. They untied the thatch and put it aside. Then the bindings holding the supporting poles were cut and the poles tied into bundles. They were the first loads carried to the plateau. A smooth track formed beneath the men's feet as they toted their loads of poles, then thatch and hides up to the plateau. The wind swayed and rustled the flax continuously, and soon the leaves met overhead and created a passage under the living plants through which they carried the last burdens of bedding, smoked meat, and coils of twine and rope.

The mate had scratched a rectangle seven paces long and four paces wide on the cleared surface of the mound. That, he declared, was to be the size of the new shelter and it would contain two rooms, one for the men and one for the officers. The castaways raised a well-braced framework over the outline in three days and covered it with a roof. The problem of the ridge presented itself. The thatch was steep enough and thick enough to shed a heavy rain, but on the ridge where each side met, it had to be covered with something. Thomas hit upon the idea of extending one side another two feet higher and thus its thatch covered the juncture. It was another week before the house was entirely enclosed and some days after that before it was finished with the inner wall and a door that could be slid into place. The officers' room was at the opposite end from the doorway, giving the captain and the mate total privacy, while the crewmen's quarters became a passageway. In addition, a small fire pit was in the men's part of the hut, taking up more space and at times filling it with an irritating haze of smoke.

Captain Tobit and the mate inspected the beach after all parts of the shelter had been carried away to make sure no evidence was overlooked. They had buried all the fire-blackened rocks and smoothed the site over with boughs of leaves. The line of charcoal marks that was the tally of the days they had spent on the island was rubbed from the rock, but they could do nothing to remove the smoke stain from the overhang. It would have to remain undisturbed; the mate supposed it might be taken for the result of a natural fire. As they left, Harrison dragged a bough along the beach to efface their footprints left in the dry part of the beach. It left its own patterns, but they expected the wind would sweep them away in a day or so.

The marks of their feet pressed into the fine soil around the edge of the lake were more difficult to remove or disguise. Sweeping the leaves over them had little effect, and a strong wind, if one ever reached in that far, would hardly erase them. A heavy rain was needed to wash them out.

"Leave them be," Mr. Morgen said, as he watched the men's useless efforts. "It will rain in a day or two. An hour of it will do more than a day's labor. No need to spend more time here. Now on to the traps."

"We can't hide them. There is no way to do that. We can only pull the sticks out. Then it will be added labor to replace them when they are needed."

"We must leave nothing the convicts might discover," the mate insisted.

"A captain coming here to wood and water will land his men where those things are to be got, not at the far end of the island where there are none. Leave the traps be," the carpenter advised. "From the bay, the pales are on the far side of the dunes, and they cannot be seen more than a musket shot away if you come to them from the far side."

"Umph," the mate grunted and looked at the ground at his feet. Then he raised his head and stared east where the shallows might be seen if the bluff did not block his view. "Well," he muttered, "we will leave them as they are. The fish are welcome meals, and, as you say, the traps are not so easily discovered."

At the new hut, each day began when the dawn light entered the smoke hole left at the peak of the gable end. Thomas or Harrison was sent to the bluff to scan the bay and the horizon for any ship that might have arrived in the night. Upon the man's return from his hike, breakfast was eaten. After the meal, Mr. Morgen set the men to their tasks and then went off around the base of the peaks to hunt more of the odd little "bears." The carpenter and Thomas scraped more hides stretched on their frames or took the finished ones across the stream to place them in the dark, tea-like water of the pools there. They weighted them with stones and marked their locations with sticks pushed into the bottom or wedged between the rocks. Soon the pools on the far side had groups of sticks around their edges. The skins soaking there were to be bedcovers if they still had their fur, or if they were unhaired, to be sewn into a sail. Part of every day and sometimes the whole of it was spent hiding at the edge of the lake to snare ducks, marching to the traps for fish, or gathering eggs, clams, and wood. On any trip around the plateau, they scanned about for bits of volcano glass, especially near the slopes of the peaks.

The crewmen used their evenings to make what parts of a canoe they could by the light of the fire. Thomas scraped flax leaves and rolled the fiber into yarns, then laid the coils aside. A winch of some sort would have to be devised out in the work yard to spin them into strands and rope. He was resolved to have all the lines and sail finished before the log was hollowed. It was tedious labor but suited to the evenings and rainy days.

One night Harrison fitted a chip of glass into the notched end of a stick. The others watched as he wrapped sinew around the stick to hold the chip in place. The following evening, when the sinew was dry, he used a bow to spin his newly made drill into a piece of dry wood, first from one side halfway through and then from the opposite side to make a complete hole. When it was finished, Thomas reached over and felt the smoothed wood in the pierced part with his finger. "Ha!" he exclaimed, "a thimble."

"Yes, to draw the shrouds and stays taut," the carpenter explained.

"We cannot make sheaves and blocks, and they are not needed for our little canoe. These will give us purchase enough. A little fat on the inside and a line will not chafe but slide through with ease. We will use one to make the sheet go double and so draw the boom in with less effort."

The two men bent over a green hide, stretched and dried on its frame, and, with the ends of charred sticks, laid out plans for the vessel. Harrison had apparently spent hours considering what was at hand and how best to use it. He would draw a detail of rigging or a point where the pieces of wood were to be bound together, then Thomas sometimes added an improvement or a new idea for how it might be done. Rope and small cordage were the key to all. Without iron, everything would have to be lashed and seized.

"It is still done so," the carpenter said, "aye, even preferred in places where the savages now have iron."

He made a list of all that was needed: the number of hides for the sail, the amount of cordage and small stuff, the boom and mast, and even the parts that might be required for repairs at sea.

"Here will be a netting," Harrison pointed out on his plan, "here between the boomkins and hauled taut to serve as a bed. Two may sleep there whilst the others sail the canoe."

"Let the boomkins extend some to the other side," the lad suggested, "and rig some netting there, too. With a man on each side, the hull will be better balanced."

Christopher looked at Thomas, smiled, and gave him a mock punch on the shoulder.

Captain Tobit allowed the work to be done in the evenings. At least he never discouraged the men or meddled in any way. He cast only a cursory glance at them and made no comment on their efforts and plans one way or the other. However, he delayed the hollowing of the hull. "That," he cautioned, "must be done last of all. The wood is dampish and any fire there will show smoke. We cannot leave a burned log down there on the shore for weeks to give witness we are on this island."

"When all is ready and the weather is promising," the mate added, "we will burn the heart out of the log. But we must keep a sharp watch for any sail whilst we do."

Thomas listened to the officers with his head atilt. He suspected they had talked much between themselves about the building of the canoe, and he was certain he and Harrison were being cozzened with the threat of Botany Bay bolters. Not every ship in that part of the ocean would be crewed by convicts. No, not one in a thousand. Why should they hide from those that could carry them home? And why was old Tobit so little interested in the plan of the canoe, the gathering of its parts, and any progress they made? Thomas didn't complain for he was content to be working on the lines and the hides and to see progress. In a few weeks those hides would be ready to be made up into the sail. There was nothing on the island that would serve so well. Mats they had considered to be too stiff, heavy when wet, and of little dependence. They might unravel at sea. A dozen skins would make a sail large enough for their needs with two or three more to replace any that might split.

"NOW WHAT'S amiss?" Harrison asked one morning as he straightened up from his work. He reached over and touched Thomas's shoulder and nodded his head toward the grassland.

The lad looked up and saw the mate had returned early from his hunt, but he carried no animal on his shoulder. His hands and feet were smeared with mud, and the knees of his trousers were wet and dirty. The captain, who had stepped out of the hut a few minutes before, looked Mr. Morgen up and down as if he was a mischievous child and demanded, "What have you gotten into?"

The mate did not reply, but held out his clenched left hand toward the other officer. Slowly, he opened his fingers and revealed it was full of some mealy white powder.

"What have you there?" the captain asked, peering closely at the substance.

"I believe it is niter," the mate answered.

"Niter, you say?"

"Yes, taste it."

The captain pinched up a bit of the powder and touched it to his tongue. His eyes closed while he concentrated on the sensation.

Harrison also reached forward and picked up a small bit of the powder.

"What do you say?" Mr. Morgen asked.

"Ump, yes," the captain answered. "It is most likely niter."

"It has the sharp taste," the carpenter agreed.

The captain rubbed the powder between his thumb and forefinger. "Where did you find this?" he inquired.

"Where the animals have their dens. They have become very shy now," the mate explained. "When I appear, they run for their holes. Most are too narrow to admit a man. One of them went into a larger one and I followed, meaning to kill him there, but he dropped into a larger space below and disappeared. I believe it is a cave that goes under the grassland. I went down as far as there was light to see. This white powder clings to the rock everywhere. If it is niter, it must leach down out of the animals' stale and manure above." Then he turned to Harrison and ordered, "Wet a piece of our twine and roll it in this find. When it is dry, touch a hot coal to it. Then we shall know if it is niter."

That afternoon the test proved their guess was correct. When lighted, the twine sparked and hissed like a fuse and boiled out little glowing beads of the melted powder. Captain Tobit stared at the last bit of the twine as it fizzled out, leaving a smoking ash. "With charcoal and brimstone. . . ." he muttered, leaving the words hanging.

"Yes, black powder." The mate replied to what he assumed was an implied question. "We may carry some of it about, and with a rock that will strike a spark, have fire with very little effort."

"There may be need for it sometime," the captain muttered.

"With this niter," the carpenter suggested, "we might speed the burning of a log for our canoe."

Captain Tobit gave a quick glance at the mate, turned to the carpenter and said, "Well, then it will be to our advantage to gather more of it."

"We will need torches to get farther into the cave," the mate explained. "Pitchy wood . . . the best to make tapers with. . . . Where might we find that?"

"Up there is the most likely place," Harrison replied, pointing a finger toward the high peaks.

"Then you will go there to find some tomorrow," Mr. Morgen ordered. "Ah, and also search for straight limbs that are springy and just so in size." He indicated the diameter he wanted by making a circle with his thumb and forefinger.

The carpenter and Thomas gave the mate puzzled looks.

"I mean to make a bow," Mr. Morgen said, to make his need plainer to the crewmen. "The animals have become chary of me and cannot be approached, though they will sit and watch at a little distance. If I near them, they now run off. It's maddening. But with a bow, I could send an arrow into them in a trice."

"Sir, we have enough hides curing now for all, and we have smoked meat for weeks ahead. There is no need to kill more of the 'bears,'" Harrison pointed out.

"Aye," Thomas agreed emphatically, "we should give them time to recruit their numbers. There is the danger you may kill them all."

Mr. Morgen took a step toward the crewmen. He raised his right hand and pointed his forefinger at them. "You mind who you are!" he growled. "Find fit wood for torches and limbs that will serve for bows, and bring them to me tomorrow!"

Thomas's mouth opened and a defiant answer almost passed his lips when he felt Christopher's strong grip on his elbow. He clenched his teeth and gave the mate only a sullen stare.

"There is a plenty of the animals. They are up there in the peaks," the captain boasted, and waved his hand to the southwest. Seeing no change in the doubting expressions of the crewmen, he added, "Those you see on the grassland are merely the verge of great herds. We could line this hut with their pelts if we wished. We may do that yet! Have no fear that they will not recover. It is not your concern."

The crewmen could only stand silently, knowing reason would not hold against the captain's belief. In addition, their footing as men in the fo'c's'le meant that their opinions were never to be considered. All blame was theirs while all credit went to the officers.

"IT WAS A curious thing, a most curious thing," the mate said to the captain in their room that night. He spoke in a hushed voice, not wanting the men to hear him. "The animal looked at me in such a strange manner. It went into its hole and when I didn't follow, it came out again. It stared at me as if it was more than a dumb beast. Then it went back into its burrow, all the while looking back to see if I would follow. Then I went in. Every few steps, it stopped and turned about, just to make sure I was there. It wasn't all that dark a short ways in. The animal didn't drop into the cave as I said today when the men were listening. It vanished, like magic. In a trice . . . gone! I waited, but it didn't return. There was no other cranny it could slip into. I looked about and that's when I discovered the cave and the niter."

Tobit rolled a little in his bed and replied, "So, you find that odd, do you? There are many things we cannot explain in this world if we don't look to find the answer in God. Our lives are ordered by Him, yet you find it odd to see a small creature leave not a trace. You believe our Lord is all-powerful, do you not?"

"Well, yes."

"Might he make that animal disappear, or even an elephant, if he so wished?"

The mate paused for a moment, then answered, "I suppose so."

"Suppose so? It follows, it follows! The only mystery here is why you cannot understand. If he makes this creature fade before your eyes—your eyes, I repeat—don't you think He had a reason?"

"A reason?" Mr. Morgen echoed.

"Yes, there is a reason in all things He does. Think on it. Read the sign in it."

THE NEXT morning, after their breakfast, Harrison and Thomas gathered a few pieces of rope, one of the baskets, and two glass-bladed axes. They climbed the familiar way, up along the cascade spilling from the small volcano. After reaching the top, they rested and viewed the panorama below them. The morning light shone into their eyes as they looked eastward. From due north around to due south, the sea was laid before them with its white-flecked waves drifting with the wind. Not even the least dot interrupted the cambered line at the limit of sight.

"No relief for us today, Chips," Thomas said, after his eyes made a sweep of the sea.

"There may be a ship to chance upon us yet," Harrison countered.

"When? Years from now, when our lives are spent? Ha! The only sure rescue is the one we make for ourselves. There. . . ." the lad said, and pointed east beyond the lower end of the shallows, "with a following wind and a little luck we may raise the coast in a few days."

"Aye, mate, I agree. No great to-do about it in fair weather, but while we work to make our canoe, there is always a chance of a ship. These peaks can be seen from a great distance."

Thomas made no reply and started walking slowly around the rim of the crater, looking over the outer edge and then in the opposite direction around the shore of the lake. The carpenter followed and watched the young sailor as he searched for something. He was baffled by the lad's curious hunt. After a few minutes he asked, "What is it you are looking for?"

"For what draws old Tobit up here. He takes his bath in the stream below. He need not fag himself to come up here for that. What is it? What makes him labor up here, puffing the whole way and smelling this sulphurous stink . . . to sulk or to pray? Isn't this where he went over the first time we came up here?"

Harrison looked in each direction along the narrow rim and then answered, "Yes, I believe so."

Thomas dropped his basket and said, "He was searching for something, and I think he found it. He looked somewhat pleased when he got back up here." He started over the side. Christopher followed, stepping and sliding after him. In a few minutes they came across a cave, hardly more than a cavity. It was six or seven yards in width and nearly the same in height. Part of the portal overhead had collapsed, creating a mound at the entrance. It was half again as deep as it was wide, and its back wall was wet in two places with little trickles of water issuing out of crevices and running down into a pool that had gathered behind the mound.

"This must be what it was. He said it was where the side of the mountain was thinner, but of what use is it? How can it help us from this island?" Thomas asked. "If it were down below and altogether dry, we might live in it."

"It's simply a weaker portion of the mountain," the carpenter replied. "Perhaps this is not what he was seeking."

"What else is here? Trees, ferns, rocks, nothing that can't be found below. He says little about the canoe and seems not interested in how we fare with the rigging. I think he is satisfied with the work because it keeps us busy at night. That makes me uneasy."

Harrison shook his head and said, "Perhaps some idea has taken his fancy. It is odd he doesn't speak of the *Dove* or our lost mates, as if the wreck never occurred. We must watch him, watch what he does, but it would not be wise to oppose him."

"You are saying we are to obey a lunatic?"

"We do not know that he is a lunatic. We cannot say for sure what his disorder is. He hungers to order everyone about. It is his only pleasure. On board the ship he took no tobacco. He drank no rum. A desire to lord it over others consumes him, and he takes every opportunity to wig us. So he appears to be some deranged, but may not be."

"Where is the difference, Chips? Mad or half-mad, the result will be all the same; we will not get home while he's alive."

"I think it is best we not grumble or appear to traverse him in any way. Opposition, even any slackness, makes him worse."

"You wish to obey him without question . . . for how long?"

"For a while yet. It is not intolerable for us to do the chores and work. We would be doing much the same if we were alone here. If a ship raises this island in the next few weeks or months, we will leave and all will be well. But if we balk too soon, it will go hard for us when we reach home."

"And in all the time we wait, he will find new ways to chafe me."

"The time has not come to set against his wants," Christopher warned with a shake of his head.

They picked footholds, gripped branches, and struggled their way back up to lip of the crater. They rested there for several minutes, panting from the exertion of the climb.

Thomas looked down the slope. "It puzzles me," he said. "Aye, I cannot be at ease when I don't know what the fool means to do."

"Come, lad," the carpenter urged, "we have our errand to finish. Pick up your things." They continued their trip around to the point where the two peaks had joined and spilled over the western edge of the small volcano. They entered under a canopy of trees, and discovered the source of the water that filled the crater, cascaded down into the stream, and, from there, spilled over the fall. Boulders choked the streambed and forced the cascade to one side or the other or split it into two or three streams. Its prattling and rumbling echoed between the two slopes and along the length the steep valley. A fine spray from its dashing against the rocks wet all the ferns growing near its path. Drops of water swelled at the tips of fronds and fell to a layer of mosses that had spread over the rocks and the ground. It was three to four inches thick and extended up, muffling the boles of the trees, and making them appear oddly enlarged for the first eight to ten feet. At each man's step, water oozed from the spongy mat and then filled the depressions left as he moved on. A soft light entered the narrow defile from above, giving the scene only diffuse shadows. Other than the white of the plunging water and the black side of a rock not covered with growths, everything was colored in greens from the darkest to the most vivid shades.

They waded across the stream to find an easier route up the peak. "Oh, oh, that is cold!" Harrison exclaimed, stepping out. "The heat in the water of the crater must come from the bottom. It must act like a kettle, warming it and sending it to the stream and the lake. There is no heat up here for sure."

Each boulder was an obstacle around which they had to find a way. They brushed aside fronds and moss-fringed limbs. Drops shaken from them soaked into their leather trousers so they became wet to mid-thigh and flopped clammily against their legs.

"This is a misery," Thomas complained.

"Right lad, let's get out of this dank hole. We will be soaked if we go much farther up. The sides are steeper but drier."

They turned to their right and immediately found they had to pull themselves up by gripping limbs and fronds as they had on the side of the small crater and on the bluffs below the plateau. Carrying the basket containing the axes and rope, Harrison was at a disadvantage. He had only one hand free. Without a good handhold there was a danger of falling over backward or losing footing and sliding down. For half an hour they struggled upward into thinning greenery and onto a more manageable slope of the peak. Thomas, panting from the difficult climb, halted at a small tree and rested. He held onto a branch and watched as Harrison caught up to him.

"Listen," Thomas whispered, "do you hear them?"

"Yes," the carpenter replied, "there are many more than we have ever heard below."

"Let's see," Thomas said and started off again.

Another fifty yards up, the woods opened out and more of the sky was visible.

Harrison pointed to the trees. "There are hundreds all about. They are all over the peak."

"Nearly on every twig," the lad agreed.

Small-bodied birds hopped along the branches only a few feet away.

They cocked their heads, eyed the two men, and then turned about to inspect them from another angle. Their feathers were combinations of several colors: black, brown, white, and blue. Higher in the trees, small green parrots with yellow breasts screeched short calls to each other. Six feet away on the ground two brown, hen-sized birds continually probed into the ferns and grasses. After poking to the right and left they moved ahead a few steps and repeated their search. One even came up to Harrison and attempted to peck beneath his foot. The carpenter held out his hand to one of the little green birds perched on a limb before him, whereupon the creature flicked his wings, leaped forward, and landed with its claws gripping his thumb. He drew his arm back and held the bird between Thomas and himself. It showed neither fear nor the inclination to escape, but inspected the men with one eye and then the other.

"Why doesn't it flee?" Thomas asked.

Harrison studied the little feathered body resting on his thumb and explained, "It is curious. It has no reason to fear if there have never been men or animals on this island to harm it. It is the same with all the birds and those 'bears.' The ducks and geese are wary for they must fly off to the Middle Island or some other place where they are hunted."

Suddenly, the lad's eyes opened wide and an astounded look spread across his face.

Harrison chuckled at Thomas. A black bird with two curled white feathers at its throat had flitted from the tree and landed on the boy's head. His chuckle increased to a full laugh when two more birds hopped forward, and each selected a shoulder to perch on.

"You make a good roost for these . . . what are they? The tuee birds. The one on your head means to make a nest of your hair. Hee, hee, hee. Or it might choose to shit on your skull instead. Haw, haw, haw!" The carpenter's guffaws sent the birds back to their tree.

He turned and looked back down the steep valley they had exited. Between the two slopes a segment of the grassland, green, smooth, and pathless, was visible. "What a paradise we have landed upon. Such a fortunate place," he murmured and pointed to the flatland far below. "A thousand or even two thousand people might settle here, live in comfort, feel secure for the whole of their lives."

"Aye, with others and with kin. But to be here alone or almost so and know you can never leave . . . that is desolation."

"Well, we must be on our way. Something for torches and something for bows, my friend."

They resumed their climb until they arrived at an opening in the trees. The valley they had left was narrowing as it neared the gap between the peaks, and the trees along the stream became a dense growth squeezed in between the sides. They had made a good choice to climb out and up the slope to the north. The stream's source was farther up in that inaccessible, mist-filled place where all the peaks met. What they sought would not be found there, Thomas thought. Pines or trees of their nature always grew in a more open place, drier and sunnier. He struck off more to the north, pushing a way through the underwood, but not ascending so much. Bit by bit, as they skirted around the peak and the greenery thinned, more of the plateau came in view, then the east cape, the bay, and the slough below the falls. The soil and cinders were becoming drier, less bound with roots and, at each step, they slipped down a few inches.

They tested the branches along their way by bending and releasing them. If they snapped back smartly, they lopped them off. In all, they cut a dozen that had a reasonable springiness. Harrison tested them all again and selected the ones with the more suitable shape and thickness. He kept six.

While the carpenter tied them into a bundle with lengths of twine, Thomas went ahead and picked at the bark of certain trees, hoping to find one that showed pitch at a break or wound. He wanted pine or like wood that could be split into slivers and bound into torches. The carpenter left his load of limbs and hurried to join the lad. Together, they went on until they came to a part of the mountainside that was composed mostly of rocks and cinders. Little bunches of grass and few ferns had gained a hold there. At the lower edge of that barren area were a few doddered and dying trees, some standing and some fallen. Thomas chose one that had collapsed onto the cinders. Its loose bark and the fungus oozing from cracks in its sides indicated rot had spread through it. He hacked at the softened wood, working around a limb to free it. Harrison wrenched the broken branch back and forth until it broke out of the decayed trunk.

"There, see the pitch that has saved it from the rot," Thomas said, pointing to the part that had just been exposed.

The carpenter held the end up to examine it closer. "Yes," he replied, "if it will split, we will have torches and they should make enough light."

They hacked out several more limbs from the downed trunks lying around the barren area and cut them into lengths that would fit into the basket. Hardened pitch had collected on some of the trees, where branches had been snapped off or partially broken by strong winds. The two men gathered a good handful of it. "If it is melted and slivers dipped in it, then bound together," Christopher suggested, "that might make them serve longer."

With that, they agreed they had succeeded well enough to satisfy the mate and their searches were over. The two rested on one of the downed trees and turned their attention to the view below. In all the time they had spent on the island, not once had they ventured so high on any peak. Everything they had needed up to that time had been found close to the shore or on the plateau. From that height, the exact circle of the bay was even more apparent. No light reflected from a shallow bottom, and the water was all a dark blue. Thomas turned to watch the cloud shadows drifting across the green velvet of the grassland. Suddenly he shivered.

The carpenter nodded and said, "Ah, 'tis much colder up here. No need for us to tarry. We have what we came for. Come, let's be off for the hut."

Thomas made no move in response to the suggestion except to turn and face Harrison. "Chips, why did you sign on the *Dove?*" he asked abruptly.

The carpenter had not expected the question and paused for a moment to gather his thoughts. "Why same as you, Thomas," he answered, still a little puzzled at the lad's inquiry. "I must labor for my tea and biscuit."

"No, I mean why did you come aboard as a poor jack? Will always swore you could be a better officer than Tobit or Morgen."

Harrison avoided the lad's eyes by pretending to search the juncture of the sky and sea for any speck. "I suppose I might have found such a berth, but not all men wish to command or are suited to it," he replied.

"You could have done so easily. Indeed, you have the very look of an officer. Anyone could say you grew to the mold."

"I was promoted to be one during the war. First mate aboard a coaster. Then we were taken as a prize off Cape May by a large sloop, though we had defended ourselves well and sent some shot into her between wind and water. But sadly, we lost two good men. One had his shoulder carried away. A splinter pierced the other man. Oh, it was a terrible thing to see. We were taken to Halifax and spent some months there. I had much time to think about what command means, and now I would never order men to do what might cause their deaths. Command means you might have to do so sometime. It was best I not become an officer again and fail my duty at some vital moment."

"But if you had captained the *Dove,* we would not be wrecked on this island, and all of our mates would be alive."

"Perhaps. At any rate, it is Tobit who must answer for this misadventure."

"He has no conscience. He feels he has done nothing wrong. The deaths of all those men and boys don't disturb his sleep."

"We do not know that. We can only guess," Harrison said and rose to his feet.

Thomas grabbed the basket and started down the slope. The carpenter fell in behind him, and they threaded their way through the trees and bushes to pick up the carpenter's bundle of sticks.

CHAPTER 11

MR. MORGEN untied the bundle of limbs and sighted along the length of each one to assure him they were true enough to serve as bows. Once satisfied they were, he next tested them for springiness by bending and releasing them. The mate then rebound them loosely and hung them from the rafters near the peak of the roof. "A few weeks up there and they will be seasoned," he muttered. "Hopefully stronger, then the 'bears' will need be wary of me."

Harrison made a wedge from a bone and, with it, he and Thomas split the pitchy wood they had brought from the peak into long slivers. These they tied in small bundles nearly a foot long. The first one they lighted burned for what they guessed was almost a quarter of an hour. With improvements in the shape and the addition of a little extra pitch, it burned somewhat longer. Whoever held the torch had to turn it to keep it burning evenly and sometimes almost invert the torch when it threatened to go out. All of the wood brought from the peak was made into torches and that gave them a dozen, out of which Harrison thought nine or ten would burn dependably for the needed length of time.

All four men set off the next day for the animals' lairs. Thomas toted a basket filled with the torches, hides, string, and earshells; the carpenter carried two half-rotted and smoldering limbs which he blew upon now and then to keep them glowing. When they arrived there, he built up a fire of leaves and twigs and from it, lighted a torch. The mate crawled in first. Harrison followed, with the torch held in his right hand and limping along on his knees and left hand. Next, Thomas dragged in his basket. Tobit entered last and balked a little at the peculiar smell he encountered.

"Feel the air," Harrison said, turning his head back to the two behind him. "It flows out and it's quite warm."

"What might cause it to be so?" Thomas asked.

"It must be the heat under the mountain that warms the lake above," the carpenter answered. "We are near to it."

Mr. Morgen eased himself down into the cave and reached up to take the torch from Harrison. He held it high after the others had gotten down and pointed out the white crust covering the rock overhead and reaching down each side.

"You see, it's all over. It's been gathering for ages," he explained. "The stale and droppings of the animals produce it, and the damp carries it down from their dens and the earth above."

"Ugh, this is a vile mess for us to walk in," Tobit complained. "We will be filthy when we get out!"

Mud four to five inches deep covered the bottom of the cave. Near the walls, it was drying and cracking, but in the center, it remained soft and coated the men's feet.

"It's best we light two," the carpenter advised and held another torch up to the one the mate was holding. "If one goes out, we will not be wholly in darkness."

The mate then turned and, carrying his torch before him with one hand and shielding it from the breeze with the other, walked farther into the blackness of the cave.

The four men shuffled ahead, alternately watching where they placed their feet in the muddy bottom and staring into the blackness before them. The rock overhead and the walls were illuminated for only a few yards. Beyond them there was nothing to reflect the light of the fluttering flames. From that void the air rushed at them like the exhaled breath of a great animal. Indeed, a beast might have been hidden in that darkness or a precipice or some unknown peril.

"There!" the mate exclaimed, pointing to something in the mud ahead. "What's that?"

They moved forward in short steps toward a gray lump resting on the drying mud at one side of the cave bottom. Upon closer approach, the weak light showed it to be the body of one of the "bears" lying there on its side with its hide shrunken over its ribs and the grimace of its shriveled lips revealing all its teeth. An eyeball that once filled its socket had shriveled to nothing, but a dense shadow in the empty space appeared as a fit replacement, a jet eye capable of superior sight. The animal appeared both dead yet aware of their presence. It had the stare of some heathen idol, which at first glance seemed impersonal, yet became accusing, even threatening, when beheld in a steady gaze.

"There is nothing that could be of use to us beyond here," the captain hissed. "This air is disagreeable as if it came from Gehenna. We do not belong here. Come, we leave now. Back to the niter. We will gather it and be done with this dismal place."

Harrison held a torch in each hand and lighted another after one of them burned low and failed. The mate and Thomas scraped the white crystals from the roof and walls and piled it on a skin spread on a rock. All that they could reach was gathered, and only in the high cavities overhead was any left. The castaways crept up and out toward the daylight, dragging two skins filled with the niter and tightly bound. Outside, they rose to their feet and looked at each other. Their feet and hands and the legs of their trousers were caked with mud. Harrison shook his head and declared, "Ah! What a mess we are."

"We have no need to repeat this chore, and a dip in the branch will clean all," Mr. Morgen said. "Now let's be on our way."

After a quick wash in the stream they returned to the hut.

The next day the mate lined up earshells around the walls of the hut and filled each with niter and water. "This will make it pure," he explained. "When this liquor has dried and made crystals twice, it will separate the niter and its effect will be increased." During the days required for the water to evaporate, Mr. Morgen spent his time gathering dead wood washed up on the banks of the stream and selecting from it all the hardest and driest pieces. He piled the chosen wood on a blazing fire and laid a covering of green boughs and earth to seal it from any air.

"There, that is to be my charcoal," Mr. Morgen announced. "You men watch that the fire does not break out while I go up to gather brimstone."

Once the charcoal was made, the mate had all the items he needed to produce his gunpowder. He thought the uncertain nature of his experiments might require some precaution and ordered Harrison to construct a small lean-to fifty paces from the hut. There he started his mixing and testing.

Thomas and the carpenter watched the mate's efforts with some amusement at first, but after the second day, they speculated on why he should work with such one-mindedness, using all the time of daylight on it and nothing else. The officer patiently devised a scale with a few sticks, string, and two squares of hide, then went to gather handfuls of pebbles from the streambed. He selected one pebble that was to be a standard and balanced the others on the scale one at a time against it. In all he ended his trials with more than a dozen small stones of the same weight.

"Proportion," he explained to the men as they watched his work. "It is all a matter of so many parts to so many parts and thorough mixing. When they are correct, boom!" That last word emphasized with a wave of his arm, he set off toward the little lean-to smiling and satisfied with the scale that was the result of his ingenuity.

Harrison gathered his beard in his hand, pulling on it lightly, and slowly asked his crewmate, "Curious, what does he mean to do with so much if he makes it work? A handful is all we need to make fire."

"Perhaps he will say it is to frighten off Botany Bay men should they reach here or some such silliness," Thomas answered. "It's just another waste of time, another thing to delay the canoe. I'll wager that even after the winter is past, that pair will find more reasons not to leave. They are conniving to some end, but what?"

"They are not about to tell us. But, no matter," the carpenter replied.

The following morning Mr. Morgen came to the fire in the work yard and picked out a burning stick. He blew on its end, looked at it critically, and went off to his lean-to. Moments later, the crewmen heard a "whoosh" and saw a thin puff of gray smoke rising from the bushes. During the late afternoon, they heard the noise of the ignited powder again and saw thicker smoke rolling upward. The mate was making progress creating his explosive. Minutes later, a report as loud as the discharge of a musket startled the men at their work. Instantly, they leaped to their feet and started toward the lean-to, when the mate came through the bushes with a slight smile forming on his face.

As he passed near the captain, he muttered, "I have it now. Yes, I have my proportions." Then he selected another stick from the fire and waved it to increase the glow at the end. He raised the stick and faced the others as if he were proposing a toast and, with a meaningful wink, said, "Now . . . now for the last trial." He turned and strode back to his experiments.

A half-hour later a tremendous blast struck the mens' clothes and faces. Dirt and rocks were flying high into the air. Some of it came down on the work yard, spattering on the men and the thatch of the hut. For the second time, Thomas and the carpenter jumped to their feet and tossed their work to the ground. This time they dashed toward the site of the explosion with the captain waddling after them. Thomas arrived first and searched around in the thick smoke. A fire was burning on the shattered remains of the lean-to. Bits of its smoldering thatch were scattered about in the bushes, and a stink hung in the air. The mate was sitting on his rump, swaying slowly from side to side. His eyes stared straightforward from his sooted face in a stunned expression. The hair on the front of his head and his beard were nearly burned off, and the buff color of the singed ends made him appear suddenly aged. His eyebrows were completely gone, increasing his look of bewilderment.

Thomas grabbed the mate's shoulder and gave it a shake.

"Arrh . . . arrh," was the only response the officer could make.

Harrison and Thomas examined his arms and legs for injuries. Mr. Morgen spit dirt from his mouth, and when he cleared it all, mumbled, "Arrh . . . the train . . . ahh."

"I don't believe he has more hurts than his burns," the carpenter said.

"The damned fool!" Thomas spat out.

"The train. . . ." the mate repeated. "Light the train . . . uh. . . . Flashed. . . . An instant."

Through the thinning smoke, Harrison searched around and found a hole a foot and a half deep three yards in front of the mate. "He buried his charge," he called to Thomas. "It went off before he intended it to and gave us our shower of dirt."

Mr. Morgen felt his chest and then ran each hand up and down the length of the opposite arm.

Captain Tobit arrived and, with a concerned look, scanned the mate and his dirtied clothes. "Are you injured?" he asked.

"Ahh . . . Ahh . . . a surprise, but I am whole," he answered as he struggled to his feet. "No doubting the power of this last mixture I've made."

The crewmen, seeing the mate was only dazed and burned a little by the blast, started back to the hut. After he had gone twenty paces, the carpenter's shoulders began shaking. A sniggle escaped his lips. "Hoist with his own petard!" he choked out. "Hoist with his own . . ." Harrison could not finish speaking while the thought convulsed him.

"Ah, yes, there is irony in that," Thomas agreed wholeheartedly and joined in the laughter. For the remainder of the day, when the men looked at each other their eyes narrowed and drew into wrinkles at the corners, yet both fought the urge to break out in laughter. Any outward show of derision would bring on ill humor from Mr. Morgen. It was much better for them to look at his singed face, remember how stupid he looked after the blast, and deliciously enjoy his loss of dignity.

Mr. Morgen reluctantly abandoned his powder-making for the next few weeks. The niter, brimstone, and charcoal he wrapped in separate hides and tucked away into a corner of the hut. The next day he gathered thin sticks to make arrows. It was a trial for him. His blistered fingers pained him when he grasped the axe and the small shafts, but he worked on and attempted to make light of his injuries while either of the crewmen were watching. They had their instructions to peel the bark from the sticks and straighten them with the aid of the fire. Harrison held them over the coals and then handed them to Thomas who bent them into alignment and held them until they cooled. When they were made as true as possible, the mate cut them all to the same length and set about making glass tips to fit to the ends.

An hour before sunset, Captain Tobit declared that the following day would be Sunday by his counting. "No work will be done tomorrow," he announced. "There is nothing so pressing it cannot wait. We must keep our obligations. What food we have will suffice. Our needs are filled, therefore the whole of the day and all future Sabbaths will be observed . . . the prescribed day of rest and worship. I will prepare the sermon and give it in the morning. The afternoon will be spent in the contemplation of the wisdom and the great works of the Lord." He then turned to Thomas and ordered, "You, make the trip to the lookout."

The lad gladly started off for the edge of the plateau for, as always, he welcomed any excuse to be away from the officers. On the island it was no different than it had been aboard the barque where he never knew when one of them would appear behind him or be standing over him as he rose from some task. There was always a look of mistrust or doubt on their faces. Not once had they shown they were wholly pleased with anything done on board. The finest piece of rigging or seamanship received only a passing grunt. To be out in the trees or marching along the empty sweep of the shore was a relief. There was a freedom he always savored when he could be sure no officer was close by. At those times the sense of being a castaway lessened, and the blue of a clear sky and the rustling of the trees in the sea wind sharpened his feeling of fine health and strength. He knew then that he could choose where his fortune lay and that he had the will to seek it.

So, he thought, old Tobit means to start his preaching again as he had done on the *Dove*. Now he didn't have his old Bible with its worn leather cover to wave at his bored listeners, but he had enough scripture in his head to rant for hours. No life . . . no life in it, Thomas said to himself. That old man's religion was not a faith. It was dried, faded, and fusty like a flower pressed in a rarely opened book. It had no meaning, no hope to carry one from day to day, through all the hard times. It was all threats of punishment for this, that, and the other, threats he took great pleasure in repeating. For Tobit, quoted scripture was a tool. He deftly found some passage to fit each of his needs, and it would come from his mouth as if spoken by Moses. He never cited the goodness of life, charity, or forgiveness. He dwelt on duty, the Day of Judgment, and the pains of Hell. Those warnings he had repeated until their words were bereft of meaning. There was no other religion but his and no other God but his. All else was falsity or artifices of the devil designed to deceive. Tobit could never imagine it possible to question his beliefs, and the conclusions he drew from them were all, as he declared, traceable to God himself.

When spoken aloud, those Biblical phrases elicited in Thomas memories of long, repetitious sermons echoing in the bare interior of the church in Stonington. He remembered the interminable hours endured on a hard pew while the hoarse-voiced preacher recited his favorite passages. There had been nothing to look at on the white walls, and his mind had receded into an imagined country, distant, unpeopled, and unexplored. He had made dream-like, effortless excursions into its hills and waterways. He had soared hawk-like over its peaks and plains until some fit of coughing by an ancient in the congregation brought him back to the stark interior of the meeting house. During the winter, he had shivered while sitting in the family slip and had hunched up and squirmed as much as he was able without drawing reprimand from Father. In the summer, the congregants were hot and beset with flies. Father and Mother never seemed to mind the pests' buzzing and had given him dark looks when he waved them from his face. The long-awaited final "Amen" was his release from boring confinement, and he stepped quickly to exit into the shifting patterns of sunlight and shadows beneath the trees and the stirring life of the Port. In the words he heard spoken each week, he could find no relevance to the farming, the fishing, and his daily labor at the bench. Their very grammar even set it aside, beyond the needs of making a living. The sermon was a pause in the week, a time that was alien to all that went before and after. As far as he could see, the lives of those in good standing in the church were no better in character than those who were excluded. The lively company of the boys from the ships was preferable to him, for many had called at places as far off as Russia, the Guinea Coast, Copenhagen, and the Indies. They were full of oaths and tales of escapades and the particulars of the strange people they had met. The reverend preached to the men who dealt with the idolaters of the east and the papists to the south and gave them warning from the pulpit to be proof against the false ideas of such infidels.

Mother and Father predictably stood for nearly an hour in front of the church and visited with friends they had not seen during the week. He dawdled on the street, glancing at the doorway until he saw Isabel come out. He fell in with her as she started for her home and had her attention for a quarter of an hour. Her pace, he was always pleased to note, was intentionally slow, and her answers to his questions were shy and tardy. Most Sundays they lingered at the hitching post before her house, saying little, but reluctant to part until her mother called her in two or three times.

He paused in his march to the edge of the plateau, closed his eyes and pictured in every detail Isabel's smooth face and her deep brown eyes. Then he recalled how he managed to lean close to her yellow hair spilling from the edge of her bonnet and catch its enticing scent. He opened his eyes and started off again. She would be spoken for by the time he returned, that is if he ever managed to return. Her father had probably chosen his son-in-law before this very moment. If I do not find another berth, Thomas reminded himself, I shall be no better than a beggar when again I step onto the roads of Stonington. Even had he not left, his chances with Isabel would have been slim. Now it was already far too late. Two years had passed. It looked as if it would take that much longer to earn wages or a lay and find his way home. She will be firmly urged to marry and have her children by another, some old widower with heavy belly and heavy purse.

Near the fall he turned and walked along the bluff to the tiers until the entire surface of the bay was visible. His last few paces to the lookout were always hurried in the hope that a ship would be discovered entering that circle of water or anchored with its sails furled or hanging in the bunts. He searched the western horizon out beyond the spit where any ship would be silhouetted by the yellowing sunlight. Not the least speck broke the finely drawn line between sky and water. To the north it was veiled with a haze. It was possible a ship was there, within that mist, and on a beam reach to the Indies with all sails set and white roll showing below her bobstay. If that were the case, then no one would be looking aft to spy the peaks of their refuge. Beyond the east rim of the grassland a portion of the dark sea could be made out. No sail there rising as it approached. Thomas's eyes moved back slowly to the setting sun. Empty . . . all empty. Every morning and evening empty, he was thinking. We must look to our own wits and strength to carry us to Cook Strait. At least that far, if not to the Bay of Islands.

He brought his hands up before him, curled them into fists and squeezed them with all his might. He then opened them and stared at the callused palms. That was the sum of two years of danger and labor in the heat of the tropics and the continual chill of the rookeries. With a last look at the horizon, he turned and walked back to the hut.

WEEKS LATER, after they had finished their evening meal, Mr. Morgen stood up and pulled a limb from the bundle he had suspended from the roof supports. "Not the best," he said after testing its resilience, "but good enough for now." He started a wedge into its larger end and split it in two, thus producing two pieces suitable for bows. With a large chip of glass, he began scraping one stick into the shape he desired, flattening it to a stave except for the center portion. By the middle of the following day he had finished the scraping and strung it with twine twisted of the longest fibers of flax. He twanged the string and pulled it to its full draw. "Smooth," he muttered, "smooth." It was evident that by the manner in which it bent, it was a decent bow about five and a half feet long. He sent several untipped arrows into a bundle of dried flax leaves he devised as a target. Fletched with feathers from a sea bird, the shafts flew accurately for forty paces or a little more. To reach farther, it was necessary to fire higher into the air, with a loss of accuracy. The wood of the bow lacked some of the springiness the mate desired, yet its range, he declared, was tolerable.

The next day he showed a wide smile as he strode into the work yard and dropped a dead animal from his shoulder. "There," he pointed to the carcass on the ground and boasted, "first shot . . . through the heart! They'll not escape me while I have these." He held up his right hand gripping his bow and a few arrows, waggled them at the crewmen, and continued, "Aye, and should any Botany Bay runagates reach this island, we will not be at their mercy. A few of these arrows shot from ambush will change their minds and shorten their visit. I would even welcome the chance."

He was well pleased with his weapon and occupied his evenings making more. He found ways to improve them and took pride in their added accuracy, appearance, and the longer flights of the arrows they shot. In all, he finished five: one for every man and a spare. He rubbed each bow with a little fat from the fowls and hung it on the wall of the hut with a bundle of a few arrows.

A calm sea, in addition to a favorable tide, was always required before the men could search among the rocks of the west coast for the sea ears. They ate the meat from those gem-like shells fewer times as the days passed. The surf along that side of the island grew higher, and now only rarely was a lesser sea running. The air at night and in the early morning became noticeably colder, and on the shore of the bay the wind increased and whipped the trees to and fro. Gusts picked up leaves from the ground and swirled them over the beach and the waves. Sea birds, driven from the wind-blasted coast, gathered behind the spurs of the peaks and flew in slow-turning flocks, showing as white specks against the deep green of the slopes and the leaden sky. Thomas imagined what the scene must be like at the great precipices that faced the south and west. Swells of that wild ocean must be dashing over the offshore rocks and spreading up the face of the cliff where they never reached in the summer. He pictured the band of froth, always there, growing and spreading farther from the island.

Though their hut was built in the lee of the high peaks and hidden in a boskage moved only by light breezes, the castaways heard a stirring one night in the thatch and a tossing of the trees along the stream. Cat's paws of air forced through the leaves of its walls spread the smoke that normally rose directly from the fire to the opening in the gable. Thomas noted the effect for a moment and went outside to see how the weather was making up. It was totally black, but he felt the wind had veered around to the north. He waited for his eyes to accustom themselves to the darkness. After some minutes he could detect the weak light from the smoke hole and some small defects in the thatch of the hut. But the bushes and trees about were lost to his sight and their existence was revealed only by the noise of their limbs creaking and the leaves rustling in the swingeing flurries. In a sudden glow of light from the hut, he saw Harrison coming out and sliding the door back into place.

"No night to be out," the carpenter greeted him. "It would be even worse were we in that sea. It will be months before we can set off from here."

"True, Chips, but even when it becomes fair weather again, I doubt our Captain Toby will be keen to put his foot into a canoe. Well, if he doesn't care to leave, we will bid him a kind farewell. I would love to do that. Leave him here to wonder if we will send back for him."

"I think it's going to stir up some. It will be wet with a boisterous ocean all around," Harrison warned.

"Yes, you can smell it in the air, even feel it. We can be thankful we have built a strong house."

For several minutes, the crewmen walked about sensing the direction of the wind and its strength. Large raindrops started falling a few at a time, scattered widely around the work yard and the hut. Both men ran back and ducked into the shelter when the storm began in earnest. A few minutes later, the first distant rumble of thunder rolled out of the peaks. The rain increased quickly. Many times during the night it became a roaring downpour. During the worst of it, the men rose from their beds and built up the fire. By its light and a flaming stick they searched the under side of the roof for leaks. They ran their hands along the peak and the juncture of the roof and walls while the rain drummed on the thatch and poured from the eaves. They found only two small trickles, near the outside walls, and those would not wet them or their preserved food. Fortunately, Harrison had suggested they double the thatch and re-tie it after the first rains fell on the finished hut. It was now several inches thick on both the sides and roof. Outside the storm wrenched the trees and dashed tons of water on every acre of the island. The cozy feeling of being safe and dry gave the castaways short shivers.

A blue-white light flared through the smoke hole in the gable end and reflected from the center wall. Instantly, a crack and rumble followed that shook the hut.

The mate ducked his head and mumbled, "Damned close." He then looked up at the roof as if he expected it to be blasted in with the next strike.

The lightning strikes came again and again. Some sounded as if they hit only a few yards distant, but most struck further up the mountain. The storm lasted all the next day without any change and did not decrease until past the middle of the following night.

In the next morning, the sun was still concealed by an unbroken layer of gray clouds, and gusts still stirred the bushes and trees. The carpenter discovered that the stream was full to the top of its banks and carried along broken limbs and uprooted plants. In the strictures of its channel and where the trees had grown low to the water, the flotsam was caught and choked up into chaotic dams of logs, sticks, whole ferns, and mats of leaves. Water, backed up by these obstructions, spread out in shallow fans onto the grassland.

At noon the mate slid the door aside again and looked at the sky and the plateau. He saw there was no more rain falling on the island and the wind had lost the energy to do more than rustle the leaves. Far out beyond the coast, a few gray smudges of rain hung between the clouds and the ocean.

"Harrison," the mate called out, "take Thomas and go to the lookout. Then see how our traps have fared."

The crewmen rolled up their trouser legs and splashed through the water spreading out of the stream and ankle-deep across the grassland. In the dips it was up to their knees. At the lookout, the men discovered nothing. They never expected to find a ship there, but they searched the sea beyond the spits. The bay was all a slate gray laced with whitecaps, from side to side and far north to the chops, miles away. No captain would have neared an unknown island in such weather unless his vessel was in danger of foundering. They started off on what was now a marked path to the shallows, one that followed a course east by north. The grass, wet and heavy with rain, had bowed over, and the wind had driven it low, lodging it in great patches.

After a quarter of a mile of marching, Thomas turned his head and was about to say something when he halted and stared. He raised his hand and pointed to the peaks. Harrison, looking puzzled and with a hesitant turn of his head, stopped and looked back. Both viewed the top third of the peaks covered with snow and standing out boldly against the dark clouds behind them.

"Beautiful," Harrison whispered.

"I cannot believe it, Chips. Are we still that far below the line?"

"There it is, lad, but I don't think it will come any lower. There is a natural mark there where the trees will not grow. I think that is as far down as the snow falls."

With the white covering on them, the peaks looked taller, and the entire island seemed larger and more rugged. The scene held their attention and they rested for several minutes before they moved on.

From the edge of the bluff they looked down on the shallows and saw the traps were damaged. Portions of the area had been changed, with one channel filled in and a new one scoured out in what had been firm, weed-grown banks. Shifting winds and currents during the last two days had created new patterns of land and water in the shallows that would remain until the next storm set upon the island.

They descended to the beach where the waves, opaque with fine sand and silt roiled from the bottom, broke upon the shore and tangles of rockweed were being rolled on and off by each swell. Part of the first trap was washed away and part was covered by a layer of sand deposited over one fence. The second trap had half of both fences in the deeper water carried away, but its apex remained intact. It would take days to repair the damage, and they would require back-loads of sticks to sink into the bottom and more to weave between them.

Thomas surveyed the damage and said, "Perhaps it would be better to begin anew."

"I think it best we not start any repair for a while," Christopher suggested. "If there are more storms this strong to come, then anything we do will be lost labor."

"Old Tobit shan't think so. He would have us rebuild it as quickly as it is destroyed."

"Come, let's see what else has happened to our island," Harrison said and started west through the dunes. He kept ahead of Thomas and then, rounding the foot of the bluff, turned and called back, "The rock is gone!"

"Which one?"

"The great one there on the beach!"

"Has some ship taken it for ballast?" the lad bantered, thinking Harrison had planned to spring some absurd joke on him. He nevertheless hurried ahead and found that it was true. The enormous stone was missing from the shore, an impossible thing! There was no evidence of it. They were less than a mile away and had always seen it as they came around the end of the bluff.

As they neared and climbed over the last dune, the mystery of its disappearance was solved. It was lying in the bay with only a small hump showing above the water. Close at hand, they saw that the storm had blown from the north at least part of the time, and the resultant waves had scoured away the cinders and rocks that supported it. It lay there like a foundered ship with the cadent waves breaking against its rough, dark surface.

Thomas stared at it. Huge and permanent, that rock had been toppled by something as yielding as water. So might the entire island be worn away and carried into the deep.

Harrison turned away and continued on along the shore of the bay. Many of the trees on the bluff had been toppled, and in their falling, had carried lesser ones down. They lay on the slope in a tangle with branches protruding and twisted at odd angles. The leaves, held up at unnatural angles and fluttering in the breeze, showed their undersides. They came upon marks where larger waves had swept up the beach and into the trees growing at the base of the bluff. The haul back of the water had narrowed the shore, and the waves now washed up and down a steeper beach.

The two men marched along and noted the damage that had been done while they had sheltered in their hut. When they reached the lake, they saw the water was dirtied with leaves, both rotted and freshly stripped from branches. Ferns, limbs, and even small trees drifted on its surface, and the rush of water at the outlet, now tripled in width, carried the rubbish into the surf. The waves in turn thrust it back onshore in heaps to the east and west of the mouth of the stream.

The carpenter watched the debris washing past and said, "We must cross and overhaul the shore to the west. There is a chance this wind has brought in something from the wreck."

"Ah, Chris, what we could do with a piece of iron, rope, or an entire sail."

They pulled off their trousers and waited for their chance when the stream was clear of the larger bits of wood and roots. Each man held his clothes under one arm and gripped the other's free hand to steady him. The water was thigh-deep, but they managed to struggle across without being knocked from their feet and carried into the bay.

From the wash marks on the bar, it was evident waves had risen and swept over into the lake during the peak of the storm. At its farther end, in the field of flax, the longer blades of the plants had been driven down in places to half their height. On the slopes of the peaks, whole patches of forest, some an acre in extent, were now chaotic masses of felled and broken trees. That portion of the island had borne the most direct violence of the wind. At the spot where the castaways had landed from the barque, trees loosened from their holds by heavy rain had tumbled from the bluff, carrying rocks and earth with them.

Harrison and Thomas stepped over some of the litter and searched out a path through the turmoil of branches and boulders. Their object was to search the shore for any bit of their vessel that might have been washed in, but they discovered nothing. Thomas looked out over the bay where he guessed the *Dove* had struck and remembered the opinion of the mate that the barque had slid down into some underwater chasm.

"Fathoms and fathoms where we cannot reach," he muttered.

He looked about for Harrison to see if he would respond to his words but discovered he was marching farther on toward the western spit. Thomas turned and hurried his pace to overtake him. They trudged through the dune field, reshaped by the winds of the last two days, and at its far border, arrived at the shore. The surf raised there was even more than they had expected. The approaching swells rose up one after another into curving walls of turbid green carrying fragments of rockweed. Each one thundered down and sent fountains of spray thirty feet high and drove smothering foam high on the beach. Beneath their feet the men felt the island shudder with the assault of the huge waves.

"The storm has knocked up a considerable swell," Thomas said loudly.

"With time enough, it might wear away all!" Harrison called back over the roar of the water.

Hour by hour, the remaining power of the storm lessened. The wind returned to its usual direction and the excess flow drained from the stream and the lake. The morning of the next day began with welcome sunshine.

Tobit and Mr. Morgen inspected the sky and, finding no indication of more rain, set off for the top of the volcano. When they reached the rim, the mate sat upon a rock and from there looked out over the grassland. Captain Tobit stood two paces away, gazing in the same direction, but he was staring intently, as if he saw more than the expanse of grass below. His eyes had a glint, a lively expression the mate had not seen before. His whole stance was straighter and firmer.

"No fairer prospect have I seen," the captain declared, after several minutes. "Don't you agree, Mr. Morgen?"

The mate rose to his feet, nodded and, with the words of one having discovered a long-sought truth, replied, "Aye, as you say, it has been waiting for us, and so perfectly formed to the purpose."

"We will build on the rock of righteousness," the captain continued, drawing himself up even more and raising his chin. "There, across this plain, we will spread our commune. There shall be orderly fields tilled with the loving labor of humble Christians. They will yield plenteous vittles for our table. Set among them will be our white houses. In the center of all, we will raise our church, it too dressed in the purity of white. There we will worship God in the true and faithful way. Such is the sole purpose of our life, that and to see that all others attend to their worship of God each day without fail. There will be no fiddling and dancing, no such frolics, no rum, no nine-pin alleys that tend to immorality or divert our time, for there are joys enough in worship. There will be no sin, can be no fleeting thought of sin. The devil, the heathen, the apostate will be awe-struck, thewless before our superior metal and our will to hold evil at bay, oh yes, even cast it aside. This will be our antechamber to Heaven. There is nothing doubting but this will come to pass. I, Seth Tobit, will order and cause this all to be." The captain held out his arms toward the grassland below, and his eyes widened as if his vision was coming into being while he spoke. His left arm fell to his side. His right arm remained extended, offering the mate his aerial creation.

Mr. Morgen had been listening intently to the captain while scanning the land that spread from the base of the volcano to the shallows. Then he turned to the captain and asked, "And about our people. We will build a canoe, sail to the Bay of Islands, and send for them soon?"

"Yes, when all is ready, true Christians, the chosen, your wife and children, will be welcome. But there is much work to be done before they arrive. First, we must divert this water from the crater to the plain."

"But it already flows to there."

"Aye, yet below its level. We would have to lift it in some fashion. If we tried to divert it from the cascade, that would require shifting those great blocks of stone. No, I have a far easier design. When I show you, you will see how all these things fall into place. It is all designed to be so: our landing on this island, the discovery of the potatoes, and here, this mountain filled with heated water. All are parts of a great design, but it is not complete. You see how it remains for us to bring it all into being, to gather these parts together in proper order and use. It is the charge given us by the Lord! We are being put to a trial. Do we recognize our role in this magnificent order of the universe? Let us not be found wanting, Mr. Morgen. You and I were not fated to be mere traders. Have you not in your innermost feeling been given to think that something greater was meant for you?"

The mate quickly nodded and replied, "Oh, yes, many times."

"So you have! I saw it in the way you stepped aboard and gave your commands. There is no mistaking those who have been raised up. Now you are aware how our Lord works. We are preferred among others, even among all those faithful to the true God. He has put this task before us. Now you and I must do our part, the glorious part. I was given a vision in which I was chosen to commence a new beginning on Earth. I did not know how it was to come about. But see how we have been thrust upon this unspoiled land by God's very hand! There is His great design in it. Thus, "*Dove*" was the fitting name I gave our vessel. It has searched out this new Mount Ararat and put it in our way. This is the noble labor given us, here and on this island.

We must use our eyes, not only to see what is before us, but also to recognize what it is meant to become! We must cleave always to the true faith. In doing so, we are assured to be given eternal life with Him. Our life on this Earth is but a misery compared to what awaits us in Heaven."

The captain beckoned for the mate to follow as he walked along the edge of the crater. He continually looked down the outside slope as he moved ahead. When he reached halfway around the crater, he exclaimed, "Aha, let me show you something!" He started over the steep side into the bushes and ferns. The mate went after him, sliding more than climbing down. When they reached the trees, they grasped the trunks and held onto them for a second as they passed to slow their descent. The rocks and cinders they kicked loose tumbled down as small avalanches, making noises in the greenery below. Captain Tobit halted by seizing a frond, then swung to his left and traversed the side of the volcano for several minutes, edging from tree to tree. He was standing before the shallow cave in the slope when the mate caught up to him. The captain climbed over the mound of rocks at the entrance and up to the back of the cavity.

"No, no, no, not by mere chance alone, Mr. Morgen," the captain called out, hammering the rock face with his fist. "If we open this and allow the lake to escape, it will flow toward the center of the flatland. It will water and warm the potatoes planted in our fields. You see how everything we have met with points to a clever design."

The mate studied the crannied rock for a minute, picking at it with a fingernail. "Ah . . . you mean to place a charge in here as the Cornish men do . . . shatter it with the might of the gunpowder. . . . So that is your purpose."

With a smile and a slow nod of his head the captain confirmed that the mate had guessed correctly. "Here," he explained, pointing to the rock, "the wall of the mountain must be weakened. It has to be so. See how the water finds its way through in places."

Mr. Morgen took a step back and, looking at the back of the cave, said, "I never thought to question it all as you do, but now I see how it all has been brought together, even this hollow is so perfectly placed. Yes, all is waiting for our hand to shape it. This island was not filled with savages, but left here vacant for us to use."

"The land will become even more fruitful under our hands, to sustain us and all our kindred. Now our designs must be composed with great care, and we must be wary of the power that opposes the goodness of the Lord."

"And how are we to know it?" the mate asked.

"By vigilance, sir, by vigilance. You know, there in Botany Bay and Van Diemen's Land they have planted all the vice and foulness of England, visible enemies of the Lord, and there on our other side in Tovy Poenamoo are the heathens not yet given the Word. But the devil works in other ways. Oh, he works best by trickery and wiles. That is when he is most dangerous and the least visible. You see how Thomas is willful and opposes me. I fear that in the future he will defy me again and altogether. He may be under the sway of some evil notion that causes him to give me such offense. We, the true Christians, are forever under siege from all directions. Mr. Morgen, we must be ever watchful."

"What are we to do now?" the mate inquired.

"Imprimus, to release the water from this side of the mountain. The plateau below here is a mite higher, thus the water can be carried farther by its natural flow. Make your mine well. Once the stream reaches there we will make furrows to guide it to all corners. When the others arrive with teams, the land must be ready for the plow. There must be a plenty of potatoes to plant. We shall have fowl and kine and all manner of beasts to provide our vittles."

The mate suddenly raised his right hand and held up his forefinger. "The niter!" he burst out. "The niter! I would not have found it had not the bear gone into that hole. He was leading me to it! Then the animal vanished in a trice. It was meant for me to find it, and it was meant for me to make the gunpowder. As you say, sir, all this has not happened by mere chance alone. It could not. Yes, this has not been a misadventure for us." He looked at the captain and saw his jaw was set firmly, yet the skin at the corners of his eyes wrinkled slightly with a suppressed smile.

When the mate returned to the hut, he immediately brought out his materials and resumed concocting his powder with added care and determination. The train by which he set off his charges continued to frustrate him. He filled small reeds with his powder and touched them off again and again. Sometimes they fizzled a bit and then would not burn further. In the next trial they might flash rapidly from one end to the other. Captain Tobit watched the mate's efforts for a short while, then wandered off, as he had no suggestions to offer.

Mr. Morgen sat and stared at his last attempt, which appeared to have hung fire or died out totally. He slapped his thigh and issued a muffled curse. A few seconds later the little squib the train led to popped.

"Damn," he growled, "it must be the niter! It is not even in its effect. What am I to do?"

CHAPTER 12

THOMAS groaned and opened his eyes. The morning light entered the hole in the gable end, and by its dull illumination he could make out the sooted thatch of the roof and the strips of dried meat hanging from the ridgepole. It was a little early, and he realized it was a dream that had awakened him. In flailing his arms about he had thrown off his fur cover and the chill air had awakened him. He reached and pulled his cover over his upper body again. A confused and repetitious nightmare in which he was building a canoe had disturbed his rest. He could never finish anything on it. Its rigging would unravel as soon as it was set up. Lashings came unknotted and the booms fell away. Then he would doggedly start again, retying everything. Sometimes he had to begin wholly anew, burning out another hull. In a better dream, he managed to finish his vessel and sail to the Middle Island, but he dared not land for the beach was lined with savages dancing wildly, waving clubs, and wrenching their mouths into grimaces. Each of their faces was covered with a blue-black scrollwork of tattoos. He would head offshore, only to have the wind force him back again and again.

From the other side of the partition came the sound of someone stirring. Thomas could be sure it was the mate, for he always awakened before the captain and made it his first duty to reach up and strike another mark on the ridgepole with a piece of charcoal. That mark Mr. Morgen so faithfully made would be the two hundred and eleventh made since their first morning. It was now July. July of 1821. Had the barque not struck upon that rock they would most likely be on soundings near the New England shore.

Enough of the hides had been unhaired for a sail and there was rope and marline to rig everything on their canoe. All that was left was to burn and scrape out their hull, but the first favorable time to set off from the island would be no sooner than four months. The start of 1822 would be nearly upon them when they reached the Middle Island or Cook Strait, and if they did not fall in with a sealer or a whaler there, it might mean weeks of coasting before they arrived in the Bay of Islands.

Birds outside burst into their usual songs, and he listened as he lay under his fur. More joined the morning's chorus each minute, and he imagined that was because the sun's light was now striking the trees behind the hut. It was a good beginning for the day, he thought, to hear all the diverse chirpings as the birds and little parrots flitted through the bushes and treetops. Slowly he stretched his arms over his head and arched his back.

"Chill this morning," Harrison said suddenly.

Thomas, not expecting that the carpenter was awake, turned and saw him peeking from under his covering.

"Aye, the coldest yet. Do you think it will get worse?" Thomas asked.

"Perhaps a mite, but it will be better than it was on Macquarie. The Fish will rise, then the Whale, and it will be warm again."

"Chris, you go to the lookout this morning and I will stir up the fire and warm the breakfast. Agreed?"

"Agreed," Harrison replied and sat up in his bed, smoothing his mussed hair and beard with his fingers. He rose and went to slide the door aside. "On my way lad," he said as he turned to leave.

Thomas arose and wrapped the fur around his shoulders, then slipped out the door. He raked a stick through the ashes and found a few embers buried in the ashes. With a handful of twigs on the gathered coals and a few puffs of his breath, the fire was going again. He placed a few limbs on it, meaning to let them burn and die to a bed of coals as usual. Earshells of potatoes placed close by would warm in half an hour, and each man could cook his meat to his own taste. The fire blazed and Thomas added his fuel piece by piece. While it burned, he went into the hut and brought out the potatoes that had been steamed in the cooking hole two days before. He laid out strips of "bear" flesh with the sticks to hold them when the coals were ready.

Mr. Morgen peered out the door and inquired, "Where's Harrison?"

"Gone to the lookout," Thomas answered.

"Ah, good," the officer said and ducked back inside.

The fire was turning into a fine bed of coals for cooking. Thomas crowded all the ends of the unburned sticks into the center, knowing once they were consumed, there would be no annoying smoke to burn their eyes. He placed the shells around the perimeter, tilting them inward to allow the potatoes to take up the heat more readily. With everything prepared, he stood near the fire with his hands open to take off the chill of the morning air. It had become comfortable on the island, more comfortable than being aboard the barque and far more livable than the miserable and stinking rookeries. He looked up when he heard an odd noise from the path to the fall. Suddenly, the bushes were thrust aside. Harrison burst through onto the barrow and staggered to the hut. He grabbed the thatch with both hands and leaned his left cheek against the wall. The carpenter's face, hair, and beard were wet with perspiration, and he gasped desperately for air.

"Chris! What's happened?" Thomas shouted.

Harrison's right hand released the thatch and pointed north. Then he held it up to indicate he could not yet speak.

Thomas looked over the carpenter's body. His face was reddened and his feet were muddied, but there was no obvious injury. The lad spun about, and dashed down through the brush until he was on the route to the fall. Seeing nothing unusual, he halted. The bushes remained motionless. The treetops swayed slightly in the breeze. He listened for several seconds, but he could only hear the chirping of the birds and the faint rumble of the cascade to the south. He turned and ran back to the work yard.

The mate and the captain were standing beside the carpenter repeating questions, but he was still unable to answer. The mate turned to Thomas and asked, "What's the matter with him?"

"He ran in here as if devils were after him."

"They may well be!" the captain blurted out, looking warily in the direction of the bluff.

Mr. Morgen then asked Harrison, "Is there danger for us?"

He shook his head once, then drew in a deep breath. Harrison's panting slowed and he leaned his head back from the thatch and breathed out one hoarse word.

"Brig!"

"Huzzah!" the lad cheered and slapped his hands together. "We are rescued!"

Captain Tobit held up his palm for silence. "Have you spoken to the crew?" he demanded.

Harrison shook his head.

"Have they seen you?" the mate asked.

The carpenter, after a few more gasps, responded, "No, ran here."

"Why didn't you go to them and let them know we are wrecked here?" Thomas demanded.

"Have time . . . they're two anchors down . . . have boat ashore," Harrison choked out. "Come to wood an' water."

Mr. Morgen looked in the direction of the bay and asked the carpenter, "A brig, you say?"

"Aye," he answered. "Hundred eighty . . . two hundred ton."

"They must have come in during the night," the mate guessed.

"I wonder why they would choose to enter the bay in the dark?" the captain muttered.

"I'll go and let them know we are here," Thomas called back as he started toward the trail.

"Stop! Stand where you are!" the captain shouted and pointed his right finger at the lad.

Thomas wheeled around and with a bewildered look on his face marched back. "Why?" he protested. "We must let them know we are wrecked here. They might sail within the hour, and this might be our sole chance for rescue."

Captain Tobit shook his head vigorously and warned, "We do not know where these men have come from. Harrison has seen them only from the lookout. They may be rogues and murderers who have taken this vessel in New Holland, as I have warned you. No! We will look them over before we reveal ourselves."

"It's a sensible caution," Mr. Morgen agreed. "They might well be convicts. If they are men facing the gibbet, they will not want witnesses to their whereabouts. We must know for sure who they are."

"Mr. Morgen," the captain ordered, "bring out your bows and arrows. Each of you men take one from the mate. We may have to defend ourselves."

Once they had their weapons, Captain Tobit led the group toward the bluff and across the stream to the west side of the fall. They moved cautiously toward the path that led down to the field of flax, hunched low and keeping behind the greenery.

"Stay well hidden," the captain whispered as though the brig was only a few yards away. "Any master fetching this island will look it over well with his glass." The four men worked their way into the ferns at the edge of the bluff and crouched there, peeking between the fronds.

"What a glorious sight," Harrison sighed.

The brig was held by her anchors fore and aft, parallel to the shore about a cable's length away. Five black squares were spaced evenly in the wide, white band painted along her wales. All her sails were furled and not simply gathered up by the clew-lines and the bunts, perhaps an indication the brig meant to remain after the wood and water were aboard. A boat was drawn up just opposite it on the beach. One sailor serving as a guard sat on the cinders and rested his back against his charge. The moored brig and the man and boat on the shore appeared out of place, almost apparitions to the crewmen. They had scanned the sea and the bay for months and had accepted that it might be years before a ship happened upon the island. Now that it was there, with its tall masts and riding quietly between its bowers, its reality was almost suspect.

"She flies no ensign," the captain noted. "Mark you, that is not a good thing."

"Still has her royals yards up," the mate said. "She's not come up from the sealing grounds."

"Aye, this time of year they surely would have sent them down, unless she has been in the low latitudes," Harrison pointed out. "Maybe the brig is in the sandalwood trade."

"Or fled here from New Holland or Van Diemen's. That brig there may be full of cutthroats," the captain warned. "With springs on her lines she may bring her guns to command the whole of the beach."

"Any master would do so to protect his men on a strange shore," Thomas said.

"Come, lads, follow me," Captain Tobit ordered. He wriggled back out of the ferns, picked up his bow and arrows, and started down the path to the flax field, slinking along in an awkward crouch.

For several yards along the top of the path, they would be visible to anyone on the brig, the shore, or the ground around the lake. They hurried through into the trees below. At several places on the descending path there were openings in the forest. The captain approached each of these and peeked out to assure himself that neither the sailor on the beach nor the crewmen aboard the brig were looking in the castaways' direction or gave any indication they had been spotted. Once he was satisfied they had not been detected, he waved the others on to dart past into cover below. Upon reaching the bottom, they were hidden in the dense stand of plants and could approach the shore by the aisles cut through the tall leaves. Harrison took the lead. He and Thomas had made other cuttings to gather the leaves and make paths to the shore of the lake to snare ducks. The carpenter instantly knew which turn to take and hopped over the stumps without a second's pause.

In a few minutes he stopped, turned to the others, and whispered, "Down, it's on hands and knees from here to the edge of the flax."

The castaways crawled through the sparser plants until they were fifty or sixty feet from the boat. They peeked between the blades of the flax and had a fine view of the brig.

The crewman guarding the boat was still sitting on the beach and leaning idly against its bow. He held a long-stemmed pipe to his mouth with his left hand and cupped his fingers over the bowl. Each puff he exhaled drifted off with the breeze. On his head was a newly painted tarpaulin hat, worn back in the usual manner of topmen and revealing his thick red hair. The skin of his freckled face had not tanned the least and the skin of both his nose and cheeks was peeling. He sat totally at ease with his bare feet pushed halfway into the loose, damp cinders and with his old jacket unbuttoned, showing part of his red flannel shirt. To Thomas, the sailor looked to be an honest tar like any of his mates who had been on the *Dove*. The man's calloused right hand, resting in a claw-like curl on his knee, evidenced rough usage. He felt a pang at the man's appearance. He remembered that, dressed in clean duck trousers and a like jacket, he had looked just so for the first part of the voyage. The young, shaven face appeared odd to him after having seen only untrimmed beards for months. The faces beside him, all hairy and seared by the sun, were those of wild men, beasts by comparison. A sharp pair of shears would have clipped away half their menace. Their hide clothes were oily around the collars and cuffs. Even rubbing those places with ashes after soaking in the hot water of the crater did not clean them properly.

"He looks just as we did when we came to this island," the carpenter whispered, "'cept he's clean shaven."

"You see the boat," the mate noted. "It's well kept. All Bristol fashion."

The hull of the boat indeed was coated with glossy white paint and the gunnel neatly trimmed with a dark green. A new hemp line was bent to the ring in the bow and the other end left inside the boat. The blades and shafts of the oars were visible where they lay across the thwarts. They had been wrapped with log line above and below where they fit into the locks, and the line worked into turks' heads. The whole of the oars had been recently covered with varnish of pine.

Beyond the boat, the brig rode easy at her cables with wavelets lapping at her sides. A band of her copper showed above the water, a clue that her hull was not fully loaded. With her head to the west she showed only her larboard to the island. The name and home port, displayed on her sternboard, could not be seen unless the men revealed themselves and went east a-ways along the bar. Several of the crew were at work bringing up water butts and stacking them at the gangway; on the far side of her deck, two boys were working the spun yarn winch, with one turning the truck and the other walking the yarns between the main shrouds and the windlass.

Mr. Morgen wiggled closer to the captain and, in a hushed voice, spoke into his ear, “She’s taut all round. Furling well done. They pulled a neat skin over them. I’d say she has able men fore and aft. Botany Bay men wouldn’t keep a vessel so.”

Captain Tobit objected, “But her crew would keep it so even if they were governed by convicts. It is their habit. There could be men holding the captain in his cabin as a hostage and making them all obey.”

The mate reached over and touched the carpenter with the tip of his bow. “Can you see the others of the crew ashore?” he asked softly.

“No sign of them, save their tracks going off west,” Harrison answered. “Must be after wood and taking measure of this place.”

The captain raised his hand slowly and pointed to the stern of the brig. “There, do you see it, aft of the wheel?” he asked.

“Yes,” the mate answered, “a stern chase, or perhaps it’s only a quaker.”

The muzzle of a small cannon just showed above the rail.

“What do you make of that?” the captain inquired, looking at the carpenter.

“It’s a wise precaution. Her ports are false, painted on. She has nothing on her gun deck, else two or three would be open and the guns run out,” Harrison explained. “They may have had deceits worked on them in the islands. Loaded with a few spikes, it would be enough discourage pirates or cannibals from getting close.”

“Or cut us all low, if there are convicts aboard,” Tobit hissed.

“That brig is our means home,” Thomas whispered. “I see nothing amiss here. That man is no different from me. If we do not go out there, we will never set foot aboard.”

"Well, lad, you may have your chance now," the captain said, fitting an arrow to his bow. By rolling around until he was parallel to the beach and lying on his left side, he could draw his weapon and aim it at the sailor by the boat. "Now," he breathed out, "keep to the larboard. I want a clear shot at him if he attacks you."

"Do you expect him to slay me for no cause?" Thomas asked.

He left his bow and arrows on the beach and rose to his feet. Without hesitating a second, he walked out from behind the plants and directly toward the boat. The sailor had his eyes closed in the enjoyment of his ease and his tobacco. Thomas kept moving ahead. "Hoy," he called softly. The man opened his eyes slowly. When he turned his head and caught the full view of Thomas, he stared, unable to move. His pipe fell from his hand and fear spread across his face.

"Hoy," the lad repeated and stopped walking.

The sailor gasped and leaped to his feet.

Thomas held out his open hands to each side, showing he had no weapons, and retired one pace, but the gestures did not calm the man. He stared at the apparition of Thomas, dressed in dirty skins, with a face burned brown, and his hair and beard bleached and frizzed by the sun. He stepped backward and reached slowly into the boat. His right hand came up holding a musket. He brought it up to support it with his left hand, and with a quick movement of his thumb, cocked the weapon.

Thomas held his trembling hands higher. "We are from the barque *Dove!*" he blurted out. He heard the snap of a bowstring. An arrow whished past him, past the sailor, and landed in the surf.

"You damned fool!" Thomas shouted as he whirled about.

Harrison leaped up from the flax, pointing to the sailor and yelled, "Drop!"

Thomas began to fall, twisting to face the bay again as he went down. He saw the sailor had the musket to his shoulder and his cheek to the stock. A jet of flame blotted out the end of the barrel and a cloud of gray smoke obscured the upper half of the sailor. Thomas felt nothing and guessed the ball must have passed over his head.

While the report of the gun rang painfully in his ears, the smoke drifted away to the east.

"No, no!" Thomas cried as he jumped to his feet again. "We are not savages!" He bowed forward slightly and displayed his empty hands again.

In one motion the sailor laid the musket in the boat and brought up a pistol. The sound of the musket shot came back, echoing off the face of the bluff and around the lake. The sailor's eyes were wide open in fright, and his hands shook as he pulled the cock back. Slowly he stepped back and pointed the barrel of the weapon alternately at Thomas and at Harrison. The terror on his face grew as he darted looks down the beach for his mates.

"We have been wrecked here . . . struck a rock. . . ." The carpenter began to explain.

Thwack! The bowstring snapped again.

The sailor was whipped to his left by the force of the arrow that struck him in the side just above his belt. His arm went up and the pistol fired into the air. He was turned around facing the bay and the brig. The glass-tipped arrow protruded three inches out of his back, just at the edge of his monkey jacket. Now hatless, he stumbled abound and faced Thomas again. The pistol dropped from his hand, and his blue eyes stared fiercely.

"God damn you!" Thomas screamed as he wheeled, searching for the captain. "You bloody devil!" he added and dashed into the flax to find the officer still lying on the cinders and holding his discharged bow. With two steps, he leaped onto Tobit and grabbed at his throat.

The mate and Harrison pulled at his arms to free the captain, but Thomas had a savage grip and was hammering the captain's head against the earth.

"Stop it! You will snap his neck!" the mate shouted.

"I want to break it!" the lad shrieked. "Blast his stinking guts! Damn him! Damn him! Damn him!" He slammed the captain's head against the beach in time with each curse.

The mate and the carpenter pried his hands loose and shoved him away, but he dived back between them and made a second attack. When Harrison and the mate pulled him off again, Thomas held tufts of white hair in his fists that he had ripped from the old man's beard. Harrison suddenly released the lad and ran out of the flax and onto the open beach. He pointed to the west where the other crewmen of the brig were shouting and running toward them. "They have muskets!" he cried out. "Quickly, back to the bluff!"

Mr. Morgen pulled the captain to his feet and towed him by the front of his jacket back into the denser stand of the plants. The carpenter followed, trying to help the mate. Thomas, instead, turned and ran out to the boat. There the bewildered tar, his face now frightfully pale, knelt on the cinders. His right hand grabbed for the gunnel of the boat for support, and he looked up at Thomas with his mouth half open as if he would speak but could not. Four men carrying muskets were racing up the beach toward the boat, but Thomas was frozen there, his eyes filling with tears as he stared at the man gripping the boat to keep from collapsing. The fletched shaft piecing the man's stomach looked ghastly.

Harrison rushed back out of the thicket and grabbed Thomas's arm. "Run, lad!" he shouted into his ear. "They will shoot you without a word!"

The cinders at their feet erupted, and grit splattered against the leather of their trousers. Instantly, there was a report from the bay.

"There, from the brig!" Harrison yelled, pointing toward the bay. A puff of smoke was drifting alongside the vessel. One crewman was aiming his weapon at them from the rail and another was ramming a ball down the barrel of his rifle. Thomas and the carpenter dashed from the beach and dodged around the thick bunches of leaves. One more shot was fired from the side of the ship, and a tall leaf severed by the ball fell against Thomas's face as he ran by. They overtook the officers in half a minute. Shouts from their pursuers diminished and then ceased as they fled.

The crew from the brig, Thomas imagined, was moving cautiously and quietly through the dense plants, fearful of ambush. Having seen

Harrison and himself so rudely clothed and bearded, they might well believe the island was home to a race of mad men. They would not follow too far inland and risk falling into a trap.

With Harrison leading the way, the castaways broke out of the flax and started up the track to the plateau. It was slower going up the grade. The mate took charge of the captain and pushed him on when he slowed or stopped. Halfway up to the fall, the carpenter halted at one of the gaps in the trees and undergrowth and peered out at the shore and the plants at the end of the lake.

"I can see no one," he said. "Perhaps they are going back. There is nothing moving."

Mr. Morgen stepped up beside him and gave a quick glance over the land and the shore. "They may be running up the path whilst we stand here," he warned. "We must get to the top where we will have room to flee. Come, lads, quickly."

The mate had no sooner started to move, prodding the captain along, when they heard a shout from below. A man was standing at the edge of the flax plants and holding a musket. In the next few seconds two more men parted the leaves and took up places beside him. The first man raised his weapon and aimed it at them, but deciding the range was too great and a waste of powder and ball he lowered it. One of the other men shouted something at the castaways and shook his fist. The third man shifted his musket and raised his right hand. Then extending his middle finger, he thrust it upward as if it would injure them.

Mr. Morgen grabbed the dazed captain and shoved him up the path. "Hurry!" he called to the others, "or they will be upon us."

They reached the top near the fall exhausted, gasping for breath, and dropped into the ferns to hide. Harrison kept a watch on the track below to warn them if any of the crew of the brig appeared. Thomas worked himself forward until he could see the ship lying in the bay. Men were standing by the cannon, but they dared not fire it while they were unaware of where their own men were.

"There is our relief," he hissed at the mate and hammered his fist on the earth. "Now they are our mortal enemies, thanks to that suspicious old fool. We could see they were not Botany Bay men. This has been a bad piece of work. That poor jack there on the beach will die a terrible death in the next day or two. He can't last much longer. That is nothing but murder."

The mate didn't look at the lad and made no indication he heard him.

It was a crime and the mate knows that, Thomas thought. How could the captain ever make such an act look just or diminish his guilt? Oh, yes, old Tobit will say he knew the man was going to fire or even claim the sailor fired first. If it ever comes into a court, he will say that, and they will believe him. He might even swear the attempt to speak to the sailor was the cause. The poor fellow was in a fright, but more soft words would have eased it, even if he didn't speak English.

A few minutes later, the mate got to his feet and helped the captain up. The two officers started for the stream where they always crossed. Harrison fell in behind them and marched past Thomas shaking his head and looking as if he had just attended a funeral. Thomas grabbed the carpenter's arm and pulled him back.

"My eyes aren't mates if old Toby's a sane man," he whispered into Harrison's ear.

He let go and watched all three march to the crossing. They were well into the bushes before he started off. After wading out on the far bank of the stream, he didn't hurry ahead to overtake the others but stood watching for a moment, then, thief-like, slipped into the bushes and headed toward the lookout.

On the beach a cluster of men was launching the boat back to the brig, but another boat was being hoisted out and that baffled Thomas. He had expected them to leave as soon as they could. It must be that they are in such need of water, they cannot even reach the Middle Island without filling their casks. What water they had must be stinking. It was a slim hope, yet he thought he might have a chance to get aboard if they stayed a few hours before their cables were heaved in.

He kept looking back toward the stream. The lookout was a bad place to be. Captain Tobit and the mate might appear and drag him away, or men from the brig could burst from the greenery, intent on swift revenge. Thomas hiked beyond the tiers until he reached a place where he could climb down the bluff. Below its edge, he found a gap in the trees from which he was able to watch the brig yet not be discovered from above. It was a refuge for the moment, but he had to do something quickly.

He must devise a plan, he thought. How might he get aboard that brig before her canvas was loosed and sheeted home? If he approached them on the beach, even alone, they will suspect trickery, and he would receive several musket balls for his pains. If he waited until they were hoisting their boats aboard and called to them from the beach, it could be the same result. They might vent their anger by firing the stern chase at him. That might be much worse if it were loaded with a sack of musket balls or spikes, as Chips guessed. If he could suddenly appear on deck, however, unarmed and after the brig was far from the island, where the crew would have no fear of a savage attack, then he might tell his story. Then if they wished to return and take revenge on the captain, all well and good. But it would be risky at best. That fool had made it so. Am I to suffer for his lunacy? he asked himself. They will leave soon, within an hour, and I will have no choice but to watch them sail out of the bay. Any report of their encounter here will warn off other ships, and then a canoe will be the only way from the island.

The thought of a canoe made him realize that setting off, even in the best of weather, would require pluck. He might be alone out there, for Christopher, despite his cheerful spirits, might not wish to go. The mate and old Tobit seemed unwilling even to consider building a boat or canoe of any sort. As desperate as he was to see home again, he was not sure he could leave knowing he could not turn back and find the island again. He well knew how it felt to be in a frail little shell, swiftly rising and falling on huge swells coming out of the west. He could only make a course by following the correct stars on clear nights, and the rising and setting sun. He would have to trust the wind had not changed while the sun was high up in the sky and on the clouded nights. There would be no land on the horizon out there to set him right, nothing in the full circle of the sea and sky to make for, no hints of where to point the bow. He might be sailing away from land and never know it. And what of the canoe? Would all the bindings hold, or would they part and his vessel fall to pieces? He might end his life lying in a dismasted hull or be eaten by some great fish.

Thomas was elated when he saw that his guess about the conditions on the brig was true. Both boats were being loaded with empty butts and more were being streamed astern of them to be towed ashore. Four men carrying muskets and hangers climbed into each boat. They were going to fill every butt aboard at their leisure and not, as he had expected, hurriedly take on only enough to carry them to the Middle Island or on to New Holland. After the boats were loaded, Thomas watched them being rowed to the bar almost opposite the fall. They must have discovered it back in its recess and thus knew the water of the slough was sweet. It was a clever move. They could get their water and yet not risk ambush from the stand of flax. Also the stern chase could be brought to bear and that more than anything would drive off attackers. He hoped the watering would take them hours, enough time to permit him to get aboard the brig, but it wasn't likely they would stay moored there as darkness came on.

At the very moment he watched the men roll the butts across the bar to the lake, he was aware that the wounded man might be dead aboard the brig or suffering terrible pain with small chance of recovery. He remembered the stories told of the men with stomach wounds during the war, how their injuries turned septic, and of the agony they suffered before they expired.

How could he ever convince that crew he was not the one who had fired the arrow? If those men knew that there were but four on the island, they might in their anger hunt them down one by one. But the way in which they held their weapons and walked about revealed they feared the woods were full of savages eager to kill and eat any stranger. Only when they felt safe and with every advantage would they listen to him before they fired their muskets. That could only be aboard the brig and only when it was far out in the bay. If he could manage to hide aboard and suddenly appear on deck, he would not seem a danger to them. Even if they did not speak English, he was sure he could make it known to them by dumb show that he was a castaway and not a cannibal.

Part of the brig's crew worked at their leisure, filling the water butts and ferrying them to the ship. They even walked along the bar and gathered what wood was there, but they never neared the heavy growth at either end. Though cautious, they showed no haste to quit the island. Some men were reeving new lines on the foremast. It was all quite odd, as if the wounding of their mate had not happened.

Thomas formed his plan. There wasn't much to it. He would work his way down to a place near the outlet of the lake, always keeping under the cover of the trees. There he would hide and watch what happened next. If the brig started to hoist her bowers, his only choice then was to hail them from the beach and swim out to her. Seeing that he was alone in the water they might allow his approach and not fire upon him. It was a desperate move, yet there was nothing else to do. It was very unlikely the vessel would remain until dark, but if she did, he could swim out and conceal himself under her channels or somewhere on board. Then, naked and unarmed, he would reveal himself before them. Surely they would not cut a man down in that condition. He must seize this opportunity or attempt to sail a hollowed log over two or three hundred miles of heaving ocean and land on a perilous coast. He was girt by those two choices.

Determined to get on board, he started directly down the slope to the shore. For more than an hour he forced a way through the vines and around clumps of ferns. He realized the brig could be leaving while he was making his way to the beach, and he took chances, sometimes leaping over low limbs where he might tumble or injure himself. Once he got to the trees that bordered the back of the beach he peeked out and was relieved to see the ship still moored. Keeping concealed from the crewmen on the bar, it took him nearly another hour to slip along to the lake. He found a good vantage-point where he could see all and watched for what the crew would do next.

The boats rowed back and forth between the bar and the brig until every butt was filled and taken aboard. Thomas knew they were near leaving when he saw them rig the tackle to hoist the first boat aboard. The timed shouts of the crew came to him each time they heaved on the bars of the windlass. The boat rose from the water and was swung inboard.

When they began with the second boat, he knew he had to run along the bar and make his plea to those on the brig. He was fearful. What would it be for him, musket balls or a welcome aboard? Out on that bar he would have no protection from their fire, and he might be wounded or killed. If they pointed rifles at him, he could only dive into the lake. That would be the end of his effort to get aboard the ship, and he must then abandon all hope in that direction.

The tackle was taken off the first boat and swung out to bring in the second one. Thomas knew it was the critical point. With a great effort, he rose to his feet and was about to step out of the bushes into full view. He didn't want to do it and stayed in his place peering over the bush at the brig. He decided not to go into the open until the men were laboring to hoist the next boat aboard, but the crew unexpectedly did no more than hook the tackle on and then went about other work. He was mystified. If they didn't take it in they would not heave up the bowers. He couldn't see any reason for it. They had filled their butts and stowed them. Why were they not taking in the last boat? Did they intend to gather wood? All their actions showed they feared to approach any bush where the imagined cannibals might fall upon them. Curious, he thought. If he were master of the vessel, he would heave up his bowers and get beyond the heads of the bay while there was still enough light and the wind held.

After waiting for hours, Thomas still saw no stir on board to get under way. He kept a close watch on the brig while the sun dipped into a layer of clouds above the horizon. Through the last dogwatch, the boat remained at the gangway and no crewmen neared the windlass. No topmen went onto the yards. Their inaction, though it fit well with his plan, was confounding. He wished the brig to remain there, but he could discover no reason why it should not leave. Twilight faded over the bay, and he felt it was safe enough to leave the cover of the bushes. With slow steps he moved into the open until he reached the outlet of the lake. The sternboard of the vessel faced him, but the name and home port were in deep shadow and even his young eyes could not make them out.

Suddenly Thomas's heart seemed to pause mid-beat. He heard the pawl of the windlass clicking as its barrel turned. The brig was moving as she veered away cable forward to pick up her other bower. She's hoisting her anchors, he thought. The one aft was being hove short. The boat will be taken in next. When her best bower comes up, she will be heading north!

He broke into a run along the beach, meaning to get as close to the brig as possible and then swim out to her. Just opposite the dark shape of the hull, he stopped. Above it, her two taunt masts and their rigging were intricate black silhouettes against the last faint light in the sky. The boat was still tied at the gangway but no longer visible. No light was set out. But that was to be expected.

The noise of the windlass ceased after several minutes and he imagined the shank painter was being passed, yet no voices came of orders given or curses shouted when things went awry. The next sound he would hear would be the windlass again as it hoisted in the last boat. When it was aboard and the crew busied forward, he must start for the vessel, for then the other bower would be coming up. With all the men moving around on deck and the topmen going aloft to take off gaskets, it would be his best chance to board.

But no more noise of any kind came from the brig, not another click of the pawl, no chant of the men as they heaved. It was uncanny. She remained there, riding by her cable from the remaining anchor, the boat at her side, and her decks silent. He waited for what seemed to him to be half an hour for the squeal of a line passing through a block or the murmur of a voice. The brig was still there but not showing a glim from a single lamp. Were they going to wait and leave by the morning light? Why didn't they hoist in the boat? It made no sense to leave it unless they meant to land again. The hull was now only a smutch with the masts rising above it. He decided to swim out and see what caused the crew to suddenly stop all work and leave the vessel as if it were abandoned.

Thomas slipped off his skins and felt the cold water moving up around his legs as he waded in. He began swimming toward the brig, wishing he could cut through as fast as he was able, but if they heard him approaching, they would make a sport shooting at him with their muskets. He had to keep his hands below the surface and paddle quietly. The silent, black form grew in size as he neared it. Only that shape and a few stars gave dimensions to the night. At closer range he made out the boat and swam toward it. Once at its side, he reached up and grasped its gunnel. The touch of her wood sent a thrill through him and his pulse pounded in his ears. He had made it! A light breeze carried once-familiar scents to him, and he rested there tallying them: tar, tobacco, wet rope, paint, all the smells attached to ships plus that of a hot lamp. His days on the island had sharpened his nose, and it was a joy to breathe in those odors. He had known them all first in Stonington when he visited the docks and then had become used to them during the months aboard the *Dove*. They meant he was only a few feet from rescue! With little effort, he could pull himself into the boat. From there he might crawl up through the open gangway and be on deck. But where was the anchor watch? Surely they would have set an anchor watch, yet no man was walking the deck fore and aft every few minutes. Were they asleep? Not possible, given the events of the day. Concealed? Yes, he was sure someone was keeping his eyes on that opening.

He wouldn't crawl into the boat. The instant he was discovered, the crew would shoot him, thinking a whole tribe had surrounded the ship and was about to board the easiest way, from the boat to the deck. He pulled himself through the water around to the stern of the boat and then up to the brig's hull. Beneath his hand, the cold copper sheathing felt solid and unmoving as a marble wall. He paddled aft under the brig's counter, forward along the starboard side, and around the cutwater until he was on the larboard side again and even with the shrouds of the foremast. That was almost a circuit of the ship. Above his head were the ends of the chain plates. He bobbed up in the water and made a grab for one, but his reach was too short.

Even if he could get up and wedge himself in between the plates and the hull, how long could he stay there? Not long. The space appeared narrow and the plates a difficult perch for an entire night. When would the brig leave? In the morning? He knew he would not be able to remain in the cold water much longer and paddled back to the bow and grabbed the cable rising out of the water. It was taut, kept so by the press of the wind on the mast and spars. He decided he must shin up it and peek over the bow to find what to do next. There was no place outside the gunnel where he might conceal himself until they were well underway. No time to hesitate after coming so far, he thought, he must do it or count himself a coward.

Thomas pulled his body up the cable far enough to get a hand into the hawsehole. By wrapping his legs around the cable he held that gain and then reached another hold above. He laid his hand on the rail, rested and listened. There were still no voices from the fo'c's'le, or footsteps, or even a stray cough. He heard only the wind in the rigging and the drops draining from his body hitting the water below. By all signs, except the odors, the vessel appeared to be abandoned. With both hands on the rail, he pulled himself higher. One foot on the cable in the hawsehole supported his weight. The deck was deserted as far as he could see in the darkness, not the least light, not even a dim reflection showed anywhere. Around the knight-heads and below the far gunnel were dark shapes that might be gear stowed there, or they might be crouching men. But nothing moved. Thomas peered at them, trying to make out what they were.

Suddenly a black shape, the outline of a man, holding some long thing rose up before him. Thomas grabbed at the object with his left hand. With his right, he gripped the rail to keep from falling backward. He could feel he was grasping a musket barrel and pushed it away from him. It discharged. The flash from the pan instantly blinded him and the blast from the muzzle sent a piercing pain into his ears and set them to ringing. The weapon was wrenched from his hand, and a half-second later his head was slammed backward. Another blaze of light filled his eyes. Intense pain shot across his mouth. His fingers pulled from the rail and he plunged backward into the bay. Cold water gurgled in his ears as he thrashed about to reach the surface. The salt-sweet taste of blood filled his mouth. Something was loose at the tip of his tongue. He spat out some teeth and felt the gap where they had been. His foot touched the hull and he kicked himself away from it. There was nothing he could see but the white light in his eyes, and he could only guess which way to swim. His head broke the surface, and, taking a gulp of air, he dived, kicking and pawing himself forward.

Just as he did so, another musket fired. He heard the ball strike, but he felt nothing. It must have stabbed into the water behind him, he thought and pulled fiercely to get farther away. Another ball hit near his head. It was obvious they had a fair chance of hitting him if they had had lanterns out. When he came up again to gasp for air, he heard a Babel of swearing and yelling but could not make out what language they were speaking. The firing and the noises of the crew were the only indications he had of where he was going. He kept them to his rear and dived again, changing direction a little to avoid rising along the same line each time. Twice more he came up for air and heard musket shots echoing over the bay. The balls struck wide of their mark. Hoping he couldn't be seen, Thomas then swam on the surface to put more water between him and the brig. The flash that had filled his eyes was fading. When he took a quick look behind him, he saw the glows of lanterns moving along the deck of the brig. They were looking in all directions. At that distance, he reasoned his head must be invisible, for more shots were fired and none hit near. The crew more likely fired to vent their anger rather than in any hope of striking their foe. Thomas slackened his pace until he ceased gasping for air. The salt water stung his wounds. He pushed his tongue out and felt his upper lip was split up to his nose. His lower teeth had been driven through his lower lip. Damnation! he cursed in his mind.

They had laid their trap well, he admitted. The boat had been left beside the brig purposely and the gangway left open to entice the imagined savages to board there. But he had chosen to climb the cable instead and thus escaped being cut in half by a dozen or more musket balls. The silent ship had been a ruse, a trap for savages. They would not know the routine of getting underway, but he did and knew something was amiss from the start.

He turned and looked at the ship again. The lanterns kept moving fore and aft. There were continual flashes and reports of musket fire as each man's weapon was reloaded. The crew must imagine they were beset by canoes full of bearded and wildly dressed men looking for victims to put into their cooking holes.

His great wish to quit the island had led him to do a foolish thing. He should have guessed they wanted their vengeance, else they would have left soon after filling their casks.

Shouts came from the brig. Then the voices were replaced by the squeal of lines passing through blocks. The clicking of the pawl came again, a certain clue the boat was being hoisted in, yet there was no rousing chorus at each heave on the bars. The song was missing. An uncommon thing, he thought, but he understood their silence.

Thomas turned and started for the shore again, moving slower now that there was little danger from the brig. Finally his feet touched the bottom and he waded up the shore.

"Fool! Fool! Such a fool I am," he kept repeating to himself as he walked along the shore, shivering and hunting for his clothes. He shuffled back and forth, thinking more of his folly than his pants and jacket. They had not been so clever as he had been witless. He had made a bad situation worse and had got split lips and lost three or four teeth. If the crew had been better with their weapons, he would have received a ball or two in his back.

The clicking of the windlass pawl came across the water again. She was heaving short on her best bower. Soon she would cast her head to starboard and be fairly underway north out of the bay. Their rescuers had been driven away. Those men would give a report of the attack here and it would work against the castaways' relief. How long must he wait until another ship fetched up to the island?

His lips throbbed and he touched his fingers to the wounds. Blood dripped from his upper lip and he could feel its warmth as it ran down into his beard. The loss of his teeth was a calamity, but he had escaped alive. Had he climbed in at the gangway where they expected boarders, he would have taken a volley and perhaps been cut in half.

The picture of the sailor kneeling beside the boat came to him. He could imagine the poor jack was now lying in his bunk groaning with pain or already mercifully dead. It was a cruel, senseless thing to do to a man who had shown no anger but only his caution.

Thomas could not see the brig, but he knew she was out there loosing her sails and sheeting them home. The four of them had watched the sea for more than half a year for such a vessel. Now it was leaving with its crew carrying the bitter memory of the attack on their mate.

His head was full of questions. Would his face mend without festering, and could he feed himself in his condition? Where could he spend the night? He swore he would not return to the hut. From that moment, there would be no Thomas Wightman in Tobit's crew. Never again would he obey an order from the captain. Tobit will make that to be desertion, Thomas thought. He will rave and quote scripture. He will swear to have revenge for Thomas's attack on him.

Therefore Thomas must find a place to hide until he left. For now, should he go to the rock overhang or to that crevice he had found the first night? The island was large enough for him to conceal himself, and he would build the vessel he and Chips had carefully planned. The others could not know what happened to him and might well reason that he had got aboard the brig. At least they would not search for him this night. Tobit would still be in fear of his Botany Bay devils.

His foot brushed against his clothes piled on the cinders. He swept the drops of water from his body and pulled the skins on.

Thomas walked to the washed part of the beach. He hadn't thought it all out, but he knew he should not leave footprints that the officers might follow. Better to leave only those leading to the middle of the bar where he had entered the bay and thus give them some reason to believe he had got to the brig. Some lair in the high peaks would be the most difficult to find, but he would have to descend to build a canoe and find food. The east or south coast would be the better choice. If he could find a cave or some such shelter well hidden near shore, then he could have more time to make his canoe. The old rock overhang would be his shelter for the night since it was on the way to the east coast. The strike of his heels on the beach jarred his throbbing wounds, and he found that sliding his feet in short steps eased the pounding of the blood. In that manner he drifted slowly toward the rock overhang.

All the queries, doubts, and carking thoughts swarmed in his head, each one pushing aside the previous one before he could settle on a solution. The worst suddenly knifed through them all, the question neither he nor Christopher could answer. If they all reached home again, could the captain have him tried for mutiny? Or was Tobit's puffing about his right to command only a ruse to rule the rest of them when he had no authority? Thomas knew he would certainly try because that hammering of his skull on the beach hurt his vanity far more than his thick head. But the question was the law. The officers might connive to tell some monstrous, infernal lie that somehow he had caused the loss of the *Dove*. There would only be Chips to speak for him. Two against two. The captain and mate against two crewmen. No question about that contest, but it was all too fanciful and looking too far into the future. None might make the shore of Tovy Poenamoo or be rescued; as Christopher noted, Tobit, being so old, might die before he returned. Thomas put that problem out of his head.

He shuffled along miserably in the darkness, searching for the opening that led to their old shelter. It was the longest he had ever taken to walk that portion of the shore. By the starlight, he noted a familiar tree that had fallen half over and knew he was near fifty yards of his goal. Within a minute he turned out of the moving foam and was feeling his way through the bushes to the back of the rock overhang.

He eased his body down and tried to find the most comfortable position in which to lie. He couldn't control his thoughts. No matter how he willed them otherwise, a parade of images always returned: the blue eyes of the wounded sailor staring at him as he held onto the gunnel of the boat; the black figure rising up from the rail of the brig; the flashes of the muskets. There was no rest for him as he lay there listening to the interminable roll and rush of the waves. He was becoming chilled. The cold air and the pain of his lips barred any sleep and any escape from the visions bedeviling him. It served no purpose to remain under the rock. He decided he might as well walk and try to warm himself. He arose and felt about for a branch to erase his footprints. That evidence of his presence must not be left. Tobit might well believe or want to believe he had gotten into the brig if he found no other sign than the tracks he had made on the bar.

Thomas backed out from the shelter, sweeping the ground with the limb. It was all done by feel and hope for he could not see a thing under the rock and only the breaking waves and dark shapes out on the beach. At the water's edge, he flung the tool into the surf and started for the eastern side of the island. He decided to follow the surf along to the dunes, then cross to the shallows. Because of the darkness and his wounds, it was easier that way than climbing the bluff and crossing the grassland. The shallows were full of fish and would provide him with food while he devised some canoe. Some hideaway beyond them and on the slope of the bluff would be the best he could expect to find without going high on the peaks.

He kept moving in the spreading waves, though the pain increased. He advanced each foot and eased his weight wholly onto it before he dragged his other foot ahead. While in that slow progression, he pushed his tongue through the opening in his upper jaw and felt the split in the upper lip again. By arching it over his lower teeth, he touched the cut there.

I was a fool, he berated himself again, a fool to believe I could get aboard the brig. I was more of a fool to think Tobit would ever allow me and Chips to sail for the Strait. The subtly malign look on the captain's beefy face in the last few weeks was evidence of that. Had he been wiser, Thomas thought, he would have set up for himself months ago and by this time would be on the Middle Island. But he was a fool no more. His future plans were settled. I will reach the Strait. I will return to Stonington Port and if Chips will not go, it will be all by my own wits and labor.

He stopped abruptly, mid-stride. White blotches on the beach before him and to his right drifted away as he walked, then remained fixed when he halted. He waited uneasily, watching the patches of white, thinking they might be a danger. There was no threat to be expected from the brig. It was on its way north, possibly passing the chops of the bay at that very moment. The captain, the mate, and Christopher were concealed in the darkness somewhere on the plateau or in the peaks. There could be no danger from men by land or sea. But what of animals? Sea elephants and seals are dark. What is white? Birds! Gulls! Here were merely a few birds resting!

He felt absurd to have been frightened like a child in the dark.

CHAPTER 13

THOMAS resumed his shuffling walk, but at a faster pace. He knew old Tobit would go into a rage once he had gathered his wits again, then simmer in silence with sullen looks after he had exhausted his swearing and ranting.

When the officers discovered the brig had quit the bay, they could never be sure whether he was aboard it or possibly concealed somewhere on the island. To oppose Tobit, to speak defiantly was crime enough, but he had battered the old man's head in such rage that he might have stove his skull had the beach been of stones. The captain would never give up the thought of punishment. His vanity required revenge, and law, he would swear rightly or falsely, gave him authority. Thus he would always watch for any sign of Thomas's presence. A broken twig, a footprint, an unburied turd, any mark he left from now on could set the captain on a single-minded search for him and perhaps be his undoing. From this moment to the day of his departure from the island, he must live like a hare, always watching for the sight of the fox.

To build his canoe in secret, fill his belly, and not alert old Toby or the mate were difficult tasks ahead of him. It was going to be a life of dodgery. For that he needed a den, a totally hidden lair, from which he could emerge at night, gather food, and work on his canoe. That shelter must be one tucked away in some crevice or covered with dense bushes. Some place on the east coast, he figured, would be the most suitable. They had seen the south coast at a distance the day they had explored from the plateau and looked for seals. It was farther from the hut, but it was rugged. From the last accessible point on the plateau, they had glimpsed the series of cliffs footed with shattered stones, always half-buried in the breaking surf, alternating with openings where the waves smashed directly against the vertical rock of the island. It was impossible to traverse. He could build no vessel there and keep it hidden. Back then he had stared at each succeeding, foreshortened profile in the distance. Only the forward edges of the cliffs had showed through the haze. The voids between those outlines, filled with mist flung from the shattered waves, had appeared compressed along the line of sight. From the nearest one, a dozen specks, a line of birds, had exited toward the sea.

He could not hide on the peaks above those precipices, though they offered the better concealment. He needed food that was close at hand. What was up there he could eat? Birds, hardly a meal in a dozen of them and a little fern root. He required vittles that could be gathered with small effort and time, for he meant to hollow his canoe as soon as he found a cave or shelter that would keep him hidden and from the rain. The east coast was the logical option, ideal for his wants. That shore was not visible except from the side of the nearest peak and the rim of the plateau. The light of his fires, made at night, could be hidden if they were close in beneath the thickets, and the wind would carry the smoke and smell out to sea. One of the scant strips of sand and cinders they had seen while on that first search for seals might serve on which to build a canoe if he found a hideaway close at hand. From there he could launch his vessel, and from there the wind would sweep him to the great Middle Island or into the Strait, perhaps to be a castaway once more. But it was known land on that side of the sea, charted by the great Cook years before. Ships now touched at those shores to wood and water and trade.

A fine gray light insinuated across the sky. Thomas was aware of the shapeless bluff that blacked out half the constellations to the south. He kept following the beach, skimming his feet through the wash of the sea. The black smudge to the east lowered, shrank in bulk as he walked, allowing the brighter stars to reappear in their old places. Now, directly to the east in the darkness lay the field of dunes, and beyond them, the shallows. Over those low parts of the island, the wind blew constantly with flurries strong enough to erase his tracks. In a day's time they might be filled in or swept away. Even if some remained they would, after a few hours, be taken for some old ones made on a trip to the fish traps days before. Confidently he veered out of the wave edges and toward the shallows.

He discovered a stride that eased the throbbing of his wound while he walked through the loose, dry material. A shorter, slower pace required less effort, and he slipped each foot ahead of the other to carry his weight in a smoother cycle. It was a long transit across the dunes and a feat for him while exhausted and in pain with each beat of his heart. He avoided the finer cinders and sand near the traps which held footprints well and skirted through the last of the dunes to the surf. From there, he waded south until he gained the rocky portion of the beach. Night was blending into the colorless hour before dawn, and, minute by minute, details of the east coast precipitated out of the haze. The shore ahead was a chaos of boulders fallen from the side of the plateau. He should be able to step from stone to stone on that side of the island and not leave any mark of his passing. Thick greenery hid the slope as it did on the bay side of the grassland, but there was no beach, only the litter of broken stone. The salt spray of the waves breaking on it kept the bushes from advancing nearer the sea. He looked at the narrow foreshore ahead, bordered by the boskage on the right and the sea on the left. By keeping closer to the foot of the bluff and near the trees, he would be concealed from anyone above searching from the edge of the plateau. The route they had taken on the plateau while searching for seals was too dangerous. Tobit may have regained his senses and, in company with the mate, might be up there at that very moment scanning the grass. He must find a den between the rim of the flatland and the sea before he reached the great cliffs of the southern shore. Some place on that long slope would be his refuge for weeks, perhaps months, until he departed from the island.

For about an hour he toiled over the lumps of stone, picking a way, placing his advancing foot firmly before committing to the hop to the next rock. The sun had ruddled the thin layers of clouds, then stealthily risen through them. His hands and face felt the warmth of its growing rays.

On the sand between some rocks he discovered a trickle of water weaving its way to the surf. It was reversed and overridden by the thin edge of each wave as it rolled in. He followed the water up into the trees until he found a place where the piddling stream fell from a mat of twigs and leaves. His swollen and painful lips denied him the pleasure of sucking up the sweet water in deep gulps, thus he had to crouch low and thrust his jaw out to catch it in his mouth.

Despite all his care, the jarring movements across the stones had kept his wounds aching. He might be able to go farther but didn't wish to. Tobit and the mate could not have the slightest idea where to look for him if they suspected he had not got away from the island. Even if they had heard the musket reports in the night, they could not have guessed why. There was no urgent reason for him to totter along in his condition. He felt safe enough and it was time for rest and sleep. He went back to the shore and between two rocks found a wide hollow already warmed by the sun. The space was filled with dry, loose cinders. Slowly he kneeled and turned around to lie on his back. A greater measure of warmth penetrated his clothing and reached his skin now that he was in the quieter air between the rocks. Two fingers of his right hand touched the caked blood in his moustache and beard.

I am quite safe, he reassured himself, and no one can see me as I lie here. I can sleep for hours. Damn him! Blast him! he cursed in his mind. He let out two deep sighs and in less than a minute was asleep.

IT NEEDED a marked effort by Thomas not to waken. He became aware of his chest rising and falling in slow, deep breathing while suspended between consciousness and a thick opiate sleep. Bird calls, joyous and querulous, filled the darkness in his head, yet he desired nothing more than to sink back into the soft nothingness. The clamant chirping from the trees and the whispering of the low surf continually nudged him upward. Blurred light slipped through his lax eyelids. He opened them fully and found his body adhered to the side of the planet; he was looking out into the sky. A few clouds were fixed there, and a gull flew across his view with its underside facing him. The directions slowly rotated back to their proper places. Up was no longer at the top of his head, but straight before his face.

Where am I? he thought.

Then he remembered lying down between the boulders to rest. He remained there for a few minutes more, not wholly awake and not wanting to exert his tired limbs. Then he cautiously raised up to sit and peek over the rocks to each end of the shoreline. There were no figures of men carrying clubs to be seen: no searchers, stepping from stone to stone as he had done. To the west, the sun was within half an hour of dropping behind the highest peak. The greater portion of the day had passed while he had slept betwixt the stones. The sun had dried the legs of his trousers, wetted in the long march on the beaches.

That was good, he noted. Nighttime will not be so comfortable and might even become a misery if he did not discover some place to shelter. Clouds were piling up and darkening in the south. A night spent shivering in the wind and rain was a wretched prospect. The swim to and from the brig and the night march had left him tired despite his long sleep. Before darkness came, he must find his crevice or cave that would at least be dry if nothing else.

The lad smoothed the surface he had lain upon with his hand, then deftly cast handfuls of the cinders about to disguise those marks. Then he stood up and strode from rock to rock to the south, always taking care not to step down and leave a footprint on the sand and cinders between them. At several places, where large rocks were visible between the boles of the trees on the slope, he made forays up to them, but failing to find a hideaway, returned to the shore.

In the middle distance, a short headland, really a spur of guano-whitened boulders against which the swells rounding the island broke into froth, ran out into the sea. In an hour he had scattered its roosting gulls and shags and crossed through its chaos of stones, some the size of a cottage. There was calmer water in the lee and a remnant of beach, but a canoe would have to be hidden in the bushes whilst a-building and launched between and over the tumbled boulders. Thomas went on searching the coast beyond. To his right, shadows gradually filled in under the trees as the sun dropped from sight. It became more difficult to see the trunks imbedded in the darkness. Finding an opening, a cave, another overhang that would be dry in a downpour, even a cramped one, became more urgent. The southern sky was filling with more clouds, creating a minatory blackness at the horizon, and flurries of wind tossed the limbs of trees and flapped the hood of his jacket. He saw no promising place ahead on the shore and climbed higher, pacing from the stones into the forest. It was a wandering route around trees and ferns from one boulder to the next. In the dimming light, he spied a group of tabular stones to his right and higher still. Upon reaching them, he discovered one that had, in its tumble from above, come to rest in a tilted position. It leaned over another block, and the space between the two was large enough to admit him. He reached in and felt the few crisp leaves on the lower stone, proof that neither rain nor dripping water reached there. It would be cold and drafty, but it would be dry and would serve. The surface of the lower block was canted, but a mat of fern fronds thicker on one edge might keep him from rolling in his sleep or sliding inch by inch from beneath the upper stone.

A blustering wind was now whipping the trees and filling the air with flurries of leaves. Thomas was sure it was going to be a wet night.

He stumbled about in the gloom, hunting for the taller ferns. When he found one, he wrenched the fronds from its trunk, stripping away the skirt of dry, spent ones that surrounded it. Darkness stopped his gathering when he could no longer locate the ferns. Twice he feared he was lost and had to search about to locate his shelter. The material he had managed to glean was enough to make a bed but not enough to provide cover and warmth. He laid the fronds out to create a level bed. Then there was nothing to do but lie on it in the dark. After an hour, no light was perceptible from any source, not even a solitary star between the leaves above. Opening and closing his eyes made no difference. It was a total blackness to him either way.

Sleep, at least a continuous, restorative sleep, was not to be his for the night. By curling up and pulling his hood over his head he felt a little warmer, but his lower legs and feet were cold. He wished for his fur blanket and the loose boots Harrison had made. With those, he had slept in comfort in the hut. Wish all he might, he knew he would be cold until the first light permitted him to see and to continue his march. He dozed for a while, only to awaken again and stare into the darkness. With the passage of the constellations hidden by clouds, no measure of time could be made. The duration of that nap and any others could not be guessed. His bed became less comfortable as the layer of fronds compressed under his weight. Pressure on each hip forced him to roll from side to side every few minutes or lie on his back. Walking about to warm his body was impossible in that blackness where he might twist an ankle between tumbled stones or be poked in an eye by a twig. Once a few yards away from his shelter, he might never find it again. It was best simply to lie there. Tomorrow night he would find more fronds and leaves and make a softer bed.

Suddenly he tensed all his muscles and raised up on an elbow. He swore he had heard a sound some yards out in the trees. He remained unmoving with his head held up rigidly the better to hear. A few seconds later he was sure of the noise, just a single one a bit closer, like a step on a dry leaf. It couldn't be the officers, he reassured himself. They would not be out in this blackness; they couldn't hope to find anything. It had to be an animal, but what animal? He had not seen the least mark of the "bears." They ate the grass and would not have reason to venture down the bluff. There had been no prints on the narrow patches of sand between the rocks, save the webbed ones of the sea birds. Could it be that parrot that Chris claimed had made the strange sounds? Might it be a cannibal, a lone one hidden in this part of the island?

His neck ached from holding his head up, but he kept his body motionless. Then there was another sound of a step directly ahead, followed by one to his left. Whatever it was, it was moving to that side. Then, oddly, he heard one far to his right. Was there more than one approaching him?

Thomas suddenly lowered his head to the fronds and rested his neck. Rain! He chuckled to himself. Rain! He realized that what he had heard was the first large raindrops spatting on the leaves and stones a few yards from him. The drops soon increased in number and became a hissing out in the trees. Many times in the night he heard heavy downpours. He then shivered from the cold and also a little because he knew he was snug under the rock. How he would have suffered, he thought, if he had not come upon the natural shelter. To be out in that storm wandering about in his sopping clothes would be hard to bear knowing old Tobit was dry and comfortable in the hut.

In these last few hours, his fortunes had gone further awry. He had been struck in the mouth, and his possible rescuers had fled from the island. Now he must conceal himself for weeks, months, on the rocky coast. If another ship did enter the bay, he would not know it. The others might be taken aboard, and they, believing he'd been in the brig, would leave him behind. Another misadventure might persuade him he had been born under an evil connection of planets. But it was not planets that had brought him to such a condition, only that pompous ass.

What else could he have done when Christopher reported the brig was in the bay? Run ahead of the others to that sailor on the beach and fall to his knees before him? Would that have made him appear less fierce, made the sailor understand his words and heed them? Tobit's demand that they look over the brig and its crew first seemed a reasonable caution, yet the instant Thomas saw the sailor sitting beside the boat, he knew the man was an honest jack. He had made friends with so many like him in Stonington Port and had lived with them on the *Dove*. No convict could dissemble to appear so, ape the manner, wear the clothes, and have them fit as they did on that tar. The clean, trig look of that ship, its taut rigging, its boat, all bespoke men in a creditable trade.

He finally fell asleep for what he guessed were longer periods, until the first light of morning came from overhead, gray but welcome through the canopy of leaves. The persistent storm during the night had thoroughly wetted the trees, and their dark trunks stood one beside or beyond another, in broken ranks, until farther out they lightened to gray and faded into the mist of rain. The downpours gave no hint of lessening soon. Thomas lay on his side, watching the large drops pelting the ferns and rocks and the sodden litter of leaves lying around them. Ah, just as well, he said to himself, it will wash away any footprints I might have missed, and Tobit and the mate will not go about searching in this weather. I can rest, let my wounds mend, lay the plans for my vessel.

Fire, he knew, would be his first need. Only with fire could he hollow the log that must serve as his hull. If he couldn't get the cordage for lashings and stays and the small stuff for lacing they had already made, he would be at pains to redo it all. He remembered how he and Christopher had planned their canoe, how, at night, by the fire, they had drawn the outlines and the many details. Eagerly, each had added his ideas of how to make each part: the spars, the steering oar, and the stays. He saw in his mind how lines led through the thimbles to go double and give purchase might last even if he sailed far into the Strait. Everything needed was somewhere on the island. Perhaps not at hand, yet in time it could all be gathered and put to use.

Thomas knew he must have a sail and stay its mast well. Without a sail, currents might carry him in any direction, and without the wind driving his canoe, he could not be sure to raise the land before his water gave out. That sail posed the greatest problem. A mat of woven flax leaves would surely be too heavy and awkward when wet by sea or rain. Nine or ten of the unhaired skins sewn together should make a serviceable sail. If it were made small, that would hinder splitting in a gust. He planned to lace it to the mast and then to the boom, angled upward, thus carrying the bulk of the sail high. When the hull dipped between the crests, she might then still have way to keep her bow to the east or nor'east. He could have his vessel all readied for the voyage save for that sail, and at the last moment slip into the hut to get the skins. Or he might meet Christopher somewhere in the weeks to come and persuade him to bring them out. One way or the other, he would have a proper sail, one that would drive his canoe to the Middle Island.

Every hour of the night would have to be spent gathering flax, burning the log, or searching for food. He mustn't move from the cover of his hideaway in the day. The entire residue from the parts and rope he was making would have to be gathered and hidden or burned. The fire must be banked before dawn to save it for the next night's use. All those precautions would require time, time that was sorely needed for the work. Certainly, the canoe could be built sooner if he was not always on the *qui vive*, in fear of discovery, but that was not the case. If he were discovered, old Tobit would crave his revenge, however tardy it might be. He would spend all effort to seize him. If the officers did take him, what would they do? Hang him? Unless they took him unawares, he was light of foot, a match for them both, and they knew it. Then, too, they could not be sure he had not gotten into the brig. Would they spend much time marching over the island and poking into thickets in search of a man who might be far away at sea? He reasoned he had a good chance to escape detection and complete his canoe. He was no poor, helpless creature. He had his wits, his strength, and his determination to leave the island at his pleasure.

Thomas sat up and eyed the thick slab above that formed his shelter. It was too high above the rest of the slope and the space beneath it too open, making it a refuge he could not conceal in any way. There was no covering of limbs, bushes, or vines he could draw about it that would not be instantly recognized as not of nature. Therefore, when the rain quit, he must find another place, a cave, another shelf of rock that was dry in the heaviest downpour, and one that was also hidden or could be made so.

Once he succeeded in that, he must burn out the hull of the canoe. A log of the proper size already near or on the shore was his object. The one discovered on the bay shore by their first shelter was ideal but, sadly, far beyond his reach. When he found one he would set a line of small fires on it. They would require constant tending and could burn only at night for any smoke was visible in daylight and would give certain proof he was still on the island. He planned to hide his little fires under trees and with mats propped around them.

If all went well and he found all he needed, he would be ready to set off by the southern summer. Even in that season, though, the weather would not always be favorable for a small boat. On the day he had spied the island, there had been a long, hollow sea running. If the troughs were deep, a boat might be becalmed, and when it rose on the crests, the wind would strike full force, straining the sail and the stays. The mast might be carried away and the canoe would then become no better than a drift log. He might fetch up on the coast of the Middle Island after many days, perhaps not alive or even in his hollowed bole. If he managed to sail there, would the Indians welcome him or knock him in the head with their stone clubs as he stepped ashore? Thoughts of landing on the coast of Tovy Poenamoo both buoyed and worried him.

He saw in his mind's eye the entire vessel he and Harrison had intended. It would have one boomkin lashed athwart the hull forward of the mast and one abaft it. They both would reach seven or eight feet to the starboard and have a spar lashed to their ends along the same line as the hull. A ship's nail heated to redness could burn holes through the hull for the lashings, but he did not have one and must make a drill with the volcano glass as Chris had done. It would all be finished in time. He knew he could do it, and well.

During the day the rain slackened to showers and then ceased. Thomas leaned from beneath his rock and saw patches of blue sky through the trees. He was not surprised that it was now late afternoon. Most of the day had passed in slow hours of dull light, and he had long since tired of lying on his bed of fronds in enforced idleness.

He crawled from the refuge and picked his way down to the rocky beach, trying his best to keep dry. All the bushes and ferns were dripping, and they loosed showers when shaken even gently. Drops pelted on him as the wind stirred the branches and leaves overhead. He hoped to find something to eat, birds' eggs or a clam hidden between the stones. There is food here, he assured himself, but it might be a difficult chore to find it on his side of the island. It was too late to explore very far, and he must return into the woods while there was light enough to find his hideaway. If he discovered a better place than what he had, well and good, but there was small chance that he might in the hours before dark. At the edge of the greenery he peeked up and down the shore for any sign of a man. Then he stepped from rock to rock until he was close to the breaking waves. With his trouser legs rolled up, he waded between the stones, searching for anything he might eat. The ache of hunger was growing in his stomach for he had last eaten the night before the brig had arrived. A few birds soared above and angled their heads to scan the foam of the waves as it receded through the channels between the stones. Occasionally one swooped and disappeared into a cleft and in a frantic flapping ascended again. Thomas couldn't make out what the bird had captured, if anything at all.

In the surf mist, perhaps a half-mile on, was a small headland of boulders, and beyond it, he spied another three times as far away. From that distance it was only a featureless burr on the coast. He selected his path with care, sometimes scanning several seconds before choosing the direction of the next step. Halfway to the spur, he stopped. No, tomorrow, he decided. The sun was behind the peaks and the whole coast was in shadow. Under the trees the cool, solitary gloom was deepening. If he turned back, he could find his shelter before the night closed in. He knelt to pull a bit of green weed from the rock on which he was standing. For half a minute he chewed it, and then pushed it out with his tongue. His supper would have to be a good drink of water, he thought, and he spat out the small bits. Tomorrow, if it didn't rain, he would hunt for something to eat.

Darkness was coming on quickly. He rose to his feet feeling even hungrier and headed back to his hideaway.

At first light the next morning, his shivering awakened him. It felt as if the dampness and cold had penetrated to the very core of his body. His whole night had alternated between naps and wakefulness. By rolling, stretching, and flexing muscles, he tried to make warmth in his body, but it helped only a little. Might as well resume his searching, he reasoned, as lie there hunching and shaking. His plan was to leave his bed there as it was until he found another dry place to shelter. Once a new one was located or built, he would return and scatter the fronds to make it appear they had fallen from their trunks. He rose and picked his way through the trees and bushes to the shore.

From the top of the largest rock about, he looked at all the horizon open to him. A ship could happen upon the island from that side as well as any other and anchor in the lee near the shallows. She might send a boat ashore, though that would do her crew little good. But there were few if any whalers or Port Jackson traders, he guessed, that traveled courses that might bring them near. The island was unknown. The brig was the only vessel to touch there since their wreck, and possibly it was the only other one ever to raise the island. He might search the far edge of the sea for years and never see it broken by a sail. No, best he follow his scheme, face the danger, and trust to his wits. He could not spare so much more time out of his life.

The sky was still in its pre-dawn gray. Light increased in the east, yet no color tinted the low layering of clouds. Mist over the surf and shore to the southwest accrued with the miles until only the brow of the first great cliff was hinted in outline. Thomas moved from stone to stone and over the gaps with chary steps, and after an hour and a half of slow progress, reached the next series of boulders that extended into the water. The coast retained its drabness until the sun's rays broke through, drove off the haze, and gave varied greens to the scrub and the treetops. The fresh light turned the sea a blue that contrasted with the dense white of the surf.

Farther down the coast, the last and longest of the spurs that caught the swells from the southwest emerged in fine details of rocks streaked with guano. It had appeared the evening before as a dark protrusion into the water's last reflection of twilight. He, Harrison, and the mate had seen it months ago from the rim of the plateau, and had noted how the cluster of its boulders curved a mite to the north, forming a slight cove. Two more hours of walking over and around the rocks brought him to the point. Once he stood on the narrow beach that had accreted on the island side of the cove, he knew he had found the best place yet to build his canoe. It was close under the trees, and they had seen only its outer margin when they were on their hunt for seals. If he could roll a log up its incline, the trees and bushes would conceal it and his fires from anyone on the brim of the grassland far above. Long, tough ribbons of rockweed anchored to boulders laved back and forth with each swell. Sticks and limbs and all sorts of driftwood were mixed with the weed surging in and out with the degraded waves rounding the last rocks of the spur. If another shelter could be found nearby, then it would be the ideal situation, but if no better den offered than his first discovery he would simply have a long walk to and from the tiny cove. Swirls of the current had carried some of the flotsam across to the beach and left it stranded there. Thomas stepped over the rotting weed and battered driftwood. Some of the limbs and logs had been in the ocean weeks and possibly for months. Little bark was left on their grayed surfaces, and their ends were rounded from striking against each other or against the rocks and sand. Some might have come from Van Diemen's Land, New Holland, or perhaps some shore even farther away. He saw in the shapes of the wood possible masts, spars, and paddles. There was a wide choice for the parts of his vessel. Several logs were buried in the sand where the beach curved out toward the rocks. Only one had enough girth and length to serve for a hull, and he would have to dig it out and turn it to prove it had no large limbs and was sound on all sides. If it was a fit log, he must roll it up under the trees and set fires to hollow it.

In a half-dried lump of rockweed, he saw something that looked odd, perhaps familiar. He dropped to his knees and pawed out a thin, white fragment, resembling a bit of eggshell. He placed it in his left hand and nudged it over with a finger. Crawfish! The name popped into his head when its other side revealed a dark greenish color and little spikes tipped with yellow. Aha! He thought, if there are crabs and crawfish and the like to be had, he could make traps of woven twigs and snare them. His thoughts went ahead. . . . And surely clams are somewhere and sea ears on the rocks farther to the south. That meant he might feed himself from the shore alone and not risk going above to the plateau for the "bear" or to the shallows for fish. Thomas rose and looked all around the cove and the wooded slope. Above him, gulls called in their hoarse voices and soared on the breeze rising over the shore and bluff. In smooth glides, they passed low over the shore to spot any stitch of food. They managed to eat and those not searching sat over on the rocks of the tiny cape and whitened them with what passed through their guts. The fitness of the cove for his needs elated Thomas. He was now master of his fate, working solely for his escape. Now all would be different. He craved to feel the scend of the sea lift his canoe and thrust him forward toward the Middle Island. The sunlit day and the discoveries raised his spirits, and the hazards of the voyage diminished. The worst of the doubts that had scurried through his thoughts at night were expelled.

He felt the scabs that covered the cuts through his lips, and then ran his tongue along to check them from the inside of his mouth. They were mending well and had not become septic. Even the soreness was diminishing. At odd moments, when he was thinking, he picked bits of dried blood from his beard.

He was still a castaway and also, if the officers suspected he was still on the island, a hunted fugitive. Had he changed his fortunes for the better or worse? Surely for the better, he told himself. There was no other choice for him once the captain fired those arrows there on the beach. Now he was free of Tobit, and all was far better with no one to thwart his escape. The rigors would ease. He would master each of the problems as they came to him. If he escaped the notice of the officers in the next few months, he would launch his canoe and make for Tovy Poenamoo. If he met with a ship on the coast or in the Strait and sent it to rescue the others, Tobit would surely look a great fool.

By the end of the day, Thomas had explored up through the trees and near the crest of the bluff for a crevice or cave in which to shelter. There were three possibilities, but each lacked some wanted feature. The one he chose was the easiest to conceal, although it was the farthest from the shore, nearly at the top of the bluff. It would take time to travel between the beach and his lair, yet if the officers happened upon his canoe during the day, they would not discover him close by. It was a cavity under a ledge low enough to be hidden under draped vines and bent limbs. Once that was done, it could not be detected even a few yards away. He could walk to and from it on downed trees and rocks and not leave an evident path of trampled earth and plants. After he had enclosed it and barred the wind with boughs and clumps of grass, it had room for little more than his bed. Though it was cramped, it was warm, dry, and, best of all, not likely to be found. The first night he slept well in what appeared to be an enlarged mouse's nest. The first need was met.

The partially buried log on the shore took his attention next, and by digging away the sand and cinders, he was able to roll it over to reveal its underside. It was split for half its length, which spoiled it for use as a hull. Not the least disheartened, he stripped off his leather jacket and trousers and waded into the water of the cove. He swam to the drift logs that heaved back and forth with the bands of rockweed. By feeling around them and along their length, he judged one to be the best. What he needed next was some way to get his log out of the water. Thomas paddled to the beach and gathered several vines hanging from the trees, and with them he made a line long enough to reach from the shore to the log. It worked well enough if he kept up a steady pull, easing the bole through the weed and flotsam. Any vigorous yank on the line of vines, he feared, would snap it, and that would mean swimming out through the weed again and retying the vine. A constant tug brought his prize into the clear and across to the beach, but to get it out of the sea and up into concealment proved much more difficult.

It had apparently been adrift for a long time and its wood was saturated. He knelt with his feet dug into the loose sand and cinders, but was unable to roll the log more than a few inches out of the water. Then he devised a parbuckle with the line of vines tied to a tree trunk, led under the log, up around the trunk again, and back to his position in the surf. It helped in rolling his log and holding the gains while he reset his lever. He discovered it was easier to turn one end up while the other rested against a limb driven into the beach. In that way, he worked the log up towards the line of bushes and trees, advancing each end about a foot to a foot and a half at a time. During the hours at this heavy task, he paused every few minutes perspiring and panting. When it rested where he wished it to be, Thomas looked at the great bulk of wood with a feeling of pride. To move that cumbersome thing from the water and up under the canopy of leaves was an accomplishment for a lone man. It could remain there and dry while he made the other parts and gathered and cooked his vittles. After two weeks had passed, he felt around the log's sides and ends to find how well the wood was giving up its water. It was drying yet needed more time before he could burn its center out.

At the end of each night's labor, Thomas smoothed every footprint on the beach and brushed them lightly with a fern frond. It was not likely the officers would ever walk the length of the coast, but they might make forays down to certain places on the shore. He could take no chances. Each evening he emerged from his den and climbed to the plateau and peeked above its edge to be assured Tobit or the mate were not walking about searching. He then descended slowly, keeping a keen eye for any broken twig or limb pushed aside to allow a man to pass. The officers would have no reason to cover the evidence of their passage while they thought they were the hunters. They would be intent on finding signs that he had not made his escape in the brig and was still wandering on the island.

A month after he had got the log out of the cove, he judged it to be dry enough to burn. He was anxious to have it hollowed and drill the holes for the stays and boomkins. The small fires he set on it during the moonless nights were well masked by the trees and the mats of flax leaves he propped beside the log. Thomas crept around through the greenery, always looking back to detect any faint glow or flicker from the fires. The burning required constant tending and there wasn't much he could accomplish while he watched that the fires didn't go out or burn too far. That was the greatest danger: to let them burn too deeply in one place and spoil the entire hull. At the first hint of daylight, he gathered all the embers and banked them in the sand. Any smoldering wood remaining had to be scraped and extinguished. He always rolled the log until the burned portion could not be seen by anyone peeking into the trees and also so it would not hold any rain falling in the night.

The brighter phases of the moon he suspected would reveal the smoke of his fires, thus he reserved those nights to gather food. Under the brilliance of a full moon he ventured along the south shore as far as the surf allowed. On a small patch of sand between the shattered boulders he spotted fragments of many dark shells. Waves dashing them against the rocks had shattered the thinner parts of their lips and bodies. What remained were the narrow, beak-like ends where they once had been hinged together. Thomas nodded as he held two in his hand. At low tide he knew he would find mats of mussels on the rocks lower in the water. It was a food he could rely on when his traps failed.

By degrees he became careless, not in leaving marks of his passage or allowing the light of the fires to escape, but in extending his hours to complete the work. Each morning he delayed scraping out the hull a bit longer and each evening he arrived earlier to build up that night's fire. Surely now old Tobit must be thinking the brig had carried his crewman away into a life of piracy or some such twaddle. In all the weeks he had been at the little cove, he had not found the least sign that another man had walked before him. On the nights lighted with a moon, the nights when he pulled his crawfish traps from between the rocks or gathered wood, it seemed impossible that the captain would be out stumbling across the grassland in a search for him. He left his nest late one day when the last of the sunlight was still on the sea to the south and east, lighting the water and moving bits of foam. He made a guess that it was a half-hour before sunset, but disregarding that, started off. All the precautions he had taken made him feel secure. He descended on one of his many routes to the beach, skipping from rock to rock and halting by habit every few yards to peer into the trees and listen. At the cove he looked north and south along the shore as always and saw nothing amiss among the rocks or trees. With a stick, he rolled the log upright and felt the hollowed portion to determine where to place his next fires.

The hull and the other parts he estimated could be ready in another four or five weeks at the rate he was progressing. Only the sail would be lacking then. That was no cause for worry, for there might be months yet while storms blew over the island, weeks in which he might lay his hands on skins or find what could serve in their place. The assembly of the canoe could be done in some two or three hours on the beach, and launching would be a simple levering of the completed vessel down across skids set in the sand. Every part of his design was going forward in its proper time and way.

His thoughts were suddenly dashed away by the sound of a little object falling through the trees near him. He jerked his head up and listened. Was it something a bird let fall, something heavier than the droppings they shot from their bottoms? Could it be a clam as he had seen some sea birds carry aloft and drop to break it? A few seconds later he heard the sound again as something fell, hitting leaves and a branch. It struck and bounced into the hollowed portion of the log. It was a pebble! Thomas grabbed his lever and leaped to his feet. As he dashed out to the open beach, he bent low and scooped up cinders with his left hand. He was ready to fling the grit into his opponent's eyes and flail away with his stick, but he found Harrison standing there with a smug look on his face. Thomas whirled about looking for the officers he feared were on the beach with the carpenter.

"Have a trust, lad. I'm alone," Harrison said, giving him a broad grin. "What's this, mate? Have you no voice?" He stood there waiting for the lad's answers. He had a net bag slung over his right shoulder and a bundled skin in his left hand.

"Christopher!" Thomas blurted out, but he said not another word. There was a strange sound to the name he had called, sibilant like old Will's words. He realized he had not spoken since the day he had parted from the others. The only noises he had made were grunts when he moved some heavy rock or rolled his hull. He had had no need to speak, and all those days alone had been spent in silence. Now he was aware his missing teeth altered the quality of his speech. He stepped forward and gave Christopher a long embrace. When they stepped back, Harrison tilted his head and stared at Thomas's mouth.

"What has happened to you?" he asked. "How did you get that scar under your nose?"

The lad opened his mouth and displayed the gap where his upper teeth had been knocked out.

"Did you fall somewheres?"

"Ha! No, I tried to make it aboard the brig, and this is what I got for my pains. I nearly got a few musket balls in my back, too."

Christopher nodded. "I thought you had made it, but wasn't sure. I watched everywhere, for any sign, and waited for my chance to come to this side of the island. I think you have put them off the scent. Your tracks on the bar were nearly washed out by the rain, but old Tobit and the mate searched up and down and at length found them. They decided then you were gone, but they keep a watch. Tobit has that suspicious nature."

"That miserable dolt! Ho! I'll lay he ranted for days after I disappeared."

"Aye, that he did. A devil, he called you . . . a fiend. Swore you were off in league with convicts and he would see you hanged if it took years. But he's quieter now."

"How did you find me? I've taken care to hide all."

"Ah, mate, I know your mind well. I asked myself, 'Now where would he wish to be?' and the answer came to me easy. . . . 'Far away on the coast where he may best hide and must be in a place where he could build and launch a boat.' Well, that's here. The mate and captain do not think as you or I do."

"Might they have followed you?"

"I have been sent for fish," he replied, holding up a net bag half full with his catch. "I could see them across the grass if they did."

"You didn't come along the shore from the shallows?"

"No, not on that rubble. I would be all day hopping over that. I walked along the edge above, keeping to the taller grass and the flax. Never fear, I have left tracks up there for every point on the card. Here, Thomas, I have brought you something." Harrison presented the skin bundle to the lad who laid it on the sand and unrolled it. The skin contained rolls of twine, several of the potatoes, and a lump of the volcano glass. Christopher then leaned over and added three fish from his net bag to those items.

"The very things I need most!" he blurted out. "Join me, Chris! You and I together will speed the work. Why spend your time serving those two?"

"If I left them, the officers must surely guess that you are still on the island. They would spend their time hunting us or lying in ambush. We in turn would have to be always dodging them, and our canoe might never be finished. Tobit must rule us by one means or another. If he cannot, he sees himself as a failure. He will not abide our independence. It's best that he believes you have escaped and he can do nothing more. From the hut, I can smuggle what you need. Then, when all is ready, I will join you and we will leave. Am I right in that?"

Thomas frowned, thought for a moment, and answered, "Yes, you are, mate. Now the skins, I must have them for the sail. If you can manage to bring one at a time, I will sew them together during the day in a snuggery I have up on the slope. Most of my nights are spent working here. Come, Chips, see what I have done till now." Thomas pushed aside a limb and led the carpenter into the trees to the partially hollowed log. "You see," he said with some pride, "I have some of it readied. The mast and booms are back there under the ferns. All the line I have made, I keep dry in my nest that's under a rock."

Harrison stepped to the side of the log and hummed a note of approval as he ran his hand along its side. It was burned for a third or more of its depth and the carpenter felt and gauged the wood remaining at the top edge. "Aye, she will ride high. That is good," he said. "You have taken good care so far."

"I have kept my fires small and far apart, fearing she might crack from too much heat."

"Even so, if she splits a little, she will close up when wet. I expect she will make some water when afloat. A little bailing will keep it down. Leave the bottom thicker as we planned. She must be stout under the mast to give the heel a good step to rest upon. You are doing well, lad. I will bring all the vittles, rope, and skins I can slip away with. But Thomas, I cannot risk coming here again. I will make a cache up there by the animals' dens. Just a pistol shot this way from them is a fallen tree at the edge of a little open space."

"Yes, I know that one," the lad broke in. "The wind carried it down, tore its roots out of the ground."

"That's it. I cannot carry what you need any closer and be absent from the hut longer. Each fourth night from now, I will hide what I can spare you under the far side of the trunk. I will leave a limb resting against the tree if I have put something there. If the limb lies on the grass, it is my sign there is nothing. You will have to make the trip up on each of those nights for there is no way I might let you know I have failed."

They returned to the beach. "You say you have a shelter of some sort?" the carpenter asked.

"Yes, closer to the top than to here. . . . A small place, but dry and warm."

Harrison then clapped his arms tightly around Thomas and released him. "Keep up your spirits, lad," he said smiling and then started back along the shore. At a dozen yards away he stopped and turned. "You will see Yankee Land again!" he called out and held up his right hand as if swearing that it would come to pass.

Something about Christopher's hair seemed odd to Thomas. Had it always been that gray? He couldn't remember it being so when they arrived on the island. Perhaps the sun had changed it in the last few weeks. Regretfully and with a slow wave of his hand, he bid farewell to the carpenter and watched him start off again in a firm and purposeful stride. He wished he might have visited with him longer. There would be little time to gam before they left on their voyage, and he missed the idle talk of mateship, even if it was only complaints and speculations. He was aware Christopher could not be long absent from the hut or his work. Tobit and Morgen were suspicious by their very nature as officers, and would keep a tally in their heads of the carpenter's errands and whereabouts.

By the time he returned to Stonington, Thomas feared he might be older than Christopher was now. Or if his fortunes became no better after he landed on the Middle Island, he might arrive there as an ancient. He might reach home years in the future and find Father had died, and all in the Port had given him up for lost at sea. There might be only one or two who could remember him as the lad who had set off for the southern fishery so many years before in the *Dove*. Isabel would have borne many children and they in turn their children, none his. It might be that no child would ever carry his name. For him there would be no young laughter to soften a songless old age. What might he become then? A morose, bent old man who would envy those who had stayed in the Port, one to hobble about and watch the moving life of which he could not be a part? Would he become another white-bearded dotard in a worn black coat who sat on a barrel and watched the lading and unlading of ships, another one living on charity with even his firewood given him? An involuntary shiver seized Thomas.

"No!" he said to himself. He would never have it so. He would venture from the island by oar and by such winds as would drive him home. There, between those islands, in the Strait, in those bays, he must surely fall in with a trader or a whaler. His plans had been made with care and all the wit he possessed, and he was following them each in turn. He had made his fires and the mats to hide them. From the volcano glass, he would chip blades and with them drill and scrape. What else might he do?

CHAPTER 14

EACH FOURTH night Thomas picked his way up the bluff to the grassland, carefully keeping to a route in the thicker growth. Once he reached the plateau, he slipped along in the shadows of the trees that bordered the foot of the mountain. He moved slowly from one concealment to the next, knowing that if the officers sighted him or any mark he had made, they would pursue him all over the island. Some nights his foray began late to avoid the moon's brightest phases. Starlight gave him just enough illumination to find his way to the cache. When close to it, Thomas watched the shadows for several minutes for any movement or dark shape that could be a man. The downed tree was as close as he wanted to get to the hut. Tobit and Morgan might wander that far some evening if they could not sleep, or Harrison might give some hint in his manner that his mate was still on the island. Caution was most needed when he was near his goal, and he sometimes suspected he saw a dark form shift beneath the trees. But thus far they had proved to be nothing, a swaying of the bushes in the wind or his imaginings.

Harrison was true to his word and filched the most needed things; on all but a few of those fourth nights, Thomas found a skin, a coil of rope, potatoes, or smoked fish. His friend understood that, by the placing of those items, he was giving Thomas assurance, heartening him to complete the canoe. Chips must now recognize the futility of obeying Tobit and want to escape to the Middle Island. A new courage welled up in Thomas when he thought of Harrison's willingness to share the trial of the voyage. If Chris was with him in the little shell it would be much easier to watch the island sink below the horizon, be borne up on those great swells and plunged into the hollows. They could divide the hours into watches, and one could sleep while the other held the steering oar and bailed the hull.

For the next weeks, each night seemed a near repetition of the previous one. His small fires burned in the log in some places while he scraped char at other spots. Before the sky lightened each morning, he scooped up the live coals, buried them in the sand, and made sure there was not the least spark of fire left in the hull. It would have been a tiresome and constant round of labor and sleep except that there was measurable progress each morning. He was proud to see the hull taking the shape he desired, with the sides as thin as they could be safely made. Thomas wanted it to be a light canoe with good freeboard and so require less bailing.

After weeks of work, the hull lay under the trees so well hollowed Thomas could lift one end an inch or two in a stiff-legged straddle. He had drilled the holes in the upper edges for the lashings. Beside it lay the mast, boom, oar, and the twin boomkins. Only the bow needed work. It was a blunt, misshapen thing that would not part the sea evenly. Thomas built a fire against each side and burned off part of it in the process of making a passable shape. For the last touches, he pecked at it with an adze fitted with a glass blade, stopping after each few blows to run his hand over the surface to feel where the next chips should be removed. When work on the bow was finished for the night and all the other parts were lying in readiness on the beach, he banked the remains of his fire under the sand and cinders. He felt pride in his achievement as he viewed every part, however rudely made, ready to lash together and become a vessel that could carry the two of them away.

Thomas climbed to his hideaway before the eastern sky lightened. He lay there and went over the plan piece by piece as he had almost every morning. The next step was to find or devise some butt or skin to carry water. Once it was made and the storms ceased, he would leave a message under the log for Christopher, instructions to fill a hide with food and steal off in the following night. When he arrived at the beach, they could rig and launch the canoe in an hour or less.

That was all the time they needed. With the canoe a hundred yards out in the surf, they would be safe, beyond the officers' power to stop them. Then let them swear and rail all they wished, for he and Christopher would be on their voyage that would end somewhere to the east and north. It had taken so many relentless hours of labor, Thomas could barely believe he and Harrison might be under sail for the Middle Island as soon as they chose to leave.

It began to rain in the middle of the night, lightly at first, then increased to a hissing on the stones and leaf litter. Thomas was awakened several times by the heaviest downpours, but there was nothing to see when he pulled the vines aside. All was black in his shelter and out. It was a close, inky blackness in which he felt immersed. The next morning brought only a sourceless, gray illumination and, out beyond the overhang of his shelter, the rain and furtive light allowed the trees and ferns only muted colors. Thomas drew the skins he had sewn together for the sail closer about his body, and watched the drops pelt down and little streams pour from the rock above. Yesterday's morning sky had been a portent and he had read it correctly. Under the low clouds, the farthest edge of the ocean had been as dark as a charcoal line drawn from the south to the northeast.

As always, he had taken the precaution to roll the hull over to prevent it from filling with water. All the lines and seizings were now stowed under it. Like any rope, they would rot if allowed to stay wet for too long. There was nothing he could do in such wind and rain. Any foray out, even for a few minutes, would have left his clothes soaked and clammy against his body. There was no possible way to build a fire and dry them, and it was too cold to strip them off and work or search about for food. A shudder passed through him when he viewed the soaked litter and the pelting rain just beyond his projecting stone.

He set to making twine, and though he sat on his thick bed of fronds and the accumulated scrapings from the flax, his bottom and legs ached after being in one position for hours. At each short break in the rain, he wandered out between the dripping trees to stretch his cramped muscles and piss.

At last all the flax he had was scraped and rolled into strands and thence into cords. There was nothing more to do but lie under the hides and sleep, dream, and speculate about what they might meet on the coast of Tovy Poenamoo.

There could be peril there. Surely there was peril there. Would they be wiser to stand off during the day and attempt to land only at night? That meant to risk going near the surf without seeing what they might encounter, currents that would carry them onto rocks or great breakers that could dash their craft apart. There was no security in any approach. They would have to make their choices when they arrived for there was no foretelling what the coast might serve them.

The downpours lasted three days, yet Thomas felt he had been confined to his den for twice that time when the rain diminished and the clouds began to break up. Just prior to sunset, he eagerly slipped out and climbed to the top of a nearby rock from which the coast was visible. The ocean reflected a blue sky except where a few ragged showers drifted down from the fragments of the storm.

His first concern now was grub after having eaten his last mite of smoked fish and two potatoes the day before. Christopher would not have left food at the cache with rain threatening, and he reckoned it best to overhaul his traps. A crawfish would do him well. He picked his way down through the trees, hopping from rock to rock. At the cove, he found the hull had fared well, still inverted with all the rigging dry beneath it. The banked fire had long since expired. He would have to start another with the drill to cook what food he might find. All about his work place, gusts of wind had twisted the bushes, bent limbs aside, and filled the crevices between the stones with fresh, green leaves torn from the trees. On the beach, he found that more driftwood had been cast ashore, forming windrows of broken limbs and rockweed.

One of his three traps anchored between the rocks to the south had been damaged by the surge of the waves. Another was empty even of the bait he had placed in it. Some small fish or sea animal had gotten in through the twigs and out again. But one trap held a crawfish of moderate size. Thomas started his fire and while it burned down to a bed of coals, he went searching along the shore.

Thomas paced along, poking and pulling at the flotsam until he found a short section of a log in which he could see the shape of the water butt he wanted. It had a split in one end. He would force wedges into it and rend it into halves, then he would burn out the halves just as he had done with the hull. A strip of softened hide placed around the edges of the hollow would make a sound seal when the two pieces were bound back in place. Dry ropes wrapped around them, he figured, would swell when wet and become very taut. It would make a better container for their water than a skin. Skins leaked, and the water might become foul and be a trial to drink.

The next evening he returned to his old routine of working and gathering food at night and sleeping during the day. While the wind and sea did not admit escape, he could make the butt or maybe two. All must be ready. There could be no delay once he and Christopher met there and pushed the canoe into the sea.

The oily neck and sleeves of his jacket were black with dirt, and in addition his clothes were sooty from working over the fire and reeked of smoke. At each sunset when he arose from his bed, bits of the fronds and the scrapings of the leaves clung to his hair and beard. Even without a looking glass, he knew he must be an apparition far wilder than when he had affrighted the sailor on the beach. He promised himself that once the water cask was made he would wash his clothes. Till then, he would only spare time to bathe.

On the next of the appointed fourth nights, Thomas banked his fire early, hoping that Christopher had left some food beneath the downed tree. Mussels and the crawfish were all he had managed since the rain had ceased. Potatoes were what he wished for most. They gave some variety to the diet of fish. Overhead, the margin of sky between Cetus and the western horizon assured him there was at least two hours of good darkness remaining, enough time to reach the cache and return to his crevice before the eastern sky lightened. He climbed the bluff at a leisurely pace and approached the rim of the plateau. Each deliberate step up revealed a little more of the grassland. He searched to the right and left, but detected no dark figure crouching or slinking about. Farther to the northeast, there was only the dim, indistinct line of low trees and clumps of flax along the stream that drained over the edge of the plateau. Faint starlight coming from between the small moving clouds was all the illumination he needed. The way was familiar enough, though he always took a different path to avoid leaving a marked route.

Thomas turned and peered down toward the shore, but all was dark there except for a small blur of white swelling and shrinking where the surf broke on the rocks of the little point. If he turned his head to just the right angle, he could hear the whisper of the waves. He stood there considering that, in a few weeks, he and Harrison would be out on that sea, in that blackness, lifted high on the swells and dropped into the troughs between them. Clouded nights would be the worst when they could not see the stars, long nights with no hint of where the Middle Island lay. Thomas gave a deep sigh, one he tried to stem but could not. Their departure time was nearing and the uncertainty of it grew in his mind. Unless they had good fortune, it would be a parlous crossing, and he and Christopher might never see land again. It might rain the entire way, and they could only huddle and shiver together under a few skins for protection from the wind. They might rue the day they set off. On the wet and clouded days, the lighter portion of the horizon at sunrise and sunset would be all from which they might set their course. There was no way to make even the rudest form of a compass. To look at that full circle of sea, devoid of any ship or faint shadow of land low on the horizon, was to be wholly lost, far more lost than if cast into a wilderness ashore. Land was fixed: its features remained in place and might be given names. Hills, mountains, valleys gave dimension and shape even to an unknown land. But one portion of ocean looked like any other.

They could only wish that the wind would keep to its usual direction and drive them toward the Middle Island. There could be no thought of return. Once beyond the sight of the island, they must make for that long coast east to northeast. Thomas hoped it would be high land that might be sighted from a distance if the horizon was clear of mists and rain.

He could never have conceived that there was such an immensity of ocean when, as a boy, he had stood staring south from the Long Point at Stonington. The weeks of sailing from the Point to the Brazils had been interminable, yet not dull. Near the line he had been awed by the abrupt rising and setting of the sun and the menace of storms burgeoning by the minute to the zenith and snapping tortured veins of lightning from their black undersides to the sea. The swelling, milk-white towers with their many shaded alcoves and the fragments of shelving clouds around them, expanded the perceived depth of the sky far more than any vacant heaven. A faint vapor hung in the wide passages between the clouds and, at the farthest distances visible, tinted the air a faint bronze with some distillation of the sun. He remembered pale horizons and the hours of sweating heat and brilliant light that had followed the thunderous deluges. In the numberless clear nights, the old, familiar constellations had edged north and new ones had arisen out of the southern ocean.

He also remembered thinking they would never reach land again while running their easting down below New Holland. The *Dove* had risen and then pitched into the hollows, day after day, night after night, toward a horizon that always backed away from them at the same speed and never revealed the least speck of an island. He and Christopher would be in much peril on that heaving ocean with no more than a tree trunk to support them. They would have only water and food for a few days. If they did not raise land in a week, their suffering would begin.

Thomas faced around toward the peak and searched the trees along the border of the grassland for any unusual shape, the dusky form of a man, anything moving. Tobit or Morgen could be crouched in the shadows of the trees watching him, but he had to take the risk to gain the skins and victuals. Then he felt foolish. How would they know where, on the whole island, to keep their vigil or at what hour he might appear. They had no cause to think he was even on the island, and after all this time must be convinced he had left in the brig. He was safe while covered by the darkness, and he repeated that to himself over and over again. That pair would not spend every night lying in wait, hoping by chance to leap upon him. No, he was secure enough, he thought, and started off across the flatland and then into the trees. By slipping from one shadow to the next, he avoided crossing the places open to the starlight. At the edge of the little clearing, he crouched in the ferns and stared into the shadows. To his left was the log, and beneath its far side was the cache. This night Christopher might have left some potatoes wrapped in a skin. Cooked or uncooked, it didn't matter. He wanted something to eat. There was plenty of time to scan the greenery, wait for a few minutes, and repeat the search. Anything larger than a bird could only be one of the animals or one of the officers. Nothing moved except the nearby branches of a tree nudged fitfully by the night air. It was all silent. The surf's rumble could not be detected so far from the coast, and no bird broke the quiet with a muffled coo or chirp. The limb lay against the tree trunk, indicating Chris had been there. Thomas was satisfied it was safe.

He rose to his feet and strode to the log. With a last look around, he leaned far over and felt the ground under the far side for what Christopher might have left there. His fingers found nothing and moved farther along. He was puzzled. His mate would not have placed the limb up there and not left something.

Suddenly he felt a hand grab his shoulder. It was a powerful grip. His heart skipped and started a rush of thumping beats. He gasped, twisted to his left, and attempted to straighten up. Beside him was a black shape. A rope was being forced over his right wrist. Instantly he yanked his arm back, but it was already held in a tight noose. His feet were kicked to one side, and he landed on his back, wrenching his arm to free his hand. Another rope was slipped around his other wrist as he fought to get up. A bright flash of light filled his eyes with a jolt of pain on the right side of his head. He had been clubbed. Before he could recover from the stunning blow, his wrists were drawn together and tied. Against the stars he could see the black shapes of two men leaning over him.

A familiar voice exulted, "Ah, a clever boy, a clever boy! But not clever enough!" It was the captain.

"Do you think we are fools?" Mr. Morgen asked. "Your mate has led us to you."

"Ha," Tobit shouted, "you would kill your captain! You would murr-der." He drew the word out as if he savored the sound of it. "Mutiny and murr-der!" he continued. "You have descended to that and so you must be punished for it." He kicked at Thomas's head, but in the dark the foot missed and caught his shoulder a glancing blow.

"We have all prepared for you. Get to your feet!" the mate ordered.

The lad rose slowly to his knees and was pulled fully upright by the mate tugging on the rope tied about his wrists.

"You have a boat a-building. Where is it?" the captain demanded.

"I have not," Thomas protested.

"What's that you say? No? Then why has Harrison left this for you?" the mate asked, holding something up to his face. "Why do you need so much rope if you are not building a boat? He has been fetching this and other truck for you."

"I have no boat," the lad replied again.

"Damn your eyes, you lie!" the mate shouted and slapped him across the face with the coil of rope.

"You are a mutineer and deserter. We will see justice done here," Tobit broke in. "You'd be a murderer! Aye, would kill your captain."

"You are the murderer!" Thomas cried out and jerked on the line tied to his wrists. "You killed that poor jack. . . ."

"What has happened to your speech? Are you drunk?" the captain broke in on his accusation.

"A gift from the crew of the brig," the lad answered. "They knocked out my teeth."

"They served you well," the mate sneered and pulled on the rope, forcing him to follow across the grassland.

"It was you who. . . ." Thomas accused him again, but stopped speaking when the captain jabbed a stick into the small of his back.

"You will be silent," Tobit snapped.

The mate tugged on the rope and led Thomas out of the trees and toward the hut. At each ten or twelve steps, the captain prodded him with the stick to remind him to keep up the pace. The men marched in a line, stumbling when their feet struck small rocks or lurching when they stepped into a depression unseen in the darkness. No one spoke. The only sound was the swishing of the tall grass against their leathern trousers.

Harrison surely didn't lead Tobit and Morgen to the cache so they might capture him, Thomas reasoned. No, he would not do that. The officers must have seen him put food aside or reckoned that a hide was missing. With their suspicions raised, it would have been simply a matter of days before they found he was making trips to the south for no need. Perhaps the mate watched Chips go toward the downed tree from the top of the little volcano. A search to find the cache would take an hour or less.

Thomas thought of bolting across the plain, but he knew he could not run fast enough with his hands bound. They had tied them too tightly to be worked free, but he tried it anywise. At least the struggle kept the blood flowing to his fingers. When they reached the hut he would plead for them to loosen the ropes. Perhaps they would do it and he then might manage to pull them off. With his hands and feet free, he was a match in speed for the mate. He had been taken by stealth once, but it would never happen again. They had mistaken their man if they thought he would submit without a fight.

He knew Tobit had something in store for him, some devilish punishment. Would it be hanging, the usual one for a mutineer, or something else?

Before they reached the hut, Mr. Morgen turned aside toward the trees. They now could be seen, faintly outlined in the intimation of light before dawn. They passed between the first few trunks and stopped. The mate pointed to something just a few paces ahead. Thomas tried to make out what it was. In the gloom stood three poles about eight or nine feet long, leaned together at their tops, and tied, forming the outline of a pyramid.

"You recognize it? You recognize the triangle?" the captain asked. "Oh, yes, you know what it is. But you must know I do this for your own good. As a Christian, I cannot abandon you to the devil and let him turn you to his hateful purpose. You must be punished in the body until you repent your crimes."

Thomas said nothing while he looked at the poles.

"You will know the triangle, my lad," the mate hissed in his ear. "Your cunning cannot help you here."

Thomas saw what was to happen. They meant to flog him. Once he was spread and bound on that frame, there would be no chance to break free. Suddenly, he yanked the line from the mate's grip and dashed toward the grassland. The mate, startled at first, pursued him and stepped on the trailing rope. Thomas stumbled and almost fell. He straightened, tried to regain his speed, but Morgen scooped up the line and hauled back on it. Thomas was jerked about and flung to the ground in a heap. Both officers dragged the struggling sailor back to the triangle and managed to pass the rope over the top of it. They hauled on the line from the opposite side until Thomas was drawn up and hanging there at full length with his hands nearly touching the bindings that held the framework together. The mate crouched at the pole on the right where it rested on the earth and reached out to get a line around the lad's ankle. Thomas kicked at him and, for a few seconds, hindered the officer from binding his leg. Tobit kneeled at the opposite side and attempted the same with the left leg. Unable to kick effectively at both officers at the same time, Thomas was finally subdued. With each leg bound to a pole, he could only move his head. He had hung there several minutes when the mate stepped up behind him and tugged at his jacket. He felt a stinging cut over his spine and then knew the officer was working with a blade of the volcano glass, slitting his jacket open so he would have a clear swing at his whole back. Ha! No half-measures for the mate. He wanted the whip to wrap around his back to the more tender skin under his arms. Would that satisfy old Tobit, he asked himself, or would he crave a worse revenge after Thomas's back was cut open?

Where was Christopher? He is my mate! He will help. He would not allow this! Thomas thought. Had they bound him someplace so he could not interfere? Surely he would come to his rescue and save him from this beating if he was able. But where was he?

Mr. Morgen finished cutting the back of his jacket and tossed the splinter of glass to the ground. Thomas could see it lying there to his right. The gray light was now strong enough to send a dull shine from its surface. The mate then tied each half of his jacket to the nearest elbow with twine.

The captain stepped under the triangle and put his face close to Thomas's. "You deserve this and more for your foul nature," he declared with measured words, "but I have an offer to make you." Tobit leaned his head back a little and considered the bound lad for a moment with his eyes sighted along his large nose. "Mr. Morgen has laid a charge of his powder up on the volcano," he announced. "You are to light the train. Do just that and you will not be flogged. You may then go your way with my leave and without your due punishment. Agree and you may take your boat and try your fortune on the ocean."

"Why should I do a thing for you? You two are a useless pair, no help to Chips and me. And why lay a charge?" Thomas asked. "What are you up to? You should want to get home, not blast the mountain asunder."

The captain leaned forward and peered at Thomas's mouth. "What did you expect from such blackguards? Well deserved, well deserved from our enemies."

Thomas grimaced at Tobit, showing the gap in his upper teeth. "They were not our enemies until you made them so. It should have been your fat face they struck. You are the murderer! Now what other evil are you up to?"

"What I do is not for you to question! Neither in this nor anything I do. I am captain and you are a mere thing to be ordered about."

"You find reason to stay here because you fear a voyage not rising two hundred mile. Aye, you fear it! You are too much a coward to attempt it. Captain Tobit must play at some mysterious game lest he be counted a poltroon." Thomas gave a jeering laugh until the captain struck at his face.

"You foul thing!" Tobit shouted. "I have made you a decent offer and you taunt me. I ask this one last time, agree to it or you will feel a hundred of my best. Your answer now?"

Thomas's mouth pulled up into a slight smile. The pre-dawn light was growing. He watched the captain's seamed face as he asked, "Why not light it yourself? Why give me leave for such a trifle? What assurance do I have that you will free me once I have lighted the train? Only your word."

Tobit, inflamed by the suggestion, screamed, "You doubt my word? The word of an officer!"

"Ha!" Thomas shouted back. "I am not such an innocent to believe all that is told to me! You see no chaff in my hair. You have too much a conceit of yourself. You cannot be without your command, your pulpit, or some power over others. You mean to have me light the train for there is too much risk. I saw the mate's trials of it. If I light it and it does what you wish, then you will find some other notion to keep me at work."

"There! You call me a liar! You call Captain Tobit a liar! You miscreant, you scorn my offer!" he shouted. His jaw closed and the muscles tensed as he stared into the lad's eyes. A flush spread on the skin of his cheeks and across his forehead. With his right forefinger rigid and almost touching Thomas's nose, he raved, "You oblige me to discipline you, you oblige me! Bring the cat, Mr. Morgen!"

Mr. Morgen stepped forward and handed him something. The captain then placed himself one pace from Thomas's left side and swayed a little to test his footing. He poked a cat-o'-nine-tails under the lad's nose and rolled it around to display its tightly twisted and knotted cords. Then he dropped the cat to his side, shook it twice to free any tangles, and made a swing at one of the poles. The tails hissed past Thomas's ear and their hard knots cracked against the wood.

"You refuse to walk in the righteous path. If you will not be an obedient Christian and serve God's will, then you must surely be one with the devil. There is no middle ground between the two. You hear me, no middle ground! You must choose between our true God and that fiend who has filled you with vanity, disobedience, and a taste for sin."

"There is no devil outside of men's skulls," Thomas spat back. "Why should there be one? Ha, yes, we must have the devil. Those who do not obey you are possessed. It must be your God or the devil. No middle ground. I must serve you or be counted evil."

"If you will not choose, this will drive Satan from you," the captain continued as if the lad had not said a word. "Yes, you understand the lash. Yes, yes, by it you will be given the Light and obey. No answer yet? . . . I will make you answer, and humbly." Tobit drew his arm back, then froze in mid-swing. "Ha!" he exclaimed. "But I am forgetting. Harrison must witness this punishment. It will have a good effect on him. He must be reminded of his place too. I will wake him and fetch him here." The captain handed the cat to the mate and started for the hut.

Thomas waited a few minutes after the captain left, then asked, "What spell has he cast on you?"

The mate did not respond.

The lad twisted to his left to look at Mr. Morgen. "You were not a bad officer. What has seized you? Now you are as daft as he. You let that fool bedazzle you."

"I have seen all," he replied, pacing around the triangle and swinging the cat in his right hand. "He has shown me what has happened to this world. It is in deep peril, worse now than ever. Apprentices run away, live in sloth and ignorance. Journeymen prefer thievery and chicanery to honest labor. People worship false, heathen gods. Children slay their parents. The devil gains more disciples every day.

You haven't the wit to know how he weaves his way among you and your ilk. It is for us who know better to set you aright. I have seen how the Lord has guided us to this place to do His will. A fortress must be built here the devil cannot enter by any of his devious ways, a place so totally given to the worship of the Lord he dare not approach!"

"So, I guess right. He has no intention of leaving."

"In proper time, but not before we have prepared the land for God's purpose. Here, this undefiled soil must serve for what the Lord intended, a place where temptation to sin is not known."

"And Tobit will rule all, oh yes! He would not have it otherwise. You will spend the whole of your days on your knees and when not digging in the earth, you will be praying and thanking Tobit? Ha! What folly! What a dull life you will have preparing for your death. You are welcome to it."

The mate stepped up to Thomas and thrust the cat beneath his nose, and warned, "You jeer. You cannot see any of that for Satan has blinded you. I realized that when you tried to slay the captain. The devil conspires with those like you, but this cat will remedy that. You will see the way when we finish with you."

"What a scarcity of wit you have! That is all Tobit's invention. If he said the sun was the moon and the moon was the sun, would you believe that too?" Thomas asked.

"I have my wits, much better than yours. No one puts a spell on me. I can see the tide of evil for myself, and you are part of it. But the world is not lost," the mate declared. "Nothing sets things aright like a good flogging." Then, with his head leaned a little forward and his eyebrows raised, he added quietly, "Or a hanging."

He said no more and stood at the side of the triangle, humming and waiting for the captain. He sang a few remembered words of a hymn softly, then returned to humming when his memory failed him.

Thomas hung there with his head down. He could think of no way to escape without Harrison's help. There was nothing to do until he arrived. Yet Mr. Morgen was a match for Christopher. With the two officers together, his chances were poor unless, by some ruse, he drew one of them off. If Christopher could get the mate to leave for no more than a minute or two, he could then overcome Tobit. With Thomas's hands and feet freed, he and Harrison could flee, and once they pushed their canoe into the surf they would be beyond capture.

Tobit's voice could be heard carrying through the greenery. By twisting his head around, Thomas could see Harrison approaching, the captain following several paces behind, spouting his favorite Biblical phrases about duty and righteousness.

At once Harrison saw the situation and dashed forward. He stopped and stared at the ropes that bound the lad's hands and feet. "You mustn't do this!" he shouted and dropped to his knees. With his left hand he pulled at the line around Thomas's right ankle. Thomas saw Christopher's right hand drop to the ground and close over the bit of glass the mate had cast aside.

"Back away!" Mr. Morgen ordered and pulled him by the neck of his jacket until he was on his feet and several paces away. "Any more of that and you will have your turn on the triangle. Don't interfere."

Harrison turned to look at the captain who was holding a heavy stick and asked, "Why such a punishment?"

"For his attack on the captain," the mate answered, "and because he is to light our mine up there on the volcano and refuses his duty. You are here to see justice done."

"No! No! You cannot do this!" he cried, wrenching himself from the mate's grasp to rush at the triangle again. This time he reached up for Thomas's hands. The lad felt the carpenter's fingers tugging at the ropes and, at the same time, the glass sliver being pressed into his right palm. His fingers curled over it to conceal it from the officers.

"God damn you!" Mr. Morgen shouted and grabbed the carpenter again by his jacket. In one continuous motion, he pulled Harrison down and flung him to the ground.

Before he could rise to his feet, the captain rushed forward and slashed at his face with the stick. Harrison rolled away with a cry of pain and then struggled to his knees, holding a hand to his face. In a few seconds, trickles of red oozed from between his fingers. He lowered his arms to help himself get to his feet and revealed that his nose had been split open. A stream of blood ran over his lips and into his beard. The mate picked up a short length of rope and started for the carpenter. Guessing the mate's purpose, Harrison pushed past the captain and ran out toward the grassland. The mate started to pursue when the captain called him back.

"Don't bother with him now," he said. "He will be coming back to aid his mate. We can snare him in good time, and then he shall learn his catechism."

"Aye, his cat-echism, and from the cat, to be sure. Its tails teach it all well." The mate laughed as he handed the knout to the captain.

Tobit positioned himself at the triangle again and swung the cat back in a wide arc. He brought it swiftly forward and the tails struck Thomas's back to wrap around his right side. Thomas had a fold of his sleeve in his mouth and bit down on it. The pain was not as severe as he had expected. Only the knots that struck the tender skin under his right arm burned hot. The captain swung again, grunting with the effort. After five strokes, he stopped and gasped, "It does not have the effect it should. There is not enough weight to it."

Mr. Morgen took the cat from the captain, snapped it in the air, and laid it across the lad's back. The mate's stronger arm made the cords strike harder, and Thomas arched his back and let out a squeal.

"You are right, it hasn't enough weight. I will soak it in the branch for a while," the mate said and started through the trees.

"And I will watch our mutineer," the captain called after the mate. "I would labor with him, but fear he is too far gone toward evil to save him by word and reason." He lowered himself to the ground, grunting with the effort and heaved a sigh as he rested his bulk there.

Thomas hung motionless from the triangle with his head turned just enough to sight past his right arm at the captain who sat Buddha-like, looking at nothing.

The ropes tied about Thomas's wrists cut into his skin. He wished he could saw through them, but he feared the captain would notice the movements of his hands, even slow, furtive ones. His sole chance for escape would be lost if the bit of glass was discovered and taken from him, yet he had to do something. Slowly, he brought the edge of the blade up and touched it to the line that suspended him from the apex of the triangle. He drew the glass across it once, then shifted his body to the right and left as if to make himself more comfortable. He hoped such fidgeting might draw the captain's eyes from the motions of his hands. Each few seconds, he swayed or pulled at his leg bonds, while he pushed or drew the blade against the rope. He felt the strands gave way a few at a time, but he knew he must not cut them all. His left hand closed over the severed part of the rope to conceal it. Tobit would be upon him in a trice and clubbing him with his stick if he parted the last strand and dropped down to slash the ropes holding his ankles. There was nothing more he could manage until both the officers were where they could not see him cutting himself free. It was a mean situation. If he agreed to light the train, they would hobble him and watch him closely, with their bows and arrows at the ready.

How was his poor Chips? The captain had fetched him a terrible blow across his face. With such a wound, he was probably too injured to return and deal with Tobit. But somehow, if he could draw the captain away, even for a few seconds or a minute, Thomas might cut himself loose and be gone. Then he and Christopher could rig the canoe and leave in an hour or two. It would be better to be sailing for the Middle Island, even in those great rolling swells, than to be hiding or waging a war with Tobit and Morgen. The captain would spend his days searching for the canoe, meaning to smash it and burn the rigging. His lunacy was complete.

"Mr. Morgen must have forgotten his errand," Thomas suddenly said to the captain.

Tobit turned his head and looked at the lad for a second, then resumed his blank stare at the bushes before him.

After a few more minutes Thomas added, "Perhaps he has fallen asleep there by the branch?"

Without bothering to face the lad, the captain answered, "Are you in such haste to be flogged? Mr. Morgen knows his duty. It is a shame you do not know yours. I doubt you would be hanging there if you had not become such a stiff-necked rascal, but I think you were meant to swing on a gibbet somewhere. Rogues such as you never die a natural death. You have set yourself against all reason and the revealed will of God."

"Where is there any reason in staying on an island no one knows of? To age and die and never see another human?"

"It is for me to see the reason. It is for you to obey. That is God's will. There are few people who have the gift to see what is meant to be in all its parts and perfection."

"Does Mr. Morgen see it? He hasn't returned. Perhaps he has lost trust in your vision and gone off somewheres."

Tobit did not answer the question or give any sign he had heard it. His jaw was thrust out and clenched in a bulldog look, his expression of a belief that was unassailable by any reasoning or doubt.

After a few minutes of silence, Thomas suddenly tittered, "Our mate has been waylaid by Christopher. Aye, fetched a stout blow with a cudgel. By now, old Chips has him tied hand and foot. That's why he has been gone so long. You'd best find and rescue him. Chips might be creeping up on you this very minute. Better take a look about."

The captain gave no more heed to the lad's voice than if he had been struck deaf.

There was nothing more Thomas could think of that would stir Tobit and send him off to look for the mate. A few precious seconds was all he desired. Four or five slices with the glass and he could be gone. On the alert, with his limbs unbound, he was a match for the mate. Tobit was too fat and short-winded and could be ignored, except that he might spot him and Harrison and inform Mr. Morgen.

His thoughts went back to Christopher. He imagined he must be lying somewhere in the trees, suffering from the clubbing, else he would be devising some way to draw the officers off.

The first bit of the sun nudged above the sea and lighted the underside of a few tattered and drifting clouds. Thomas could see more now. He hung his head back and looked at the crudely hacked ends of the poles, their bindings, and the rope that held him upright.

He considered his chance of cutting the last few strands and freeing his hands and feet before Tobit was upon him. But he saw that opportunity had not yet arrived. He dared not risk having the glass taken from him. Patience, patience, he reminded himself. They might yet leave him alone after they had flogged him to their satisfaction. The glass was the key to escape. He must keep it even though he must suffer the whip.

There was a shuffling in the bushes, and the mate pushed his way through, swinging the cat in his right hand. The captain rose to meet him, took the cat, and tried a few swings with it. He grunted approval with a nod, handed it back, and ordered, "Start with fifty, Mr. Morgen."

The mate went to his station at Thomas's left. Tobit strode over to a spot just a pace from the lad's right side and assumed his quarterdeck pose with his arms folded across his chest, head high, and a detectable lean back to counter the weight of his paunch. Mr. Morgen swung his arm aside, and then, in a wide circle, brought the cat hissing forward to spread and wrap around Thomas's back.

"Eiyee!" the lad screamed and arched his back. He had bitten the fold of his sleeve again, hoping the tense grip of his jaw muscles would prevent his crying out, but the soaked cat and the mate's stronger arm made fiery lines on his skin. It was twice as painful as the dry scourge, and he wondered how many lashes he could suffer before he gave in and agreed to light the train. He had no hope of lasting long with the mate swinging the cat.

"That's it, give it your best, Mr. Morgen. There is much evil in him, arrogance, pride!" the captain shouted and waved his fists. "Two . . . three . . . four . . . five. . . ." He counted each stroke as the tails left crisscrossed patterns of bright red welts. He stomped his feet, almost in a dance, to his shouts. "Yes! Yes! That's it. Beat him, beat his black soul clean! Ha! Yes, beat him, beat him!"

Tears ran down Thomas's cheeks and into his mussed beard each time he squeezed his eyes closed in the tense half-second before each strike of the cat. He shrieked with pain when the tails laced like hot wire across his back.

After the twenty-fifth blow struck and the mate drew back for the twenty-sixth, Tobit held up his hand to stop him. He took a step forward and spoke into the lad's ear. "Are we ready to listen to reason?" he asked. "Have you been given enough wisdom now to abjure the devil and do your duty?"

Thomas leaned his head back and turned it slightly to look at Tobit with a slowly opening right eye. He said nothing. His face was shiny with tears and perspiration.

The captain reached up and touched a forefinger to one of the trickles of blood creeping down Thomas's back. He held it up for the lad to see the red drop on its tip.

Thomas closed his eye and turned his head forward again.

"You mock me!" Tobit shouted. "You mock me. Just as you did every Sabbath aboard the *Dove*. When I read from the good book, I saw it in your eyes, always sneering. Inside, you were mocking me and therefore mocking our Lord. You are a confounded infidel, a godless wretch! Proceed, Mr. Morgen."

"I give over," Thomas said softly.

Tobit turned his head and leaned closer as if to hear better, then asked, "I hear a voice peeping, like some little bird. What is that you wish to say?"

"I give over," the lad repeated.

"What is it? What am I hearing from this pagan? Speak a little louder," the captain demanded.

"I will light the train," the lad muttered a bit louder.

"Ahh, he sees reason. This is most astonishing for one so filled with scorn and evil, is it not, Mr. Morgen? Instruct him how it is to be done."

"Your hands will be kept bound," the mate explained, "and there will be a long rope hitched to one leg. Attempt to run and we will trip you up. There, just short of the mine you will be given an ember to light it."

"There is no need to keep me bound. I have said I will set it off."

The captain moved closer to Thomas and declared, "We have no faith in what you say. You do not trust the word of an officer, so we in turn have less reason to put trust in a common sailor. You would dash off the moment you were set free."

"I must be unbound or I'll not do it. You mean to keep me prisoner after I light it."

"It will be done as we say. Proceed Mr. Morgen until he agrees to it," the captain commanded.

The interruption had given the mate a respite and, meaning to lay on afresh, he twisted his whole body to the side. His arm was up and tensed to make the next stroke, but he halted in that pose when a tremendous boom echoed across the side of the volcano and then returned, rolling again and again from the higher mountains farther back. Mr. Morgen remained in his stance with the cat drawn back ready to lash Thomas's bare back again.

Tobit glanced up in the direction of the slope, though he could see none of it through the wall of leaves. Then the two officers stared blankly at each other as the rumble died away.

"The mine. . . . It's . . . it's . . . the . . . mine," the mate stuttered.

The captain rose up on his toes in an absurd, witless effort to see over the trees. "Damn! Harrison has touched it off!" he shouted and rushed off through the bushes.

Mr. Morgen flung the cat to the ground and followed the captain. In seconds they were swallowed up in the branches and leaves.

With one slice of the glass fragment, Thomas cut the last few rope yarns that suspended him from the triangle. He leaned over and sawed at the bindings of his ankles, first the right and then the left. His legs were free, but his wrists were so tightly bound he was unable to get the blade close enough to draw it across the ropes. He sat on the ground and bit at the knots, wrenching his head from side to side to work them open. His missing front teeth unexpectedly made the task easier, allowing the remaining ones a closer bite on the ropes. Gradually they pulled open and he shuffled his hands out. With a leap up, he was running after the officers, but after a few paces he stopped. His split jacket tied to his elbows flopped at his sides and annoyed him. One wrench at each tie and they tore loose, then he was on his way again.

Christopher was his greatest worry, now that he was free. He wondered, as he dodged around ferns and ducked under tree limbs, how the carpenter had managed to find the mine. He guessed! Tobit's curious descent down that slope on their second day ashore was the clue. Chips guessed it was placed in the cave they had found before they climbed the peak for pitchy wood. Hurrah! He had hit on the ideal ruse to draw the officers off, to remove the true cause for the flogging. At the pool at the foot of the cascade, Thomas stopped. Where was Chris now? He would surely not return along the trail just after the blast and risk encountering the officers. Chips would hide and watch to see if the mate or the captain or both went by, to discover if their mine had succeeded. If only one passed him, Chris would then go back to the triangle to help free Thomas from the one remaining as a guard. He would go there in any event to be sure that Thomas had freed himself. He expected to meet Harrison coming as fast as he could down their old route. He then started off again, hopping up from rock to rock and pulling at each limb and frond that would aid his climb.

Now that Tobit knew to a certainty that he was building a boat, he would not rest until he discovered it and burned or broke it up. They did not have any time to spare. He must find Christopher and rush to the cove. The mast had to be rigged and the canoe launched within the hour. Otherwise it might become a battle fought with bows and arrows and clubs.

As he passed the midpoint of the climb, he saw that something odd was happening to the stream. The water no longer dashed over the stones in a white froth, but now only flowed around them. Its volume diminished as he got higher, draining as smaller rivulets in channels that twisted around each obstruction. The sides and tops of rocks once washed or under the water for years were now exposed. Mosses that had spread over the surfaces and had been constantly splashed by the stream now dripped and trickled their absorbed water. Once Thomas broke out of the trees and reached the lip of the crater, he saw that the level of the lake had dropped. It was shallower at the outlet and unable to feed a full cascade anymore. The channel, bordered by thick stands of ferns on each side, now spilled a stream just a few inches deep.

Thomas stopped and uneasily scanned the way ahead but saw no one on that rough edge. He should have met Christopher before he had reached the top. Had the officers made a prisoner of him? No, his mate was cleverer than that. He would not take some other way down through the woods, for he knew moving through that tangle on the side of the mountain was too slow and that they must launch their vessel quickly. Once they had captured him at the cache, Morgan and Tobit had some idea where to search for the canoe. All his labor making it would be wasted if it were found.

He must act swiftly and join with Christopher. Surely he would have returned down along the cascade once the officers went past. Something was wrong. Perhaps he was still hiding, for some cause, in the ferns just below the rim of the crater. Thomas moved ahead, hopping lightly to avoid the sharper pieces of lava and searching the ferns and bushes on the slope for any sign of his shipmate.

Tobit was wholly seized by his lunacy, and the mate was under his spell. Had they both eaten some strange plant that had stripped them of their reason?

There was a roar in the air, and a wavering echo of it from the next slope. Thomas stopped and listened. It came from below, where he expected the mine had been placed. There was nothing to be seen from the lip of the crater. Cautiously he started over the side, first through the low band of ferns, then into the bushes and trees. He picked up a dead limb thinking he might have to use it as a weapon if he met with the officers before he found Christopher.

The loose cinders and leaves rolled from beneath his feet. He nearly tumbled over, but grabbed a frond to keep him upright. The roar grew in volume as he descended through the steeply pitched forest. Between the limbs and bushes below him and to his right, he saw the source of the noise, a swift, brown stream of water a yard across shooting out into the treetops. It was airborne for fifty feet and then broke into steaming spray as it plunged back into the forest.

After another minute of sliding and falling Thomas grabbed a limb to halt himself. Below and close by the flying water, he spotted Tobit and the mate. They were searching through the ferns about them and stepping up on half-fallen trees to peer into the forest farther away. They talked and gestured to each other, but nothing could be heard except the roar of the escaping water and their actions appeared to Thomas, peeking through the bushes, as mere pantomimes. The officers must have reasoned that Harrison, after lighting the train, would stay on the side closer to the hut, for they knew his whole purpose of igniting the train was to divert them long enough to free his mate. Thomas scanned through the trees to the north, looking for any bent fronds or other traces of his passing. Harrison must have climbed up and waited for the officers to rush along the top and then return along the trail to the plateau. That was surely what he would have done, but there was not the least sign. Thomas started down again, slowly on the unstable cinders, peering into the woods after each few steps. Could Christopher in some manner have gotten back to the triangle without passing him? Impossible, he thought.

He saw that the captain and the mate had given up their search and were watching the stream shoot with tremendous speed from the hole blasted in the volcano's flank. Awed and fearful of the power and danger of the water roaring out, they backed away a dozen paces. From the point where the plunging stream struck the slope, a gully was being washed deeper by the minute. Loose chunks of lava and cinders tumbled into the water and it poured down through the forest as a semi-liquid avalanche, ripping even the largest trees from the earth. Their roots and limbs threw sprays of dirty water and mud into the air as they tumbled over and over.

Thomas was about to slip away when he noticed a dark mass in the top of a tree that had been partially blown aside. The trunk leaned away from the stream of water. The lump, partially hidden in leaves, might have been the nest of a large bird, built up with a mass of twigs, yet they had never seen a bird that would make a nest that size in the mountains. Thomas's heart thumped when he spied a hand hanging from that shapeless mass. He dashed down toward the tree, breaking through the bushes and ferns and grasping at fronds and limbs to keep from pitching head over heels. The captain and mate stared at him in open-mouthed surprise as he swept past them. They recovered, and both officers started in pursuit.

Thomas reached the tree, which leaned precariously. Water was splashing over its exposed roots. The lad leaped onto the bole and climbed to the branches and there found Harrison face down against the trunk. His clothes were wet and splattered with reddish mud. Thomas positioned his feet in crotches of the limbs to get a good footing and slipped his hands under Harrison's arms. The mate moved under the tree when he saw Thomas was attempting to lower the carpenter. Thomas lifted his friend and slid his feet over the side of the trunk. With his arms raised, the mate readied himself to receive the body. While Christopher was being shifted about, his arms and legs flopped, unwilled, doll-like. Thomas tried to lower Harrison slowly, but he could not move to get to a better position or kneel to put him closer to Mr. Morgen. His grip failed and Harrison fell onto the mate. Thomas grabbed a limb, swung once on it and dropped onto the slope next to Tobit.

CHAPTER 15

MR. MORGEN fell backwards, landing on his back with the body of the carpenter lying full length on top of him and their two faces pressed together. The officer grabbed Harrison's shoulders to push him up. When the body was at arm's length from his, he screamed, "Oh God, what have we done? What have we done?"

For several seconds he was immobile, his eyes wide open, staring at the head above him. Drops of blood fell from the carpenter's face onto his. "Ah . . . ah. . . ." The mate gasped and rolled to his left to cast the body off.

Harrison landed on his back at the base of a fern that held him from sliding farther down the slope. The body had an unnatural stillness and lay in a close, flaccid contact with the earth. There were no eyes or even eyelids in the sockets. The cavities were filled with cinders and bits of lava blasted into them by the force of the explosion. The skin of his forehead was covered with gobbets of thickening blood. His teeth showed through the black grit in his mouth in a ghastly and frozen grimace. Most of the nose was torn away, revealing the two separate openings.

Thomas gasped and let out a moan. With Christopher's face now a vision of death, he was hardly recognizable as his old mate of the *Dove*. Thomas kneeled down and placed his hand on the carpenter's chest but felt no heartbeat to reassure him that Christopher was alive. There could be no doubt that his shipmate had died at the instant of the explosion or soon after.

Thomas looked up accusingly at the officers. "The blast has done for him!" he barked. "This is what you meant for me. You daren't light it yourself, but you would risk another's life for your mad idea. You are daft, aye, and cowardly withal. You speak of a murderer. If there is one on this island, it is you!" He jumped to his feet, and thrusting his finger at the captain, shouted, "Yes, you, a double murderer! And all the deaths of the crew are on your head."

Mr. Morgen, unnerved and with his jaw agape, stared at the carpenter. His right hand wiped away the blood that had dropped from Harrison's face onto his forehead. The captain's eyes, though he looked toward the body, were focused as if it were much farther away.

Suddenly a rumbling came from beneath their feet. A portion of the slope under the rushing water was giving way, and the volume of water shooting outward instantly doubled. The tree that had held Harrison's body shivered and eased lower. The side of the volcano vibrated with the force and speed of the flying, brown stream. Farther below, more trees were torn loose and carried down the slope in a tumble of broken rocks, mud, and froth.

"Take his legs!" Thomas shouted over the roar of the water. "Quickly, or the mountain will fall from under us!"

The mate grasped the carpenter's legs, and Thomas slipped his hands under his arms to lift the body. In that fashion they managed to carry him, but it was impossible to go up the slope with that burden. Even climbing alone, it was two steps up and one step sliding back in the loose material between the trees and bushes. Their only choice was to travel diagonally along the side of the volcano toward the hut. The two men struggled, stopping time after time to put Harrison down and clear a way through fallen limbs and ferns. Tobit, with staring and obtuse eyes, lagged behind, and the mate paused several times until he caught up close enough to see them and follow. Thomas cursed to himself because he could not carry the carpenter's body alone and go off, leaving the captain to blunder about through the forest to fall somewhere and break his neck.

The mate halted at a tree that had toppled across their route, its top leaning on the limbs of the trees growing lower on the slope. They placed the body on the ground and rested for a few minutes. Before they started again, Thomas climbed onto the trunk and walked shakily along its length to the higher end where he could see the land below, close to the foot of the mountain. A fan of turbid water and mud was rapidly spreading from the foot of the volcano and out onto the flatland. More trees, limbs, roots, and all were tumbling and being driven down with the rush of water. At times the boiling flood came out colored brick red, then shifted to brown, and for moments even changed to near-black. Its flow did not slacken as Thomas expected it would, but kept increasing in volume and spreading across the flatland.

"The side of the volcano must be collapsing!" he shouted to the mate. "We must hurry before we are taken down with it!" He ran back along the bole and jumped to the ground.

They lifted Harrison over the tree, crawled over it themselves, and resumed picking their way along the mountainside with their load. After a few minutes, the mate turned and nodded, indicating he wanted to go back for the captain. The lad rested while Mr. Morgen hurried back to the toppled tree. The mate found Tobit pacing back and forth on its far side, maundering as he went.

He reached across and grabbed the captain's sleeve. "Over here, quickly," he called, "or we will be carried away and drowned!" By persistent tugging and cajoling, he got the captain to crawl over the trunk and walk toward Thomas. The three of them worked their way through the thicket for a quarter of an hour, then suddenly broke out and found themselves near their old route along the cascade. From there on it was much easier going. There was no need to force their way through bushes or climb over more downed trees.

An hour or more after they had started, the mate and Thomas arrived at the hut and laid Harrison's body on the ground in the work yard. The two men were exhausted. The mate dropped and sat on the ground. Thomas stood over the body, panting, and stared at the still form. Christopher must have known how much peril there was in touching a glowing coal to the train, he reasoned, yet he was willing to do it to stop the flogging. Why had he not tried something else? A club? Two against one. . . . No, they would have had him beaten and trussed up in a minute. Had he returned with a bow and arrows, the officers would have known he would not use them. They would have seen it as an empty threat and defied it in a second. But what other thing might he have done? He could think of nothing.

Captain Tobit wandered into the work yard and glanced at the others with vacant eyes. After a minute he walked to Harrison's body and stared at it.

"See what your madness has done," Thomas growled at him.

The captain gave no sign that he had heard the lad and kept staring at the body. Thomas turned from the captain in disgust and went searching around the hut. He returned in a few minutes with two earshells. One he tossed toward the mate, and with the other, he began to scrape a hole in the soil and cinders of the work yard. Mr. Morgen stepped over, kneeled, and dug silently at the opposite end of what was to be the grave.

After several minutes, Thomas glanced up at the mate who kept his eyes on his task. There was still a broad smear of Harrison's blood in the center of his forehead. The sight of the carpenter's battered face must have shocked him into sensibility. All in one moment, Mr. Morgen must have seen Christopher's death as the result of Tobit's conceits, bluster, and folly. That fact had to be apparent to the officer now while he ruefully dug with his shell. His face certainly revealed no sign of the surety and arrogance it had shown that morning.

Here Christopher was dead, and the sailor from the brig had probably died long since, expiring in a fever and terrible pain. Two more men killed in addition to the crew of the *Dove*. So many had died as a result of the captain's arrogance and wild fancies. Thomas looked up and saw him wandering around the hut. He moved just as he had the night of the wreck, with no purpose or will to his walk. At each terrible event, the captain had drifted off into some strange dream, like an opium-eater. With Tobit in that condition and the mate no longer under his spell, Thomas would return to his little den, though he must still be cautious. He could not imagine the mate now falling under the sway of the captain again. The sight of Christopher's ghastly face had broken that forever. The mate should want to quit the island as soon as possible. Well, *he* was going to leave as soon as the chances of the storms lessened. The officers might do what they pleased. Even if one or the other changed his mind and asked to go with him, he would refuse and could refuse as long as the canoe was hidden from them. It was small for two men and would be impossible for three. If he made it to the Middle Island alone, it would serve them justly if he did not send relief. That would be good payment for the stripes he had received that morning.

Thomas's temper burned as he remembered the flogging. He knew he would have been dead at that moment if he had given over and lit the train! His anger grew as he scooped up the soil with his shell and flung it aside. He had time to dwell on it now that he was not struggling across the slope of the volcano with Christopher's body. He became furious and dug into the earth, attacking it as he wanted to attack Tobit. What an officer! Haughty and sneering when all went his way, so sure of all he said, speaking in words that brooked no denial, yet hopeless and confused when everything went awry. He craved to strike that jowly face, but there would be small satisfaction in thrashing one so befuddled and helpless. Let him regain his senses, he swore to himself, and he would serve Tobit as the captain had served the poor sailor from the brig. He could bash his head in and feel no regret.

As the grave deepened, the wave of outrage in Thomas was subsiding. He and the mate were tiring. When it was hip deep, Thomas ceased digging and crawled out of the hole. He stood at its edge and looked down into the excavation. It should be deep enough, he decided. There were no animals on the island that burrowed. The "bears" took advantage only of the natural cavities, thus there was no other reason to go deeper. But he could not allow Christopher to be placed in that rough hole with nothing to shield him from the dirt to be cast upon him. Some sort of coffin was needed. That meant making planks, which was impossible. They could burn a log out as he had done with the canoe, but the body would rot and stink before one was ready. There must be a substitute, something to keep all the rocks and lumps of cinders from pressing against his limp body and his once-gentle face.

He left the mate, who was cleaning out the last of the loose earth, and entered the hut. In a minute he came out carrying one of the adzes. He walked into the bushes and returned several minutes later bearing an armload of fern fronds. Then he jumped into the grave and spread a layer of them on the bottom. The mate pulled Harrison's body to the edge and, with his help, Thomas awkwardly lowered it onto the fronds. The lad went for another batch of the greenery and on his return dropped them at the edge of the grave and climbed into the hole once more. He grasped Harrison's hand and held it for half a minute.

"Goodbye, old mate," he whispered to the unhearing ears. "You gave your life for me. I could not have asked for so much." Then he placed the carpenter's hands flat on his chest and spread a covering of fronds over the body. He smoothed Christopher's tangled, dirtied hair and bloodied beard as best he could, then laid the last few fronds over the face. When all was done, Thomas climbed out and began the job of filling the grave. The work went slowly. At the end of the task, Thomas took great care in shaping the mound of soil and cinders, patting it all over with his earshell.

He sat back and was wiping his eyes when he became aware of the captain standing beside him. Turning his head and looking up, he saw Tobit holding two sticks tied together to form a cross. The captain extended them toward the grave, without a word, proffering them to be used as a marker. It was an unsure move, made twice as if he were begging for them to be accepted. Thomas rose to his feet and stared into Tobit's eyes, still empty of any wit or capability. He grabbed the sticks from the captain, wrenched them until the cord holding them together broke, and then pitched them away, one in one direction and the other in the opposite direction. Then he growled, "I will return here some day and see to it that there is a proper marker set upon this grave."

He spun around and stalked to the hut. Inside, he found his old fur blanket, and then searched about for anything else he could use: skins, rope, twine, potatoes, and smoked fish. These items he placed on the fur and gathered up its edges to form a bundle. The officers watched but spoke not a word as the lad shouldered the load and walked past them.

After marching a few minutes through the grass, he pulled the bundle from his shoulder and carried it in his hands. It had settled against his back and irritated the welts. Thomas was heading for the shallows at the far end of the island, leaving the officers with another vague guess as to where his hideout lay. He had not gone a half-mile when he discovered a sheet of red-brown water creeping through the grass. It flowed an inch or two deep and spilled into each depression it reached. He knew he would have to keep going to the northeast or even make a wide detour to the north, for he guessed the small streams that drained to the east must now be full to their banks, making them at least waist-deep. They would not be safely fordable with a torrent in them rushing toward the coast. He padded through the spreading water and veered to this left when it became deeper than his ankles. He might as well take that course, he thought, for if the mate was watching perhaps it would confuse him. A third of the way across the plateau he had reached the upper end of the second stream, stopped, and dropped his load to take a rest. Behind him he discovered that a deep vee opening had been washed in the side of the volcano. At its lower end, the water of the lake was still rushing out. All the greenery and earth in its path had been carried away. Entire trees were half-buried in the delta of mud and rocks that had formed where the flood met the flatland and spread out into slower-flowing streams. He wondered how much longer it would take to empty the lake. If the side of the mountain continued to wear away, then the water would not cease flowing until it reached the level of the plateau or the cavity was entirely voided.

This was not how he had wanted their situation to end. Christopher could not have known the officers were suspicious, and he had to take some risk. *No!* he suddenly thought, Chris did not have to take that risk. He could have lived without the extra food Chris had brought. That was only to allow him more time to work. He could have left off making the sail. It would have been much wiser to take all the skins the night they planned to leave. They could have sewn them together and fixed them to the mast once they were beyond the surf. But it was too late for such caution. "Impatience! Impatience!" he accused himself. Poor Christopher was now buried back there because he had not been clever enough to think all through to the end.

He turned and resumed his slow crossing of the plateau. Since Christopher was dead, he had to rethink his plans. He would not leave immediately, but when the weather promised a several good days. With only one in it, the canoe would be lighter and perhaps safer. The Indians of the Brazils wandered miles out on the ocean with their flimsy creations. His was sturdier and so he should not be less brave. Even if the winds were blowing fresh and the swells were high, he would launch if the officers came to his side of the island. For some undefined reason, he didn't think they would, yet it would be wiser to trust the ocean rather than the captain's whims. For the present he would remain concealed and finish his work. He meant to continue all the precautions he had taken before.

Thomas continued beyond the second stream. For at least half the way to the shallows he could be seen if he were walking upright. Tobit might regain his senses and return to his old tricks and madness. When he looked back to the hut and reckoned he could not see a man if one stood there, Thomas turned toward the east coast. He didn't plan to descend to the shore and make that laborious trip again, hopping from stone to stone, to his retreat. He would wait till sunset when he couldn't be observed from any distance and then return along the plateau's edge and reach it with far less effort. Most of the flood would be drained by then, he imagined, and the streams he must cross would be fordable. Upon nearing the rim of the flatland, he determined to take a rest. He dropped his bundle to the ground and looked across the grass behind him the instant he arrived. Then he sat on the ledge and watched the waves break below.

Twelve hours ago he had been nearing the cache, expecting to find useful parts for the canoe and a little food. He leaned forward, held his head in his hands, and rocked side to side. It had been an unbelievable day, a horrid day. His capture, the flogging, Christopher's battered face, all those events and images returned to his mind one after another. It had been a continuous, sickening nightmare. He was exhausted in body and felt he could endure no more in his mind. There was no urgent reason to move or do anything in the next few hours. He grabbed his bundle and picked a way through the trees until he found a level place hidden from the ledge above. A long sigh escaped from him as he settled on his left side for a nap. His back and right side had received the worst of the flogging. The branches and leaves above patterned a mottled, moving shade over his body. Sleep came over him easier than he expected despite the pain of his back, and he never awakened, even for a moment, in the next few hours.

The sun had gone behind the peaks and the air had cooled by the time he stirred into a groggy consciousness and sat up. There might have been dreams in that heavy sleep, but he could not recall the least fragment of one. He picked up his bundle and climbed back to the edge of the plateau. Cautiously, he rose step by step and scanned over the grass from the shallows to the peaks. The water had widened the breach through the side of the volcano and it was filled with a mist that extended out over the mud and debris on the flat. The cooler afternoon air had precipitated it from the warmed floodwater. Thomas calculated that, with no figure wading through the grass in the distance, he could start back on his trek along the rim of the bluff to his den. He hoisted his load and began walking to the south. By keeping to the edge, he could travel with ease, and should he detect the officers on the grassland, he might simply climb over the bluff and conceal himself in the trees.

Thomas came to the first of the runnels. It had been filled with the lake's dirty water, but it had now drained away and was low enough to be waded, though still double its usual depth. Farther up its bed, the bushes and flax plants on the banks had been forced down, with many even uprooted and carried away by the speed of the flow. Mats of twigs and grass were washed against the trunks and caught in the limbs of the small trees that had withstood the deluge. Down on the coast the surf showed a brown tinge and, just beyond, a discoloration to the green swells. Thomas estimated it had to have been a great bore to have carried so much sediment across the breadth of the flatland and then down through the rocks and trees of the bluff to the sea. He found that the next branch, having received more of the flood in a direct line, had had the lower portion of its channel scoured clear of any greenery and the underlying rock of its banks exposed. The height from which the lake had escaped had given it great impetus, and, where the rush of water had spilled over the bluff, it had torn a swathe through the trees the entire distance to the beach below. A lesser cascade still poured over the edge. Piles of ferns, limbs, and clumps of flax were deposited on the rocks of the beach. Flotsam churned in the dirtied waves for a quarter of a mile along the shore. Thomas waded across what had once been the idling stream that flowed from the plateau. Even now, after much of the flood had drained away, it was still knee-deep and four times as wide as it had been before the deluge raced through it. He could feel he was walking on a smooth layer of limestone. All the cinders and porous rocks that had composed its bed had been scoured away.

It amazed him that such a mite of the mate's rude black powder, just a few pounds, had caused all the destruction he saw. It had to have been cleverly placed to have such an impact. It had worked like a small round shot striking a ship's rudder and having an effect all out of proportion to its size.

He continued on to his hideaway; and there, to his relief, he found nothing had been disturbed. The den had a homey feel, though it was only a space under a rock with windbreaks formed of matted bushes and weeds at each side.

It had been an unbelievable day. He could never have imagined in the dark hours of the morning that all those mad events would come to pass. He stowed his bundle at the back, but he suddenly felt a weakness and shaking in his arms and legs. Food was what he needed at that moment. He pulled the hide back out and opened it. The potatoes were no problem; he munched them skins and all. Fish were not as neatly eaten. His fingers picked one out and placed it on a scrap of hide. He pinched up bits of its flesh and put them into his mouth. The spiny bones he felt with his tongue and pushed them out of his mouth. Those he placed on a corner of the hide. At the finish of his meal, he rolled up the bones and the head in the fish skin. He would carry them to the beach and bury them as he had always done to keep his den clean. Thomas stretched out on his mat of leaves and ferns. Having lost an entire night's sleep, he needed more rest.

Four hours later when he opened his eyes again, he could see a little by the last of the twilight. He remained lying on his left side and stared at the gloom. No birds called, and there were only murmurs of the surf below. He pulled aside a few of the vines hanging over the entrance to his den. Outside, there was enough of the faint light to give gray shape to the larger rocks. Tree trunks were indicated by what they obscured, standing as dark and vaguely outlined sentinels of diverse sizes and inclinations. It was a familiar view, one he had stared at often before he fell asleep and upon awaking. There he was safe and dry in his hideaway. It was something to be thankful for, and also that he was fit and able to sail his canoe despite a sore back.

When the light increased enough the next morning, Thomas poked into his collection of tools for his bone needle and then took his jacket off. His first chore of the day was to sew up the long cut the mate had made. The mended jacket rubbed against his cuts and welts and for two days he went about without it while he worked.

Now it was all a matter of patience. Everything was in hand: the hull, the spars, sail, water butt. Only some days of calmer seas were wanting. They might be weeks away, or the swells he watched from the shore might draw out lower in the next few days. They could never be expected to abate entirely, as no land impeded their course as they skirted Van Diemen's Land and rolled on to break against the Middle Island. Their drift, added to the wind, would help drive the canoe all the more swiftly. The voyage would be days and nights of sailing. He could not expect to stay awake the entire distance to the farther shore. Would his vessel hold a course while he dozed off, or would he have to lie to? That would be a danger in itself. The canoe might capsize if it swung broadside to steep swells while he slept. A line towed astern might keep it before the wind. He would have to give it a trial.

The look he had seen in Tobit's eyes, staring and bereft of any expression more knowing than that of an ox, was the reflection of a mind empty of resolve. He reasoned the captain was now less of a threat to him for some days to come. His spell over the mate was broken and he couldn't carry out his fool ideas without aid. Still, Thomas would be cautious and remain out of sight.

Considering all, he made the choice to rig the canoe. If the weather changed abruptly, he would be ready to launch. He would continue to gather his grub and cook it after dark, but the log had been hollowed and there was no need to work on the canoe at night. Now the remaining items, the paddle, another water butt, and a bailer, could be made in the daylight under the cover of the bushes and trees. If the canoe were rigged where it lay, the officers could not see it unless they came upon it while hopping over the rocks along the shore.

Thomas picked his way down to the shore, following one of his many routes through the trees. The hull was as he had left it, and nothing that he could see had been disturbed. He knelt beside it and ran his hand over the bow, trying to imagine how it would part the waves. Aye, the whole canoe must be readied as soon as possible, he thought, for there was some possibility old Tobit could regain enough of his wits to make a good guess as to where it was and still have the wish to destroy it. He might have to leave despite the weather, for he could not protect his vessel and, at the same instant, gather his food or sleep.

With no one to help, he knew it would be awkward to step the mast with the hull upright. Another man was needed to hold it in place while he rove and tightened the lines to make the mast stand true. Thomas rolled the hull on its side and placed the heel of the mast in the center one of the shallow pits he had drilled in the bottom to receive it. With the mast lying on the beach, he rigged the shrouds and stays. The thimbles worked better than he expected, and, with their purchase, he drew the lines taut until the mast was held rigidly in its place. It was stepped three feet forward of the middle of the hull, and he estimated that should allow her to steer easy when before the wind.

Before falling asleep that evening, he reviewed what he had accomplished and made his plans for the work yet to be done in its proper order. The boomkins or outriggers were to be lashed to the hull next. They had to be stoutly bound to the spar at their outer ends for it would be a disaster if they broke or unraveled while at sea. He could mend the lashings on the hull, but if those out on the spar loosened, they would have to be retied while he floated in the waves. Thomas used a stick as a heaver in a loop of the bindings to haul them taut and as many wraps as he could reeve through the holes drilled for them. Christopher had proposed to place the spar on the starboard side. It would make little difference in running before the wind, but if they were forced to coast along to find a beach or run for the Strait, the wind would be much on the larboard beam or quarter. If it was built so, he thought, then the canoe would be less apt to upset in a sudden gust. Thomas had seen those frail craft only a few times off the Brazils. Other than their hulls, they appeared to be a collection of sticks with each one carrying a sail that was a geography of rags sewn together. He had considered the Indians there to be mad to risk their lives so far out in them. Now he wasn't mad, but he was desperate enough to sail two hundred miles or more in one.

One of the two sticks he had selected for the boomkins had a bend in its smaller end. He heated the other stick in the fire and bent it to match the first. These he mounted athwart the hull, one forward and one in the wake of the mast, so that on an even keel their ends drooped to the spar alongside. The spar had been a fortunate find. He saw how he could use it the instant he saw it floating in the tiny cove. It had two stumps of limbs on the same side to which he could bind the ends of the booms. That would leave its surface uncluttered with bindings and allow it to cut a clean furrow through the water. It was a guess how it would work. The hull might not ride level and thus carry the mast canted. When the time came to launch, he planned to lever and skid the completed canoe into the cove. Any changes could be made while it floated there an hour or two before he sailed.

The knowledge that he could never turn back and find the island became a greater worry as the vessel took on more of its shape each day. On the sealing grounds, he and his mates had constantly rowed a boat carrying skins and oil out to the *Dove* from various places along the shore. Twice they had been capsized, but the barque or the island had been close by.

Once over the horizon there would be no clues as to where the island lay. The canoe could probably sail well on the wind, yet without a compass or any means to navigate, it would be impossible for him to find his way back.

He and Harrison had planned well, but they were unfamiliar with such craft and problems arose. After the boomkins were lashed in place, he began fitting the boom for the sail. Then it was evident some changes had to be made. The shrouds, it appeared, would work better if they were farther apart and that required another stick lashed athwart the hull to spread them. The backstay needed to be raised higher with a gaff to allow the boom to swing from side to side. Thomas was heartened and later on even felt a bit proud each time he found a solution for the problems of the rigging.

At the end of ten days of work, interspersed with foraging for food, the canoe stood in the twilight nearly ready to launch, even with its sail laced to the mast and boom. Three extra saplings were tied across the outriggers and parallel to the hull. They could be used to replace a mast or the boom and were a handy place to lash his extra rope and tools. The food he intended to hang from the mast in a skin to keep it clear of the spray of the waves. He sat in the canoe as he had done many times, and imagined being on the swells far out at sea. He reached forward and passed the sheet under the aft outrigger to hold the sail where it would be for most of the voyage. With one turn around the end of one of the saplings, he could hold that line for hours without fatigue and yet haul it in or slacken it in a trice. The water container was tied off with a lanyard and lay on the bottom within reach. For days and nights, he would have to sit there tending the sheet and steering oar. His place in the stern had to be comfortable, but he found his head bumped the backstay, although the gaff now held it higher than before. The answer was to move forward. The remainder of the day he worked devising a backrest tall enough to lean his head against and allow him to sleep. It also permitted him to sit another foot and a half ahead with everything even closer at hand. For a little comfort he padded the seat with wads of ferns and would add his folded fur blanket over them when he departed.

The canoe might hold a course with the sheet and oar tied off, but that was speculation. He must plan to guide it all the way to Tovy Poenamoo. Something towed astern would slow the canoe but should keep it headed downwind and permit short naps. He would only discover how well that worked when at sea. All those concerns bothered him more each day. When there had been no vessel to consider, he hadn't dwelt so much on the dangers and believed the chances were much in his favor. With the canoe completed and resting on the beach, he sat in the stern and felt some disrelish at the idea of leaving. He was growing more aware of what a precarious adventure it would be, with the risk of capsizing or the wind veering or even failing. Anything was possible: a sudden gale, the appearance of a sea beast that could smash his frail little craft to slivers, or a slow death from thirst.

It was now a wait for the calmer seas. He had to prepare and keep a store of food at all times. He couldn't salt any of it unless he had a larger supply of water in the canoe. In the weeks following he must attempt smoking fish and the flesh of the sea ears. Some night, later on, he would cross the plateau and gather potatoes from around the slough. Those would keep and could be prepared in a cooking hole as they were needed. He busied himself with gathering his vittles and adding little touches to the canoe. A method of holding the steering oar had to be devised. Thomas brought a cord from the larboard gunnel, took a turn around the tiller arm of the oar, and hitched its other end to one of the saplings on the outriggers. He found that the blade of the oar could be moved, set to any angle, and not slip.

Each day he inspected the water container, added more if it had lost any, and moistened its bindings to keep them tight.

Thomas returned to his den one evening and stretched out on his bed to sleep. He was just about to fall asleep when the rock beneath him shuddered once. In an instant he sat up, and asked himself, had he actually felt that? . . . Or was it part of a dream?

CHAPTER 16

HE REACHED up to touch the slab above to see if it was not sinking over his small space. Only once had he experienced a shaking of the earth, and that had been many months before on Macquarie when he was gathering up skins on the shore. A strange rumble had preceded it, coming through the ground toward him from the south end of the island. The rocks beneath his feet had miraculously swayed from side to side. Reports of earthquakes had been brought to Stonington, but it was beyond his conception then that the solid rock of the earth could move and even shake enough to tumble mountains and destroy buildings.

He had looked at his mates and they had stared back wide-eyed. He had known instantly what was occurring, though never having felt an earthquake until that moment. Even before the evening meal was eaten that night, Gabe started one of his long tales. "Oh, that was just a mite of an earthquake, a shiver not worth noticin'," he began. "Now when I was just a little chip of lad, I was sent as steward aboard the *Nantasket* out o' New London. Capt'n Fletcher. We made port in the Kingdom of Naples the day before the great earthquake happened there."

He managed to go on for an hour, giving all the details of the voyage, the crew, their cargo, the harbor, the character of all the people he met there, and the mountains inland, before he related any one thing about the earthquake. Like a mummer, he waved his arms to illustrate the fall of houses and the roaring fires, and how the earth opened up in many places. "Just like a splitting mainsail," he had explained, his eyes shifting from side to side and his hands held far apart to indicate the width of the gaping holes. He swore men fell into those chasms and the ground closed over them. Steam and boiling water shot from the earth in other places. The old fellow talked and gestured there in the blackened interior of their hut. Only his face and hands were visible in the wavering firelight and that made the descriptions of the disaster seem all the more impressive. “All those terrible happenin’s,” he announced, with a finger pointing upward, “was because the Lord was so long vexed with popery. He caused it all to happen, just as he done in Lisbon.”

“Then why did the Lord send an earthquake to the Protestants in the very same year if that was his purpose?” Jack had asked from the other end of the hut.

Gabe tilted his head and remained silent, but couldn’t think of any ready answer to the man’s question.

Thomas wondered how much of the calamity Gabe had actually seen. Or was some of it exaggerated stories he had heard there and in other ports and confounded in the telling? He described an enormous wave sweeping into the harbor and carrying boats far inshore, but never explained how his own vessel had not been stranded with the others. None of the crew believed the whole of Gabe’s stories, but none except Jack spoke his doubts openly. The old man was very salt, a good storyteller, and must have earned many a drink in the taverns of New York and Boston. And all of them, even Jack, preferred to be amused by his endless tales, however suspect, than just to stare into the fire in silence before they went to sleep.

Thomas decided to make a foray to gather potatoes at the next waning moon, and to that purpose he wove a net bag to carry them. Since they were miles away, he planned to gather half a hundredweight if he could find that much. They kept well and he might eat a few each day or so. Just prior to quitting the island, he would cook the remainder. He awakened in the middle of a night when there was only a sliver of moon, and with his bag and a stick to dig, he started off for the north coast along a route that avoided a direct line to the slough. It curved out into the middle of the grassland and would pass no closer than a mile of the hut. His pace was rapid and constant until he had crossed about a third of the way. At that point he noticed a sound in the air. As best he could guess it came from the crater. It was most like distant thunder or frigates, far out at sea, firing at will. A small white cloud lay directly over the top of the volcano, and some of the same vapor issued from the gash in its side. The stream from the high peaks he knew was pouring into the empty or near-empty crater. It had to be the internal heat of the earth being cooled suddenly that created the rumblings and the white cloud. Thomas resumed his trip, thinking that fire and water must be contending mightily against each other. In time, when the lower parts of the volcano cooled, he expected the thumps and rumblings would cease.

Though it would be a much easier route, he avoided their old trail and kept farther out in the grass. He arrived at the edge of the flatland to the east of the lookout point. From there he scanned the bay below, which was only a black void edged with a fuzzy white surf at the base of the bluff. No light, not one glimmer from a binnacle showed, but then he didn't expect one, only hoped. The empty bay renewed his feeling of isolation. It might be a dozen years before any ship might sight the peaks and then have a reason to land. He descended through the tangle to the shore and then west to the slough. There, by the faint moonlight, he found the potatoes had spread all around and covered its shore with a complete tangle of vines since he had last seen the place. It was easy to gather enough potatoes, and it took less than half an hour to fill his bag. For another half an hour, he wandered out and along the surf to see if there were any more changes on that part of the island.

With his load over his shoulder, he climbed back to the plateau. He became curious about what was happening within the hollow mountain, and on his return across the grass he veered closer to it. The rumblings were louder and more distinct as he neared. The wide semi-circle of mud was still soft. That and the debris of trees and rocks now blocked a closer approach. He stopped and listened intently. The only noise he had ever heard that he could compare it with was the thumping and rumbling when the blacksmith plunged a red-hot plowshare into his quenching tub. Mixed with that was a hissing, surely the result of a violent meeting of intense heat and cold water. Beneath the soles of his feet there was a vibration in the very soil of the plateau. Here was the mightiest tension between two forces imaginable, one that might burst forth like an overcharged cannon. Yet all fires expired in the end when their fuel was spent. So must this one. He had no good reason to get closer and went around the mire and tangled bushes and trees to continue on his way.

But events in the volcano did not carry forward as he had expected. Two days later Thomas felt the ground shake once more. The shocks came again and again until after a week, the island shuddered nearly every day and each time a bit longer. Curiosity drove him to climb to the plateau in the daylight and peek over the edge. He was astounded by what he saw. There was no longer a cloud over the lower peak. In its place a column of gray smoke boiled from its interior. It rose up and was carried off to the north and east by the wind. Infrequently, a huge puff shot skyward. After several seconds he heard a muffled blast echo across the flatland. It was like watching the *Terror* fire its stink pots into the Port during the war, except that the smoke and reports from the mortars of the bomb ship were not a twentieth of what the volcano sent forth. Each morning he made the short trip from his tiny lair to the edge of the plateau to see if the eruption was lessening or increasing. Its level of violence seemed to remain the same for a while, but what was disturbing was a shift of the wind.

During the months of their stay on the island, on some days the wind had ceased and even blew from the east. When it shifted, the changes never lasted more than twelve hours. During the rains it veered from the southwest to the north and returned at the end of the storm. One morning he saw the smoke being drifted west up over the high peaks and around them. Several times during that day and those following he watched and expected the wind to change, but it did not return to its old direction for more than two entire days. He realized that if it did so while he was at sea, that would be a disaster, blowing him westward where there was no land for more than a thousand miles. He doubted he would have enough water to last even if he was drifted directly back and then on to the Middle Island. The voyage seemed far riskier now that he had learned the wind was not as dependable as he had thought. In the last months he had considered the trip would not be an easy thing, but for the first time he saw the whole peril in attempting to reach Tovy Poenamoo and the Strait.

While he watched the volcano and waited for the time to leave, he kept working on the canoe. He realized one day that if a storm came upon him on the water or if he was entering the surf to land, the sail might have to be doused quickly. He could pull the boom up with a lift, but it would still billow and catch enough wind to keep the hull moving ahead. If it was bent to hanks, he could let the halyard run and drop the sail, but he had laced it to the mast. As he climbed up and down between the shore and his den, he wondered what could be used to make hanks. Withes heated and bent into circles should slide up and down the mast, but there was no way to fix the ends together that would support much strain. Then he hit upon notching them and cutting a groove for seizings to lie in. Made so, they could not slip open. He cut and formed a dozen of them, more than needed, but extras might be a wise precaution. He tried pulling a few apart and found the hanks were stout enough to hold until the sail itself tore. When he had made them up around the mast and seized the hides to them, he took his place in the canoe and let the halyard run through its thimble. The sail dropped to the boom, with the hanks clattering. When the halyard was pulled the hides rose right to the peak. He was pleased. It was enough sail to drive the canoe, but not so large as to be unmanageable or tear. A small sail was less apt to lay his vessel over in a sudden gust.

His last need was the bailer. Many times while he was making the other parts and rigging the canoe, he puzzled over how best to fashion it, until one day he passed an old tree lying on the slope. Its weathered bark was peeling away from the trunk. The curl of the bark suggested how it could be made. Soon he had fashioned two bailers with pieces of bark firmly bound with cords into a cone. He used one of them to scoop the rainwater out of the hull and found it worked admirably. Each one he tied to the canoe with a lanyard, like every other loose item in it. Once anything went overboard, he knew he might never retrieve it.

From the moment he had finished the bailers, Thomas was merely waiting for the moment when better weather would come and hold. The canoe, with its sail hoisted, rested just within the trees, ready to be worked down to the water. Even the limb to lever it was cut and trimmed and lay alongside. Only the food and the extra skins, rope, and twine were kept out of the rain up in his den. Unable to sit idly and watch the swells roll by offshore and the rain come down every few days, he burned off a short section of log and began another butt. The supply of water he carried might mean the success or cause the failure of his voyage. He wanted to work on only that which favored his chance of reaching the Middle Island.

In the next ten days, the booming from the volcano increased perceptibly. One morning he was awakened by it, and climbed up for a look. As he stepped above the edge he saw that the nature of the eruption had changed since the day before. With each blast, in addition to the smoke, stones were being cast out. Flung up and out, they left a line of dust in their wake, then arced down to the grassland. A new crater was building quickly over the old one. It appeared that the eruption would last longer than he had anticipated. Thomas was fascinated with the sight, and sat for an hour. When the rolling smoke shot skyward, a dull red glow within it faded quickly. He would have to come up at night and watch, he was thinking. It would be fireworks for him. If the rocks became hot enough, they might make a show, flying up like rockets. Ha! Exciting, just like 1814, but without the danger and destruction.

Out of the corner of his eye, he thought he saw movement. He turned to his right and, after a few seconds, spied a dark speck inching along the edge of the plateau toward him from the northeast. It could only be one of the officers. Thomas slipped back over the rim and found a thick bush to hide behind. It was almost half an hour before the figure was close enough to be recognized as Mr. Morgen. The officer made no effort to conceal himself and walked with the shambling gait of an exhausted man. Every few minutes he stopped and, holding his hands to his mouth like a speaking trumpet, yelled down the slope. Thomas studied the mate and, as he neared, saw that his hair and beard were thickly dusted with gray ashes. There was even a layer on the skin of his forehead and on his clothes. Mr. Morgen looked as if he had been rolled in a barrel of sweepings.

"Thomas!" the mate yelled, but his voice was hoarse and strained from constant calling and did not carry far.

Thomas stayed hidden and let him pass without revealing himself. The agitation showing on the mate's face, Thomas decided, was not a try at deception. He twigged no danger from a man so distraught and fatigued. There was also a hunger in that face and much fear. He watched the mate move along the edge to that point where the steep slope of the high peak covered the level ground and blocked him. The mate rested for few minutes, turned back and repeated his calling. Thomas waited until he was twenty yards away, then he climbed onto the edge and stood up squarely before him.

"Oh, Thomas, Thomas," he gasped, running forward, "you must help me!"

The lad did not reply and stared at the mate's dirtied face. From the inside corners of his eyes, tears had trickled down to his beard, making two crooked rivulets bordered with damp ashes.

The officer waited for an answer, but getting none went on talking, "The captain will not move, not for anything. Rocks are falling all about the hut, but he will not budge."

"Tie the fool up and drag him away," Thomas said curtly.

"I have tried that. He fights me. Somehow he has gotten a strength, a ferocity. He is now a match for me, aye more than a match."

Thomas stared at the mate for a moment and declared, "Leave him."

"I cannot do that. The rocks come at us like broadsides. Two have gone through the roof. He is a fellow being, Thomas."

"And was I a fellow being when you flogged me?"

The mate ignored the lad's question and asked, "Thomas, won't you help, only to get him out of danger? I beg you."

"Ah, do you? Beg, is it? Beg? Not ordering? Old Toby orders well enough. Have him order the volcano to cease. If that fails, let him pray. As for me, I will sit here and await results."

"I have spent hours looking for you, hoping you would help. Let's move him far enough to be out of danger. You are a stout lad. It is so little to ask, so little to do to save a life."

Thomas raised one eyebrow and spoke with an airy politeness, "What a memory you have, Mr. Morgen." Then his voice dropped into an accusing tone as he spoke. "My mates there at the bottom of the bay are nothing to you now. That poor jack skewered there on the beach, you put out of your mind. What little it would have been to ask to save their lives and Christopher's life. Ah, but now you cannot forget your humane duty to your dear captain."

"Thomas, I could do nothing about your mates then and I can do nothing now, but we can haul the captain from danger," Mr. Morgen pleaded in his last try. He could see in the lad's stony look that it was useless. He lowered his chin to his chest and walked slowly toward the center of the grassland. He turned back once and each man stood motionless looking at the other across a distance of fifty yards. To the mate, the lad's adamant refusal was still evident on his face and in his stance, and he slowly resumed his trip back to the hut.

Thomas watched him until, at a half a mile away, he faded from sight in a sudden drift of fine dust from the clouds above. He couldn't figure out why the mate put his life in such danger for that lunatic. Was he again under his spell? How could such a capable man. . . . Ah, but he had lost his arrogance and showed some small sign of being contrite. Did he think saving old Toby could atone for what he had done?

His thoughts trailed off as he turned his attention to the eruption. Some of the stones cast out must have become very hot. All around the cone on the slopes of the higher peaks were thin columns of white smoke, rising out of the trees. That meant the rocks were now heated enough to char the leaf litter, but that the forest was still too damp to burn. If there was a similar effect on the plateau, the smoke and dust falling across that part of the island concealed it.

Tobit might be destroyed by his lunacy as poor Chips had been. If the mate did not come to his senses, he could be struck by a rock or choke in the smoke. If the eruption continued much longer, the cinders and dust would certainly cover the slough and the fish traps with a heavy layer. The potato plants would die and the officers would have to dig deeply to reach what was left. Only the clams and earshells would remain as ready food. The officers might even starve.

He had learned one thing from the encounter: the officers were no longer a threat. It meant he could set a fire openly in the daylight and that the canoe could be skidded nearer the cove and left in sight. Thomas went directly to the beach and gathered short pieces of drift logs and rolled them up the beach. He placed them across a line drawn from the hull to the water and then dug a trench for each log and buried it, leaving only an inch or two of its side showing. They were spaced so that the hull would always rest on at least two of them at all times.

Wet wood slides well on wet wood, he repeated to himself as he poured water on the exposed sides of the logs from a bailer. Thomas had removed his jacket and was panting for breath and wet with perspiration when the canoe finally balanced on the first skid. Once it rested on two of them, it levered smoothly down the slope. Thomas halted it when the bow was at the high tide line. There it was at last, a few feet from the sea with the sail flapping in the breeze. He tied the sheet off to the larboard to keep the sail ashiver and allow it to dry after any rain. That was better than letting it drop into a heap. The leather was not too well tanned and it might rot in places. Thomas looked with pleasure at the tautly rigged vessel ready to enter the sea. He had created it, not having seen one closer than a musket shot. Now he was more in control of his fortunes and all by his own wit and efforts. Perhaps in two weeks he would push it the last few feet and float it in the cove. If the wind would just hold steady for a few days, it would carry him to the Middle Island.

He was well aware the waves altered the beach easily during storms, and the earthquakes, he suspected, might do even more. He got out his long line and hitched one end of it to the canoe and the other to the nearest tree he could reach.

With that done and a last look at the canoe, he started up to his den.

MR. MORGEN pulled the hood of his jacket over his head and wandered under the clouds of smoke and ashes looking for the hut. His throat was dry and he coughed constantly, though he breathed through his cupped hands. For brief moments the cloud rose or shifted to one side or the other, and he was able to see parts of the high peaks. That allowed him to correct his travel. He reached the bushes and trees along the branch, and seeing some familiar trees, he was able to turn in the proper direction. When he found the hut, it had a heavy layer of ashes on the thatch, and the sagging roof looked as if it would collapse if it was not cleared off soon. Upon entering the dark interior, he could barely distinguish the captain lying on his pallet with a hide pulled over his head.

"Captain! Captain!" he choked out and shook him, fearing the man might have suffocated while he was away. The mate heard a faint groan. "Captain," he repeated hoarsely, "I have found Thomas. He is on the south coast. There are no rocks falling there and no ashes. Let's go there before it is too late. Hurry!"

The captain stirred slowly and sat up. "How many times have I repeated it? You lack comprehension, Mr. Morgen. You lack comprehension. It is the very danger itself that keeps me here. You may go if you wish, but I must remain. It is the Lord who casts these stones at me, and I must remain here armored with my faith only." Tobit finally peered up at the mate through a dusty atmosphere made even darker by the volume of ashes falling over the hut. "I must bear my trial as did Abraham, and like Abraham must not flinch or doubt in the least. I am chosen. My faith will not be found wanting."

"You will be killed if you stay here another hour!"

"I shall not be harmed as long as I believe. You cannot see that!"

"I see you wish to be a martyr!"

"You deceived me. Some small adversity and you prove not to have the faith."

"It's not a question of faith. You leap from a cliff and you will surely die. This is no different. You stay here, and the volcano will kill you in one manner or another."

"If I jump from a precipice, that is my doing, but this volcano is of the Lord's making. I must not betray myself and retreat from it."

"You see all has gone awry. You cannot build your holy community, lord it over your parcel of worshipers, and order every hour of their lives, so you will become a martyr. But here there is no one to watch. Who will know and admire your great sacrifice? Well, I will not be the one. You weave no more spell over me. You talk of deceiving, yet you made me look a dolt and caused Harrison to be killed. Oh, we are different. We are chosen ones! How did I ever come to believe such piffle? We are no different than any others. I have done my best to save your old carcass and I take no more responsibility for you."

"You have none! You have shown yourself not worthy. Go! Go to the security of the coast. Consort with that heathen. Leave me to prove myself to the Lord and join with Him in heaven."

Mr. Morgen stepped back, picked up a fur, and beat the dust from it. Then he pressed it to his face and stalked from the hut. Outside, he discovered the smoke and ash had increased and he could see only a few yards ahead. It was thicker than any fog he had encountered, and if he attempted to cross the plateau to the south or east coast, he knew he would be lost out there after a dozen paces and end up wandering in circles. The only guide he could have was the branch and the bushes growing between it and the grassland. Walking in the empty bed of the stream would be the surest way to reach the northern shore.

It would guide him and he would arrive at the waterfall. From there he could go down the trail to the flax field and reach the western shore. There, the wind would certainly be blowing the smoke and ashes away. A ship might be nearing or even in the bay, attracted from a distance by the smoke mounting to such a great height. When the eruption was finished, he could return and discover if the captain had survived.

A cascade of fine ash fell from the bushes as he trudged through and disturbed them. His bare feet stirred up more clouds. In the bed of the stream, in its scours and around large roots, were signs of water. Damp patches indicated the few pools that remained. The mate leaned over, pushed the ash layer aside and dipped up a handful of water. It relieved the intense choking and dryness in his throat for a short while. He put the fur tightly to his nose and mouth and started off again, trying to move faster over the rocky bed. With each breath now came a burning sensation deep in his chest, between his lungs. For some reason, he was becoming light-headed and had to hold onto a branch to steady himself. Something other than the dust and ashes was stifling him. He must get to the clearer air he expected to find at the waterfall. Not many more minutes and he would be overcome, collapse, and die there. He forced himself to move again, reaching from limb to limb with his free hand to keep him upright as he stumbled through the haze and snowing ashes. The trees that met over the streambed and the dimness caused by the ash fall gave the mate a feeling of moving through some internal space.

"One step more . . . one step more," he chanted to himself as he placed each foot into the flour of ash covering the gravel. Finally, he wasn't able to move and could barely stand on his feet. He took shallower breaths and found his lungs burned less.

"Damn," he muttered, "all has gone over to leeward!" He gripped a limb for a few minutes and slowly looked around in the ash-filled air. "The trees must be on my right, they must always be on my right," he muttered to himself. "I must touch them with my right hand. If I turn, I will be lost. The trees must be on my right." He felt that the few minutes' rest had helped him and began walking again. One step, a pause. Step two and another pause.

For a count of fifty he kept it up, then rested and started his pacing again. The ash alternately thinned and thickened. When it lessened, he moved faster; and when it snowed down heavier, he resorted to counting his steps and pausing between them. It had been more than an hour since he had left the hut. He could swear to it. Yes, he was sure he had been walking for more than an hour. It was about a mile or so from the hut to the fall. He should be there. In one of his stops he believed there was a slight lightening of the haze ahead. That sent a rush of energy through his frame. Bit by bit, the glow increased. He was nearing the fall! It was there just ahead! The air no longer burned in his chest. The ashes were clearing quickly.

Suddenly, he could see the tree ferns at the head of the fall as faint outlines in the smoke and ash. When he broke out into the clear, he felt as if he had escaped through a true tunnel. He turned about and saw, behind and above him, dense, gray and white clouds shooting up, swift and violent as the discharges from mortars. They boiled to the zenith and were carried over the remainder of the island and the sea to the northeast. Ash rained out of their bottoms as their edges expanded north and drifted over the eastern spit and the shallows. The mate walked out near the head of the fall and sat on the bank of the dry stream, coughing and breathing the cleaner air. From there, it was clear for him to go down to the western spit. That would be the safest place on the northern side of the island. The sole threat to him would be a shift of the wind to the southeast, and that they had rarely seen. The mate rose to his feet and turned to start toward the trail on the slope.

Just at that moment the earth jolted beneath him. A half-minute later, a tremendous blast slapped against his clothes and the side of his head. A growling and rumbling came from the direction of the volcano. He jerked about to face its source. A cloud fifty or sixty feet high was bursting through the streambed toward him. On the outside it was gray, but glowed red within like hot coals in the remnants of a fire. He instantly felt a fierce heat preceding it on his face and saw whole trees and ferns burst into flames as the red glow reached them.

In a fraction of a second the mate spun around and was dashing down toward the overhang of the fall. The first tier was only four feet down. Then a leap of six feet, and his teeth slammed together from the shock when his feet struck the rock. The impetus of his stride carried him over and onto the last shelf, but there his legs collapsed beneath him and he tumbled headlong over the edge with his arms spread and his body turning. The rush of air fluttered his burning sleeves and whished past his ears as he dropped, meteor-like, trailing smoke, toward the dark remnant of the slough, hundreds of feet below. A long shriek of pain echoed in the void and faded away.

CHAPTER 17

THOMAS was approaching his little den when he heard the huge explosion. A few seconds later he could see thick, gray clouds, by far the largest yet expelled from the crater, boiling into the sky above the top of the bluff. Instantly, he scampered up to the flatland to see what was happening. Enormous billows of smoke shot skyward and drifted to the northeast as he reached the edge of the plateau. Another cloud, lower, had boiled out of the cone and down the slope, then fanned out across the flatland with a bright fringe of orange preceding. It had an odd progression with the bottom portion scooting forward a little faster than the top, reversing the roll of a wave coming ashore. An intense heat radiating from its leading edge caused the grass to burst into flame yards ahead. The boiling, gray mass left behind rose, swelling many times in volume.

That will be the end of Tobit and Morgen, if they didn't reach the coast, Thomas thought. Roasted alive if they hadn't the sense of a hare.

The speed of the clouds shooting up from the crater was evident from how they rolled higher than the peaks in a mere count of five or six. He stood there and watched blue-white bolts of lightning jag through their roiling sides. After the expected seconds passed, thunder cracked and rolled to him across the plateau. The air was filled with those peals and the booms of the eruptions.

From then on, day or night, there was no respite from the blasts. In the dark, the glowing red fountains of cinders and flashes of lightning filled half the sky to the north and were more impressive than any fireworks he could imagine. Rocks thrown from the crater glowed red, even a bright orange, and left trailing sparks as they were thrust skyward and pulled back to earth. Enough of them had landed to dry portions of the forest and set trees afire on the high peaks. The island shook with every blast from the crater, and, in almost every hour of the day and night, earthquakes rocked it.

Thomas wondered if it would ever stop. His apprehension grew when he made his next morning's visit to the shore and discovered the constant shaking of the island had caused the outer edge of the beach to subside into the cove and left the canoe floating except for its stern. Might the very rock of the island do the same, sink beneath the waves? As each fit of shaking ensued, he wondered if it would increase to such violence as to sunder the island. Or might the continual blasts carry it away into the surrounding ocean? Chris had said it happened to a great mountain that once stood where the bay was now. They had seen the result from the side of the peak, and knew the center of the bay was deep, beyond the reach of the lead.

Thomas watched the canoe half-floating in the waves. It was his chance to try the hull in the water. He pushed it the rest of the way out and was pleased to see that the hull and spar rode well and evenly on the water. The mast canted some to the starboard and he waded in to set up the shrouds again. His weight in the stern brought it down some, though not so much as to concern him. Long naps would be possible while he leaned back and cradled his head against the backrest. He could reach forward to tie off or loosen the sheet, but that he shouldn't have to do until he came onto the coast. The tedium of sitting so long would be the greater trial.

For the last month, the swells had become the focus of his keener watch, and on those days when they were lower in height he was tempted to leave. Each time, for no definable reason, he changed his mind at the last moment. Then, without exception the following day, the wind would freshen and they became high as before.

The next day the fury of the earthquakes increased, and huge stones were jarred loose from their places on the bluff. Some crashed down, knocking trees and ferns aside, and then landed as far out as the surf. Thomas, fearing that the upper rock of his shelter might shift and crush him, moved down to the shore with his skin robe and chose a sleeping spot out on the spur that formed the cove. It was a narrow patch of sand in a crevice. No large rocks, he expected, could roll that far. If it rained, he planned to rig his robe up as an awning over the canoe and sleep in the hull. A few hundred feet to the east along the shore and just within the trees, he remembered a stone lying at such a slope that beneath it there was always a dry spot. He had found it on an early search, but then it had seemed too small and easily discovered, and he had dismissed it as a hideaway. He carried the food and his little skin of tools and cords there to store them closer at hand.

Several times that day he looked at the canoe and then at the waves and wondered if it was not the time to leave, but the hope that the eruption might wane kept him waiting on the shore. The smoke, rising to greater heights, spread not only to the northeast but also to every other direction and blotted out the blue of the sky. Everything within sight, the trees, the rocks, even the skin of his hands, took on strange orange tints from the light filtering through the cloud. By the next day the dirty black layer had expanded until the island received its only light from a band around the horizon. Except at dawn and in the evening, the sun appeared to be a dull red ball, fixed glare-less and impotent within the cloud above. Nights became totally black except for the frequent flashes of lightning and the reddish glow that was weakly reflected from the smoke above seconds before the sound of each blast.

On Thomas's last trip up to the rim of the grassland he discovered that the mountain had grown three times in size since he saw it last. Huge stones were being flung out, turning end for end. When they struck the earth, they bounced, rolled several times, and lay smoking on the plateau like roasted carcasses. The decision to leave had to be made soon, for each day brought some new violence from the crater, and each day the black cloud covered more of the sky. About two hours after its rising, the sun dimmed until it was no longer detectable through the smoke even as the dark red disc. It reappeared late in the afternoon. The band of clear sky along the southwest horizon narrowed, allowing the island nothing brighter than an eerie twilight through the entire day. That night Thomas lay on the shore that constantly shuddered beneath his body and listened to the thunder from the lightning and the blasting of the volcano. The island had lost all its solidity. If the eruption did not cease, the great mass of tremulant stone and earth might sink beneath the sea at any moment.

There was one stranger sound coming to his ear. It was difficult to separate it from the noises of the eruption, but in some brief seconds, between claps of thunder and the deep rumbles, he heard the single thrums, spaced at intervals, that Christopher had said came from a parrot. After minutes of listening he could swear it was there out in the trees. He couldn't mistake that peculiar call they had heard and puzzled over the morning of their arrival. Not once in the months since then had he heard it repeated. Now it was there again, much nearer than the first time, sounding between the blasts and cracks of thunder. He scanned the bushes intently, but in the last of the dim light he detected nothing.

In the morning he awoke to find a portion of his robe and the rocks and sand all about covered with white, pea-sized pebbles. He wondered how they could have fallen without waking him, until he picked up a handful and saw that they were lighter than cork and appeared to be a hardened froth. A handful tossed up fluttered down like bits of paper. The cove was covered with a blanket of them inches deep, muffling the waves rolling to the shore. He went to the canoe and found it half full of the little white bits. Scooping them out, he uncovered the water butts lying there. Then he remembered it was time to take them to the stream and fill up the amount that had seeped out.

Water was becoming another worry for him. The little stream spilling over the edge of the plateau had begun to wane soon after the eruption started. On his arrival there he found it was now reduced to a trickle, yet he managed to fill his containers to the top again. He might have to travel farther north along the rim to the next stream if that one failed. What would he do if all the water disappeared from the action of the volcano? Crossing the flatland under the falling ash to get to the slough was impossible. If, by some miracle, he got there, its water might be gone or covered with mounds of ash. Little by little, he felt he was being forced from the island and must set off into the long, deep swells if the eruption didn't stop soon.

In the middle of the day, Thomas heard something crash through the canopy of leaves. He stood up, faced the slope, and waited for a minute. His eyes searched the black clouds overheard. It had to have been a heavy object to make such a racket. Off to his right, something streaked down, hit, and bounced into the layer of white particles. Thomas ran toward it and heard a hissing in the damp edge of the beach. He knew that stones were now being cast the three and a half or four miles from the crater to the cove. Instantly, he saw that the choice to leave had been made for him by those deadly missiles. He scooped up his fur robe, tossed it into the canoe, then bolted down the shore. He had to retrieve his food and tools and start his voyage before he was injured or his canoe destroyed. On his way he heard more rocks plunge into the trees and the surf each ten seconds or so. Some came in twos and threes. The food and equipment were bundled in their skins, each with a cord attached to tie them to some place in the canoe. Thomas grabbed them without another look about and raced back to the cove, leaping from rock to rock. When he reached the canoe he tossed the two bundles into the hull. With practiced hands he untied the line from the tree and swiftly coiled the rope as he walked into the water. In one stride he shoved the canoe seaward and leaped into the stern. He seized the paddle and started rowing madly, bending forward to plunge the blade in and draw it back with the whole of his upper body. He needed every bit of his strength to force the hull through the waves and keep it from swinging to one side or the other. Once out of the cove, Thomas pulled the sheet in and the sail began to drive the canoe forward on a close reach.

Rocks shot into the sea around him, and the geysers thrown up were illuminated only by the narrow band of sky ahead. A pair landed several yards beyond the bow and another hit between the boomkins so close as to throw water on Thomas's clothes. A stone the size of an apple splintered the edge of the gunnel and fell into the hull forward of the mast. It still had some heat despite its long flight for miles through the air and gave off wisps of steam as the bit of rainwater in the bottom washed fore and aft. Fountains were being thrown into the air from the swells as far as he could see. Thomas guessed some shot up twenty to thirty feet into the air. Each one marked where a stone from the volcano plunged like a meteor into the sea. If a large one struck in the hull, it would hole it like a round shot or rive it from end to end. He doubted he could return to the island or drift on its wreckage to the Middle Island. Any second, one might crush his skull.

With the force of the sail added to his paddling, the canoe plowed through the mat of white cinders toward the lighted horizon. The mast being stepped forward kept the bow falling off the wind, but he managed to hold his course by taking a wider sweep with his paddle and drawing the stern back in line. Once out of the blind spot below the bluff, he allowed himself a quick turn of his head and a glimpse of the island. In that half-second a blast of cinders glowing red-orange shot from the volcano to equal the highest of the peaks.

Thomas kept up his rhythm and counted his strokes: reach forward, pull back, reach forward, pull back. One . . . two . . . three . . . four. By his guess, he had paddled about a quarter of an hour when he finally reached beyond the mat floating on the waves and saw no more rocks striking the sea ahead. He was panting and counting to himself: 520, 521, 522. . . . Perspiration ran down his face. Suddenly, he laid the paddle athwart the canoe and leaned back in his seat gasping for breath, but he sat up and paddled again when the hull swung parallel to the crests of the waves. With the bow brought up again, he set the steering oar to counter the canoe's want to veer from the wind. The helm needed constant attention as the bow quartered up over the swells and down their far sides.

Every few minutes, he turned about to watch the eruption. Each detonation sent a jet of red-hot ash skyward from the mountain. It quickly cooled and a gray-white cloud twisted and rolled to the zenith.

Constant rumbles came across the water, forming a background to the sharper blasts and thunderclaps. It was three and a half to four miles from the eruption to the island's shore, and he guessed he had traveled three or four miles from there due south. So he made his position to be six to seven miles from the volcano. At that distance it was surely safe, and the only peril from then on was from the waves and weather.

The few pieces of gear he had tossed into the hull had to be carefully stowed. The coil of rope and his tools he lashed to the saplings as he had intended. The food was a problem. He had thought to fix it to the mast as that was farthest from the reach of the water, but it would interfere with lowering the sail. His best choice was to tie it to the backstay and let it dangle there. It was merely a few pounds of the sweet potatoes, some cooked, some still raw; and he had only to reach up for them. The water butts were lying at his feet within easy reach with their lanyards tied to the aft boomkin. One of the bailers was just forward of the butts, and the spare one was bent to the heel of the mast. The robe of furs he folded and placed as an additional pad under his bottom.

Once all was secured, he settled into his seat again. If the wind was blowing from its usual direction, he was going south, give or take half a point or a little more, for it was impossible to hold the short hull on a steady line. The sea came at him at an angle and lifted the bow away from his course, and as it passed under the canoe, started a slide down the other side. The mast was always pitching from side to side and the forestay edging back and forth before the distant swells and the horizon.

Hour after hour he sailed, and nothing changed except the quality of the light. For days the smoke had created and continued the menacing darkness over the entire sky, except for a strip on the horizon from due west around to the southeast. The light entering below the cloud in those directions had by contrast become increasingly bright to the eye. A mile above, the black clouds appeared to have solidified to form the roof of an enormous cavern; the low band at the west and south was its entrance and his first goal. The increase in the eruption and his sudden departure had changed his plans. He could not sail before the wind and be drawn into the black, choking curtain falling to the north and east, but must continue south until he had a clear sky overhead. Only then would he dare to head northeast with the swells or east until he fell in with the Middle Island. From that point on he could only guess what he might do. If the coast was ironbound or the natives appeared to be troublesome, he must sail farther north. How far, he did not know. Then again a desperate need for water might drive him to land sooner.

His jury-rigged butts had held well so far, losing only a small amount over several days. The little water that raced from one end of the hull to the other kept their bindings wet and taut. If his supply lasted long enough and the weather remained fair, he might even reach as far as the Strait. He decided then not to drink until the next day.

He recalled the story Christopher had heard from an old hand. It was an odd tale about ships that whaled in the bays of the Strait and even landed men to work from shore. Besides them, there were men there who had deserted other ships and runaway convicts who lived about the Middle Island. The man claimed they had got their own boats, harpoons, lances, and try-pots, and took whales all on their own account. There were even coopers to make and repair their barrels. Once or twice each year they sold the oil rendered and the bone gathered to whale ships that called.

It was a fanciful story told in some rum shop, and he thought it might or might not be true. If it were true, he would reach the Strait in some fashion and live with those men and sign on one of the whalers when they called. It sounded simple and quite easy to do, but he knew it would not be so. There were the natives and a great distance between him and the Strait, and those whalers might not even be there when he arrived. If he fell into the hands of the savages, they could make a slave of him or do worse if they wished.

The sun reached the thin, brown edge of the smoke low to the western horizon. The orb increased in brightness, shading up from red to red-orange as it slipped from behind the cloud and touched its lower rim to the sea. It shined through the slot between earth and smoke cloud with rays parallel to the surface of the ocean. Off to his left, each bit of foam carried up on the crests was caught in a crimson light for an instant, then winked out as it sank. When the canoe dipped into a swale, none were visible. When it rose, the brilliant red specks reappeared: two or three here and two or three there, blinking on and off, each with its own rhythm, on the black water. When rising on each crest, the mast, sail, and stays were also reddened by the glow and stood out vividly and eerily against the sooted gulf beyond and above.

Thomas glanced back every few minutes to see if the eruption progressed or declined. Of course he knew it wouldn't change in a few minutes. He scolded himself for thinking it, but the fire fountains there still called his attention. By taking into account the miles he was now distant from the island, he guessed that they exceeded the height of the peaks before they cooled to drab clouds boiling upward. In a way the blasts seemed to fill the entire sky, reaching his ears from the north, east, west, and from above; he sensed that, though muffled by distance, they were enormous.

The twilight was fading along the horizon and soon he would have no beacon except the red showers of the volcano growing ever more distant astern or some minor star ahead just below the fringe of the smoke. It was obvious the canoe would never sail on a reach without his hand constantly on the steering oar correcting its course. Throughout the night there would be no sleep for him, and at some time his sole hint of direction might be the wind on his beard and cheek. Tomorrow he would turn downwind, restep the mast, and then try towing something astern to discover how the canoe would hold a course while he dozed off. It meant many trials, for too much aft would slow him needlessly, and too little might not keep the bow pointed where he wished.

The saffron glow in the west muddied and expired. There was no longer an ocean or a sky: only absolute blackness about him. Unable even to see the sail or the food bag dangling before him, it was as if he had been struck blind. A sudden giddiness seized him, a sensation that he was plunging into an enormous abyss. Thomas grasped the edges of the canoe, then ran his hand over the steering oar and the taut backstay above his head to reassure himself that they were still there and he was still sailing. Never had he experienced being so alone nor, he would readily admit, felt such fear eating deep in the core of his body. If only Harrison was in the canoe with him, or even the mate, a voice would make the blackness more bearable. Living alone on the island and searching about for food by starlight had been no great problem, but now there was no firm earth to walk upon and he would be confined to the aft end of the hollowed log until he had crossed two or three hundred miles of ocean. His crude vessel rose on invisible swells, then fell forward into an emptiness, thrusting into a black void that might hold any number of dangers: currents to carry him out of his course, unknown rocks or a whale or great serpent that might shatter his frail canoe. Storms could toss him about like a leaf in a millrace. Even though he and Chris had spoken of the voyage at first as they would some boys' escapade, now a dull, heavy ache settled in his stomach and his hand trembled on the steering oar. For the first time he admitted to himself that he was risking the possibility of death. Had he moved too quickly, made an incurable error? Should he have taken shelter somewhere and waited for the violence to ease and stop? It was that cloud above, that unnatural black sky that frightened him most. What if it covered the last bit of daylight and there was no longer a sunrise or sunset? That would be the end of time.

The volcano glowed fitfully from behind him, but its flames, now distant and partially hidden in their own clouds, hadn't the power to make the mast, the backstay, or the bag of potatoes detectable. It was the only evidence that a firm surface of the Earth still existed in the blackness. In the opposite direction a few faint stars did wink low along the horizon. By leaning to the starboard and looking past the sail, he kept the forestay moving back and forth, eclipsing and revealing the brightest one. By that maneuver he kept the vessel heading south and perhaps a little west. He imagined his wake must look like the trail of a snake, but it didn't matter. That star might rise and be hidden behind the cloud or might set before dawn came, and then the next brightest one would become his guide. He noted again how the wind felt on his face and pressed against his whiskers as he sailed south. That feeling, he knew, must be remembered if the cloud covered that last chink of sky and there was no longer a hint of a star. The thought of losing those few faint twinkles terrified him, and his whole body shuddered for a second.

There was no way he could estimate his progress without enough light to see one or two of the white bits of cinders still lying in the hull or some strand of rope tossed ahead of the canoe as a marker. The seconds it took to pass the hull divided into its length would give something better than a guess. In the end he gave up the thought of doing it in the morning when he could see. There were too many things that might change, the current, wind direction, leeway. It would be an impossible task to cypher his progress to the Middle Island. When there was still light on the horizon he had guessed his speed to be three to three and a half knots, but the seas were angling toward him and so may have deceived his eye.

"Days and nights," he mumbled to himself, "this is going to last for days and nights, and it's going to be difficult to go for a walk."

Suddenly, a red-orange light illuminated the tip of the sail and mast while he was at the bottom of a swell. The hull rose on the next crest and the vessel and the entire sail caught the glow. Thomas twisted to look astern. A flame wavered there, as bright and of the same color as one shot from a forge by the bellows' exhaust. In an unthinking move he put his palm out to shield himself and noticed that the fire was as tall as his opened hand. Considering his distance from the island, the blast had to be great enough to sunder the peaks. Christopher had been right about volcanoes casting out their entire bulk as mountains of shattered stone for miles. He thought he must be at a secure distance, having sailed for four to five hours. If he had made his least guess of three miles each hour that should be about twelve miles added to the seven miles at the point where he stopped paddling and relied on the wind alone. That would make the volcano no less than nineteen miles away. There was a good chance he was even farther from it. He turned forward to use the intermittent light to see how the bow met the swells. It was almost quiet with only the sound of the wind around the sail and a little slosh of water along the side of the hull. He expected to hear something of that great explosion. For about two minutes there was silence in the north with not even the most distant rumble. He then considered he was beyond the reach of the booming of that eruption.

But a few seconds later a blast slammed against his head and back and slatted the sail. He heard it and felt the concussion strike his body in the same instant, as he would the firing of a nearby cannon. It rumbled from the right and left and across the entire sky. After he had gathered his wits, he thought, That's the last of it, both the island and the eruption. The mate and Tobit were surely killed, as he would have been had he stayed. No place on the island was shielded from such an explosion. Ha! He had made the right choice. There could be only small remains, a few burned and riven rocks at most. Now, the worst of that was over for him and he should be able to see the ocean better tomorrow. The black cloud would blow away. The sky would be its wonderful blue again, and he might turn east directly to his goal. Yes! He had done well to escape the island when he did. A few more hours' delay and his body would have been shattered and roasted. Now his greatest worries were only the weather and his supply of water. Despite his hurried leave, he was doing well, with the canoe moving under his control. Aye, he might shift the mast aft some, but if he turned downwind in the morning, it wouldn't be necessary. Indeed, the canoe should steer easier then.

He would have a tale to tell when he returned. It would rival all the stories told by the blockade-runners and the privateers. Those were the escapades of ships' crews, or most of their crews. When he reached the Middle Island, it would be all by his own doing. Except for the skins and lengths of rope Christopher had smuggled to him, he had built his vessel alone. He had done it with only fire and chipped glass blades while concealed on the south shore and fearing discovery every hour.

Yet he would also have to carry the news home that he was the lone survivor and that the others, every other man and boy aboard the barque, had been lost. There would be many saddened families in Stonington, Mystic, and New London when he returned.

Some curious captain might search and find the remains of the island: some shoals and scattered spires of rock, perhaps a little more. That would give much authority to his story. Some day he hoped to find the crew of the brig to tell them the whole tale and that the man who had attacked their mate was dead. Captain Tobit and the mate were surely killed. Neither man nor beast could have survived such a blast, even had they fled to the farthest end of the island. All the powder gathered from a thousand frigates and 74s could not have made but a small part of that destruction.

He remembered once more that, in the morning, he must find out how long the canoe would hold a course going off the wind while he slept. With the skins driving the hull and the spar being dragged through the water, it might veer one way or the other going downwind. The oar turned to correct that might never hold it exactly true. A towed line, if long enough and bent to the end of the boomkin that held the shroud out on the larboard might balance the spar and keep a truer course. At night he could nap, perhaps an hour or two at a time. The drag of it had to be borne if he was to get any sleep. It was far better than lying to all night. Then at dawn, he must take the line in and steer with the oar and so increase his speed.

Thomas heard a sound from aft, but it was a steady murmur, wholly different from the blasts and booms that had come from the volcano. He glanced back and saw nothing. The murmur grew into a deep grumbling. In another look, he thought he saw something lighter along the horizon, but the night was so dark he doubted his eyes. The noise approached swiftly and became a roar only possible from a huge plunging wave. The hull lifted by the stern and he felt seawater pouring over the sides, filling it. Then he felt the canoe being thrust forward at an ever-increasing speed. He was moving so fast that the wind from ahead swung the boom back amidships and bumped his head. He could hear the sail ashiver a foot away. The roar was all around him. The canoe tilted to a nearly vertical position, and Thomas, fearing it would pitch end for end, leaped free to port.

Instantly, his ears were filled with cold, gurgling water. He came to the surface, wiped the wet hair from his face, and reached around for the canoe. The rumble of the wave sped away from him and nothing showed in the blackness all about or above. Several more waves lifted and dropped him, but none were near as high as the first. The spasm of panic seized his chest. If he swam in one direction to find his vessel, chances were much against him that it was the right one. The longer he waited to find it, the farther it might drift from him. If he did not find the canoe, he was doomed to swim about until he weakened and drowned! Dawn showing through the chink to the south and west would reveal the hull only if it rose on a swell at the same moment he did. He wondered if he could last until daylight. He cursed himself for waiting so long to leave! The tremendous blast had thrown up the sea into a monstrous wave. Damn! Damn! Damn! If he had just sailed a day earlier. . . . He could not be more than a few feet from the hull, but in which direction was it? If he listened, perhaps he could hear the water sloshing around it.

For a minute, he treaded water and concentrated on what he could hear. To his right he thought there was a faint gurgle. Cautiously, he kicked and pawed in that direction. One, two, three, four, five kicks, then something bumped against his cheek. He reached up for it. Ha! It was the blade of the paddle. Slowly he pulled on it, hoping it was still tied to the canoe. It came to him freely at first and then stopped. It was attached! He was going to pull himself to the canoe with it, but realized a mere strand might be all that held it. He ran his hand along the cord until he felt the edge of the hull.

The gunnel was under the water! The canoe had been overturned! The worst had happened! How would he ever get it righted? If the mast and sail were still in place there below, they would be a great stop-water and no man, however large, could force it upright. All the rigging would have to be taken loose, and perhaps even the boomkins unlashed before he could roll the hull. Nothing could be done in the dark. He crawled up on the exposed bottom and lay along its length with arms dangling in the sea. It was going to be a night of misery with no relief from his awkward position except to turn his head and rest the other cheek against the hull. Sometimes he brought his hands up and laced his fingers together. That made a pad for his face, but in a few minutes they ached and he had to drop them into the moving water again. He felt his cold, clammy leather clothes against his skin. Their first nights on the island had not been as terrible as this. At least there they had been secure. There was the earth beneath their feet on which to move about to warm themselves and ease their stiffened muscles. Now all he had was the log under him and a slim hope he might repair his canoe. All night he would be numb with cold, and then helpless with spasms of shivering.

He had to piss and rolled a little to one side, but he couldn't balance on the hull and get the knot loose with one hand. The pressure and the pain were too much to resist, and he gave up and let the hot fluid spread around his groin. At least an animal didn't have lie in its own water, he thought. He was in a worse condition than any animal, and unlike them, much aware of his awful plight. He shivered so violently he was unable to fall asleep, and that made the time of darkness interminable. There was nothing to look at, nothing to hear except the occasional slosh of water against the spar and hull as they were lifted and dropped by the swells.

Only memories served as diversions from his misery, and throughout the night he recalled being a boy in the Port with an endless round of school, work, and church. He knew all the houses, the ropewalks, and the kiln. His father had sent him on many errands and he learned how to cut through backyards, the marshes, and garden plots, and hop over stiles to each destination and return. He went as far as Mystic to fetch and deliver parcels and messages. It had seemed a dull existence compared to the lives of the coasters during the war. Even after the war's end, a vessel's departure from the docks was the start of an adventure for some of his friends. They went to South Georgia, Spain, Surinam, and Africa. Some made many times more than wages when they were allowed to carry something on their own account. The opportunity to go asealing from New York had been offered him twice before, and both times he had to remain in the shop when other boys even younger than himself set off for the fishery. They had better fortune than he had met with. They had become mates aboard ships. He had ended his first voyage clinging to a log in an empty sea hundreds of miles from another soul. No one would ever learn what happened to him and all those aboard the *Dove*. Perhaps he should have kept at home. Perhaps it was just the time he left that had decided his terrible fate. Mother's death had done away with his father's last objection. She had lain in bed for days, red-faced and with her hair wet with perspiration. Each day she had moved less and looked at him with glazed eyes. At the last, Mother closed her lids as if there was not enough energy left in her body to raise them. The next year to the day, Father had let him go. Had he sailed sooner or later he would not have gotten a berth on old Tobit's barque. If another had been placed in his way, he might have returned and had some hundreds of dollars paid him.

Thomas recalled everything in his life up to the time that the eruption had driven him from the island. He remembered all the roads in Stonington and pictured in his mind all the buildings or empty lots along them. He listed all the names on the lasts in the racks on the walls of the shop and matched each to the face of its owner. The effort was difficult to maintain; yet, except for a few short lapses, it diverted him from his low spirits. Isabel's image repeatedly came before him, but she was always walking with her parents, her plump-faced mother and her father, all too conscious of his footing, and always dressed to prove it. The face of everyone he knew appeared in his mind more than once, and he remembered all the farmers, fishermen, and their wives and children. The Benedicks, the Browns, the Pendeltons, the

Chesebros, the Miners, even Rhoady Owens, so meanly labeled a lewd woman by the pastor. In his mind he pictured himself walking past each of their houses in and near the Port. On and on they came to him until there were no more to recall. Hours of darkness had passed, many hours. Surely the night must be nearly over, he thought.

There was a possibility that the smoke had spread even farther and covered that last sliver of sky. He dismissed the idea. One final blast from the volcano had surely ended it, he thought. The huge wave that had hurled the canoe forward and capsized it when he was nearly twenty miles from the island was evidence of its violence. There could be little left of that fair piece of land, perhaps just another circular bay with a few rocks around its outer edges. Such a huge explosion could have shattered the peaks and cast them far over the ocean.

Thomas looked for the least graying of the horizon. Without light to see the state of the rigging, he could not plan what to do next.

He thought the inverted canoe was holding parallel to the swells most of the time. They were coming from starboard. That should put south toward his feet and he favored looking that way over the other. Once, when he did look in the opposite direction, he noticed a faint, but only the faintest, band of gray. His mind would not accept that as south. It might be that the smoke had risen to the north after the last of the eruptions. He wasn't even sure that he was seeing any light. Perhaps he was just hoping too much that it was dawn, yet the band remained there and became undeniably lighter than the black all around.

It had been a horrible night, the longest and most miserable he had ever spent. He could wait now. Once he knew the sun was rising somewhere, he could find the patience to lie there until the light increased. Yet it was not right. The growing band could not be southerly. He kept thinking that until he realized that he was lying face down with his head in the opposite direction, not sitting face up, and so, with the swells coming from his right, it was south or more accurately southeast. It was such a fool mistake to make. He wasn't thinking clearly. How could he get so confused so easily? When he sat up and faced the thin band of light, it all fitted into place with the swells approaching from starboard. An irregular sea was running with some waves at different angles. Gray light was coming through a slit, and that slit was to the southeast, if the waves were still heading northeast.

When he was barely able to make out more of the surface of the water and the spar, he saw no floating tangle of sail and lines. There was a good chance that the mast was unbroken. By leaning over and feeling beneath the surface, he could unhitch a stay and a shroud from the hull and allow the mast to come out of its step and so not hinder rolling the hull. Only then would he have the least chance at repair.

The glow at the horizon grew quickly and Thomas guessed the sun was rising. He knew that after the first hour, the light would not get much brighter, and he put his plan to the test. Just the taut feel of the lines let him know the mast was still in place. The wet ropes were difficult to loosen, and it required several tries on the forestay and one shroud before the mast came free. After he succeeded, he rested for several minutes on the overturned canoe. The hull was free to be righted. He ran his hand under the saplings and untied his coil of rope. It had to be passed around the spar and that meant a dip into the sea. He slithered in, passed the line and was out of the water in four or five seconds. The next move was more difficult. With both lines in his right hand, he had to rise to his feet and balance himself at the same time. Once he stood, with his legs spread and feet secure, he leaned back and used the ropes to hold him steady. The canoe was always shifting in response to the slope of the swells, being both a hindrance and help. If he heaved back on the rope when the spar was lifted, it should aid in the turning.

The first three tries raised the spar out of the water, but they didn't bring it high enough. Thomas saw that by creating a rhythm, leaning back and forth and giving it a final heave at the moment the spar was raised by the wave, it might flop over. On the next attempt the spar passed the critical point and started over. The turning hull rolled his feet to the side and he plunged straight down into the water. The spar cleared his head by inches and slammed onto the surface. It worked!

He cared not a fig that he had to take another dip. The turning of the hull was his saving. He grasped the gunnel with his left hand and felt around with his right for one of the bailers. The hull was full to the top with water. He pulled himself along the side until he discovered a bailer, its lanyard tangled with the lines of the water butts. After carefully freeing it, he rapidly dipped the water out. The sea was chilling him and he pulled himself up with shaking arms and climbed in when the hull was still a quarter full. The remainder could be scooped out while he sat in the stern. Each time the bow went up, the water rushed aft and he got a full bail to pitch over the side. In a few minutes most of the water was gone.

Thomas pulled the butts back into the canoe by their lines and learned the wave had given him another disaster. The containers had remained tied to the canoe, but their plugs had been knocked or pulled out. He had no water at all! Just to be sure he tasted the little water remaining in them and spat it out. "Damn!" he swore, "nothing but seawater!" Could he still make the Middle Island alive in a few days? Could he reach it before he went mad with thirst?

In the weak, gray light he started his overhaul of the canoe. He found the bundle with his tools still lashed to the saplings, but the sack of potatoes was missing. So, in all, he had lost the food, his pad of ferns, the robe of furs, and, most valuable of all, the water.

Thomas stripped off his clothes and wrung what water he could from them. They remained damp, yet were more bearable when he dressed again. The intervals of his shivering became shorter and finally ended.

The sail was lying alongside. Some of its skins were ripped from the hanks on the mast and from the lacing on the boom. Only the lower third still held fast. The soaked skins were heavy, and it was awkward to lift the boom and pull it across the hull. This time he would set the heel of the mast farther aft. He pulled up the lines of the backstay and shroud he had unhitched and held their ends in his right hand. It took delicate balancing to stand and hold the mast up while the canoe pitched in the swells. Then he had to tie the lines off with shaking hands. Thomas managed it after many tries, first the backstay and then the shroud. Once the mast stood by itself, he made final adjustments, easing one shroud and tightening its opposite. With that part of the rigging done, he could sit and repair the sail.

He put his idea of the previous day into action and bent one end of his long line to the canoe. The remainder, with several knots tied in it, he cast astern. With the wind pressing against the mast and its rigging, the bow swung slowly downwind. The swells came from astern, lifted the canoe, and ran on, leaving it to drop into the trough. He crouched on the gunnel, feeling ill-omened and miserable at the loss of his water while he worked his bone needle and twine through the skins. He knew he mustn't consider all lost. At least the damage to the sail was repairable, and the chances still remained that he could reach Tovy Poenamoo. His spirits were raised some hours later when the last stitch was knotted and he put the needle and line back into his bundle of tools. He picked up the halyard and sang softly, "Oh, Louie was the king of France before the Rev-eye-lution." Then in mimicry of hauling on lines aboard the *Dove,* he hoisted the sail with the chorus, "Way, haul away, haul away, Joe." Thomas adjusted the sheet in and the canoe responded, picking up speed.

He gathered in the line trailing astern and turned the bow to sail due south again toward the lighted horizon. In the opposite direction it was still black, and there was not a speck of the island or even much of the dingy sea to be seen, even when he stood on the gunnel.

Throughout the morning the canoe drove from beneath the dense cloud with its dirty edges and neared a band of limpid sky that widened by the hour. The ocean regained its accustomed hue and the happy, rhythmic glints of sunlight reflecting from its waves nearby. He turned to the sun that warmed his face and hands and smiled. The sight of the blue overhead and in the sea elated him more than all else. How strange, he thought, that the ominous black above could sink his spirits so low and the sunlit sky could raise them so high. Man belongs to the day. He is not a bat.

Either he was making good progress, or as he thought more likely, the eruption was ebbing or possibly over. It didn't matter which to him. Thomas wore the bow through the eye of the wind and then around to head east. With the boom full out to the starboard, every inch of the sail drew. He leaped to his feet when he saw how the hull and spar were driving through the water. Ha! All afluking. . . . I'm on my way again, he thought.

Next he stepped on the gunnel of the canoe and looked to the horizon like an impatient child, though he knew he had days to sail before he could possibly see the Middle Island. At least a hundred and eighty to two hundred miles of rolling ocean lay before him, perhaps more. He turned slowly, searching the farthest edge of the ocean a bit at a time for any minute, hazy indication of a ship. The most likely direction would be to the south. It would be a sealer like the *Dove,* making north for a China cargo. Yet he had to admit, only one or two, if any at all, took that course in a year. The other gangs on Macquarie and Brister's had come from the Derwent and Port Jackson and would return there with their oil. Perhaps a flax trader might be standing off the coast, but they would have to chance almost directly upon him. His little sail was invisible at a mile distant and what officer would be looking in his direction with his glass and at the right moment? A whaler would be most likely to spot him. They always had a man in the crosstrees. He could only search the distant edge of the sea every hour and hope, while knowing he was only a speck of life floating in an infinite ocean.

With the loss of his folded fur and the padding of ferns it was a discomfort to sit for hours. There was always a skim of water in the hull, impossible to scoop up, and so his bottom was continually wet. If he made a thwart by cutting up one of the saplings he could only sit on it while awake, but at night must sleep in his wet seat in the hull. He could expect boils.

Warmth from his body and heat from the sun drove some of the dampness from the leather of his clothes. He pulled the hood of his jacket over his head and vowed not to open his mouth. The sun would beat down, and without a drop of water, thirst might drive him mad before he reached that other shore.

For hours the water seeped down out of the raised sail and dripped from the boom. With the effect of the wind and sun, the head of it showed some drying by midday.

He hoped there would be stars to steer by for most of the night. If he grew tired, he could cast his line out and sail safely to the leeward while he slept.

Evening came on and he knew it would be a far better night for him despite being cold and cramped in the stern. While awake, he paddled a few minutes at a time to warm himself. The stars were now revealed in larger portions of the sky and the constellations gave him assurance he was sailing for the Middle Island. Before he went to sleep, he threw out the knotted line and then let the wind carry him somewhere between nor'east and east.

Morning came on misty and gray. An hour later it cleared and revealed that the dingy cloud of smoke covered even less of the sky in what he could assume was the north.

The canoe drove over dark swells. He wished he had a larger sail or a speedier hull, but remembered they could have their dangers. Flecks of foam rode on the surface and gave him a good sense of progress. Thomas watched one as the hull slid past it. He couldn't resist the urge to count the seconds for it to move from the bow to the stern. One . . . two . . . three . . . about four seconds. The hull was sixteen or seventeen feet in length, according to his pacing of it. If it was sixteen feet long and it passed the foam in about four seconds, that would be four feet, perhaps slightly more, traveled each second. Sixty seconds times sixty minutes yielded three thousand six hundred seconds. Thomas leaned forward, untied his bundle of tools, and loosened the drawstring. From the mixture of bone needles, extra hanks, coils of twine and cord, and two adzes, he selected a blade of glass. With it, he scratched numerals on the blade of the paddle. Four feet each second times the three thousand six hundred was fourteen thousand four hundred feet. Divide that by six thousand feet, and he calculated his speed should be near two and a half miles each hour at the very least. From the way the hull cut through the sea it looked as if he was making better time, three miles maybe. He wasn't adding the current for, though it was there, its speed was not known.

After they had landed on the island, the mate claimed his last calculation of the distance to Tovy Poenamoo had been 185 miles. When sailing around the sealing grounds, he had been vague about their position, but Thomas believed the figure of 185 miles. After the wreck, Mr. Morgen no longer had a reason to give dubious answers. That supposed 185 miles traveled at two and a half miles each hour would require about 74 hours. Three days. It would take that much time if the wind did not fail, yet the canoe would not be driven due east but to the north and south some. It would add to the distance he must sail, perhaps a day at the most. The line astern at night was sure to slow him. Add another twelve hours. His last drink of water had been two days before so that would make it six days and a half without water before he reached any shore. He expected he could manage that but would suffer. If the wind failed, or a storm arose, it could be longer. His life depended on the wind: too much, or a lack of it.

CHAPTER 18

THOMAS rested unmoving, death-like in the stern. The damp, imperfectly tanned hides he wore had begun to smell. From the shade of his hood he stared at his knees showing through the holes worn in his trousers. Smaller but like holes were started in the elbows of his jacket. He might have found time in the last few weeks to sew new clothes and groom himself, but the canoe, its rigging, and the growing blasts of the eruption had claimed all of his thoughts and left him with little desire. Now, with tangled hair and dressed in ragged, greasy clothes, he might be taken for the most desperate lazar in India.

A beggar he certainly was, begging fate for wind and current to carry him swiftly to the Middle Island. And, once he gained its shore, he might have to beg chance or the charity of the savages for his life. Yet he would not beg to a god. If there was one, he must be wholly indifferent, far above any entreaties, for he allowed too much evil to exist, permitted mean men to invoke his name to shame others and to carry forward their greedy schemes. He had seen too many of the petty and peevish spouting righteousness in Stonington. Freethinkers suffered only at the hands of believers and not those of any god.

He glanced at his right hand resting on the arm of the steering oar. Its back was tanned to the color of cherry wood and the palm was callused and cracked. It bore several cuts as did his left hand, made while working with the glass tools. The sleeves of his jacket and the legs of his pants were almost dry and showed a faint bloom of salt on their dirty creases. He was being pickled like a cod, a dunfish soaked in brine and hung in the wind. And he might well look like one when he reached the shore, all dried and ready to be boxed. He forced the thought out of his mind and watched how the hull was lifted on each swell and driven ahead by the wind. The sail was small but working well. It was no time for melancholy while he was progressing, minute by minute, toward his goal.

Throughout the day the most difficult thing was to sit there, only shifting his legs and stretching his arms. Without the padding under him, his bottom bothered him more. About every hour he rose up to scan the horizon. Sometimes he stood for almost a quarter of an hour, holding onto the backstay and nudging the steering oar with his leg. Then he would step to the mast, and even around and forward of it, to inspect the bindings and the forestay. He needn't do that more than one time each day, but it was an excuse to move about. Once, as he passed back between the shroud and the mast, his foot slipped and he plunged chest-deep into the water but managed another grab for the shroud. He hung there for seconds with his heart pounding. If he had gone completely under, he might not have come back up in time to grab the gunnel. Without being on board, the canoe would have sailed on. He didn't know for how long, but with the cord holding the steering oar it might continue for hours, canting off to one direction or the other. He would have been left behind like an anchor buoy bobbing in the swells until he weakened and drowned. Once back aboard he untied the end of his long line from the aft boomkin, and rehitched it by the bight to give him two free ends: one short line to tie about his waist and a longer portion to drag astern. Then he set himself a rule never to stand without a firm grip on the backstay or the mast. A sudden lurch could easily cast him overboard.

He removed his clothes and wrung as much water out of them as he could. They were uncomfortable to put on again, yet the heat of his body might dry them before night.

At sundown he ran his tongue through the gap of his missing teeth and found his lips were stuck together with dried saliva.

In the short naps that night he had many dreams, some he remembered later, some hardly recallable at all. One recurred three or four times. In it he was walking under some trees on a bright day. By the look of the leaves above, pale green and translucent between him and the sunlight, it was spring or early summer. Yes, he knew it had to be late spring by the smell of the air and its feel, warm and soft on the skin. A child, a girl wearing a bonnet, was leading him along the main road. He could never see her face, but he saw and felt her little hand holding onto his and pulling him slowly forward. There were others along the road, all people he knew, but they stood unmoving in their various places in doorways and by fences like statues. He and the girl never reached their goal, for he always awoke before they had gone a dozen steps.

When he opened his eyes, he gazed up at the broad, ebony night, an entire dome prinked with stars of all magnitudes, winking, sparkling. Each one had a sharpness he had not seen since passing through the tropics. The beauty and simplicity of the night awed him and, for the moment, sunk his nagging sense of peril. The black expanse of the sea rising and dipping as far as he could see fined him down to a single fleck on the globe. He was moving on it but held tightly to its surface. Sitting in the hull and staring out into the farthest depth of the universe, he grasped the immense turning of the earth to the east. At dawn the sun would not rise out of a flat sea; the planet would carry him around, out of the shadow and into its glare. From dawn he would be taken to noon, to sunset, and back into night again.

Something carking and unnamable bothered Thomas as the light increased in the first minutes of the fourth day. Through the long predawn gray he made out that the swells no longer had peaks but rounded backs. They swept on, raising and lowering the canoe smoothly. No little bits of foam rode on the sea, and the boom didn't strain at the sheet as it had. After the sun broke into sight showing the bow was within half a point of his desired course, it also confirmed how much the canoe had slowed. Thomas pulled a sliver of wood from where the stone had struck the hull and pitched it ahead. It required more than eight seconds to pass the stern. Calculations yielded a speed of one and a quarter miles each hour. Not even a decent walk, he thought. He could paddle to increase the speed, but that labor under the sun would cause a greater thirst to come upon him, and sooner. There was nothing to do. Just wait. Have patience. Hope. The wind might freshen again before long and drive the canoe three, four, or five knots an hour.

What he wanted just then was a drink. The sharpening need for water had come upon him the day before. It was going to be a trial to keep his mind off water. He would start right then to repeat the exercise of memory he had made while lying on the overturned canoe. Anything would do, even the recitation of multiplication tables. He would scan the waves for any bit of driftwood or rockweed or search for the long-winged mollymocks soaring low just ahead of the swells. They were the only life to be seen, for in all the hours he had sailed, not one fish or dark shape had he spotted beneath the sea. Mollymocks were magnificent to watch, though they were rare, only one or, at the most, two appeared in a day. They swept high, dived, and glided within inches of the swells that bore them up magically without a touch. In a few seconds they were gone, not having given more than a beat or two of their wings. Oh, if he could only fly with such little effort, like those stern-eyed birds! He would rise into the sky until he saw the coast. Then, on great wings, he would glide to plant his feet on the Middle Island.

The black cloud of smoke had retreated to a corner of the sky. Was that a sign the eruption was truly over or that he was sailing in the wrong direction? How could he know? Was that smoke still in the northeast or had he passed under it all in the night and it was now to the south of him?

High clouds gathered in the afternoon, but not dense enough to promise rain. That brought the thought of water. Damn! he swore to himself; that reminded him of the burning in his throat and his thickening tongue! How could he take advantage of it if it did rain? Could he catch it in the sail? It would have to be a long, heavy rain to wash all the salt out of the skins before he could drink it. How could he fill his containers? The bailers! Yes, they could be his funnels. Let it run from the sail into a bailer and then pour it into his butts. Or he could make a larger hole in its end and use it as a funnel. Ah! Yes, he could manage if it would only rain as it had on the island, downpours that lasted for hours. He would then be wet and cold, but knew he could endure that far easier than the endless burning of his throat.

The cradle-like rising and falling of the hull caused him to nod off time after time. His many wakenings in the night, when he had to paddle to keep warm, robbed him of half his sleep. Each time he jerked his head up in the daytime, the canoe was squinting off to one side or the other, not pointed east where he wished it to be. Several times it gybed, and the slatting of the sail and rocking of the hull stirred him from his naps. To drag the rope astern and sleep during the day wasn't a choice he liked. Better to splash seawater on his face, keep the vessel moving before what breath of wind was offered and be awake to watch for a ship or land.

For the rest of that day nothing changed: nothing of note happened. Swells passed beneath him. A hazy sun above the clouds inched through its arc and drew out each hour into what seemed like three. Thomas sat in the twilight, his mind teetering between awareness and sleep and feeling he could will it in either direction. He could dream while his half-open eyes watched the bow and spar push through the water and the last tints of orange and red fade from the clouds.

The pattern of the previous nights went on unchanged: set out the line, sleep, and when the chill wakened him, paddle for a while. Once when the light of a partial moon or the discomfort of the sores on his bottom aroused him, he discovered his fragile creation of a log, sticks, and hides was ghosting over the long, low swells. Only a faint air kept the sail from hanging slack. The height of Sirius showed him he had slept about an hour or more and how many hours there were yet to endure before dawn. From those stars he could see his course was still toward Tovy Poenamoo.

Suddenly, he turned his head quickly to the right. From the corner of his eye he swore he had seen a movement close by. The spar trailed its barely detectable wake. Aft of it there was no resting bird or driftage on the surface. There was nothing, no silent mollymawk sweeping a foot or two above the water in that or any other direction. Each time he wakened he sensed a dark, furtive movement somewhere at the very edge of his vision, never in a direct line of sight where he could confirm or disprove his suspicion. Perhaps it was the mere wish to see something other than the inky sea about him. Perhaps it was the solitude working on his mind. He had heard that some men did go mad after living alone for long times. They behaved like animals, nay worse than animals. They dressed in rags, lived in their own filth, and in the end they destroyed themselves. Or did they live alone because they were already mad? If Christopher had been there to share the voyage, it would be much easier. A companion to speak with was always a comfort. They could talk of the voyage, of when they might return home, how they might replace the loss of their shares, a thousand things that would shorten and enliven the hours as they had on the barque.

What was he thinking? Christopher was not even alive! His battered body was buried back there on the island if any of its blasted rocks remained. Now he was alone and had no choice but to sail on to the end of the adventure or of his life.

He awoke once more and saw by the stars that the east would lighten in an hour. This time he could see a dark form of a man sitting on the spar. That was absurd! It would not bear the weight of a man. He blinked and the blurry figure vanished. Was he going daft? Was the thirst playing tricks with his eyes?

The fifth day commenced, streaking the clouds with gray and then pink. Thomas pulled in the line and looked over the sail and rigging. The wood of the hull and boomkins was damp with a faint dew as it had been every morning. Even had it beaded up into droplets it would be of no use to lick it. Every bit of the canoe had its coating of salt from the capsizing. With the rise of the sun, the day would become more of a misery than ever. He wondered how much suffering he could endure. He tried blocking out the recurring images of cool streams in his mind, but his patchy thoughts could not keep together. The burning sensation and the swelling in his throat always brought him back to the craving for water. If only the stopper in one of the butts had held, he could have made it last till he reached the shore. One sip, just one sip was all he wanted at that moment. Perhaps the suffering might end before he died. Would his thirst cease and a final comfort be his? Would his head then fill with visions of his boyhood, the rivers, the woods, and the low coast of Connecticut?

An hour later he felt himself fading into a sleep. Let the canoe drift to the starboard and be damned, he thought. Damn everything. He didn't much care and allowed himself to slip under. It would be better if he did. Dreams were now preferable to wakefulness, if they were pleasant ones. He did dream in fitful, disjointed episodes, one coming upon another. Between each, he raised his head slightly and saw swimmy visions, through slightly opened eyes, of the bow rising and dipping and the sail pulling at the sheet.

At sundown he awakened fully, but he wished he hadn't. He felt in the very core of his body that he might not last many hours more. But was he that close to death? It had only been a few days. Surely he should be able to last that long. Had it been longer? Might he have slept whole days without waking? Yes, that might be what happened. Even had he made marks to count the days, he would never know that he had slept an entire day or even two. Had he confused how long he had been at sea? It had to be that. The morning of one day mated to the evening of the next and the hours between not recalled, lost. Strange, so strange that a man should know precisely when death was near. Or was he already dying. Was he fading from life unaware and now merely living out the last dream of his existence? His body to shrink to a little tough flesh covering his bones. All piety and prayer futile, a sham. All sinners and saintly men to suffer the same fate . . . no heaven . . . no hell. What would be next? Just his thoughts drifting on forever . . . drifting through black space? On and on for ages until, by chance, they encountered some distant comet or unimagined planet. Or would they fade, recalling less and less, aware of nothing until all evaporated like water on a hot stone? Was he going daft from the thirst? If so, what mad thing might he do next?

In the last of the twilight, the canoe was heading a little to the starboard of his course. He leaned over the side and faced the streaming water. Drink it and go insane! That was the caution given him by the old hands. Two of them were men who had survived shipwrecks and founderings. They had told of the vacant or mad look in the eyes of those unfortunates who yielded and drank seawater. They had listened to their ravings that a lush island was but a few miles away or that a ship was bearing toward them. But he couldn't stand many more hours of the intense burning in his throat and furry feel in his mouth. Breathing was an unending labor, hour after hour. The lump in his throat swelled and hardened. He craved to feel cool water passing down his gullet, even if it was salt! Who was dependent upon him and his earnings? Not even his father. He would leave no widow and child to live by charity. Father would never learn how he had suffered and, aye, at the last found no reason to suffer more. He would not be the only one from the Port to sail off and leave no trace behind. It would be only a few more hours or a day for him. Too bad he was to end his life in such a miserable fashion . . . had been so many hopes . . . such good hopes . . . had so much to look forward to. He cupped up seawater in his left hand and was about to sip it but stopped. His fingers relaxed, allowing the water to drain away. He rolled back into his seat and promised himself he would try to last the night. Cool air . . . yes, the cool air . . . if the Middle Island was not in sight in the morning, he would drink from the sea . . . might be a chance he could drink . . . not go mad before he reached the coast. How long would he last? Half a day . . . a whole day?

A series of images came before him throughout the hours of darkness. He could not determine if they were nightmares or waking visions. A water butt with brass hoops polished to a shine balanced on the forward boomkin. That was impossible, he thought, and it promptly disappeared. Minutes later, the vague figure he had seen on the spar appeared there again and, detail by detail, formed itself into Christopher. He sat there stiffly with his legs covered up to the knees by the moving sea. His bloodied face was just as Thomas had seen it last in the grave, with the nose split open and the eye sockets packed with grit.

"Have I failed you lad?" he breathed. The cinders fell from his mouth as he spoke. "I am most sorry for it if I did."

Those were the words he would surely have spoken were he there and alive. Then Jack appeared directly before him, squeezed into the hull between the mast and the after boomkin. He calmly drew on his long Dutch pipe and expelled the smoke into the wafting air, smiling after each puff. Nat was seated on the boomkin between Christopher and Jack, kicking his bare feet in the water. He stared at Thomas with his head atilt and his curious, impudent look of a billy goat.

Ghosts! Ghosts! Thomas thought. He wanted to scream, "Go away! Go away!" But he was unable even to emit a croak. He waved his hand at them as if he could sweep them from his vision. It did work! Each time he waved, the specters became fainter and at last disappeared. Why did he see them? Was he to join them soon?

Christopher then reappeared on the spar. "You must not give over, lad. You must not give over," he pleaded, holding a hand out toward him. Thomas wanted to protest that he had suffered all he could bear, yet he could only think it. Christopher must have guessed what his reply would be for he waggled a finger at him as he would an erring child. He swept the carpenter away again with his open hand.

In the first light, Thomas grabbed the backstay and pulled himself to his feet. He stepped onto the boomkin before the mast and looked in a full sweep from north, to the east, and then to the south. Rise, Middle Island, he pleaded in his thoughts. Oh, rise from the sea! Save me from this torture! Then he scanned aft to make doubly sure no land or a ship had appeared in that direction. There was a little nib there! Yes, he was sure of it. Right at the very edge of the horizon. A mite darker than the sky. Ah, ah, yes, the royals of a ship! Next her t'gallants, topsails, and courses will rise and look grand standing straight for his little shell. His way must be stopped. He must not sail on before her. Thomas drew the sheet in and loosed the halyard. The sail dropped and draped over the boom. When he looked aft again, the nib no longer interrupted the clean line between sky and sea. He held his hand over his eyes for several seconds and looked again. Nothing! Two more times he made a search of the entire circuit of the ocean hoping for any light or dark fleck to appear. Oh! I am going mad; yes, this is how it must begin. Seeing what one desires most and seeing it when it was not there. So now he was approaching that condition of those men that raved in their thirst. Without thinking, he hoisted the sail and set the sheet again.

Reluctantly, he returned to his seat to wait for the first beams of the sun to glance off the tops of the swells before he fulfilled his intention to drink. High overhead, light already rouged the underside of long, thin clouds. A few minutes later he leaned over the side of the canoe and placed his cheek next to the steering oar. His jacket hood excluded the glints of the sun and much of the light from above. Nothing showed in the water below. It was like peering into a deep well. His lips were almost touching the surface of the water. He ached to suck up a draught and feel it go down and quench the burning as it went. If he did not land soon enough after he drank, he would die. But it was not death, a black, dreamless void or the supposed punishments of a hell he feared. It was the expulsion from his young life, the loss of all his future sunlit days, the smiles of friends, the grip of willing hands. Yes, there was no one dependent on him. . . . There were children to sire, to become his welcomed charges. He could not imagine their faces, though he could hear their babble of words in high-pitched voices calling from somewhere, not out there on the swells of the sea, but across a great distance, from no fixed direction and in no appointed hour in time. Somewhere they were playing, leaping, squealing in their delight of being alive. Again, he was under the trees in the moving patches of shadow and brilliant sunlight and the little girl in the bonnet was once more pulling him forward along the road lined with the clapboard houses. If their hands parted, he would die and she would never be. She would fade from his sight, as had the shades of the night before. He could never then send something of himself, the arch of his eyebrows, the shape and spread of his hand into the years ahead. No! No! He had neither fear of a hell nor expectation of heavenly reward. That was not the question there on the heaving waves of the vast ocean. Cling to me, child! Oh, grip my hand little one! We need an abundance of days to be lived and savored, not stern warnings about sin and endless harangues to piety and thrift. Thrift? Hah, nearing death, what did a man truly own? His name and his memories. Yes, that was all. Even in the midst of life those were all that mattered . . . keep your gold . . . your properties . . . bills of exchange . . . give me that little hand . . . that is all I prize.

A wavelet slapped the side of his chin and he jerked back a few inches. Shocked back to the present, he remained in that pose as the seawater dribbled from his beard. He gasped for air quickly and deeply, as if he had been running a long way. Shivers went through his entire body for a moment and then he lurched back into his seat. How much longer could he stand it? How many more hours could he hold onto life? When was the escape from agony more desirable than life?

Something was drifting along the side of the canoe and he watched it with absent eyes without recognizing it. His mind was on his thirst and the little girl. As it passed aft he saw it for what it was, the least bit of foam. He then became aware that the wind had increased and the canoe was traveling faster. The few bubbles had come from the bow pushing more rapidly through the sea. Another few hours, he said to himself. I'll give it till midday.

Thomas pulled in the trailing line and then struggled up to stand on the gunnel. He scanned every point of the card. A vessel might overtake him or cross his wake. An hour later he saw several birds to the north. They were flying low over the water and toward the windward with even beats of their wings. Not mollymocks, he thought, for they are solitary and soar for much of their flight. Are they flying to land, he asked himself, or are they going to search out their food? Yes, there must be land to the leeward! Birds go out at first light and return at sunset. By midday he was pulling himself up by the shroud to search the horizon ahead at what he guessed was each quarter of the hour. The hull was cutting a wonderful furrow, and the smacking breeze promised to hold until night at least. Going at this rate he might make twenty-five or thirty miles before dark. It was no time for despair.

Within another hour, he detected a thin line, a ragged, white scratch in the blue ahead, exactly on the horizon. He kept watching for it each time the canoe rose on the peak of the swell. Was it fog or a layer of clouds, peculiar ones, dense and creamy white? Were his eyes and mind now failing him again, creating some new fantasy? He wanted to see the dark shape of Tovy Poenamoo there. Had the wind veered sixteen points and blown him back to the island that was now nothing save a reef and high surf? But there was no island. No! No! No! The wind blew from larboard of the sunset and toward the sunrise sky. It hadn't shifted! He went forward and stood on the gunnel again. The white line seemed fixed, unchanging in shape or position. Clouds moved, sometimes slowly, but they moved. He picked out the highest point along the line and stared at it to see if it would rise, spread, or alter its shape in some way. It rose. The entire line rose evenly and did not change proportions. Another dark line appeared below it.

Then it came to him, and there was a sudden filling of his heart and a pause before it beat again. After a few seconds, he slowly closed his eyes and pressed his forehead against the mast. Snow! He wanted to shout it, but he could not. Snow! I have made it! The words echoed in his skull. I have made the coast! I am to live again! I . . . am . . . to . . . live . . . again! I will not perish in this little hull. I will not shrivel and turn black. No, no, no, I will step ashore on the Longpoint! In a few hours he would be on that land gulping cold, sweet water from that melting snow. He lifted his head to look again, to stare at its solidity, to make sure the serrated, white line hadn't evaporated or drifted away. It was there, solid as rock. Indeed, there was rock beneath it all. What a trial it had been. Suddenly it seemed absurd that a few hours ago he was ready to drink the seawater. The worst was over. In some fashion, he would find the whalers or traders or even travel on to the Bay of Islands.

The mountains gradually rose higher and higher, with the snow covering only their top quarter. While lifted and dropped by the waves, he stared at the wonderful vision, but he knew he was most likely to come onto the coast late, just as it was getting dark. The wind that was driving him so well was sure to raise surf. A night landing on an unknown shore was not what he wished. He was weak, very weak, from thirst and hunger. He might last another day at sea but want strength to swim if the canoe was overturned. He decided to keep his offing until the moon rose and then run in at the first likely place. If he waited until dawn, the swimming would be more than he could manage. Now, just keeping his head above the waves would be a trial. He was a stout lad when the barque struck the rock and his muscles had carried him from the wreck and through the surf, but now he had been without food and water for about six, seven days, even eight or ten days if he had confused his count. Now he felt the weakness in his quivering arms. He had to run the canoe straight in and hope it didn't capsize or strike on rocks. The sole choice left to him was where he would run in.

The mountains gained in height and the snow on them glowed orange and roseate in the last light. Their peaks and ridges were starkly outlined in their finest detail against the darkening sky and became reassuring and beautiful to Thomas after his long, desperate searchings of the empty horizon. The snow, the rocks, the trees, everything of the earth was beautiful to him for it meant relief, escape, and his continuance in life. He would remember that sweet, sublime panorama to his last day.

For a short moment he forgot the craving for water when dozens of sea birds in diagonals of dark specks flew overhead toward the coast. As the twilight spent itself, the range dimmed and loomed above him.

The thunder of the waves striking the shore proved he was nearing his goal, and yet it warned him of a barrier being thrown up and holding him off. He was close, so close, but had to be patient until the moon cleared the peaks and spilled its weak light onto the shore. He turned west to quarter the swells and eased the sheet to drive her just enough to give the canoe way through the water and steer. Inwardly, he laughed a little at the thought that, in making that board, he was sailing away from the island. He kept standing off and on until the moon made its appearance. Its light spread over the snow of the mountains, turning it a ghostly white. At the edge of the lower hills, he could barely make out a thick, dark forest growing close to the sea. There seemed to be no clear space in from the surf. The best view he could manage was stepping up on the hull when it lifted on a wave, and that revealed little more than when he sat in the stern. Nothing was visible on the shore except waves dashing against a point of rocks to his right. A landing there would leave him battered if it did not kill him. If I keep going north, he was thinking, and find another such small headland, perhaps there'll be a chance there is a beach between them or at the least, fewer rocks.

Farther up the coast, a half-mile by his estimate, the land seemed lower and there were narrow openings back in the trees. That might mean a low shore, perhaps with a beach. That was it! No more waiting! When he arrived opposite the openings in the forest, he untied the rope from around his waist, slipped off his pants and jacket, and bound them tightly into the line to make a stop-water. That would hold the stern to the wind and keep the canoe from veering. There wasn't enough strength in his arms to keep the craft on course with the paddle. If the canoe rolled over, he would fight to keep afloat and let the waves carry him toward the beach. If it came to that, he hoped the surf would also send the canoe in that he might retrieve his clothes. They were hardly better than rags yet would be sorely needed.

He turned the bow straight for the surf and waited until he was almost in the breakers before he threw the stop-water astern. Then he watched each swell approach, lift him, and roll on. He was hoping to keep the waves from breaking onto the canoe. Suddenly, he saw the danger. Behind him a great hill of water was rising and tipping forward. It was too near. There was no escaping it in the canoe. Thomas pulled the slipknot loose that held the halyard. He stood up and dived away, taking a deep breath before he struck the surface. The wave thundered down squarely on him and his vessel. Cold water tumbled his naked body, first one way then the other. One moment he gasped air, then was smothered in froth and bubbling water. He tried swimming toward the shore when he could see it crazily rising and falling. More than half the time his head was covered by a wave rushing over it. He swore he must not drown there at the last moment. He could not be dealt such a terrible fate now, so close to land.

Suddenly the waves threw him onto the shore. Then they boiled over him, drew him back and cast him up again twice more before he could crawl from their reach. His beard and his long strands of hair dribbled water alternately into the spreading waves and, when they drained away, onto a pebbly beach as he rested on hands and knees. The stones to each side of him growled as they rolled down with the retiring waves. The solid, unmoving earth beneath him and the foam racing up and back on each side created vertigo in his head. From a fear of falling, he only moved his right hand ahead, then his right knee. He repeated the moves with his left hand and knee. For several minutes he struggled up the shingle surface. Thirst alone drove him, gave him unexpected strength to wobble to his feet. Water was there somewhere. He swore he could smell it: clear, sweet water he could gulp down and put out the burning.

He staggered inland through clumps of grass, the first growth he met with. He halted and gripped the stems with each hand. There was a sudden thrill in the feel of them. They were the ground tackle that held him to the Middle Island, an assurance that he was truly on land again and not in one of the mad dreams he had had during the long nights. After a minute he let the grass slip from his hands and moved farther in. Then he entered some low ferns. He wrenched a frond off and licked it, but the night air hadn't begun to make dew. He tried chewing the rib as he walked. It was woody and his teeth broke it into a wad of slivers. No relief came from it. It yielded no moisture and tasted strange. Farther in, waist-high ferns brushed against his bare skin. He encountered others that were ten and twelve feet tall as he pushed his way through the underwood. In the dim moonlight he saw something he never expected. Ahead were trees like those he had seen in the Brazils, except the fronds did not droop but appeared stiff as if their ends had been cut off. Yes, they were the palms or perhaps what were called cabbage trees. The noise of the surf had diminished to a rumble. He stopped in the mottled, shifting moonlight and shadows and listened for the sound of running water. He heard only the wind in the leaves and stumbled farther on though he had no idea which direction he was going. The ground he was walking on sloped up, so he reckoned he was going away from the shore. He was surely gaining a little elevation with each step. The bushes were thicker and scratched and poked his skin when he pushed ahead. Roots almost tripped him. It was irking to be staggering about on the Middle Island and still suffering from thirst. In Dusky Sound, at its south'ard end, they had met with streams and cascades at every turn and filled their butts only a few paces from the boats.

By the moonlight he saw that the ground was lower to his left and headed in that direction. That was where he would find water and he forced limbs aside to make a way down. It was a wandering route he took, turning right or left as he found openings between the bushes and clumps of flax. He descended to a level ground where they all grew a little more than head-high. If he continued on, keeping the mountains to his right, he should meet with a stream. The earth and leaves he walked on felt soft and even wet under his bare feet. The scent of water came to his nose as he approached it. Then, there before him, between some small bushes, was the moonlight rippling in a puddle hardly a fathom in length. It was not the clear, gurgling stream he had dreamt of so many times. Thomas collapsed onto his knees and sucked at its surface. He held the first gulp of water in his mouth and let it loosen his swollen, sticky tongue. The liquid worked its way down and quenched the terrible burning, but his nose and the puckery taste told him there were rotting leaves in it. He wasn't repelled the least and kept drinking it and even swallowed the smaller bits of the leaves with the water. If there were tadpoles and fish in it, damn but he would swallow them too! Then he forced himself to raise his head, knowing he must not drink too much at first. Sip, sip, he told himself. Sip and wait for a while. He got to his feet still not sated, but remembering the cautions of his old mates, managed to hold off a few minutes before he dropped down and took the next drink.

The knowledge that there were endless amounts of water to drink on the island gave him a new strength, but it also returned the other craving, hunger, which hadn't bothered him as much. What would the forest around him provide? There had been clams, earshells, and many fish at Dusky. He had no hook and line, or seine, but surely those earshells must be here on the same island and the clams too. It didn't worry him. There was food. He would surely find it.

He worked his way back to the shore and stumbled about until he found the patch of bunch grass again. He crouched in it to keep warm. It worked for a while, but he was eventually seized by fits of shivering. After a few minutes he got up and returned to the puddle for more water. Thomas repeated the routine through the night. The trips to the water and back created some heat in his body.

Just prior to the setting of the moon Thomas took his last drink and faced north. He started forward to explore the low ground by the last of the light. There must be a sizeable stream there somewhere, he thought, one that had washed through and created the flat ground. Progress was slow between bushes and over patches of boggy ground. He reached a slough and a taste of its brackish water was proof it ran to the sea. There was soft mud along its bank and his feet squished ankle-deep in it until he arrived at the shore. Waves were breaking on a bar across the mouth of an inlet. If he had taken the canoe a little farther along, he would have landed on that bar. He watched the surf as he marched south to keep warm. Thomas sensed a slight lightening of the sky and turned to his left to search the flatland behind the beach. Spiky outlines gradually appeared in the misty light, odd things for which he could not account. They might have been an abatis or the forts of the Indians, but he well knew they always built on some cliff that made any approach perilous and so were easily defended. Under the lightening sky, piles of logs and limbs resolved out of the murk with ends salient from the masses at every angle, to the right and left and toward him and away. The driftwood had been twisted and battered in the rivers of the island and the surf. Now, long after having been rolled twenty to twenty-five yards ashore by storms and neap tides, the piles rested, isolated in a field of rank grasses that extended far back to the dark edge of the forest. Sun, rain, and salt air had weathered the wood to a silver-gray, some indication of how long they had rested there undisturbed. Again, he had been thrown onto a land untamed in all its aspects, from the high, white peaks to the tumbled boulders of its coasts. There was no visible evidence of men yet. That was a boon for now, but he must prepare to meet the savages that inhabited the land.

The stony shore on which he had landed, he guessed, should be farther to the south; and he was surprised to find it after walking only a half-hour in that direction. There was nothing to be seen farther down the beach. The canoe had not yet washed in. It could not have drifted too far in the few hours he had been on land. He would have to wait.

The first rays of the sun overtopped the mountain crests and spread a clear dawn over a wild coast. Green waves rose in glinting detail and dashed toward his feet. Dense swathes of trees to the north and south reached close to the milky surf. There were old snags in the forest but not one small opening that might have been cleared by an ax. Thomas searched it all for any mark of the savages. He saw no paths worn into the soil and grass. They might only come there at certain seasons and he might not meet them before he had repaired his canoe and sailed up the coast.

By the increasing light he discovered his paddle had washed in with the waves. The lanyard that held it to the canoe had parted. He spotted the canoe itself yet farther to the south. It was drifting in upside down. As he approached, he saw that the long line and his clothes tied in it were being rolled inshore and out with each wave. Thomas waded in, seized the line and pulled the canoe higher on the beach as each wave partially lifted it. The mast had snapped and the rigging was a tangle, but it was repairable. All the bindings on the boomkins and spar still held firmly. Once he found food he would start his repairs.

He did not doubt sailing was the swiftest way to the Strait. Travel on the land would mean crossing rivers, scaling cliffs, and breaking a way through tangled forests. If he came upon the Indians, they might make a slave or a meal of him.

Thomas freed his pants and jacket, wrung the water out, and spread them on the grass to dry. The canoe must serve him again, and he meant to get it farther above the reach of the waves, though for now it was safe.

He made another trip up to the puddle and discovered by the dawn light that in the darkness he had been drinking water that was black as coffee. It was standing water, with an infusion of all the rotting leaves lying in and around it. He was disgusted with its appearance. Drink much more, he thought, and it would tan his guts. At once he went off looking for something better. Farther across the flat he found a small stream that fed into the inlet. It was slow-moving and tinged brown, but it had less taste of the leaves and was satisfying as it went down his throat.

Thomas wandered back to the shore and stood there with his feet in the wash of the waves and facing into the wind. A rush of thoughts came to him. He, the last of the entire crew, had survived by the merest chance. How fortunate he was to be alive there in the early light, even though naked and shaking with cold. His hair hung in damp strings. His lips were swollen and split, and in the splits, he felt beads of dried blood. Flakes of skin were peeling from his burned nose. Did they make a more frightful appearance, he wondered, than the paint or tattoos such as the Indians wore on the island? He was alive. What did it matter that he looked more of a savage than they did?

Out there, far beyond the meeting of the sky and sea, were the shattered remnants of the little island and the remains of every person who had sailed with him on the *Dove*. Christopher would always be the first to be remembered, the one quietly seeking the peaceable way, always seeing the better side of all. Even that mound in which he had buried him must have been carried away, and perhaps there was nothing left on which he could place a stone. The ghastly vision of Christopher's face as he lay in the grave burst into his mind. Poor Harrison had done his best and lighted the train, even knowing it might be faulty, yet hoping the blast would draw the officers away. There was no way to repay that great sacrifice, save by telling his story back home. That would be little enough. Funerals and memorials were for those who survived, for they did small good for the dead. He felt a warmth rising in his eyes. The horizon he had stared at for so many long days ceased to be that sharp, inviolable division between the darker colors of the ocean and the paler blues of the lower sky. It blurred. Closer before him, the green walls of the rising waves and the white of the surf swarmed together.

He knew he would have many more trials before he stepped ashore in Stonington. Such was the lot of men who risked their lives for their wages. Those of great fortune need not know such danger and hardship. It was the way of the world.

What a story there would be to tell if he reached home.

GLOSSARY

Argo/Argo Navis	An old constellation now divided into the smaller Vela, Puppis, and Carina groups.
Barque	A three-masted vessel, square-rigged on the fore- and mainmasts, but not on the mizzen.
Bay of Islands	An early port in the North Island of New Zealand.
"Bears"	Marsupial animals akin to the wombat.
Bligh's Islands	The Fiji Islands.
Board	The distance covered by one tack.
Bower	An anchor carried at the bow of the ship.
Bowse	To tauten with a tackle.
Black oil	Oil rendered from other than sperm whales.
Brazils	An early name for Brazil and, by extension, much of South America. Also, the whaling grounds off Brazil.
Brig	A two-masted, square-rigged vessel.
Brister's	Bristrow's Island, Auckland Island.
Cable length	From 100 to 120 fathoms.
Caboose	A house on a ship's deck that contains the galley.
Cape South	Now South West Cape, the southern tip of Stewart Island.
Cat whipper	A shoemaker.
Channels	Planks set edgewise to the hull of a ship to spread the shrouds.
Chains	Iron plates to which the shrouds are anchored. Also, the channel that spreads them.
Clapmatch	A female fur seal.

Cooking hole	A covered hole in which heated rocks cook food. The Maori *umu* or earth oven.
Crawfish	A form of lobster.
The Cross	The constellation of the Southern Cross.
Derwent	A river and estuary in Tasmania.
Dusky	Dusky Sound in New Zealand.
Equinoctial Line	The Equator.
First rate	A large warship.
The Fish	The constellation Pisces.
Five Fingers Point	A landmark at the entrance to Dusky Sound.
Flax	The flax lily, *Phormium tenax.*
Fouled hawse	When a ship has two anchors ahead and their cables are crossed.
Full and by	Sailing close-hauled on the wind.
Gam	When two ships meet at sea and the crews visit.
Girt line	A line rove through a single block to hoist light rigging.
Glass	A telescope.
Grating	Open latticework to cover a hatch opening.
Great Southern Sea	That part of the Pacific Ocean that reaches to the Antarctic Coast.
Hanger	A short sword.
Hawsehole	The hole through which the cable leads to the anchor.
Ironbound	A rugged, rocky coast.
Jackstays	Rope, wood, or iron fixed along the top of a yard to which the head of the sail is bent.
John Company	The East India Company.
Knight-heads	Timbers that support the bowsprit on each side.
Longpoint	The port of Stonington, Connecticut.
Macquarie	A sealing island 800 miles south of New Zealand.

Masy Foora	Corruption of Mas Afuera, an island of the Juan Fernandez group.
Matanzas	A sugar-producing area of Cuba.
Middle Island	The South Island of New Zealand.
Motoo Eetee	In Polynesian, little island; a rare usage in North Island Maori.
Mount of Pelee	Volcano on the Isle of Martinique.
Nankeen	A durable cloth from China.
New Holland	The original name of Australia.
On beam ends	A vessel on her side. For a person, it is to be in a bad situation.
On soundings	When close enough to the shore to make soundings with the lead.
Overhaul	To inspect. To pull a line through a block to make it slack.
Oriental Navigator	Sailing and trading instructions published in 1801, 1806, and 1816.
Oyster basket	A woman's genitalia.
Piragua	A dugout canoe.
Parbuckle	Rigging to roll heavy, round objects.
Plaguey	Harassing; also an intensifier.
Port Jackson	The site of the first penal colony in Australia.
Port William	A sealing port on the northeast coast of Stewart Island.
Pup	A young fur seal.
Quaker	A dummy cannon.
Rockweed	Kelp.
Ropewalk	A long, straight path where ropes and cables are made; usually covered with a narrow building.
Santiagy	Corruption of "Santiago de Cuba."
Sea ear	An abalone, the *Haliotis iris.*

Seventy-four (74)	A warship carrying 74 guns.
Shank painter	A chain securing the anchor to the side of the ship.
Ship-keeper	A man hired to watch a ship in port when no one else is on board.
Small stuff	Spun yarn, marline, sennit, etc.
Spar deck	Main deck.
Sojer	A corruption of "soldier." To call a sailor a soldier was an insult.
Superior metal	A ship that can throw a greater weight of round shot has superior metal (i.e., firepower).
Ticket of leave	Parole given transported criminals in Australia after serving a portion of their sentences.
Tierce	A barrel.
Temperance ship	A vessel that serves no alcoholic drink out to the crew.
Train	A fuse to a charge of black powder.
Train oil	Oil rendered from sea animals.
Tovy Poenamoo	Sometimes spelled "Tavai Poenamoo." The South Island of New Zealand, also called the Middle Island.
Tye block	A block by which the topsail yard is hoisted.
Van Diemen's Land	Tasmania's early name.
Warp	A line fixed to a buoy, dock, or anchor and drawn in by the windlass or capstan to move a ship short distances.
Weather gage	A ship with the weather gage is windward of an opposing ship. Generally, to have the advantage.
The Whale	The constellation Cetus.
Whampoa	The area of old Canton, China where foreigners were permitted to do business.
Wig	An old male fur seal with a thick mane.